CHAOS THEORY

For Dad,

Who thought I was funny (in a good way) and
wanted me to be a New Yorker cartoonist.

Think of this book as a cartoon with far too many words
and not nearly enough pictures.

Hopefully you would have liked it.

DISCLAIMER

Normally, this is where you'd read:

All characters appearing in this work are fictitious. Any resemblance to real persons, living or dead, is purely coincidental.

Which, for the most part, is true. In this work, however, a little more needs to be said.

Several of the characters here are clearly named after and based on real persons, i.e., the famous ones. That said, those actual portrayals are entirely fictitious, satirical, and do not depict actual events or words spoken by those individuals. Think of them as fictional versions of those persons, capable of actions entirely inconsistent with the real individual, existing in a parallel universe that has little or nothing to do with reality, similar to FOX News, or MSNBC. Some of the people I unfairly caricature are actually very smart, talented and, hopefully, able to laugh at themselves.

Chaos Theory

Oh, and if you're wondering about those quotations. They're all taken from Bartlett's Book of Pseudepigraphic Quotations. Which is to say, the person quoted almost certainly said those words, although perhaps in a different order, with a different meaning, and not all at the same time. This means they might not be, strictly speaking, true. As Pope Benedict IX once said, "To err is human; to lie, divine."

PREFACE

[SPOILER ALERT]
This book contains the meaning of life. So stop reading now if you want to, you know, wait until 'the end' to find out. Either way, you may leave a little disappointed.

I always wanted to write a book about the meaning of life. The problem was, I didn't know what that was. I still don't. So I decided to write about that instead. As with my first book, *The Siege of Walter Parks*, this was actually conceived many years ago. In fact, it was authored way back in 2004 when the Earth was young. It was written originally as a screenplay, although I made no attempt to sell it. I considered it unsellable and wrote it entirely for my own amusement. By lowering the bar to such a level, I figured, success was guaranteed. The ending was based on a dream I had. In my wife's words, I have weird dreams. She says that, not because they're full of odd ideas and images, everyone has those. It's because they tend to have actual story lines and structure. I have no idea how common or uncommon that is. All I know is it means I get to write things in my sleep. Like most people, even if I remember my dreams when I awaken, they tend to melt from memory like a dusting of snow in the light of day. This dream, on the other hand, persisted like oobleck. So, I wrote it down. That makes this book, arguably, some sort of therapy—for me, that is. You're welcome.

Enjoy.

CJR

ABOUT THE SCIENCE

Since this book is called *Chaos Theory*, it seems appropriate to comment on the science, specifically the math and physics, involved.

There isn't any.

Okay, technically that's not true. For the most part gravity and light operate according the laws of physics. The characters walk on the ground and have mass. Numbers go up, as well as down, and only occasionally from side to side. It's only towards the end that reality gets tossed out the window like a houseguest who has overstayed his welcome. Still, if you purchased this book hoping to learn about mathematical chaos theory, or learn anything at all really, you have made a very poor selection. I suggest you return it for a full refund and write an angry review on your bookseller's website. Feel free to throw in a few personal comments about myself as you imagine me to be.

Chaos Theory

It's fair to say that, when grouped with other authors who have written about chaos theory, I am uniquely qualified. Whereas they presumably all have degrees in mathematics and other "relevant" education, I have a BA in English. Among them, I stand alone and probably facing in the wrong direction.

I made up the principle premise of the book, called 'Loose Thread', out of whole cloth, as it were. I was therefore, somewhat surprised when recently Stephen Hawking stole my idea and alarmed the world by claiming the Higgs particle could be unstable and transition to a lower energy state*, effectively making this a textbook. I was surprised for a few reasons. First, while originally written many years ago, this book was unpublished. I can only conclude, therefore, that Stephen Hawking has hacked my personal laptop in order to read my stuff. Secondly, I was surprised and horrified by the notion that somehow something in the book was even theoretically plausible. If so, the author regrets the error. Fortunately, other physicists seem to think Hawking is wrong on this and I, for one, choose to believe them. In fact, I'd stake my reputation as an English major on it.

Anyway, the point is, the math and physics in this book, as in real life, are just metaphors or plot devices, specifically the kind that explode.

* Yes, I know he wasn't the first person to postulate this, but he was the first famous person to do so, and I live in Los Angeles where that's the only thing that counts.

CHAOS THEORY

By Colin Robertson

Edited by Dr. Neil Robertson

PROLOGUE

Truman Gorge Road, Michigan. Sunday, December 6, 1959, 07:45 hrs.

Two things happened that morning that had never happened before anywhere, anytime. In the tens of millions of snowflakes that fell that morning, there were two that were completely identical. Examine them under a microscope and you'd see every crystallized timber of frozen water was exactly the same in both size and shape. They were, to the smallest detail, perfect twins descending from heaven. The first flake was obliterated when it hit a tree branch. Its twin, unaware of the first flake's existence or tragic death, as snowflakes tend to be, evanesced into a snowbank on the edge of the gorge. That was the first event. The second happened as follows...

Truman Gorge is a giant two hundred foot deep scar in the Earth's crust left over from the glaciers' retreat at the end of the Ice Age. Back then, snow and ice stood two miles thick and reshaped the land with the weight of their passage. Today, the infestations of humans who occupy the planet complain about a mere six inches of snow and fret at the thought of having to scrape frost from their windshields.

That morning, the forest had been silent, still and cold. Suddenly, the rumble of motor vehicles split the silence and grew rapidly louder. A small convoy plowed its way down the snow shrouded gravel road that ran along the gorge's eastern edge. The vehicles were US Army—an armoured truck escorted by twin jeeps, front and rear. On the radio, Frank Sinatra crooned.

Once I was happy but now I'm forlorn,
Like an old coat that is tattered and torn,
Left on this wide world to fret and to mourn,
Betray'd by a maid in her teens....

The truck driver was thirty-five years old, moustached, and balding. For a Sergeant, that put him well past his prime. Most of his contemporaries had left the army after the war, but not him. He had nothing else to do and nowhere else to be than right here, singing along with the radio, badly. His passenger was a young Private, a draftee. The Private frowned. He frowned a lot, so this was not surprising. He'd become quite good at it and took pride in his ability to make the world aware of how he often did not approve of the way it went about its business. At that moment he was frowning with extra vigour. The tinny sound of the radio was driving him to distraction, but not nearly as much as the Sergeant's singing. The Private ground his teeth and glared furiously past the windshield wipers as they swept millions of unremarkably unique snowflakes from the glass.

It was no accident that this convoy was small and traveling on a quiet Sunday morning along an even quieter country road largely avoided in winter by sensible travellers. All of this was done to avoid attention. Despite these efforts, the convoy's passing did not go unobserved. Standing like stumps amid the black trees were two men, far enough from the road to remain unnoticed themselves. One of the men was older, with thinning grey hair. The other was nearly twenty-five-years his junior and just past his prime. They had not happened upon the convoy, whose very existence was known only to the highest members of the military and the White House. They'd known it was coming. They had been waiting for it.

Inside the truck cab, the Private continued to glower with the expertise of a practiced glowerer. Everything was annoying him now, including the rabbit's foot charm that swayed and bounced below the rearview mirror. The motion of the jeep escort ahead telegraphed every uncomfortable pothole and bump that was to come. Most annoying of all, the sergeant seemed utterly oblivious to the Private's disapproval. He actually appeared cheerful as he sang along to the radio. "...He'd fly through the air with the greatest of ease, that daring young man on the flying trapeze. His movements were graceful—"

At that moment the song dissolved into static.

"Ah Hell!" the Sergeant growled and whacked the radio. "How can everything be all clear and then just go all to fuzz like that? God Damn!"

"Must you?"

The Sergeant looked surprised. This is the first word the Private had spoken in over an hour. "What? You don't appreciate my singin'? Well, maybe if you joined in, son."

"I don't want to join in."

The Sergeant fiddled with the knob but succeeded only in changing the quality of the static. He turned the radio off. "It's the goddamn trees. We're just too deep in the woods now, damn it!"

"That! That is what I mind—you taking the Lord's name in vain."

"That's what you mind?" The Sergeant stared at him incredulously. He studied the Private for a moment, looking him up and down like a lepidopterist studies a butterfly before deciding it's nothing more than a common *danaus plexippus*. "Let me tell you somethin', son, when you've been on the beaches of Normandy, dredging Hell's cesspool without your hip-waders, when you've seen that Satan wears a swastika on his sleeve..." The Sergeant tapped an imaginary armband on his sleeve. At that moment the truck hit a frozen log in the road and lurched towards the ditch. In the back of the truck, a crate, labeled 'United States Military—Top Secret', tested its redundant harnesses. With both hands back on the wheel, the Sergeant returned the truck to the center of the road and continued, "...then, and only then, can you tell me not to take the God Damn Lord's name in vain."

The Sergeant had indeed seen Nazis in Normandy. He had also seen one of the most famous Nazis of all 'up close and personal'. After the war, he had been detailed to guard Hermann Wilhelm Göring at his trial in Nuremburg. The former Reichsmarschall had largely ignored him as a lowly private at the time, instead choosing to befriend Lieutenant Tex Wheelis. Göring said only one thing to the then-private during his entire course of duty. "You should grow a moustache. Men would respect you more." Göring himself was clean-shaven. When he'd arrived in prison, Göring was fat and wore nail polish. He'd lost the weight since the start of the trial, but not the affectations or ability to inspire awe. Three days later, to avoid death by hanging, the Nazi would take potassium cyanide—death by his own perfectly manicured hand. In spite of it all, the Sergeant, took his advice.

The Private gave the Sergeant his most withering gaze.

"Fine, fine, I'll try to—" The Sergeant slammed the brakes. "Oh Christ! I mean crap! Ah Hell." The heavy truck heaved to a grinding halt, inches from the back bumper of the front escort. One of the soldiers in the jeep watched this with only passive concern, stolidly bracing himself for the possible impact by tightening his lips around his cigarette. When the impact did not come, he pulled it out of his mouth and calmly exhaled twin plumes of smoke from his nostrils.

The driver of the jeep had already left the vehicle and was standing in shin deep drifts assessing the state of the bridge ahead. Only the steel beams of the superstructure were visible. The roadbed of the bridge itself was completely covered in six feet of snow. The driver waved and lifted his walkie-talkie to talk. His radio-modulated voice entered the truck cab, "Definite no-go, Sarge, over."

The pinprick of orange fire swelled at the tip of the other soldier's cigarette as he inhaled. He pulled the cigarette from his mouth and examined it as if it were something interesting. The man's obvious indifference to the situation annoyed the Private even more. The Sergeant picked up the receiver, "Roger."

"Can't seem to reach HQ on the horn from here, either."

"Roger that, hold on."

"Roger."

The Sergeant released the button and considered the situation.

"We'll have to turn around," the Private said flatly.

The Sergeant snorted. "Fine, you can do the driving. Wake me up when you finished backing us up the forty miles through these woods, cuz you sure as Hell ain't doin' a three-point-turn."

The Private looked out of his window. The soldiers from the rear escort had also left their vehicle and were now engaged in informal calisthenics to return circulation to their feet. Behind them, the long plowed path they'd created along the gorge edge was already being obliterated with rapidly falling snow.

"I, uh..., um. What do we do?"

"Well, for starters you can reach in the glovebox for the map. Maybe we can find ourselves an altern-o-teeve."

"We can't do that! HQ gave us a very explicit route to follow."

"Yeah, well, so apparently the weather didn't get the orders. Remember? It wasn't supposed to snow today."

The Private frowned with disapproval.

"Son, let me tell you somethin'. Sometimes in the real world, mice and men and most especially soldiers need to make changes to the best laid plans."

The Sergeant reached past the Private, into the glove compartment and pulled out a badly folded map. He opened it, turned it over and studied it for a moment. With his little finger tracing the red road line, he picked up the receiver once more. "Pandora to Escort 1. We got a change of plans..."

Ten minutes later, the three vehicle convoy came to a halt once more, this time in front of a much smaller bridge. On the side of the road, a fallen sign lay half-buried in the snow.

"You want to get out and see what that says?" the Sergeant grinned. "You know, to make sure this is it?"

"It says this is the Old Gorge Bridge"

"You're sure?"

"I can see the word 'Old'. Plus there were no other bridges on the stupid map."

"All right, then."

The Private looked at the wooden bridge. The frozen support beams extended from a mere six inches of snow on the roadbed. "I don't get it. Why was the other bridge buried and this one's fine?"

"Gorge winds. They move the snow in mysterious ways. No rhyme, no reason."

The front escort driver looked back at them through the warped plastic rear window of the jeep. The Sergeant nodded and gave him a thumbs-up. The convoy rolled forward.

Seen only by the snowflakes that covered its face, the sign did indeed read "Old Gorge Bridge". It also included other fascinating details, such as the year of its construction, 1890, as well as its estimated physical capacity of 12,000 lbs. Of course, what makes these details even more interesting is when you consider other factors such as the weight of the snow accumulated on the surface of the bridge, and the weight of the truck, jeeps and men inside. Add to this the age of the structure and its shameful neglect since the construction of the newer bridge and you have a very interesting situation indeed. As the truck's wheels crunched cautiously across the bridge surface, the wood beams creaked and bowed in protest.

"Just for the record, I still don't like the idea of taking an alternate route," the Private muttered. He imagined an inquiry later, standing in front of Major Dolkin's desk. The Major would commend him on his attention to orders. "I'll put that in my report," the Major would say with a nod.

The front jeep rolled safely up onto the far side of the gorge as the truck reached the middle of the bridge. The Sergeant shook his head with a smirk. "Duly noted in the cover-your-ass file."

There was a massive cracking sound. Beneath the roadbed one of the sixty-nine-year-old support beams gave way with a *snap!* The bridge tilted ten degrees with a stomach wrenching twist. The Sergeant slammed on the brakes as the truck rocked uncertainly.

"Jesus Christ!" shouted the Private.

For several seconds the two soldiers sat frozen in the truck cab. They watched their collective breath cloud the cold air and listened to the pulse in their ears. They watched each other from the corners of their eyes.

In the back of the truck, their cargo remained firmly in place, although now tilted at that same ten-degree angle. The clamps, designed to withstand thousands of pounds of pressure, were doing their job easily. The bridge, however, was not doing its. Too much had been asked of the old wooden structure and more supports began to split and snap. A long hairline crack raced silently along the center support beam. Suddenly, the bridge lurched sickeningly sideways, sending the Private crashing into the passenger door, cheek pressed against the glass, while the Sergeant hung from his seat belt above him.

At both ends of the bridge, the escorting soldiers paced anxiously, trying to figure out what they could do to help.

"Do we have rope?"

"No."

"Why don't we have rope?"

"Who the Hell cares? We don't."

There was a massive *CRACK!* and the bridge twisted back the other way causing the truck to slide hard against the super structure. The Private, who was not wearing a seat-belt, slid hard against the sergeant. His lips pressed against the Sergeant's cheek in a forced kiss. The tilt was enough to allow the two soldiers a terrifying view of the abyss. The Private watched as a passing snowflake fell towards the icy black river rushing below.

The Sergeant gently pushed the Private back to his side of the cab. "Okay, we're going to get out of this son, you hear me? We just gotta do it real slow and gentle-like."

The Sergeant pushed the gas pedal down, coaxing the engine to life. Despite the steep angle, the truck rolled forward. Slowly, the truck inched up the tilted roadbed towards the edge of the gorge. The bridge creaked and groaned ominously. The Private closed his eyes and prayed, "Our father, who art in heaven, hallowed be thy name..."

Then came the reassuring sound of tires on gravel as they reached the far side of the gorge. "Oh thank-you, Lord!" The Private turned to the Sergeant and said, "Now do you believe in the power of prayer?"

At that moment the bridge behind them collapsed with a crash and, as only the front tires of the truck had safely reached solid ground, they suddenly found themselves hurtling backwards in space.

"Oh Jesus!" the Sergeant yelled.

"Oh God!" the Private screamed as he literally hit the ceiling.

A moment later, the sixteen-tonne truck careened off the rocks in the river below, rebounded off a gorge wall where an outcrop sheared through its side, and landed in the water with a great splash. The Private was thrown free on the first bounce and hit the granite wall where his skeleton shattered on impact. His body then flopped onto a snow bank and dyed it bright red. The Sergeant's limp corpse hung from the driver's window as if leaning out to stare at the still spinning wheels.

There was now a twelve-foot gash in the steel armoured siding of the truck. Out of this gash, a lone canister rolled and dropped with a small *kerplunk!* into the water. Despite being made of metal, thirty centimetres high, and of clearly solid construction, the canister bobbed back to the surface and proceeded to float. It was then swept swiftly away downstream with the current.

Back at the top of the gorge the escort soldiers swore, paced, and shouted to one another across the empty space and the tragic wreckage below. They knew something important had just happened. They believed it was the death of those two men. They had no idea.

CHAPTER 1

Don't worry, it's organic. - Eve

The most unexpected moment at the 1988 Olympics in Seoul, South Korea was not the result of a surprise medal win or an athlete's triumph over adversity. It didn't even occur during competition. Instead it came during the opening ceremonies. The performance was to culminate, as all such ceremonies do, with the lighting of the Olympic flame. After arriving in the stadium, a team of torch bearers were lifted on an elevator platform to the rim of the massive brazier that was to serve as the centrepiece for the entire quadrennial event. For the hosts it was to be a moment of triumph; for their guests, a moment of inspiration. It was all perfectly choreographed in every respect—except, that is, for the doves. The enormous flock of doves, released earlier in a gallant gesture of peace, had not left the stadium as expected. Instead, they had chosen to alight atop the highest perch available to them, the giant ceremonial torch. Now, as the torch bearers arose, they desperately attempted to drive off the birds, to little effect. What to do? The world was watching, and the show must go on, so the torch bearers did what was required. The horrified audience was thus treated to the sight of flaming doves firebombing the assembled gathering of politicians, dignitaries and Olympic athletes. It was, without doubt, the largest dove barbecuing event in broadcast television history.

It was at that moment that Charlie Draper first suspected that no one knew what they were doing. He was thirteen-years-old at the time and was beginning to realize that adults weren't as in control of things as he'd been led to believe. Now, as a forty-year-old man, sitting on the cold metal seats of the waiting room, Charlie knew that this was true. He was an adult, and had lost any sense of being in control. On a TV in the corner of the waiting room, an older man was playing baseball with his son and grandson while discussing the benefits of a new drug treatment for chronic obstructive pulmonary disease, or COPD. For a brief moment, the man wandered away from his family to talk directly to the camera about the drug's many side effects, including the possibility of a 'fatal event'. His son and grandson seemed oblivious to this odd behaviour. A moment later, the three generations were hugging and laughing in the dugout, while enjoying pepperoni pizza.

Charlie's brain wasn't functioning very well right now. He was trying desperately not to think of *anything*. Most of all, he was trying not to think about why he was here. He thought about what it meant to be a father. He'd never had a son. He'd sometimes wondered what that would be like. Charlie had had a daughter. Had *had*. That was the thought he didn't want to think. Had *had.* He didn't know that for sure. It wasn't official. That was why he was here. The world as he knew it was crumbling like sand, but it wasn't over yet. Charlie tried desperately to hold the castle together, but the sand kept spilling between his fingers.

"You can come in now, Mr. Draper," said the coroner's assistant.

Charlie rose numbly to his feet and walked inside.

A moment later, the world *would* end. This is the story of what happened next.

CHAPTER 2

"Water, water, everywhere, but not a drop to drink."
– Thales

Truman Gorge Road, Michigan, Summer, Yesterday.

The gorge looked unchanged from how it had looked fifty years ago. It also looked unchanged from the fifty years before that. In fact, the gorge looked mostly unchanged from how it had looked for the past millennia. This was hardly surprising as, in geological terms, millennia are but minutes. On a cosmological scale, the gorge had only just blinked into existence and, sometime soon, would blink out once more.

"Five bounces!" shouted thirteen-year-old Alex Graham triumphantly as he watched his stone skip across the river's surface, before sinking with a splash.

"Luck," sneered his friend, Gerald Allen. "You just found a good stone is all."

"Yeah? Then, I guess I keep finding good stones."

"Exactly, luck!"

The two boys had been picking their way along the riverbank looking for dead animals. Their goal was to find a still-dying animal that they could experiment with. History, however, had taught them that corpses were far more common. 'Plan B' was to find a fresh corpse they could hook up to a car battery that Gerald had found in a ditch the week before. They would then electrify the dead possum, or whatever it was, and bring it back to life. Alex, who was somewhat squeamish, had raised concerns that such a plan would just cook the creature, but Gerald was confident the scheme could work. He'd seen it in a movie.

"I smell skunk!" Gerald shouted excitedly.

"Ick," said Alex, "won't that just stink?"

"Re-animated skunks don't stink," said Gerald emphatically.

"Oh." Alex couldn't argue with that. Clearly Gerald knew more than he did about reanimating animals, and Alex didn't want to appear ignorant. The two boys scurried rapidly over the rocks, trying to avoid dipping their shoes in the black water. Alex and Gerald had become friends at school. On the surface, they were an unlikely pair. Gerald was tall and lanky, with red hair and freckles. His height meant that he could pass for sixteen or older. Alex was several inches shorter with sandy brown hair and could pass for younger than he was. They'd met in detention at school. Alex had been caught carving his name inside his desk for "immortality", as he'd explained to the principal. It was Alex's first time in detention, but hanging out with Gerald ensured that it wouldn't be his last. Gerald had 'anger issues' and a long history of after-school incarceration. Most often, this was the result of setting various objects on fire as part of an ongoing experiment to see what was and was not flammable. Alex had always had trouble making friends. Gerald never even tried. So, as a couple of misfits, they'd hit it off and never acknowledged the fact that they were more or less friends by default.

Gerald, with his long grasshopper legs, bounded quickly along the treacherous riverbank. Alex struggled to keep up with him. The taller boy paused to sniff the air before turning to scramble over a boulder twice his height. "It's over here!" he shouted. Gerald stood atop the rock and pointed down the other side. "I need a stick."

Alex tried to climb the sheer surface but found that the handholds that Gerald had grabbed so easily were just beyond his reach. He tried to shimmy up, only to fall backwards onto the riverbank where the gravel stung his hands.

"Help me up!"

"Go around."

This wasn't as easy as it sounded. Between the boulder and the gorge wall was the worst kind of bramble—the kind that tears at clothes and gets Mom mad as Hell. The alternative was to wade into the freezing ankle deep water on the other side. He might have felt like a modern-day Odysseus, caught between Scylla and Charybdis, had he bothered with the assigned reading for history class. Instead, he simply felt frustrated. "Help me up," Alex pleaded once more.

"Jesus, you should see the maggots on this thing!"

Alex considered his options. He could do nothing and be called a "puppy" and a "loser" for the rest of the day, or he could walk around. He considered removing his shoes, but he knew that the water would be icy cold and the river bed was a mosaic of sharp stones that could easily slice open an unshod foot. He looked again to Gerald, but Gerald was gone, no doubt climbing down the other side. Alex needed to get there too, if he wanted to get in on the poking.

Alex stepped into the rushing water and felt it instantly flood his shoes. It was so cold it made his feet hurt. He resolutely trudged forward. He needed to move as quickly as possible, without slipping and falling into the cold current. As he rounded the boulder, the water reached his calves. He was forced to balance against the stone to avoid being swept off his feet by the fast flow. "Son of a bitch!" he shouted.

"That's you!" Gerald shouted back from the other side and laughed.

Suddenly, a stone shifted under Alex's foot. He stumbled, but caught himself with one hand plunged into the river, while the other frantically gripped the boulder's surface. "God damn it!" His sleeve was completely soaked. As Alex sought to pull himself up, something caught his eye under the belly of the rock. It was the cold glint of steel. He peered to see what it might be. It was obviously some sort of a container; wedged under the rock and half-submerged. Alex's arm and feet were freezing and he probably would have dismissed the object as worthless river junk, except for one thing. Where the light struck the steel, two engraved words were faintly visible, 'Top Secret'. "Hey," Alex yelled, "I think I've found something!"

"Better than a skunk with no eyes?"

"Um... yeah, I think so."

* * *

After persuading Gerald that his skunk-poking stick might, in fact, have broader range of function, Alex had used it to dislodge the canister from its place under the boulder. Alex had then carried the shiny steel cylinder to the shore, where Gerald had taken over. Gerald wiped the river slime off with his shirt and opened his eyes in surprise. "Not just Top Secret," he exclaimed, "'Property of the United States Government: Top Secret'. This is awesome!"

They both examined the metal object. It was remarkably pristine. A clear seam suggested where it might open. Gerald gave the top a twist in an attempt to unscrew it. When it failed to budge, he tried again, harder. He grunted and strained until his face flushed. "Goddamn it!"

"What do you think's inside?" asked Alex.

"I have no idea," said Gerald. "Hey, let's smash it with a rock!"

"Wait, it's my thing... let me smash it."

Gerald looked at Alex, fighting the urge to simply shove him into the river. "Sure, whatever." He dropped the canister on the rocky river bank, and both boys cast about for an appropriately sized stone. "There!" said Gerald.

Alex picked up the rock. As luck would have it, the rock in question was a perfect likeness of Henry Moore's sculpture, *Composition 1932*. Arguably, since the rock had been carved by water and wind over thousands of years, Moore's piece was the replica. Regardless, neither boy paused to appreciate the rock's form. Instead, Alex simply dropped the natural artwork on the mysterious container. The rock bounced harmlessly off with a loud *ding!*

"No! No, no, no!" shouted Gerald with disgust. "You need to hit it hard!"

"I... I thought it might explode," explained Alex sheepishly. "I mean, we don't know what's inside."

"Never send a boy to do a man's job," said the red haired boy with a sigh.

"What if it contains something radioactive?"

Gerald rolled his eyes. "Then we get super powers! Don't you know anything? Jeez, Alex, sometimes you're such a retard!" With that, Gerald lifted the rock high above his head and threw it down hard. The rock rebounded off and hit Gerald in the shin, causing him to drop to his knees in pain, "Double goddamn!" The metal canister, apparently unharmed, bounced and rolled towards the river. Alex stopped it just as it reached the water's edge. Gerald winced in pain and fought back tears. "Stupid frickin' piece of trash!" he snarled, scowling ruefully at it.

Alex examined the canister closely. "It's not even scratched!"

"Who the Hell cares?"

They both did. After several more attempts to twist, dent and pulverize it, all without causing the slightest abrasion, the two boys stood sweaty and panting over the apparently impervious object. "Well, I guess that's it then," said Alex.

Gerald started to nod—then his eyes lit up. "I got an idea," he said with a devilish grin.

*   *   *

Alex carefully placed the mysterious canister in the bottom of the metal garbage can. The two boys then began dumping in the fireworks. Gerald had an astounding collection of 'recreational explosives', from Roman candles to something called 'Dragon Eggs'. Alex had no idea how a teenage boy managed to acquire so much industrial-strength firepower. Fireworks were more or less legal in Michigan, but many of the ones Gerald stockpiled were not. Still, he explained, those were the ones most likely to be effective in blowing up their intended target, and anything else for that matter. "Of course, we really ought to be using nitrate fertilizer," Gerald added wistfully.

"Fertilizer, why?"

"That's what McVeigh used, in the Oklahoma City bombing. Kaboom!" he shouted in Alex's face, waving his arms for effect.

Alex wiped the spit from his cheeks. "Really?"

"Yeah. Don't you know anything, dipstick?"

Alex, rather than risk confirming his dipstickiness, began enthusiastically dumping even more fireworks into the trash can. Once they'd crammed in as many explosives as they could manage, the two boys stood back to admire their handiwork. Gerald pulled out a silver lighter he'd stolen from a pawn shop. On it was a picture of a nude Betty Page looking seductively over her shoulder. Gerald had no idea who Betty Page was, but had declared her to be "hotter'n Hell!" He flicked the wheel and raised the flickering flame above his head. "Ready?"

Alex gave a quick nod. "I was born ready," he said.

"You were born an idiot."

* * *

Claire Graham stood over the kitchen sink. She was busy banging two store bought pizzas, which had become frozen together, on the edge of the counter. She did so in the hope of separating them, preferably without leaving the toppings from one attached to the bottom of the other. Her attention, however, was on the 13" TV in the corner. On the fuzzy screen, Duke Norman, the televangelist, made an impassioned plea. At well over six feet tall with broad powerful shoulders that stretched the confines of his suit, the African American preacher looked more like a football player than a pastor. "And I welcome each of you to join me, Reverend Duke, and my Holy Church of Preordination, for a very special sermon on how you can help fight the spread of evil in our streets, in our schools, and in your very own home. You have to choose to be chosen, my children! Now, be sure to tune in—"

Claire changed the channel to cable news. A weatherman smiled and waved his arms in front of a computer generated map of a world that wasn't really there. As the meteorologist spoke, tiny smiling suns popped up across the state, winking as they did. "Okay then, as we bring up our Doppler radar long term forecast, we see nothing but sun, sun, sun for the next seven days, and the foreseeable future after that. So, don't forget the sunblock, folks!" The phone rang, and Claire answered. It was her friend Annabelle. "Uh-huh?" said Claire, "Getting dinner ready... Oh, yeah, well, he's hanging out with Gerald again... Gerald? Gerald Allen. All - en. Yup, that's right, Mike and Doreen's kid... No, he's not a weirdo. He's a little weird, but not a weirdo, per say... Yes, there's a difference." The news moved on to a report on the Pō Lights, who were now apparently predicting the end of the world. Not necessarily soon, they said, but eventually. What is it with crazy religious nuts and Armageddon?" thought Claire, tapping the mute button. Annabelle was now listing her suspicions about Gerald and the whole Allen family. There was no interrupting her once she was on a rant. Meanwhile, Claire decided that the pizzas were clearly going to require a little more culinary finesse. She drew a knife from the drawer and began chiseling between the frozen discs. Finally finding good purchase, Claire paused to hammer the knife with a meat-tenderizer mallet. *Whack! Whack!* Claire suddenly realized that Annabelle had stopped talking and was waiting for her reply. "You're probably right, Ann," said Claire. "I mean, Alex is basically a good kid but—"

At that moment, two things happened. First, the pizzas flew apart. Second, a massive explosion of fireworks came from behind the garage. *BA-BA-BA-BOOM!* Claire stared slack-jawed through the kitchen window at the billowing smoke and continuing display of pyrotechnics. Multicoloured fireballs and incandescent flares shot across the lawn, ricocheted off the house and nearby trees, and set fire to the postbox. As the display died down, a haze of gun smoke and the stink of sulphur filled the air.

"Annabelle," said Claire, "I'm going to have to call you back."

* * *

"You, inside!" Claire swung open the door to her son's bedroom and pointed, just in case there was any doubt. Alex scowled and shuffled past her, his clothes reeking of brimstone and smoke. At thirteen, he'd already mastered the teenage sulk. As he entered, he artfully turned to avoid her seeing the towel-wrapped bundle hidden behind his back. "And don't come out for anything,"

"What if I gotta pee?" said Alex with a smirk.

"Don't be an ass," Claire snapped. "You're so like your father."

"I wouldn't know."

Claire rolled her eyes. She'd heard it all before. "Well, here's an idea, take a shot at something he never accomplished and grow-the-hell-up. You almost set the damn house on fire." She gave her son a last glare, then slammed the door.

"Bitch," he muttered.

"I heard that!"

Alex shook his head and waited for her to charge back through the door. After two minutes, he decided she wasn't going to. He turned and dropped his carefully concealed bundle onto the bed. The towel fell away, revealing the shiny steel canister within. It still looked as good as new. Tentatively he reached out and touched it. "Ow!" The metal was still hot from the fireworks. For a long moment he stared at it, uncertain what to do next. His mother had sent Gerald home and, along with him, any ideas he might have had about the object. Alex tried to imagine what might be inside but quickly realized he didn't have a very good imagination. It looked like a thermos to him, so he could only envision it containing coffee or chicken soup. He supposed it might contain some more exciting liquid such as acid or nuclear waste. He wasn't convinced that Gerald was right about nuclear waste being a good thing. He then considered something else. It might contain nothing at all. In school they had been reading *Le Petit Prince*, the story about the Pilot who lands in the desert and meets the Little Prince from another planet. The Little Prince demands that the Pilot draw him a sheep. The Little Prince proves impossible to please, however, rejecting the Pilot's first two attempts. Finally, the Pilot resorts to drawing a picture of a box and tells the Prince that his sheep is inside. "That is exactly the way I wanted it," says the Little Prince. Alex decided that the canister might be like the sheep. It might be more exciting left unopened. Opening it might lead to disappointment, like Christmas presents. Still, not opening it wasn't very satisfying either. The only way to ensure he got something good from it, he decided, was to sell it. He could sell it as it was, unopened. Let someone else blow it up with fireworks, he thought. He woke his computer from sleep and quickly typed "www.ebay.com". I'll set a minimum bid of fifty dollars, he thought. For fifty bucks, who cares what's inside?

Chaos Theory

Alex quickly filled out the details of the auction, describing the canister exactly. By this time, it had cooled down enough that he was able to handle it freely again. In the light of the window he caught the glint of engraved letters he'd not noticed earlier, burnished by the heat of the fire. "USWR No. 34567234X". He transcribed them into the online description ending with a simple disclaimer, "Don't know what's inside, can't open it. Could be empty, no promises. Buy at your own risk. NO REFUNDS!!!" He then clicked the mouse, sending the auction live. For a while, Alex stared at the screen as if expecting something to happen. He'd set the auction to expire in one week. He glanced at his watch. One minute had passed since the auction had begun. He looked at the screen—0 bids. "This is stupid," he said. Alex turned off the computer monitor and turned on the TV instead. Someone was trying to eat an entire jar of mayonnaise before a timer ran out. He was halfway through and already looked as if he might be sick. Awesome, thought Alex.

CHAPTER 3

"Home is where the heart is" – E. A. Poe

The Berghaus Hotel in Germany had first been built in 1890 as a luxury sanatorium. The mountain air, thin with oxygen, thick with pine, was seen as the ideal antidote to bronchial infections and other maladies. Even shrouded in snow, as it was today, it held a breathtaking panoramic view of the bright green fields of Bavaria below. This vista was considered a perfect panacea for any problems of the mind that visitors might suffer. Of course, if that failed, its plunging cliff-side patio offered a different sort of relief for the deeply depressed and had done so on more than one occasion. Either way, once the Berghaus's patients checked in, they knew they would soon be leaving their troubles behind. During the war, The Berghaus's relative seclusion had made it an ideal retreat for Hitler's inner circle. Often, they would stay there, while the Führer and a select few stayed at his private chalet, the Berghof, just an hour's drive away. The Berghaus, it was said, put the 'party' back in the Nazi Party, with the late night sex romps for the would-be rulers of the world and their eager consorts. Following the war, its image tainted by Nazi frivolity, the Berghaus was largely forgotten. It suffered years of neglect and the loss of a wing to fire before finally being bought, restored and relaunched in 1976 as a grand hotel once more. The stigma of war was then far enough in the past to be dismissed as mere history. Now, it served, not as a retreat for convalescents, but primarily for business men seeking to find a discreet location for their indiscretions.

Inside, the lobby had been faithfully restored to prewar opulence, complete with ornate gold leaf moulding and Bavarian blue carpets. The morning tide of guests checking-out was at its height. The lounge was open for breakfast at that time. If a guest asked, however, he could always order a drink. So it was that a waiter carried a stein of Bitburger, and a glass of Perrier, to a corner booth. There, Mathias Boltzmann sat ensconced, receiving his newly arrived friend and business associate from America, Carl Weiss. "Pröst!" said Mathias with a warm smile as he lifted the glass of sparkling water. Carl grinned back, clinked his glass and took a deep draught. It had been a long flight, followed by an even longer drive up the tenuous mountain roads. For a moment, Carl simply savoured the bright pilsener. It felt good to be back in Deutschland.

Both Carl and Mathias were businessmen and had done deals together many times in the past. While American by birth, Carl's Germanic name was no coincidence. He liked doing business with Germans and considered his heritage to be as much a part of his identity as his official nationality. Carl was convinced that the Germans' loss of World War II was due to a simple "lapse in judgement." Hitler, he believed, had fallen victim to hubris, what with taking on too many fronts and his unfortunate obsession with exterminating the Jews. Carl argued, however, that hubris was an imperfection of greatness. The true takeaway of the war wasn't that Germany had lost, but that for a while it looked as if Germany would win. Hitler stood alone against all of the other countries of Europe, and had very nearly triumphed. Technically he'd had the Italians as allies, but they were the clown princes of the continent and didn't count. The British resisted, of course, but they were a lost tribe of Germans. Carl truly believed that World War II confirmed, rather than belied, the truth of Germanic might. He'd made this belief incarnate in his own way, by building a sizeable fortune as the largest independent distributor of "Genuine German" brätwurst in the mid-western United States. There, he was known simply as "the Sausage King". Flush with profits, Carl soon found himself looking to expand his business dealings beyond big sausage. He met Mathias Boltzmann at a Republican fundraiser in New York. With his silver hair, fierce black brows and handsome face, Mathias reminded Carl of Gregory Peck. Mathias Boltzmann had the sort of magnetic presence that made men feel lucky to be the object of his attention. Mathias complimented Carl on his 'tiny wiener', referring to his new line of cocktail sausages. "It's small," he said, "but quite delectable." The two men hit it off both personally and professionally and, when Mathias offered Carl the opportunity to invest in his business dealings, Carl leapt at the chance. Mathias was, at this point, already the largest independent illicit arms dealer in the world. Carl was unfazed by either the illegality or immorality of the business. "If I gave a damn about how sausage was made," he said, "I'd never have gotten into the wurst business in the first place!" If anything, Carl was invigorated by the arms-length element of danger and enamoured of the sheer Aryan might of his new found friend. "Now Mathias, what is this thing that has got you so excited you would actually leave your precious Monaco retreat to tell me?"

Mathias smiled. His eyes twinkled under his bushy black brows as if enjoying a private joke. He then nodded and slid a thin silver laptop onto the table. He lifted the display as if unveiling something of great, but solemn importance. Its screen showed an eBay auction page. Mathias gazed at Carl with piercing blue eyes and said simply, "This."

Carl looked at the web page. It was offering what looked like a simple steel canister for sale. Carl peered at it more closely trying to discern its value. "What is this? It looks like a... martini shaker?" Carl glanced up at Mathias, who was clearly amused by his response. He considered the possibility that the German was playing a joke, and that the joke was on him. No, he decided, he'd given Mathias too much money over the years. Whatever the man thought of him privately, he surely wouldn't have called him here to humiliate him. It would simply be bad for business. He looked at the page again. "The top bid is $62?"

Mathias nodded. "My bid."

The amount made Carl even more confused. What item for sale on eBay for $62 could possibly be of interest to Mathias Boltzmann? "Surely this is a joke," said Carl, "Unless..."

"Unless?"

"Unless, you know something that the seller does not?" said Carl. Mathias's grin widened. Carl couldn't help but feel that he was being toyed with, but his curiosity had the better of him now, so he didn't care.

"My dear friend," said Mathias, "when you've facilitated the cross-border exchange of surplus military hardware as long as I have..."

"You mean, dealt arms."

"Finc. When you've dealt arms as long as I have, documents and information also have a tendency to fall into one's hands. Information that may, at first, have no immediate value. Such were the papers that led me to this. I am, perhaps, the only person alive who knows what this is, and let me assure you, this is no martini shaker. This? This is something wonderful."

Carl studied the photo again. It had evidently been taken with the canister sitting on the edge of a desk. In the background, he could just make out a poster of a Rastafarian monkey smoking a bong.

CHAPTER 4

"It's a party line." – J.E. Hoover

The front of the CIA Headquarters in Langley, Virginia was designed to look friendly and approachable. From its own freeway exit sign to the arching glass canopy entrance, the facility more closely resembled a suburban shopping mall than a spy agency. Like a shopping mall, the agency included an actual Starbucks location. Here, however, in the interest of national security, the baristas were forbidden to write the names of customers on the cups, despite the argument that their spelling could be seen as a form of encryption. Still, the building design was better than the F.B.I.'s headquarters in Washington, where the J. Edgar Hoover building most resembled a stack of giant concrete waffles. It was also less unsettling than the black box that served both literally and metaphorically as the NSA's headquarters in Maryland. The CIA Headquarters was not so much a statement in modern architecture, as a redaction.

"Okay, so what is it exactly?" asked Charlie Draper, as he and Alicia Tremblay made their way down the long windowless hallway. Charlie hadn't been there in months and so found himself noticing the collection of regularly spaced photographs decorating the white walls. The images were uniformly black and white portraits of white men in black suits. Even if they were in colour, Charlie mused, how would you know? The subjects were CIA officials and senior agents from the 1940s, 50s, and 60s. One of the photos reminded Charlie of his father, except that his dad had worn glasses while this man did not. Charlie's actual father had been a cattle auctioneer in Houston and, without his glasses, he used to say he couldn't tell a Brahman from a Beefmaster. Charlie was lucky for being born in the era of LASIK eye surgery. A doctor had fired a light beam into his cornea and corrected his vision forever. Despite his perfect eyesight, Charlie had no interest in the classification of cows, or any other livestock for that matter. He was not his father's son. His father had said so himself. At age eight his father had told Charlie bluntly, "You're my second favourite son." In any circumstance this would have been a hurtful thing to say; Charlie, however, was an only child. His mother had tried to persuade him that his father was saying that he was "second to none," but Charlie knew that wasn't true.

"We don't know what it is," answered Alicia. "We need you for clearance. George found it."

Charlie didn't know who 'George' was but assumed he was an analyst. "Well then, what does George say it is?"

"He doesn't, I mean he won't. He'll only tell you."

"I see," said Charlie when, in truth, he did not. None of this made sense. Of course, it didn't help that this was his first day on the job. He'd been on a leave of absence for the past five months and wasn't supposed to return for several more. Something had happened, however, with Doug Cranberry, the official who had been running the cyber-espionage division— something embarrassing. All Charlie had been told was that it involved "3D midget call-girls," whatever that meant. He assumed it was code for something else, or at least he hoped it was. Doug had resigned a few days ago. Charlie, having once worked for a software company, was perceived as the best and, probably, only qualified choice among senior agency officials. So they'd asked him to come back early and take charge of a team he'd never met. Not to worry, he had been told, "the unit largely runs itself." It was seen as a cabal of computer geeks who were accustomed to working for people who didn't understand what they did. Of course, normally an incoming director had time to get up to-speed, sit in a few meetings and at least read a dossier or two before taking the wheel. Charlie felt as if he'd woken from a dream to find himself driving a car, at night, with no headlights.

"So who exactly is this George?"

"You don't know?" Alicia stared at him to see if he was joking. Charlie's blank stare answered her question. "They really did drop you in dark didn't they? Hmm... Well, you'll meet him in a moment. It's probably easier that way."

"Can you at least tell me where George found it?"

"On the internet."

"Well, that narrows things."

They'd arrived at the elevator at the end of the hall. Alicia pressed her finger on the down button, which doubled as a biometric scanner. The white disc lit up, scanning her fingerprint. "Access denied," said a computer-generated female voice. Alicia pressed her finger once more. "Access denied," said the voice again, sounding, in Charlie's opinion, a little self-satisfied. Alicia sighed and gave the console a hard smack. "Access granted." The elevator doors opened, and they stepped inside. Alicia ignored the numbered floors, which only went up, and inserted a passcard instead. The elevator began to descend.

"And when did you find it?" Charlie asked. He hadn't much luck finding out what, who or where it was and decided that this was the only question left to not get answered.

"Ninety minutes ago," said Alicia.

"Wow, specificity. It's fortunate I was nearby."

"Very."

"I was shopping for socks."

Alicia looked at Charlie wondering why he'd shared this with her. Charlie wondered the same thing and decided he hadn't a clue. He sometimes felt as if he were an undercover alien who'd forgotten how to communicate with humans. Lisa, his wife, had always been so much better at it than him. She could talk to anyone, including perfect strangers. She called it 'the gift of the gab'. She'd passed that gift onto their daughter, Faith. Faith could hold an intelligent conversation from the moment she could string two words together. Charlie, on the other hand, had always been the master of awkward pauses. Despite being conventionally good-looking, in college he'd been mostly dateless. Girls would want to talk to him, and he'd respond with "um... uh..." He knew that the words most often used to describe him by girls were 'boring' and 'disappointing'. Lisa was the exception. Lisa was able to get him to talk before he started to think too much. That was the trick of easy conversation, he'd learned—avoid thinking.

Talking to Lisa was somehow effortless, and he'd loved her for it. Of course, at the funeral no one had expected him to talk. Not that he was thinking much either. It felt that day, as if his brain had been vapourized. It still did. Charlie Draper had a smoking crater between his ears. Now and again, the smoke still made his eyes water.

"We're all very sorry for your loss," Alicia said softly.

Charlie nodded. The elevator doors opened, and they stepped out.

The room looked like a university computer lab made entirely of metal. Dozens of PCs manned by dozens of young men, mostly about college age, glanced up as they entered. The analysts then quickly returned their attention to the screens before them. This was the secret cyber lab. There were three other less secret cyber labs in the building with the unimaginative names of Cyber Lab 1, Cyber Lab 2, and Cyber Lab 3. This lab was different and its existence was known only to a select few. As the confidential dossier on it explained, the only people who knew of it were a handful of senior officials; its direct manager, Alicia Tremblay; and the highly skilled personnel who worked there. There were, of course, also the day janitor, the night janitor, and the guy who restocked the soda pop machine, but that was it. Such was the reality of running a massive intelligence facility. There were cleaners who had higher access levels than half the management staff. Someone, after all, had to empty the wastebaskets. The name of the super-secret lab was Cyber Lab $\sqrt{-16}$.

"So, who's George?" Charlie scanned the young men for someone who looked like he might be named George.

Alicia pointed to the far wall, which Charlie now saw was made of dark glass. Behind it, in shadow, was a second wall made of racked 1U computers stacked in columns. Joined as a cluster, they each served as neurones in a single super-computer brain. Through the dark glass the machines themselves were almost invisible, but the blue-white LED indicator lights created the appearance of an organized array of stars. It was a galaxy created by a God suffering from OCD. "Meet George," said Alicia with a smile. "George surfs thousands of webpages per millisecond, intercepts emails, accesses blogs. He's basically a specialized search-engine but instead of giving you the top twenty sites on whatever, he looks for the top twenty terrorists. He knows pretty much everything published or communicated online. He hacks systems without any human help. That's why we call him George, as in *Curious George.*"

"Ah," said Charlie, "I was thinking of a different George." Charlie gazed at the starfield that was George and wondered what he'd gotten himself into. Everyone knew the political explosion that the NSA's PRISM program had created, once exposed by Edward Snowden in 2013. Similarly, the domain of the CIA was, ostensibly, limited to foreign intelligence gathering. In practice, however, the line between foreign and domestic was often blurred. Foreigners corresponded with Americans, travelled to the United States, owned US companies, and so on. "Doesn't this contravene the idea that the CIA isn't supposed to spy on US citizens?"

There were chuckles around the room, which Alicia silenced with a harsh stare. "We're not spying on US citizens," she explained, "we're spying on suspected terrorists *among* US citizens. We just don't know which is which until after we've looked. It's like using a trawl net. We sweep the ocean floor and throw back any innocent dolphins that get caught."

"Don't the dolphins usually die in a trawl net?"

"The point is, George is a black box. We don't get to see what he sees unless he identifies it as a possible concern. It's exactly how Google works, they don't read your emails and search results, their machines do. So that makes it okay. Only after George finds something algorithmically suspicious does he send it to a team member. That agent then uses human judgement to determine if the issue is 'actual' or not."

"I see," said Charlie. George was different from PRISM in that its information gathering didn't require the cooperation of private partners or even CIA agents for that matter. Somehow, it acted autonomously. George wasn't human, so it couldn't break the law by itself. If George raised an alarm, a warrant could no doubt be obtained from the FISA court making it legal to look at what it had found. Charlie wasn't sure if that made it better or worse.

"So he—it found something 'actual'?"

"Paul, show Mr. Draper what George found."

One of the young men nodded and clicked his mouse to bring up a browser window. In it was an eBay auction page showing what, to Charlie, appeared to be one of those reusable steel coffee cups sold at Starbucks. He leaned over the agent's shoulder for a closer look. Instead of the Starbucks logo, it had the words "US Government" and "Top Secret" clearly engraved on its side. "Okay, so it looks like something. Army trash maybe? Do we know what it is?"

"No idea," said Paul as he cracked open a Diet Coke and took a sip. "George won't tell us."

"The thing is this," said Alicia, "George has a huge database of stuff to look at. Much more than we know or have access to. When George finds something he ranks it from one to ten in importance. One being, say, a Muslim buying a handgun illegally. Ten being known terrorists building a nuclear bomb in Albuquerque."

"Okay..."

"Most of this stuff is harmless. We get a lot of red herrings. So being, well, a bit understaffed, we only look into the fives and above."

"Got it," said Charlie, " so... what ranking did this get?"

"Eleven."

Charlie smiled. He then realized Alicia wasn't joking or, if she was, had great deadpan delivery. "I thought the rankings only went from one to ten."

"So did we."

* * *

Charlie and Alicia sat in the Meringue conference room. All of the conference rooms in this area had been renamed after desserts as part of a more 'family friendly' initiative. The NSA PRISM fiasco had put the whole intelligence community on the defensive. So the CIA was trying proactively to soften its image. Of course, no actual families were allowed into the area, but still, the idea was to make them feel welcome should that change. Whenever the agency attempted to soften its image it usually ended up looking desperate or creepy instead. Charlie thought of last year's attempt at a neighbourhood open house. All of the staff wore stickers that read "Hello my name is...", but with their actual names redacted out with a black bar. Still, the confectionery conference room names served another purpose as well. It was felt that, should the rooms ever be referred to in the context of, say, a Senate inquiry, dessert names might make the proceedings sound a little less menacing. So, next to Meringue was S'mores, where many of the most lethal oversea drone attacks had been planned. On the other side of the hall was Twinkie, booked for the week by Narcotics. Finally, there was

Chaos Theory

Cream Puff, where a review of the effectiveness of water boarding was currently underway. Faith would have loved this, thought Charlie. The image of his daughter's face popped unwillingly into his thoughts. He remembered her eating s'mores on a camping trip, marshmallow dripping on her shoes. *Not now*, he said to himself, forcing the image from his mind.

Charlie and Alicia faced a teleconference screen filled with the looming face of CIA Director, Robert Morely. The problem with the 70" high definition screen, Charlie decided, was too much detail. For example, Charlie could see that the CIA director wore contacts and had a plethora of old acne scars. When he wasn't talking, Morely's jaw moved up and down with the mesmerizing motion of a cow chewing its cud, only in this case, its cud was tobacco. "George who?" he said in a thick Kentucky drawl.

"George the computer, sir," offered Charlie.

"Ah right, George. So you think George ID'd it by the identi-fo-cation numbers?"

Charlie glanced at Alicia, who nodded and said, "Yes, sir."

Morely considered this as he unwrapped and stuffed another wad of chewing tobacco into his mouth. He did so without removing the plug that was already there. "I thee," he said, the additional tobacco somewhat impairing his speech. Charlie wondered if the excessive chewing was a sort of nervous twitch and if so, why the Director was so nervous. Did he know something they didn't? At that moment a woman leaned into view on the monitor and whispered something into Morely's ear. His face went grim and paled noticeably. "I thee," he said and crammed a third plug of tobacco into his mouth. He waved the woman away and stared at the screen, brow furrowed, cheeks stuffed like a chipmunk. As he chewed, Charlie watched in 1080p as a trail of yellow nicotine spittle ran from the edge of his mouth.

Morley wiped his chin, smearing rather than removing the liquid. "Mow wiffen Chawee. Tha's a' odc id mumba buh i' is vawid."

"The number's valid?"

"Yeth, we weed to recova tha' i'em a' any coth't."

"We need to recover the item at any cost?"

"Yeth!" shouted the CIA Director impatiently, spitting on the camera lens. Despite his stern front, he was clearly unnerved. This made Charlie nervous as well.

"Right," said Charlie. "The problem is, sir, there's only minutes left before the auction ends."

"So wha' a' you goo-ing abou' it?"

Charlie paused to mentally decipher Morely's garbled words.

"Well?"

"We've already dispatched a team, sir. They should arrive at the listed address in Michigan in ..." Charlie glanced at his watch, "...one hour, and fifty-five minutes."

"Goo. Wha' elf a' you goo-ing?"

"Um, well, we're, um... bidding on it, sir."

Tom Morely studied Charlie. Sitting in his Washington DC hotel room, he was viewing them on his laptop. The two agents looked small and insignificant. Too small, too insignificant, he thought. The CIA Director nervously mashed another wad of tobacco into his mouth and considered what to do. "Goo," he said.

* * *

Alex and Gerald stared intently at the computer screen, waiting for the eBay page to update. "Your connection is a piece of crap," muttered

Gerald as he tongued the hole of his pop can.

"I know," said Alex.

"You should get cable. DSL sucks."

"Your cable is out all the time."

"Yeah, but it's fast as Hell when it works."

The first six days the mystery canister had been up for auction there had been a total of six bids and a few random inquiries from army-surplus nuts, driving the price to a total of $62. Suddenly, just an hour before the auction was set to end, the price had jumped to over $200. The webpage loaded. Gerald almost sprayed Dr. Pepper out of his nose. "Holy crap!"

"A thousand bucks!" shouted Alex. He couldn't believe his eyes.

"Keep it down in there!" his mother yelled through the wall.

"Sorry mom!" Alex put his finger to his lips to silence Gerald, who wasn't even supposed to be there. Gerald had snuck over after Alex had emailed him that the price was climbing. "I'm gonna be rich!"

"A thousand dollars isn't rich. Anyway, half of that's mine!"

"Yeah, right."

"If I hadn't made you go around that rock—"

"Holy crap, two thousand bucks!"

Alex blinked at the pixelated numbers on his screen in amazement. He glanced at the silver canister sitting on his dresser. The gleam of light on the top rim seemed to wink at Alex knowingly. "I wonder what's inside that these people want it so badly?"

"Money," said Gerald.

"Really?"

"No, dumb-bum, the hopes and dreams of suckers. If it was money, we'd keep it. Anyway, hit refresh."

* * *

Alicia crouched down beside Paul, the analyst, who entered their latest bid on the eBay auction page. Charlie observed from behind. He was still not convinced this wasn't some sort of hacker prank or bizarre bug in George's programming. The problem with black boxes, he knew, was that they're black boxes. Nobody really knows what's going on inside the damn things. They simply spew out results without repercussion, like a late night psychic hotline or the FCC. They become like the obelisks in *2001: A Space Odyssey*—powerfully mysterious and utterly confounding. Unlike the obelisk, George wore his stars on the outside, but Charlie still had no idea what it all meant. "How are we doing?" he asked.

"Currently at $9,350," said Paul. "You want to stop at 10k?"

"No."

Alicia and Paul both stared at Charlie.

"We can't lose this," he stated emphatically. He realized he was biting his nails and shoved his hands into his pockets. "Keep going."

Paul nodded and upped the bid. The screen refreshed. "Ten thousand," said Alicia. "This is crazy! What lunatic would bid that high besides us? Not that we're lunatics, I mean, but—"

"Someone else who knows what it is," said Charlie. He ran his fingers through his hair as he tried to consider the possibilities. "Who could know what this is besides us?"

"Well, technically, we don't know what this is."

"Morely does." Charlie had seen fear in the Director's eyes. He'd also seen half-chewed tobacco stuck between the Director's teeth whenever he spoke. Charlie banished the entire unsettling image from his mind. "But, yes... exactly."

Paul waved at them, "Auction ends in one minute. We need to put in our maximum bid, or we could lose it. I could put in a million bucks."

"Put in a trillion bucks."

"I can't, the field only accepts ten characters. So, the most I could put in is nine-billion, nine-hundred and ninety-nine million, nine-hundred and ninety-nine thousand, nine-hundred and ninety-nine dollars."

"Do it."

"You're the boss." Paul dutifully entered the long string of nines, then clicked the "Place Bid" button.

Alicia stared at Charlie, "That's more than our entire operating budget!"

"Auction's closed!" shouted Paul. They all stared at the screen, waiting for the result.

"It's the property of the US Government, we're not going to have to pay. Plus it's not even that much by Fed standards."

"And eBay only increments your bid to the amount needed to win," said Paul. "We'll owe far less than that."

"You couldn't have told me that before?" said Charlie. He realized he was chewing his nails again.

"I thought everyone knew that." As Paul spoke, the screen refreshed. "We won! For... twenty-million and ten dollars? Holy crap!"

"Congratulations," smiled Alicia, "I think you just became the single highest online auction bidder ever."

"Pay it," said Charlie.

"What, now? We have time."

"Now."

"Why?" asked Alicia.

"Because someone else was willing to pay twenty-million dollars to get this thing. So lets lock it down. We'll get the money back. Go on, Paypal it." Charlie pulled his jacket from the back of his chair and turned to leave. "Meanwhile, I'm going to Michigan."

"I hear it's nice," said Paul.

CHAPTER 4.6692

"...and, if I turn it upside down, it spells *BOOBIES!*"
– M. Feigenbaum

The rain was oppressive in the sort of way that rain is. Not content with merely landing on you like most forms of weather, rain insists on soaking through your clothes, making them cling cold and wet to your clammy skin. In this way, rain wasn't merely oppressive. It was downright rude. At that moment, however, Alex loved it. It was invigorating. Its sensory assault seemed to affirm his very being by defining it with a feeling of wetness. Even the invisible man becomes visible in the rain, he thought. Alex sometimes thought of himself as invisible, at school, at home. This was not one of those moments. This was a moment where he felt alive.

"You don't have to send it today, dickweed!" shouted Gerald.

"I told you, I don't want to risk it," said Alex as he charged down the gravel side road. The two boys dodged pothole puddles as they made their way through the colonnades of tall trees. Alex glanced at his watch. If they didn't hurry, they would miss it. Alex had been begging his mother for years to move closer to town, and she'd always told him that she preferred the isolation of the woods. The truth was, they simply couldn't afford it.

"They've already paid you, so what does it matter?"

"It matters," said Alex. He was scared that if he did anything wrong, the millions might vanish. It was all so surreal. Technically he had been paid. It was all right there, in his Paypal account. Still, he couldn't actually withdraw it yet. Apparently, such a large amount required some sort of hold. Now, he felt a desperate need to keep up his side of the bargain. With that kind of money he could buy his mom the home they'd never dreamed of. Despite all of their arguments, Alex loved his mother. As much as he made her unhappy, he wanted to make her happy.

The boys reached the last dip in the road. Alex managed a controlled descent on the wet gravel. Gerald wiped out, rolling painfully over the small stones. "God damn it! This is your fault, Alex!"

Alex ignored his fallen friend and sprinted towards the main road. He could just make it out between the trees—the white metal frame of the USPS truck. "Wait!" Alex yelled. He reached the asphalt road just as the mail truck started to pull away. "Wait!" he cried, frantically waving his arms. The truck's brake lights brightened. The truck pulled to a stop. Alex, ran alongside to where the driver sat. The postman watched him, bemused, through rain speckled glasses. "Yep?"

"I've got a package," said Alex, panting to catch his breath. He then offered up the white plastic shopping bag he'd been cradling.

"You want to take it out of the bag?"

"Oh, yeah." Alex tore off the water soaked bag and handed him the brown paper parcel. The postman peered at the entire book of stamps that coated one side. "Is that enough?" asked Alex desperately. He glanced at Gerald who had arrived now beside him, looking as pissed-off as possible.

The postman shrugged and tossed the parcel into the back. "Probably."

Alex opened his mouth to object but, before he could say anything, the driver put the truck in gear and pulled away. Alex stood slack-jawed on the shoulder. He turned to Gerald, whose normally curly red hair was now plastered across his forehead. "Do you think that's enough?" asked Alex.

"How should I know numb-nuts?"

"What happens if it's not?"

"Then, they return to sender, and we sell it all over again... or whatever." Gerald turned around and stomped back down the side road. He'd had enough of Alex running the show. He wasn't even sure how that had happened. Somehow Alex had stopped letting him make all the decisions and where had it got them? Freezing their asses off in the rain like losers, that's where. "Come on!" Gerald growled.

Alex suddenly felt deflated. With the canister gone, the whole thing seemed like a dream. It had to be a dream; it made no sense. He trudged slowly up the road and, for the first time that day, felt cold and wet.

* * *

Colonel Rynard Gruber did not move. A single raindrop hung from the tip of his long aquiline nose but did not fall. More rain beaded on the camouflage grease paint he wore on both cheeks. Spread out on either side of him, hidden under the shadows of the forest ferns, huddled a small contingent of men, stock still moss covered statues in the garden of good and evil. They were invisible, save for where the rain drops defined them. "No sign of the boy," said a voice in Rynard's earpiece, "he must be away from the windows."

Or not at home at all, thought Rynard. Never assume, it makes an ass out of you and me. A British man had told him that once. That man was now dead. The Colonel had killed him when the man assumed he would not. "You've made an ass of yourself," Rynard had said, as he pulled the trigger.

"Should we move in?" asked the voice in his ear.

It was Braun. He's an ass too, thought Rynard. "No. We wait until we see him. We wait all night if we have to."

"Yes, sir," said Braun.

The boy's mother was clearly visible in the yellow light of the kitchen. She was washing dishes and staring wistfully out at the rain. She was looking right at them, totally oblivious to their presence. A large mosquito bit into Rynard's forearm, right into his tattoo of a modified Nazi SS symbol. Rynard watched the mosquito fatten with his blood and did not move. This was nothing to him. He'd once crouched for two days in the basement of a latrine, covered with cockroaches and maggots, while awaiting his mark. When the target had finally entered, the man never saw it coming. Despite the victim being over two hundred and fifty pounds, Rynard managed to drag him through the twelve inch toilet hole and suffocate him in sewage. As a result, the body was never found. It was ridiculous and sublime. That was Rynard's favourite kind of kill; the kind where the victim simply vanishes. Murder can be elegant in its own way. Rynard firmly believed that killing was an art form. He'd come to see death as an end in itself. Belly bloated, the tiny bloodsucker flew away. Rynard mentally congratulated the mosquito as being the only creature to draw his blood and live. He glanced back at his tattooed bicep where a welt was already forming. A US Customs official had once stopped him, upon noticing the apparent Nazi insignia on his arm. Rynard pointed out, that it was not a pair of S's, but a pair of dollar signs. Rynard felt no fealty to the Führer, only to the almighty dollar, euro or whatever other currency he was being paid in. The customs official had waved him through; there was no arguing with dollar signs. Rynard wore one other tattoo. It read simply "Anna" in Schaftstiefel Grotesk type. Rynard raised the binoculars again. The target's mother looked tired. She placed the last dish on the rack, turned away from the window and was gone.

The rain began to let up.

"We have the boy, approaching from the main road."

Rynard smiled with satisfaction. "Wait until he's entered the house, then we go."

A minute passed.

"He's inside."

"Go."

Fourteen soldiers materialized out of the wet woods.

* * *

Alex and Gerald stood dripping in the front hall. "Wipe your feet!" shouted his mother from the living room, "and hang up your coat!"

"Sure mom," said Alex. He carefully hung the dripping jacket on the hook. A pool of water instantly formed on the floor below.

"Such a good boy," said Gerald with a sneer.

"I'm sneaking you in aren't I?" said Alex. He'd first checked to make sure his mother was in the other room watching TV before inviting Gerald inside. It was risky, but easier than having him climb over the woodpile outside Alex's window. Still, if his mother caught them, she'd take his internet privileges for sure. "I'd get a Mustang," said Alex, continuing their conversation from before.

"A Mustang?" said Gerald with a snort. "You're such a hick! For that kind of money you get a Porsche."

"Oh..."

"Or maybe a Bugatti."

"Yeah, you're right," said Alex. He had no idea what a Bugatti was, but wasn't about to admit that. At that moment, what looked like an unmarked pop can rolled across the carpet and stopped at his feet. "Ger, what's that?" asked Alex.

"What's what, dickwee—"

The gas grenade exploded with a *FOOOM!*—filling the room with white smoke. Alex and Gerald gasped and choked before dropping to the floor.

"What the Hell is going on?" said Alex's mother as she stormed into the hall. Claire found herself walking into a cloud of knockout gas, halothane mixed with potassium chlorate and lactose. Claire was lactose intolerant but, really, that was the least of her concerns. Her first thought was that the boys had been playing with fireworks again. She carried this misconception with her all the way to the carpet, where she landed with a *thud!* There she lay, unable to move but still vaguely conscious. Her anesthetized brain continued to function in a detached, unemotional way. She watched, curious, as a troop of Neo Nazi mercenaries dressed in camouflage gear and gas masks exploded through every window of her home. Two of the soldiers appeared above her. Each held an MP7 suppressor-tipped submachine gun, or 'personal defence weapon' as the NRA preferred to call them. The soldiers gazed down at Alex's mother through mirrored plexiglass face masks. Claire could see herself in the reflections. How embarrassing, she thought, my hair is disaster. Somewhere, in the back of her brain, terror clawed at the lid, trying to get out. The soldiers spoke to one another through their masks. Their voices sounded like garbled announcements from a subway train PA system. Claire wanted to say something they could understand, to bridge the divide. "Mind the gap," she said. The glass faces looked down at her obliquely. Claire's final fleeting thought was how the glass particles from the windows looked like glittering snow on the men's shoulders.

Rynard entered the hallway, wearing a simple rubber gas mask and goggles. He snapped his fingers, pointed to the boys, and flipped his hand. Two mercenaries rolled over the bodies of the unconscious boys. Rynard studied their faces. He then twirled a single finger in the air. The men immediately set about ransacking the small house. Rynard checked the gas meter on his wrist. He lifted his mask, inhaled, held, and remained conscious. "Clear." The men pulled up their own masks, then continued with the task at hand, overturning tables and slashing sofa cushions.

One of the soldiers reached the fireplace and paused to pick up a snow globe sitting on the mantle. Inside was a plastic four leaf clover and the words "Good Luck!" in green celtic script. The soldier shook the sphere and watched, amused, as snow fell inside. Rynard cuffed him on the back of the head and snarled, "Get back to work!" The soldier dropped the glass ball to the floor and scurried to search a nearby closet. The snow globe bounced and rolled to rest at the toe of Rynard's boot. The Colonel saw the inscription and scoffed. He didn't believe in luck. Nor did he believe in fate. He thought that people who said "everything happens for a reason" were idiots. A South African game warden had said it to him while arresting Rynard for smuggling. Moments later, after disarming the warden and turning the gun on him, Rynard repeated the words back to him. "Everything happens for a reason," he said. "In this case, the reason is ten million euros in black rhinoceros horn." He then shot the game warden between the eyes. Rynard smiled at the memory of the look on, what was left of, the man's face. Rynard kicked the snow globe away. He then turned and joined in the search himself. He was never above getting his hands dirty.

*   *   *

Using a pair of tongs, Charlie picked up the cracked snow globe from beneath a smashed IKEA *Söderhamn* chair. He peered at the message inside. If we're lucky we'll get some prints off it, he thought. He placed it gingerly into a ziplock evidence bag. "Looks like they beat us to it," said one of the agents.

Charlie peered about the small home. The power was out. The interior was lit in stark relief by the crisscrossed beams of floodlights they'd erected to aid in the search. The cold night air blew freely through the shattered glass windows, billowing the drapes, and scattering loose papers. Outside, the dark woods, wild, harsh, and impenetrable, formed a black mass against an eigengrau sky. Hours ago, this was a cozy family home, he thought, if only for a single mother and her son. The sense of violation was stark—drawers dumped, upholstery torn, lighting fixtures pulled from walls. Charlie shuddered. He also felt disappointment. They were too late. There was no sign of their objective and the only two people who could tell them about it were dead. Charlie considered again the bodies of the mother and her young son. Both had been forced to the floor somehow, then shot between the eyes. There was no sign of struggle. The bullets had passed clean through their skulls and penetrated several inches into the floor. Armour piercing ammunition with no armour to pierce. Charlie rolled the young man's head with his toe and tried to look for a hint of resemblance to his mother. They had nothing in common, other than the new family trait of a bullet hole through the forehead. Red hair, thought Charlie, he must have got it from his father. Everyone said Faith took mostly after her mother, save for her eyes. She'd had Charlie's eyes. Charlie stopped himself from thinking about it. Nobody had his eyes now. "I'm not so sure," said Charlie.

The agent looked at him. Around the house, a small team of CIA operatives picked through the wreckage, gathering any possible clues in ziplock bags. Charlie nervously touched the gun in his pocket. Despite working three years as a field agent, he had never once carried a gun. The agency had no domestic law enforcement mandate—that was FBI or DHS territory. Charlie had tried to suggest bringing in the bureau but Morely, predictably, said no. He'd claimed there was no time, but the reality was that Morely was an agency man, and old habits die hard.

"Whoever did this was a professional," said Charlie, "and there were several of them. It's messy... but methodical. It's also complete. They didn't stop part way through as if they'd found something. So, unless it really was in the last place they looked..." Charlie's iPhone chirped. He peered down to see he'd received a new message on CIM, the CIA's encrypted messaging app. It was a photo of Claire Graham, in her pre bullet-in-the-face days. She looks nice, he thought, like a good mom. He swiped to the next photo. It was of Claire with her arm around her son Alex. Alex looks a lot like his mother after all, he thought, but nothing like the boy on the floor. He glanced at Gerald Allen, with his red hair, hazel eyes and tomato soup seeping from the hole in his forehead. Nope, thought Charlie, nothing at all.

CHAPTER 5

"Do I really sound like that?" – R. M. Nixon

The President of the United States sat at the head of the White House Situation Room table. Also present were; Jim Hornswell, Chief of Staff; General Frank Troy, Head of Armed Services; several other advisors and security staff. Teleconferenced in on the big screen was CIA Director, Robert Morely who, on direct orders of the President, had left his chewing tobacco at home. Instead, the director was chomping furiously on a piece of nicotine gum.

"Indestructible?" asked the President, skeptically.

"Yes sir, but I assure you; we have our very best people on it."

"Like who?" asked Jim.

"Charles Draper. Good man."

"Never heard of him."

"Yes, well, with all due respect, sir, do you know any of our senior staff?"

The Commander-in-Chief waved this off. "What about nuclear weapons? Can't we just blow it to Hell? As a preemptive last resort, of course." The President was still not buying this 'indestructible' nonsense.

"No sir, definitely not. Once opened, it cannot be stopped."

"Sounds like a Senate Inquiry," laughed one of the staffers. His smirk vanished when no one else joined in.

"Even controlled nukes?" asked the President.

Morely, who was used to working with politicians, responded as if the question made perfect sense. "No, sir."

"What about uncontrolled?"

"An *uncontrolled* nuclear strike? We hadn't actually considered that, but... no. Honestly, any use of nuclear weapons could actually make the problem worse." He resisted the urge to ask the Commander-in-Chief if even knew what these terms meant.

"Damn," said the President. Deflated, he took a sip from his coffee. The nuclear option was the one trump card a President was always supposed to have at his disposal. Finding out it was useless was like playing four aces at poker, only to be beaten by four monkeys. "I mean what the hell are four monkeys?" demanded the President.

"I'm sorry sir?"

"What? Oh, nothing. I just... I just never saw a problem a nuclear weapon couldn't fix," he muttered ruefully. "Okay then, it looks like this going to require some out-of-the-box thinking."

A murmur of agreement went around the table.

"Well, those are your orders, people," said the President of the United States.

Those in the room looked at each other, searching for someone among themselves who knew what this meant. Frequently they didn't understand what the President was saying. They simply played along, knowing that, most of the time, it didn't matter anyway. A former staffer once compared meetings with the President to watching a David Lynch movie. It looked like it meant something, but maybe it didn't. Either way, you sure as hell couldn't admit you didn't know or you risked looking like a fool. In Washington, being a fool was fine, looking like a fool was not. This time, however, there was no faking it—someone had to actually do something. "I'm sorry, what are our orders, sir?" asked a junior staffer. While secretly grateful that someone had spoken up, the others glared at him with contempt. The young man suddenly felt like someone who'd inadvertently volunteered to be a participant in an ebola vaccine trial control group.

"You heard the President, think out of the box!" roared General Troy. "You need him to zip up your fly for you too, soldier?"

"Um... I'm not a soldier," said the young staffer, thus ensuring that this was the last time he'd ever be invited to The Situation Room.

The General sneered, "And you never will be."

The President rose to his feet, buttoning his jacket as he did. "Report back to me when you have answers," he said. The others stood accordingly and remained so until the President and his Chief of Staff had left the room.

* * *

The President entered the Oval Office feeling irritated. He then proceeded to pace back and fourth as he attempted to grapple with a problem unlike he, or any president, had ever faced. He remembered what a life coach, and former lover, had once told him years before. The word for "crisis" in Chinese, she said, was a combination of the words "danger" and "opportunity". The President pondered how the danger part was always apparent, while the opportunity part was often elusive. He also thought about how the English word "brunch" was also a combination of two words, "breakfast" and "lunch". The President of the United States then realized he was hungry. He pressed the intercom. "Judy? Send in some grilled cheese sandwiches."

"Yes sir. Any particular type of cheese?"

"The best, of course—American."

"Yes, sir!"

The President turned to his Chief of Staff, who had been standing by patiently "Now, where were we?"

"You were ordering sandwiches."

"Before that."

"Averting Armageddon?"

"Yes, exactly." The President walked behind his desk, placed his hands on the back of his chair and hung his head. Jim was used to this pose. The President did it when he considered serious policy decisions, when he prayed, and when preparing to break wind. Sometimes he did all three at the same time. "I just don't get it," the President confessed. He and Jim went way back. Jim had helped him run for governor. His Chief of Staff was one of the few people he could be completely honest with.

"What? Oh the weapons? Well, nuclear weapons are a wonderful thing, no one's saying they're not, but—"

"No, no, no! I mean, why is this happening to me? Why is it

happening during my term? It's not fair."

"You're right, sir. It's not fair for anybody."

The President began to pace again. "What I want to know is, how did it even get out? And how did anyone know what it was? None of us seemed to know what it was."

"Well, we're not sure, sir. I mean it was the Cold War... it was top secret... it was embarrassing when it was lost... Perhaps they figured it was gone for good, and hoped and prayed it would never be found? Swept it under the rug, as it were."

"But it's the most dangerous weapon ever devised!"

"Well, yes, in theory. It's never actually been tested. Look, Mr. President, they probably figured no one knew it existed, so no one would look for it. No harm, no foul."

"Someone knew it existed!" snapped the President.

"Yes, Mr. President, apparently so," Jim agreed, "but, you know, this could work out well for us. I mean, you can take command and look 'Presidential'. Don't change horses in midstream and all that. It could help us win a second term."

The President stopped pacing and considered this. After a moment, he began to nod, slowly at first, then with enthusiasm. "You're right! It could define my legacy."

"Indeed, sir."

"Assuming we actually avert Armageddon..."

"Well, either way, really—but yes."

The Commander-in-Chief resumed his pacing, this time with growing excitement. Suddenly, the President's eyes lit up and he began waving his arms as if directing planes at an airport. "I've just had a... a...

what's the word? Starts with an 'R'...

"Revelation?"

"No, no. Rrr... rrrrr..."

"Realization?"

"Rrrr..."

"Recognition?"

"No, no, no," The President thought hard for a moment, then snapped his fingers. "Epiphany!"

"My next guess."

"I've had an epiphany. This is no accident."

"It isn't?"

"No. This... this is why God made me President. This was what I was chosen for!"

The Chief of Staff hesitated. The President was a man of faith and that faith had been a guiding light for many of the choices he'd made, first as governor, then as a presidential candidate. Jim, on the other hand, put his faith in poll numbers and back room deals. Still, years of working together had told him when to step back and let the President's authenticity shine through. The people sensed the sincerity of his faith and so far it had never failed them. "Perhaps you're right, sir," said Jim, nodding his head in agreement. "Lets run with that."

"This is about *Judgement Day*, and I don't mean the next election."

"Alleluia, Mr. President."

"Hallelujah, Jim."

CHAPTER 6

"Will you accept this rose?" – Henry VIII

The Sunny Side Motor Inn was one of those ignorable roadside motels whose primary clientele were people who had misjudged how far they would get that day. It was near nothing, had no particular appeal, and rarely had more than two or three cars in the lot. Today, however, was a banner day at this unremarkable lodging. For the first time since the World Pog Convention was held there in 1992, there was a 'No Vacancy' sign hanging out front and tired travellers would simply have to drive on. Normally, this would be something to celebrate for the owner and manager of the Sunny Side Motor Inn, Donald Crane. Don, however, was spending the day stuffed inside the motel ice machine, turning blue.

On the front door hung a sign that said in orange on black letters,

"Be right back!"

Don, like Claire Graham before him, had a bullet hole between his eyes. The position of the hole made it look rather like a tika mark, the symbolic third eye of Hindu culture. In gaining his third eye, Donald had time for only a single flash of insight before his brains were blown out. His single flash of insight was, "Say, that looks like a gun..."

Since Don was indisposed, a mercenary named Alphonse Drek was now covering for him behind the front desk in the motel lobby. Everything about the lobby was drab; from the ash grey carpet to the green paisley wallpaper and matching drapes. The mercenary's task was simple; tell any weary travellers there was no room, and shoot any who seemed suspicious. It was a simple enough assignment, but Alphonse was feeling despondent. He had discovered that the late motel owner had kept an Elvis shrine in the back office; complete with hundreds of photos and memorabilia on a tiny corner altar. Alphonse too was an Elvis devotee, although not to the same religious extreme. The innkeeper seemed convinced that Elvis Presley was the Messiah himself. Of course, it was Rynard who'd actually shot Don, but still it made Alphonse sad to see a fellow fan slain. He softly sang *Are You Lonesome Tonight?* to himself in requiem, as he oiled the muzzle of his FN P90 machine gun.

The rest of the troop was divided into three adjacent rooms on the upper level. Their flight home was not until tomorrow. In the meantime, they could relax. In room 203, two of the men were watching television. The old antennae TV initially showed nothing but static. "If I wanted to watch snow, I'd have stayed in Stuttgart!" the soldier named Jan shouted as he drew his pistol to shoot the set. Before he could pull the trigger, fellow mercenary Johann demonstrated that he could make the TV work by tying a wire garrotte between the rabbit ears. "Ich bin ein MacGyver!" he declared. What Jan and Johann did not know was that one percent of all TV static is background radiation left over from the Big Bang that created the universe 13.7 billion years ago. Of course, even had they known this, they wouldn't have cared. The mercenaries changed channels until they found static organized in the form of a reality TV show called *The Bachelor*. On the show, more than two dozen women compete for the love of one man. In theory, the winner got to marry him. In real reality, almost none of the network arranged marriages worked out. You had a better chance of finding marital bliss with a mail order bride from Moscow. Still, the show was a great way to unwind after a kidnapping. On the screen, the Bachelor kissed his date. It was a passionate kiss and the two Germans watched intently while sharing a jumbo bag of Cheetos. This in itself was an act of disobedience. The Colonel always insisted that the men eat only organic food. Jan and Johann didn't know what Cheetos were exactly, but were fairly certain they didn't qualify as organic—or even food for that matter. "Goodnight," said the Bachelor.

"Are you kidding me?" yelled Jan, throwing up his hands.

"Dummkopf!" said Johann. "She would sleep with you! They would all sleep with you! Ahhh!"

The woman smiled coyly and squeezed the Bachelor's hand one last time.

"At least grope die boobies!"

"Ja."

"How stupid are these Americans? If Germans made this show it would be nothing but sex."

"Or the Italians."

"Yes, the Italians would do a good job."

"But then they would get married and fat."

Jan snorted with laughter, "Ja, is true!"

"Can you please keep it down?" said Elias. Elias was the third soldier sharing the room. He was bent over the bathroom vanity, trying to expunge camouflage paint from his cheeks with makeup remover and cotton balls. Jan and Johann were still wearing their greasepaint and sweaty fatigues. They can keep their clogged pores, thought Elias, nowhere does it say a soldier of fortune can't have clear skin.

There was a knock at the door

For a moment, no one moved. Slowly, Jan and Johann's hands fell to their firearms.

There were three more short knocks.

The men relaxed. It was one of their own. Still, rules were rules. Until visual verification was obtained, a certain amount of caution was required. Both men rose to their feet, hands on pistol grips. Johann spied Elias's gun on the top of the TV. "Annie, get your gun!"

"I'm exfoliating!"

"Get your gun, Fräulein."

Elias turned to face them, fingertips covered in microdermabrasion cream. "First of all, whoever it is, he knew the knock, so he's one of us. Second of all, even if it is the police or whatever, they'd have to get through you to get to me. So what do you care?"

The two mercenaries exchanged glances. "What if it's the Colonel?" asked Jan.

Elias paused. He hadn't considered that. He delicately picked up his pistol with his pinky finger through the trigger guard. "Fine."

Jan nodded and peered through the peephole. He instantly recognized the bald pate of Dr. Holtz. "It's the professor," he said with a laugh. Elias tossed his gun on the bed and returned to the bathroom mirror. Jan unlatched the door and waved Dr. Holtz inside. The doctor, dwarfed by the muscular mercenary, nodded meekly as he entered. He wore coke bottle glasses and nervously stroked a small goatee. The beard itself was grey, but his moustache was stained cigarette yellow from too many late nights in the lab. "I need to see him."

"What for?" asked Jan.

"Ja, the Colonel said he was going to question him himself," said Johann.

"Well, he changed his mind," said Dr. Holtz assertively. It was hard to be assertive when staring up another man's nose. The soldier's nose hairs were perfectly manicured, Holtz noted, just as the Colonel required. Rynard believed that good discipline began with good grooming. He had once yanked off a soldier's unkempt beard with his bare hands. "He wanted me to question him first, to see if I could learn anything technical about the device." The two men eyed him skeptically. "Ask the Colonel yourself if you don't believe me," said the physicist. He pointed to the hotel phone, daring them to call.

Jan considered this a moment, then nodded. "Fine. He's in the bathroom, chained to the toilet."

"Is he okay?"

"Of course."

"Maybe a little wet," grinned Elias, "Jan's aim is terrible."

"Ja, is true," agreed Jan.

The men laughed. Holtz forced a smile.

The toilet was in a separate room next to the vanity and shower. Jan opened the door to reveal the young boy cowering beside the toilet as promised. Inside, a small window offered a second story view of telephone wires and slate sky. Holtz studied the boy. Other than a black eye and bruised temple, he seemed fine, physically anyway. He reached for Alex's face. The boy whimpered and shrank away. Traumatized, thought Holtz, who wouldn't be? Handcuffs held the boy's hands tight around a drainpipe in the floor. Holtz noted the red welts where Alex had strained against them, no doubt for hours. "Give me the keys."

"Why?"

"I want to interrogate him as a boy, not a dog!" He tried to sound authoritative, on the theory that soldiers responded better to orders than requests.

Jan snorted. He then leaned in close and pressed the key into Holtz's hand. "You'll get better obedience from a dog."

Holtz waited for the soldier to go. When he realized the mercenary had no intention of leaving. "This is a private interrogation," said Holtz emphatically.

Jan stared at the scientist, trying to decide if he cared enough to argue.

"It's almost time for the rose ceremony!" Elias shouted from the other room.

"Whatever," said Jan. He then turned and headed back to the bedroom to watch the rest of the show.

Holtz closed the toilet door and quietly locked it. He then turned to face the quivering boy. "Chocolate?" Holtz said in crisp English. He offered Alex a bite of dark chocolate wrapped in foil. Alex stared at Holtz as if the professor had offered him arsenic. "It's good. It's German." The boy shook his head. "Eat it," Holtz insisted, "you'll need your strength... and energy." Alex cautiously accepted the candy, never taking his eyes from Holtz's. He took a bite, then another and another, until the bar was gone. He hadn't eaten since yesterday. "Now, Alex, you need to listen to me," said Dr. Holtz firmly. "I am your friend, your only friend, and we haven't much time."

"Where's my mom?" asked Alex.

"I don't know," the professor lied.

"Who are you?"

Dr. Holtz took a cigarette from an inside coat pocket. He lit it as he spoke. "My name is Dr. Rudolph Holtz. I am a physicist and mathematician from Leipzig." Alex had no idea what or where Leipzig was. The professor paused to exhale, savouring the flavour of the tobacco.

Alex began to cough. "Could you not do that? Smoking will kill you, you know!"

"I should be so lucky," said Dr. Holtz with a chuckle. "Anyway, to answer your next question, you have to trust me because you have no other choice. If you do not, the Colonel will be in here shortly and he will question you. Colonel Rynard Gruber is a soulless man who believes in nothing. His type of interrogation quickly degenerates to the removing of fingernails, fingers and other parts of the body. Things much worse than your dreaded second hand smoke." The professor took a long drag on his cigarette while he let this sink in. Alex's brain tried to grapple with the idea that he seemed to have landed in some torture horror film, complete with Nazis and mad professors. "Now then, give me your hand," said Dr. Holtz. Alex stared at him as if he were mad. "I'm not going to cut off your fingers, boy, I'm going to release you. Quickly now!"

Alex nervously held out his hands. The professor parked his cigarette in the corner of his mouth, and proceeded to unlock Alex's handcuffs. "I'm going to quit after this one," said the Professor with a wry smile, "and this time, I mean it."

The handcuffs fell from Alex's wrists. The boy immediately began to rub the painful welts. "What's going on?" he asked.

"The item you found is extremely valuable and extremely dangerous. So dangerous, that it simply cannot fall into the hands of one such as Mathias Boltzmann."

"Who's Mathias Boltzmann?" asked Alex. Someone had turned on the radio in the next room. What followed was a chorus of falsetto voices singing along in German accents, badly off key. Holtz smiled kindly at Alex. He had been afraid the boy might be too traumatized to absorb anything at all. "Boltzmann is an arms dealer and a very successful one at that. Colonel Gruber and I work for him."

Alex's brain slowly clicked into gear, "So, then why are you helping me?"

The doctor paused. His expression grew dark. "Because I have children myself," he said, "It is for them that I must... quit smoking."

Alex stared at the professor, confused by the course of the conversation. "So what now?" he asked.

"Now? Now, you must go!" Dr. Holtz nodded toward the small window above the toilet. "Too small for a man," he said, "but not too small for a lad such as yourself."

Alex stared at the window. He then stepped up onto the toilet and peered out to the alleyway below. "Are you out of your freakin' mind? That's a twenty-foot drop!"

"There is mud, you see? The mud is soft from the rain; it will break your fall."

"More like break my legs! No freakin' way!" said Alex adamantly. He wasn't exactly scared of heights, but he wasn't fearless of them either.

Fingers shaking, Dr. Holtz took a long drag on his diminishing cigarette. He stared fiercely into Alex's eyes and spoke with punctuated precision. "Boy, Alex, listen carefully. This is the sort of man that Colonel Rynard Gruber is. If he decides you are worth less whole than the sum of your parts, he will not hesitate to dismember you. You understand? If you do not jump now, you may soon have no legs left to break."

* * *

In the motel bedroom, the three mercenaries had largely forgotten Dr. Holtz and Alex. Having given up on television, they had turned to the radio instead. The 1991 hit, *I'm Too Sexy* by Right Said Fred blared at top volume. Jan and Johann sang along, while Elias danced on the bed in his underwear, waving his MP7 submachine gun in the air and shouting "I'm too sexy. Ja! I am too sexy!"

Colonel Gruber entered the room. The men froze. All three mercenaries, veterans of countless gunfights and clandestine operations, were momentarily petrified. They then snapped to attention. "What is this?" Rynard demanded.

"I'm Too Sexy, by Right Said Fr..." Elias trailed off as he realized the Colonel was staring at him.

"Sorry, sir," said Jan. "We were, um... uh..."

"Raising moral?" suggested Johann meekly.

"I see," said Rynard. None of them had learned to read the Colonel.

This was what kept them on their toes. Rynard might accept their explanation, or he might shoot them all for insubordination. It could go either way. The only thing they knew for certain was that, if it came down to the three of them against the Colonel, they would lose.

Suddenly, there was a loud *KLANK!* from the bathroom. It was the sound of a heavy porcelain cistern lid hitting the floor.

"Let go of me!" they could hear Alex yell. "I said, let go!"

* * *

Alex lay facedown in the mud of the alleyway. His body reverberated with the impact of landing. After a moment, the pain came. "You broke my damn leg!" he yelled.

"Go! While you still can!" shouted Dr. Holtz from the window above.

Alex was angry, but also terrified. He pulled himself to his knees and was surprised to discover that, while his shins ached, his legs did not appear to be broken after all. He tested this theory with a step. It was painful, but not unbearable. "Run!" the Professor pleaded. "They will kill you, boy! Run!"

"Break it down," ordered the Colonel.

Inside, Dr. Holtz braced himself against the flimsy motel bathroom door. *Whomp!* Johann kicked the particleboard. The impact nearly dislodged the door from its hinges. It held only because the professor had buttressed his legs against the opposite wall.

"Again!" shouted the Colonel.

Holtz chewed the butt of his cigarette and braced himself.

In the alley below, Alex broke into a lurching run.

Johann kicked the door again. Once more, with Holtz's help, it continued to hold, albeit barely.

Rynard placed his hand on Johann's shoulder as the mercenary prepared to kick the door a third time. "Wait." The Colonel drew his treasured antique Mauser C96 semiautomatic pistol. He then fired three evenly spaced shots through the bathroom door.

Dr. Rudolph Holtz slid to the floor. All three bullets had punctured his back. "Ungh..." he gasped. Ungh? He was going to die and this, he realized, didn't even qualify as a last word. Rynard kicked in the door and rolled the dying physicist out of the way with his boot. Dr. Holtz landed facedown on the tile, staring at the bottom of the toilet bowl. There he tried to think of something more profound to say and, in a flash of inspiration, he did. It was something poetic and beautiful. It was something that somehow summed up his life's achievements, terrible failings, and ultimately noble death. When opened his mouth to speak, however, he found that he could not. The second Mauser bullet had punctured his lungs. Instead of words, Holtz simply gurgled and spat red phlegm. "Guh," was the best he could manage. Oh well, he thought. He remembered how his mother used to serve him oatmeal porridge before school and how warm it made him feel inside. He felt warm inside now. That, of course, was the feeling of his belly filling with blood. He remembered the meadow outside the kitchen window. He remembered the flowers. Mutter, meine Mutter, he thought, can I have some more porridge please? Jackboots stomped past his eyes as they shuttered for the last time.

"The window!" said Jan, stating the obvious.

Rynard stepped up onto the toilet seat and stuck his head out. Limping down the alley, in a broken trot, was the boy, wincing with every step. Alex glanced back over his shoulder. For a brief instance, his and the Colonel's eyes met. Even at a distance, Alex was struck by the German's piercing blue eyes—their icy hue the exact colour of a nuclear cooling pond. Like the metaphorical pool, the German's eyes were clean and clear, with something deadly lurking in their depths. Rynard tried to reach his arm through to fire his pistol, but discovered he could fit either his head or his arm, but not both. Enraged, he turned back to the anxious soldiers. "Get him!" he snarled.

Alex now realized he'd run the wrong way. Neither the motel, nor the neighbouring buildings offered any escape routes. The only door he'd found had been locked. Now, it was taking too long to reach the alley's end. He'd be spotted for sure. For a moment he hesitated. He then heard the rumble of a truck behind him and dove to hide amid a collection of trash cans.

Cautiously, Alex peered out to see the source of the sound. A hulking green garbage truck, barely able to fit the narrow alleyway, rumbled towards him. He watched as the truck rolled past his hiding place, then halted with the hiss of air brakes. Two garbagemen, who had been riding the tailgate, jumped down. Both men were huge. Despite being dressed in dingy green coveralls, they looked more like linebackers than city workers. Alex decided he would leap up and beg for help as soon as they came over to collect the garbage. The garbage men, however, did not come towards him. Instead, they seemed more interested in what was happening in front of the truck.

Rynard approached the garbage truck with one arm raised and an anxious look on his face. Jan hung back, hands casually behind him, hiding his semiautomatic from sight. Johann and Elias had taken the long way around to cut off any possible escape. "Hey!" Rynard shouted with a perfect mid-western American accent. "Hello there!"

"Yo," said the truck driver, leaning from the cab window. The two other garbagemen, curious and happy for a break from routine, wandered up the side of the truck.

"Have you seen a young boy?" said Rynard. "He's my son, and he's... well, he's been a very naughty boy."

The driver, whose name was Irving, eyed Rynard suspiciously. Irving, the garbageman, had been named for Washington Irving by his mother who'd felt he had poet's eyes. As a young man, Irving had tried to live up to his mama's aspirations, but soon found it hard to make poetry pay the bills. He learned that few believed that a six-foot-four black man from the projects could be interested in anything poetic that wasn't rap. So, Irving had found work instead as a security guard, a mover, and now a 'waste removal engineer'. Still, his notebook full of poems sat below the dash, ready for use in case inspiration struck. During lunch breaks Irving would recite the poems to his coworkers. On more than one occasion, he had brought them to tears. After Irving's death the poems would be found and published in The New York Times under the title *Too Beautiful for Words*. As a result, Irving would eventually go on to posthumous fame. Eventually being sometime next week. Now, as he sat peering over the wide truck steering wheel, Irving's poet eyes told him not to trust the man standing before him. There was nothing he could put his finger on, but his sensitive soul told him that something was off. Despite Rynard Gruber's relaxed stance, the Colonel could not hide his powerful, spring-loaded physique or multitude of scars on his shoulders, neck and chin. He looks like the god of war carved from a block of ice, thought the garbageman poet, and where

Ares went, Phobos, Deimos and Enyo were sure to follow. "Nope," said Irving, "and I wouldn't tell you if I did, cuz it looks like you're fixin' to do him harm."

"What?" said Rynard, who appeared hurt by the accusation. "Not at all!"

"Uh huh," said Irving. He exchanged glances with his fellow garbage men who grimaced at Rynard accordingly. Even at six-foot-two, Rynard Gruber was dwarfed by the men. He was also twenty years older, as evidenced by his almost entirely grey buzz cut hair. It never occurred to the three garbagemen to be afraid of him.

"I'm sorry to hear that," said Rynard with a sigh of resignation, "and I'm sorry to make such a terrible mess."

Irving glanced about. "What mess?"

"This one." In a single swift motion, Rynard drew his pistol, fired three shots and returned the weapon to his shoulder holster. The Mauser, fitted with a custom-built silencer, ensured the executions were soundless. The speed meant that, even were witnesses present, they would not be sure of what they'd seen. Irving was thrown back in his seat, left to ponder the sky with dead poet eyes. His two coworkers stood a moment, mouths agape, brains obliterated, before collapsing to the ground one at a time. Rynard waved his hand and Jan jogged forward. On the other side of the truck Johann, Elias, and another mercenary, named Rupert, approached. As they walked, they scanned nearby windows for anyone unlucky enough to have seen what had happened. They had all been ready to help had the Colonel needed it. They knew he would not. One of the garbagemen moaned. Rynard stared, dumbfounded. How could he still be alive? After a moment, the man's eyes blinked.

"God damn it!" swore Rynard.

"He'll die in a moment," said Jan.

"It doesn't matter. It needs to be instant. If we don't stick to the rules then they're all just meaningless deaths. Now, I'm back at zero." Frustrated, Rynard emptied his pistol magazine into the garbageman's body, causing it to convulse before lying still.

"Still, twenty-three is a new record..." said Elias.

"Don't try to make me feel better," snapped Rynard. "It should be twenty-four. Scheiße!"

Rynard approached a cluster of steel garbage cans stacked against the wall. It was the only possible place for the boy to hide in the entire alley. The Colonel gave them a hard kick and sent them clattering over. Nothing. Rynard glanced up and down the narrow lane. For a moment, he was puzzled. No, he realized, it was not the only place. Rynard calmly pulled a silver cigarette case from his pocket and extracted a Villiger cigarillo. He then struck a match against the iron frame of the garbage truck and neatly lit the tiny cigar. Across Rynard's neck ran a long purple scar from an old machete wound that had never fully healed. As he inhaled, smoke seeped disturbingly from the seam. In spite of his mantra of clean living, the Colonel allowed himself this. "Some men smoke after sex, I smoke after homicide," he'd say, "It's really my only vice." Rynard leaned casually against the garbage truck's rear loader. "Not a very good hiding place, Alex. You know this, ja? It puts you in a... what's the word? A compromised position."

Alex's blood froze. Still, he did not move. He had completely covered himself with trash in the hope that somehow they would not think to look inside the truck itself.

"Do you know what this does?" asked Rynard. Alex opened a single exposed eye. The Colonel was waving his cigarillo at a bright red button on the tailgate frame. "You see this button?" Rynard paused to take a drag. "Well, it triggers the trash compactor. The one inside the truck, I mean. Do you know what happens to little boys who are hiding inside when this happens? Hmm? They turn into even littler boys. The kind I can take back home to Germany as carry-on luggage."

Alex's heart sank. "What do you want from me?"

"I want you to come out."

"What if I refuse?"

"Haven't I made that clear? Either you come out voluntarily now, or I scrape you out later—with a spoon."

Alex started to stand up.

"Wait," said the Colonel. "First, I want you to tell me something. I want you to tell me where you put the item you listed on eBay."

Despite his terror, Alex realized this was the only bargaining chip he had left. "I don't know what you're talking about."

"No? Okay, my mistake. Jan, I guess we got the wrong boy."

"How sad," said Jan with a grin.

"Terribly sorry for the mix up, Alex. But not as sorry as you, ja? I mean, you must be crushed." With that the Colonel slapped the red button. The hydraulic pistons jolted to life and slowly the massive steel packer panel began to rise. Alex rolled backwards into the hopper with a shriek.

"Are you crazy?" Alex screamed as he tried to scramble up through the shifting trash. He found himself grabbing fistfuls of wet coffee grounds and cardboard.

"Maybe a little."

Chaos Theory

Alex reached up to grip the lip of the closing compactor's jaw. "Help me!"

The Colonel took a casual drag on his cigarillo, then said calmly, "No Alex, you help *me.*"

Unstoppable pressure crushed Alex from below. Through the closing metal maw, he saw the Colonel's ice water eyes studying the sky impassively, as if hoping to spot a passing bird. Alex felt himself being swallowed alive. He watched as the metal teeth slowly moved to close. In seconds, his fingers would be severed, but he could not bring himself to let go. He screamed, "Okay! Okay!"

"Where is it?"

"I mailed it!"

"Where?"

"Somewhere in Washington!"

"When?"

"Today!" Alex screamed. He felt steel clamp down on his skull.

Then, it stopped.

The hydraulic press reversed and slowly, mercifully, the compactor opened once more. Squashed pieces of debris dropped from the ceiling of the unit. Alex lay flat, panting, heart pounding. Powerful hands gripped his shirt and dragged him out of the garbage. He landed hard on the asphalt, covered in wet orange peels and eggs. The mercenaries stood over him. One of them chuckled. Rynard wiped his hands with a white handkerchief.

"You're going to let him live?" asked Rupert in German.

"For now."

"What's next?" asked Elias.

"Load in the others and crush them. It will slow the police."

"And then?"

"Then?" Rynard took a final drag on his cigarillo before tossing it into the back of the truck. "Then, we go pick up the mail."

CHAPTER 7

"No one takes the time to write letters anymore."
– T. Kaczynski

The woods seemed less dangerous by day, but no less impenetrable. Charlie Draper sat in the back of the black SUV as it rolled along the forest road. He studied photographs of the crime scene on his iPad. A pile of papers and packages of physical evidence sat on the seat beside him. He had to work quickly as it was only a matter of time before the inevitable carsickness set in. Charlie had never been able to read in a moving vehicle, and it was long enough drive to the airport even without feeling queasy. The images on the screen could create a sickness all their own. The body of Claire Graham, splayed on the carpet, brown hair matted with blood. The body of the unidentified boy, head turned, mouth open, gawking at eternity. Charlie felt that edge of panic he always felt when there was no obvious next step in an investigation and the clock was ticking. He had never felt good at his job. He'd done well, and been promoted up to the level of director. Still, Charlie felt as if at, some point, he'd be found out as the fraud he was, a boy pretending to be a man. "Promoted beyond his level of competence," he could hear his father say. His father had made Charlie feel as if he'd been promoted past his level of competence since graduating kindergarten. Charlie had promised himself that he would be a better father than that. Of course, his father's child hadn't died, so there was that.

Charlie felt the pang of sickness at the back of his throat. He'd learned not to fight it. Back when he had a sense of humour, he used to say, pain I can handle, but nausea makes me sick. He put the iPad down and turned his attention to the collection of ziplock bags containing evidence he'd felt worth a second look. He opened the first bag. It contained a pen and a religious pamphlet from the Pō Lights. That was probably nothing. The Pō Lights were worse than Jehovah's Witnesses and Mormons combined when it came to knocking on doors. He'd found a copy of *Are you the Messiah?* under his own front door more than once. He looked at the next sealed bag. It contained an empty book of stamps. It was an odd thing to have taken, but he'd learned to listen when his right-brain said, "do it." Now, Charlie's left-brain tried to see if its sister hemisphere knew what it was talking about. Left-brains could be incredibly impatient with right-brains, which often seemed happy to loll about and daydream. While the left-brain worked dutifully away at a problem, doing math and checking off lists, the right-brain often seemed to respond with, "I'm sorry, what was the question again?" Worst of all, once in a while the right-brain would pop out some absurd suggestion that would turn out to be right. It was infuriating. The left-brain even tried to argue that the whole left-brain right-brain paradigm was an over simplification that was no longer seen as true in modern neuroscience, but the right-brain didn't care. It simply went on existing, in a paradoxically conceptual kind of way. Every right-brain was a left-brain's idiot savant conjoined twin. It was a discipline that not everyone could master—to relax, and let one's idiot half loose. Now, Charlie's right-brain was saying something. It didn't come up with an answer. It came up with a question. "How long do you keep a book of stamps after you've torn all the stamps out?"

"I'm sorry, sir?" asked Bill, the agent driving the car.

"Never mind. Just turn around."

"Yes, sir."

* * *

"Thank-you, Mrs. Simmons, you drive safe now."

The elderly widow smiled and waved goodbye as she turned away from the post office service counter. The Carlstown United States Post Office had served Carlstown and much of the surrounding county for over fifty years. Due to recent government cutbacks, it also now served the village of Eastbrook and what used to be Wilborough. The postal worker, Ed, nodded to the next customer in line. At the next window over, his coworker, Sheila, was weighing one of a dozen packages for Wilborough resident, Douglas Hicks. Doug, an aspiring author, was shipping out dozens of copies of his latest manuscript to prospective publishers. This was his reference book of 'asymmetrical palindromes'. He hoped it would go on to become the definitive collection of what he called 'linear linguistics'. It was certainly the only such work.

"Doug, you know you can't ship overseas without a customs form," said Sheila.

"They're just documents," he said. Doug was careful, as always, to construct his sentence as an asymmetrical palindrome.

"You still need the forms." Sheila looked at a message on her computer screen. "Network's down, Ed," she said. "Any idea why the network's down?"

"Nope." Ed smacked the side of his console with the toy gavel he kept for when he wanted to lay down the law with quarrelsome customers.

"Still down?"

"Yup."

"Better call IT, now we've tried everything."

The double front doors flew open with a powerful boot kick, shattering the inset windows and knocking a picture of the President of the United States off the adjacent wall. Colonel Rynard Gruber entered, brandishing his MP7. Fourteen heavily armed commandos rushed through the doors behind him. The men fanned out to tactical positions around the room. One of the soldiers stepped on the President's face in passing, crunching the glass under his heel. Moments prior, the soldiers had cut the phone line to the building and jammed nearby cell towers. "Everybody get down!" Gruber shouted in accented English.

Immediately, the post office customers fell to their knees, with the sole exception of Mr. Helms who was hard of hearing. "Get brown?" he asked.

Rynard grabbed the old man by his collar, threw him to the floor, and snarled, "Get down."

"Oh!" said Mr. Helms, nodding, "That does make more sense."

"Spread out, and search for the device," ordered the Colonel in staccato German.

"What?" asked Mr. Helms.

The soldiers moved towards the service counter. By this point, the postal workers had recovered from their initial shock. Sheila and Ed reached for the AK-47s each kept under the counter in a box of unsold Y2K Crisis Commemorative Stamps. While technically against Post Office policy, every working member of the Carlstown post office was heavily armed at all times. Long before the open carry practices became popular in Texas, Carlstown postal employees embraced the belief that guns, in general, were a good idea. It is a little known fact that most postal workers across the country pack heat, and many post offices are better armed than most police stations. The official motto of the Postal Gun Association, was "a disarmed postal worker, is a disgruntled postal worker." Of course, this is was all kept quiet because "a few bad apples" on "a few multiple occasions" had decided to shoot up their colleagues. To some, this made the very notion of having a militarized postal service seem like a bad idea. A new proposed motto paraphrased the words of NRA President Wayne LaPierre, saying, "the only way to stop a bad postal worker with a gun, was a good postal worker with a gun." As the PGA handbook put it, "It isn't a question of if a contingent of armed soldiers attack a USPS office, it's a question of when." Now that a troop of armed European mercenaries had actually stormed the Carlstown post office, that particular scenario-based training seemed like a very good idea indeed. Feeling at once both elated and vindicated, Ed and Sheila simultaneously swung up their weapons and unleashed a barrage of bullets at the startled soldiers. Despite their kevlar vests, two mercenaries crashed to the floor amid the terrified customers; one dead, the other with multiple fractured ribs. Rynard and the remaining soldiers reflexively kicked over tables, took cover and returned fire. Armour piercing ammunition tore up the post office service desks in a storm of wood dust and shredded envelopes. Even Mr. Helms covered his ears.

"From our cold dead hands, ya damn Ruskies!" shouted Ed.

"We're German!" shouted one of the soldiers indignantly.

"Oh. Well then, from our cold dead hands, ya damn Krauts!"

In the back office, three more postal workers leapt into action, grabbing an assortment of armaments from their storage lockers and break room. Mail sorter Andy Burkowitz gleefully shoved shells into his double-barrel shotgun. "This..." he chuckled, "is why I joined the United States Postal Service!"

Andy and his colleagues kicked open the double doors connecting the sorting room to the front desk. Shielded by a pair of metal carts, they opened fire on the enemy. One of the mercenaries panicked and unloaded his clip into a cleaning closet behind the counter, exploding a case of Fabreeze air freshener. The seductive scent of moonlit lavender descended over the battlefield. The air reeked of death and spring flowers. Andy laughed at the feeble attempt by the soldiers to use wooden tables as cover. Having emptied his shotgun, he turned to what he called his 'big surprise'. Andy raised a SMAW, more commonly known as a 'rocket launcher', to his shoulder and pulled the trigger. Unfortunately, in his excitement, he failed to actually aim. As a result, the rocket flew over the soldiers' heads, shattered the front window and hit his own 2012 Chevy Cavalier in the parking lot. "God damn it!" he swore as the resulting fireball sent his front hood flying fifty-feet into the air. The shockwave a moment later blew in all the post office windows, showering everyone in the room with glass. Hmm, thought Andy, might be a good thing I missed.

Chaos Theory

*   *   *

Charlie heard the explosion from behind the trees, a half-a-mile away. The black SUV swerved into the post office parking lot, just as Andy Burkowitz's hood crashed down through the windshield of Mrs. Simmon's car. Mrs. Simmons was already dead. Mrs. Simmons had been shot in the back of the head by Rynard after confirming for him that this was the only post office for miles. Consequently, she was unconcerned as a sheet of automotive steel, built right there in Michigan, severed her and her seat in half. "Jesus Christ," said Charlie.

Charlie was not alone. He arrived with the two other SUVs full of armed agents he'd ordered to rendezvous with him en route. Since domestic law enforcement was beyond the CIA's mandate, Charlie had also contacted the local police. Consequently, there were two police cruisers already in the parking lot waiting for them. The officers had arrived only moments before and had not even time to take stock of the situation before the errant RPG had obliterated all common sense from their brains. Officially, the police were there to make any arrests. Charlie, however, had decided he was damned if he was going to have his men unarmed given what he'd seen at the Graham house. The four policemen stared blankly at Charlie as if awaiting an explanation. "Get down!" he ordered.

The spell of shock broken, the police and ten CIA agents all took up defensive positions behind their vehicles. "What the hell is going on?" yelled Police Officer Stan Mitchell.

Charlie wanted to admit he had no idea, but he knew he had to appear in charge right now. "Just stay down," he said firmly. He'd never been under fire before. He'd always wondered how he'd react. He was terrified, but functional. So now I know, he thought. Charlie gave hand signals to the

CIA field agents, telling them to fan out to surround the facility. He had no idea what was going on inside the building, but there was no way whoever was inside was getting out without his say-so. The agents rested on their haunches, ready to make the fast crouching run required to flank the structure. Charlie gave the nod. As the agents started out, a massive hail of bullets flew from the post office windows, shattering windshields, puncturing car doors, and rattling nerves. The agents ducked back to where they'd started. Evidently, thought Charlie, they've got us pinned down.

The truth was, the people inside the post office had no idea they were even out there. The volley of gunfire had been a coordinated attempt by the employees to drive back the Germans. The postal workers, while able to put out a massive volume of bullets, weren't particularly efficacious with their aim. Most of the gunfire had hit the interior ceiling, raining dust, and debris upon all concerned. The rest had landed outside in the parking lot. A few stray bullets had hit the floor wounding a carpet salesman named Don, and striking Doug Hicks twice in the chest. The aspiring author died, sputtering deliriously, "Evil, a sin, is alive."

Finally, there was a pause as everyone seemed to reload at once. The Germans had superior training and experience, while the postal workers had better defences and more firepower. There were now three dead mercenaries. Sheila was alive, but lay on the floor against the wall. She had a hole in her shoulder and a badly mangled hand spouting gouts of blood. She was in shock and could only wonder where her wedding band had landed after her ring finger had been shot off. The brief lull also allowed the dust and gun smoke to dissipate as shredded ceiling fans did their thing.

"It's the PGA!" yelled one of the local police officers, finally able to catch a glimpse inside.

"The Professional Golfers Association?" asked Charlie in disbelief.

"The Postal Gun Association," the officer explained.

"Oh," said Charlie, as if this made perfect sense.

"They've got way more firepower than we do," said another officer.

Suddenly, there was a massive barrage of bullets from inside the post office. Every window shattered from every pane. Inside, walls disintegrated and furniture turned to mulch.

The gunfire lessened, lessened again, then stopped.

Silence.

A tinkling crash sounded, as the last glass shard fell from its frame.

Silence.

Charlie, the agents, and officers waited. Common sense said the shooting should start up again, but something told Charlie that the shooting was done. Trails of gun smoke could clearly be seen drifting from the open windows. "On my signal," said Charlie.

"We should wait for backup," said one of the officers. The others nodded their agreement.

"You wait for backup," said Charlie. He looked past the police officers to his own men. "Now."

Charlie made a crouching dash towards the building's front steps, using the cars for cover as best he could. He felt a clear sense of urgency. Something told him that he had no time to do this by the book. The agents, caught between a sense of self-preservation and not wanting their boss to go in alone, followed more cautiously, guns raised.

Charlie scrambled up the steps on his knees and rolled to just under one of the front windows. He listened for a moment, before peering up over the sill. Inside, the air was still thick with particulates. He could make out eight bodies immediately, six civilians in the middle of the floor and two postal workers behind the counters. The first was Ed, whose corpse had been shot over a two-dozen times. The second was Sheila, maimed arm at her side, a single bullet hole between her eyes. Charlie recognized the tikka-mark precision of the wound. A ceiling light fixture crashed to the floor, breaking the silence.

Charlie motioned the agents forward, then arose himself and stepped through the now doorless door frame. Gun ready, he stepped over the bodies of post office customers. Charlie sniffed the air, puzzled. Despite the hanging clouds of gun smoke and the blood soaked floor, the scene smelled inexplicably fresh and clean with just a hint of floral essence. A glance about seemed to confirm everyone to be dead several times over. Suddenly, one of the presumed corpses sat bolt upright. It was Mr. Helms, covered in ceiling plaster and someone else's brains, but somehow miraculously unscathed. "Who the hell are you?" he shouted. As a result of the gunfire, Mr. Helms was even deafer than usual.

"Quiet!" whispered Charlie.

"Wyatt? Who the hell is Wyatt? Wyatt Earp, maybe. It's like the OK Corral in here!"

Charlie held his finger to his lips, gave him a look meant to convey the peril of the situation and hissed, "Quiet!"

"Oh, *quiet*. Well, that makes more sense."

Behind the service desk, Charlie discovered four more bodies. They were the postal workers. Three of them had been shot in the head. I don't need to be a forensics expert to sense a pattern, thought Charlie. At his signal, the men flanked either side of the double doors behind the desk. It was the only possible avenue of escape. Charlie kicked the doors open and rapidly aimed about the sorting room. The room was large and well organized. Engines whirred, powering unsorted mail onto an untended conveyor belt. The floor was covered with letters and packages tossed from overturned bins. Someone had ransacked the room, and had done so quickly. Charlie felt the same sinking feeling of being too late.

From the loading dock beyond came the sound of a starting truck engine.

Throwing caution and common sense to the wind, Charlie and the agents ran to the loading dock, just in time to see a postal truck peel out of the gate. Charlie looked to a second parked truck. Its tires had been shot to shreds. "Out front!" he yelled.

The CIA agents leapt over the carnage in the lobby and out the front door—as the postal truck roared past the surprised local police and disappeared down the road. "Follow them!" Charlie shouted.

* * *

Moments later, Charlie was bouncing wildly in the passenger seat of the agency SUV. They rode dangerously close to the back bumper of the police car in front of them. The local officers knew every turn and hurtled dangerously over the twisting gravel road. Charlie's driver, trained in pursuit, struggled to keep up. Beyond the flashing lights of the police car, Charlie could just see the fleeing postal truck roof. "They can't be allowed to escape!"

"They won't, sir. There's nowhere for them to go."

As if to erase all doubt, a roar from above signalled the arrival of the helicopter Charlie had called in. He knew there was no way for it to land in these woods, but it would ensure their quarry would have nowhere to hide.

He glanced up to see the steel undercarriage of the chopper through the treetops. Adrenaline rushing and heart pounding, he realized he was enjoying this. For the first time in months, he felt alive.

All at once the road made an unexpected turn in a most unhelpful way. The driver of the postal truck banked hard, but not before leaving the road entirely and crashing into the brush. It then came to an abrupt stop. The truck had developed instant engine trouble—the kind caused by having a tree stuck through its carburetor. A low branch from the same tree had also shattered the windshield. The driver, amazingly uninjured, staggered from the passenger-side door and attempted to flee into the forest.

The pursuing vehicles stopped. Police and CIA agents spilled out.

"Freeze!" yelled one of the officers, levelling his gun on the suspect. The fleeing driver stopped where he stood and raised his hands.

The others focused their attention on the smashed postal truck. The lopsided wreck was now still, save for a single rear wheel spinning slowly in the air.

"You're surrounded!" yelled Charlie. "Come out with your hands up."

There was a long pause. Everyone waited, weapons drawn. Based on what they'd seen at the post office, most expected the unseen assailants to come out, guns blazing.

"I said, come out with your hands in the air!"

Another minute passed. No one moved. One of the rear doors had been flung open on impact. Charlie stepped slowly sideways, gun raised, to position himself to peer inside. After several steps he was at an angle that allowed him to see half of the interior. It appeared to be empty save a few spilled mail bags. He leaned slowly over to get a better view.

"It's empty," he said. "It's empty," he said again. It dawned on him that somehow he'd been duped. "God damn it!"

"Turn around, with your hands up!" one of the officers shouted at the driver. The driver did not move. "I said, turn around!"

The driver slowly complied, revealing himself to be a terrified thirteen-year-old boy Charlie instantly recognized as Alex Graham.

CHAPTER 8

"Here kitty, kitty..."   E. Schrödinger

1988 was the year Charlie's father decided to give his thirteen-year-old son one more chance to prove himself. Ever since Charlie had learned that chickens were the direct descendants of Tyrannosaurus Rex, he'd felt better about being a disappointment to his father. Despite this, it was impossible not to yearn for the chance to change that. He therefore could not say 'no' when his father offered him a summer job. "The whole point of having a son," he told Charlie, "is to live on through him. A father's son makes him immortal. In other words, if you fail at this, you're pretty much murdering me." Charlie's father came from the Sun Tzu school of parenting.

The debacle occurred on Charlie's second week working at his father's industrial cattle farm. Since starting the job, Charlie's thirteen-year-old self had found that he identified more with the cows than his coworkers.

Chaos Theory

His coworkers were adult men who scowled and swore. The cows, on the other hand, were completely content and apparently oblivious to their ultimate fate. Charlie found himself exchanging glances one morning with a cow while mucking out the pen. The cow watched him with her large brown cow eyes and wondered about nothing. This, of course, was what all cows wonder about. Zen Bhuddist's could only hope to achieve the same sense of nothingness a cow attains every minute of every day. "Oom," said the Cow, backwards, while meditatively chewing her cud. Charlie was no animal rights activist, nor even a vegetarian. He was, however, a thirteen-year-old boy, idealistic and somewhat impulsive. In an act of inspiration he decided that the cows needed to roam free. He unlocked the gate and told them to "Make a run for it." The cow's being cows simply stared back it him. He was forced to lead and shove them through the gate, until some sort of flow started and the animals began to exit in force.

Of course, being a thirteen-year-old boy at the time with no actual interest in farm work, Charlie didn't know much about cows. For example, he didn't understand that they were thoroughly domesticated animals and had virtually no instinct for self-preservation. They certainly had no comprehension of what to do on an interstate highway. Faced with the headlights of an oncoming tractor trailer, one can only assume their last thoughts were, "Oom," backwards.

"You're not my son," his father said with disgust, standing amid a heap of once valuable cow carcasses. "You're just like your mother."

* * *

Forty-year-old Charles Draper sat in a borrowed office. He was looking at Alex Graham, who was looking at an image projected from a laptop on a desk. The projection showed a grainy photo of Colonel Rynard Gruber, ten years younger, taken in Prague by a parking lot security camera. When the photo was taken, the Colonel had just executed a Greek businessman and stuffed him in the trunk of his own car. He had then driven the car to a long term parking lot near the airport and boarded a flight to Moscow. This ensured that the crime and this photo were not detected until his trail had long gone cold. Despite his having been paid a half-million dollars for the job, the soldier of fortune had used an internet discount coupon to save twenty dollars on the parking spot. Rynard Gruber was, if nothing else, pragmatic.

"You're sure that's him?" asked Charlie.

Alex nodded. An untouched doughnut sat in front of him.

"Not hungry?"

"It's grape jelly. I hate grape jelly."

"Oh. We'll get you another one."

"They said it was all they had."

"That can't be right." They were sitting in the Carlstown Police Station, having commandeered several of the offices for agency use. Surely there must be more doughnuts in the break room, Charlie thought, it's a police station for Christ's sake. First, however, Charlie needed to make a phone call. He picked up his encrypted cell and called Robert Morely's assistant, Herbert Chow. "Hi Herb?"

Herb responded with his customary "Yo," followed by the crunch of potato chips.

"We're dealing with Gruber."

"As in the baby food?"

"No, that's Gerber, I said Gruber, as in Colonel Rynard Gruber."

"Who the hell is that?"

"A mercenary known to be in the exclusive employ of Mathias Boltzmann."

"And who the hell is that?"

Charlie sighed. Boltzmann was on the agency top watch-list. Chow should know him. He could hear Herb licking the potato chip flavouring from his fingers. "International arms dealer. Known as the Walmart of Warlords, the K-Mart of Coup d'Etats and the Amazon.com of Armaments." This last reference was surprisingly accurate. Boltzmann's brazen approach to the business was unrivalled. He was the first weapons smuggler to go online, with a fully functional website operating out of Romania. Charlie had visited it and, despite its total lack of ethics, it was hard to argue with its customer service. After adding a dozen canisters of chemical weapons to his cart, the website had helpfully suggested that "Customers who bought sarin gas, also bought wing-mounted crop dusters."

"Oh... *that* Mathias Boltzmann."

"Pretty much means Project Loose Thread is unraveling."

"Jeez. Bob's gonna be pissed."

"Yup."

Charlie hung up the phone. He realised that he was holding his breath. He forced himself to exhale. "It's not the end of the world" was something people said to put negative events into perspective. After all, compared to the end of the world, what could be that bad? Now, it was literally the end of the world, or could be, if Charlie failed to recover the lost device.

"Can I see my mom now?" asked Alex.

Charlie stared at him blankly. He'd forgotten that the boy didn't know what had happened to her. Alex had been unconscious when Gruber had dispatched his mother and friend. Charlie opened his mouth to speak. He hadn't a clue what to say. It's not the end of the world? The world can end in different ways. Charlie knew that first hand. He looked at Alex's hopeful face. In the boy's mind, his mother might still be alive. Now, it was Charlie's job to kill her with certainty.

Outside, in the police station break room, one of the officers reached for a doughnut. "Grape jelly again?" he groaned.

"They're all grape jelly," said the front desk clerk, who had come in to get a can of Mr. Pibbs from the pop machine.

"Why?"

"The chief only likes grape jelly."

"He only ever eats one! So get one grape jelly and the rest glazed."

"I suggested that, but he said he doesn't know which one he'll want."

"Oh," said the officer, "well, can't argue with that."

Across from the break room, through the half-closed blinds of a borrowed office, Alex Graham put his head in his hands and began to cry. Charles Draper stood still for a moment, unsure what to do. He then shook himself from his trance, walked around the desk and gently stroked Alex's hair. He did so stiffly, awkwardly, as if trying to recall something he'd forgotten. The boy collapsed into him, sobbing uncontrollably.

CHAPTER 9

"Are we not men? We are DEVO." – R. Santorum

When the President first took office, the Camp David Situation Room looked nearly identical to the Situation Room at the White House. That meant the requisite presidential blue carpet and solid wood table surrounded by comfortable leather chairs, all in boardroom brown. The First Lady, determined to put the 'camp' in Camp David, had ordered the room redecorated in 'country rustic'. The cabinets had been redone shaker style, the walls wore a summer floral print, and the dark wood furnishings were replaced with wicker. With her famous attention to detail, the First Lady even insisted that lemonade be offered as the drink of choice whenever the room was in use. That and her famous caramel fudge squares, of course. The result was a comfortable, homey feel that made launching cruise missiles seem a little less grim and a lot more Martha Stewart. Thanks also to the First Lady, *The Secret* was mandatory reading for the President's entire staff. *The Secret,* authored by an Australian television producer, enjoyed a cult following for its premise that you simply had to will the universe to bring good things to you. "The 'law of attraction' worked for me, let's make it work for America," she said. "It's science!" When the President's Science Advisor tried to tell her that this was not how the actual law of attraction worked, she told him that it certainly would not with an attitude like that. The following week, the Science Advisor was replaced, along with the Camp David Situation Room side table.

"A complete dossier on Mathias Boltzmann is in your briefing documents," said Secretary of State, Sarah Maxwell.

"I haven't had time to read it," said the President. "Brief me on what's in the brief, but keep it... short."

Sarah nodded. It was hard to focus and look at him at the same time. The Commander-in-Chief had developed a cowlick that stuck out like a weed from the top of his head. He was blissfully unaware of this and, in Sarah's opinion, looked completely ridiculous. Sarah petted her own head in the hope of inspiring him to do the same. The President only stared at her, as if wondering if she might be a giant house cat in disguise. You can't tell the President of the United States he has a cowlick, thought Sarah. As the Commander-in-Chief spoke, the tuft of hair waggled back and fourth like the tail of a happy dog. God help me, she thought, he looks like Tintin. Sarah didn't exactly look up to the President to begin with. She secretly shared the opinion that he was a sort of idiot savant, minus the savant part. She did, however, like being Secretary of State and, since their political futures were entwined, she'd learned to work around him. Sarah also had to admit that

Chaos Theory

The President did have some sort primal political instinct that served him well. Years in government had taught her that a good political gut was better than brains. K Street was stuffed with brilliant former candidates who didn't know when to keep their mouths shut. Secretly, the Secretary of State wondered if she too might have wound up working in a political think-tank had she not tied herself to the 'Idiot Savant in Chief'. Go team, she thought. "Mathias Boltzmann is well known to us, Mr. President," said Sarah. "He's also well known to terrorist organizations around the world. They call him the 'Walmart of Warlords', selling more than fifty-million dollars worth of weaponry in the last year alone."

Jim Hornswell cleared his throat. "Actually, the real Walmart sells a lot more weapons than that. Boltzmann would be more like the Costco of... Conflict perhaps?"

"Jim?" said the President.

"No, it's true, I mean the sales figures aren't public, but—"

"Jim," the President said again, this time more pointedly.

"Yes, sir?"

"Nobody cares."

"No, sir."

Sarah concealed a smirk. It amused her to see the President scold his Chief of Staff. She hated Hornswell's pedantry. She believed her own laser-like focus and all business approach would favour her in the end. "The point is," she said, "Boltzmann is extremely well connected and has sophisticated channels for moving an item, even one as hot as this."

"But how did he find out about it? I mean, my understanding is that this was the most top secret of top secret things. The very toppest top of top...secretness."

Jim cleared his throat. "Technically, there can only be one top," he explained, trying to be helpful. "I mean, all of the other things would be near top, or second to the top, so not really..." Jim trailed off when he realized the President was simply staring at him. "Sorry, Mr. President."

The President of the United States turned away. He wanted to gaze out a window reflectively. Since there were no actual windows in the Situation Room, he was forced to gaze at a mirror instead. This meant that his reflection was more literal than expected as he found himself gazing at himself. He saw, for the first time, that he had a cowlick. Gee whiz, he thought, I look like Alfalfa from *The Little Rascals*. Why the heck didn't anyone tell me? He shot a suspicious glance at Jim Hornswell. Jim, he realised, could pass as a grown-up version of The Little Rascals character Spanky. For the first time, he wondered if his Chief of Staff truly had his best interests at heart. The President of the United States licked his hand and pressed the cowlick firmly into place. That should do it, he thought. He lifted his hand. The disobedient hair immediately popped up again. The President scowled and pressed down more firmly. Sarah and Jim watched in uncomfortable silence. When the tuft sprang up yet again, the President began vigorously slapping himself on the head in the hope of beating his scalp into submission. Finally, he pressed down with both hands until his head began to hurt. He then, tentatively, lifted his hands away and noted with satisfaction that the rogue hair stayed flat. When in doubt, he thought, use force. He had been ready to resort to a hammer if needed. He wondered what had happened to the real Alfalfa. Had he decided to check, he would have learned that the actor who played Alfalfa, Carl Switzer, died of a gunshot wound to the groin over an altercation involving a lost dog. The court ruled the death as self defence. The Little Rascal had been armed with a switchblade knife at the time.

"We don't know Mr. President," said Sarah, "communist spies in the fifties, perhaps?"

"Ah, so the Russians are involved."

"Perhaps. But, it could also simply be a case of former staff with loose lips. After this many years, who knows? We really have no leads. We do know the scientist who invented Project Loose Thread disappeared."

"Disappeared?"

"Yes, sir. Dr. Rupert MacGuffin. He quit shortly after the project was completed and moved back to his home in Scotland."

"Ah, so the Scots are involved."

Sarah wasn't quite sure how to respond to this. "Hmm, yes, well, I suppose that's possible. Anyway, he began conducting some rather crackpot experiments over there. About six years ago, we learned that he'd vanished."

"Vanished?"

"Without a trace."

"Ah ha!"

"Mr. President, I realize that sounds very mysterious but, to be honest, I wouldn't be too concerned about him. From what I understand, he went off his rocker in the years preceding. 'Sad' was the word some of his colleagues used to describe him. They said his work at the time was more fantasy than physics."

"I see," said the Commander-in-Chief. He then stared off into space as if seeing a path unseen. "I see," he repeated, his countenance both serious and thoughtful. At that moment, the President's cowlick sprang free once more.

He looks like a kind of unicorn, thought Jim.

CHAPTER 10

"This is your chance to get in on the ground floor..."
— V. Lustig

The Marina Bay Sands Hotel in Singapore looked like a large ship marooned atop three giant pillars high in the sky. This was no accident. Someone had actually designed it this way at a cost of eight billion dollars, making it the most expensive casino hotel ever built. Each of the pillars were separate hotel towers. The boat that bridged them was the so-called 'Skypark'. The Skypark included trees, restaurants, and a resort sized infinity pool overlooking the Malay Peninsula. Despite the premium prices, the poolside was packed. If the hotel was architecturally ludicrous, it was ludicrously successful.

Mathias Boltzmann stood at the edge of a precipice. He glanced down at the city streets below. A section of the Skypark's glass safety barrier had been removed, leaving nothing between Mathias and oblivion. He loved this. The opportunity for imminent death made him feel alive. He confidently raised the Famars Rombo four barrel shotgun to his shoulder. "What do you think, Carl?" he asked with a grin. Mathias's teeth were bright red, making it look as though he'd been drinking blood. In truth, he'd simply been chewing betel quids, a local leaf stimulant often compared to chewing tobacco. It was a bad habit he indulged in only in Asia.

"Twenty miles per hour," said Carl nervously. "No, twenty-five."

"Ten," said Mathias. He chuckled. Despite his efforts to conceal it, it was obvious that Carl was afraid of heights. The stocky American refused to come within a few feet of the ledge and cowered each time the wind blew. Fear makes him over estimate its speed, observed the arms dealer. Fear makes fools of us all. But what, he wondered, does Carl fear the most? "Pull!"

The slight Asian hotel employee on the platform behind them, released the lever. The metal arm snapped, sending a clay pigeon high into the sky. Mathias smoothly followed its arc for a moment, then squeezed the trigger. Boom! The skeet, a tiny black spec against the purple twilight, was instantly obliterated. Mathias nodded with satisfaction. "Your turn."

"No, it's fine," said the American, "I'm happy just to watch."

"Nonsense," said Mathias. "Here."

The arms dealer tossed the ornate shotgun to Carl, who had no choice but to catch it. "Okay..." he said reluctantly, "I'm a bit rusty."

"Take as much time as you like." Mathias gestured to a nearby waiter who stepped forward to hand him back his drink. Mathias swirled the fifty-year-old Macallan Scotch a moment, before taking a sip. "And as many shots as you need," he said. He then added with a wink, "I know where to get more ammunition if we need it."

Carl smiled nervously at the joke. He wasn't a bad shot and could normally hold his own. He'd grown up in a family where learning to handle, clean, and reassemble guns blindfolded was a given. If he ever so much as left the safety off, his father would box his ears until they bled. He'd killed his first deer at the age of twelve and had routinely entered target practice tournaments. Carl never won these contests, but always landed safely in the middle of the pack. The problem here wasn't the gun. It was the gulf of space between the Skypark and the Earth below. If he stared down too long, he'd start to swoon. He'd start to feel as if the building were leaning forward into the void, trying to spill him off. Still, he had to shoot, Mathias had left him no choice. Carl took a small step forward, clutching the gun in a death grip.

"You need to get closer than that," said Mathias, burying his nose in his whisky to hide his amusement. "Right up to the edge, Carl. That way, if it falls below, you can still get it. I promised the hotel that nothing would hit the ground, so it would be most unfortunate if something did."

Carl took a deep breath. There was no way he could back out now. Staring straight ahead, he stepped forward to within inches of the edge. He'd been told once that, the reason some people fear heights wasn't the fear they might fall, but the fear they might jump. It was *thanatos*, they said, the Freudian death urge, which compels a part of us, in some perverse way, to seek oblivion. As the seemingly infinite space yawned before him, Carl knew that this was true. He braced himself against himself, and waited.

Of course, the hotel didn't normally allow guests to shoot guns off the roof. Mathias Boltzmann was no ordinary guest. Mathias had a great many powerful friends throughout the Pacific Rim. As a result, he'd reserved an entire section of the Skypark for his own private use. Ostensibly this was for meeting with clients. That, however, could be done anywhere. In reality, Mathias simply enjoyed doing things that others could not. He never looked at the throngs of tourists lying poolside outside of his cordoned-off domain, but he knew they were looking at him. They were wondering who he was, and he basked in their wonder. Mathias held his hand aloft, but did not lower it. When he did, the servant would release the skeet. For now, however, Mathias savoured his drink, and his friend's fear.

Carl's arm shook. The longer he waited, the worse the shaking grew. He felt the wind trying to push him from his perch. Another few inches and he would be hurtling through empty air to the pavement below. Carl glanced down. Directly beneath, a toy red hotel shuttle drove along a grey road. If he fell, he might also land in the adjacent water, but he knew that, from this height, it might as well be concrete. "Well?" pleaded Carl.

Mathis smirked and dropped his hand. "Pull!"

The servant released the lever and once more a clay pigeon was flung into the void.

Released from the pressure of waiting, Carl was relieved to focus squarely on the tiny target. Once he had a sense of its trajectory, he aimed ahead and fired. The skeet continued on its way, unharmed. Humiliated and afraid that a miss might mean having to go again, Carl returned his bead to the skeet. Gravity had taken over, and the small projectile was now dropping fast. Carl aimed, adjusted, and shot once more. The skeet wobbled, indicating a graze from a stray pellet, but remained intact. This was a four-barrel shotgun, so Carl still had a chance. Keeping his eye on the plunging black pill, he aimed low. The city swung into view, and he prepared to shoot again. This time, he was determined not to miss. He tracked the target relentlessly until he was suddenly yanked upwards and flung his hands wide. The shotgun flew from his grip and flipped out into space. He was hanging over the edge, staring at asphalt, and water, one hundred and ninety-one metres below. His heart stopped.

"Ziehen!" someone shouted in German. "Pull!"

It was Mathias who had a hold of his jacket. The hands of the hotel servants joined in. They pulled him back to the safety of the roof where he collapsed in shock. He was hyperventilating. His heart pounded in his chest. It's trying to burst out, he thought in a horrified stupor, like that alien from that movie. "What happened?"

Mathias, still panting from the effort, began to laugh. "You crazy Texas fool!" he said, "You have terrible aim, but you get an 'A' for trying, and a 'D' for almost dead."

"I don't understand..."

"You followed that stupid skeet right off the roof! If I hadn't caught you..."

"You saved my life?"

"I suppose so," said Mathias with a shrug. "Anyway, you've earned your drink."

Carl continued to sit, splayed out on the terrace tile. Outside their allocated area, some of the tourists who had witnessed the incident pointed at him and babbled. He peered over the open edge and felt oddly unafraid of it. On the roadway far below, a small group of individuals had gathered around to inspect the shattered shotgun that had fallen from heaven. One of the servants helped Carl to his feet, where Mathias handed him a tumbler of Scotch. Mathias watched as the American drank, emptying the glass but not gulping it. Carl felt that he could taste every ounce of sherry cask in the luscious whiskey. He almost instantly felt drunk.

"Now," said Mathias, "enough fun and games. I invited you here for a reason."

* * *

Ten minutes later Carl was waiting in the living room of Mathias's penthouse suite. The interior was off-white modern, replete with off-white luxuries that included an off-white Steinway Grand Piano. While he waited, Carl casually played *Birch Canoe*. It was the only piece he knew. He noted that the fine piano had not been tuned in some time, and sounded a little off. One of the keys made no sound at all. He was not entirely alone. An imposing man in a black suit stood in the corner. The brute had a shaved head that bore a striking resemblance to the inimitable statues of Easter Island, had the statues worn sunglasses and spiderweb tattoos. Outside on the balcony stood a second guard, scanning the sky. An RPG lay at the ready by his feet. Carl knew Mathias to be anything but paranoid. Despite his enormous wealth and most-wanted status in more countries than he could count, the arms dealer often traveled alone. The idea that Mathias felt the need to guard against aerial assault intrigued Carl. What was going on?

"Okay," said Mathias, swinging wide the french doors leading to the office. He smiled warmly and waved Carl inside. Mathias then turned and pulled the double doors closed behind them. The hotel had spared no expense in furnishing the place and wanted its guests to know it. The office was tastefully opulent, centered by a large desk carved from a single slab of mahogany flown in illegally from Brazil. On the desk sat two large platters, one gold, one silver, both conspicuously covered with domes. The domes were large enough each to conceal a suckling pig.

"I've got it!" shouted Mathias triumphantly. "I've got it! I've got it! I've got it!"

"Got what?" asked Carl.

Mathias beamed, relishing the moment. "Loose Thread!"

Carl had no idea what this meant. Mathias clearly seemed to think he should. "What?" asked Carl.

Mathias hesitated. "Do you mean, 'what I can't believe it?' Or, do you mean 'what is Loose Thread?'"

Carl hesitated, then sheepishly admittedly the latter.

Mathias deflated, then became annoyed. "You don't remember that website I showed you last time?"

"Oh... right, the can... thing on eBay!" Carl had never known Mathias to be trivial. Despite this, he had dismissed his friend's explanation of the online auction as pure fiction. It was simply too preposterous. Mathias, after all, had described the canister as 'far more powerful than an atomic bomb.' How could a weapon of such awesome potential be on eBay for less than the cost of a case of bratwurst? "I'd forgotten what it was called," said the American meekly, "but, yes, of course, I remember. How exciting!"

Mathias accepted this with a nod. "Well then, let me show it to you!" Barely able to contain his excitement, he walked to the desk and reached for the gold platter. He turned back to look at Carl, and grinned once more. With a dramatic flourish of his hand, he lifted the dome. Carl, suddenly cognizant of what the platter contained, flinched, and stepped back. What was revealed was anything but threatening—an innocuous steel canister looking exactly as it had on the auction webpage, but smaller. If anything it looked even more like a Starbucks coffee mug in reality than it did in the photo.

Mathias laughed. "It's quite safe, my friend! Besides, if it were to go off, stepping back would hardly save you. Nor would leaving the country, for that matter."

Carl stared at the shiny cylinder, suddenly fascinated. "Is it... true?"

"True? True that opening it could destroy the earth? I certainly hope so. Otherwise, I'd be quite the fool. Caveat emptor and all that, I suppose. Do you think me a fool, Carl?"

Carl looked aghast at the thought. "No, certainly not! It's just so..."

"So unbelievable? I understand, but I assure you, I've done my due diligence. It's quite real. Here, take a look for yourself!" For the second time that day, Mathias tossed a weapon towards Carl. Carl caught it in his arms as if it were a baby thrown from a burning building. "Jesus Christ, Mathias!"

Mathias laughed. "I told you, it's quite safe. You couldn't open it with a sledge hammer if you tried. I've had it thoroughly examined. It's made of osmiridium, is structurally engineered to be uncrushable, and has a childproof lid."

Despite these assurances, Carl examined it with care. The container appeared utterly unremarkable. It was hard to imagine an exterior that better belied its promised potential. Just as in the photographs, the outside was smooth save for the inscribed serial number and 'Top Secret' labelling. The canister was a contradiction. It felt at once both old and new, otherworldly and oddly familiar, harmless and yet utterly lethal.

"I know," Mathias snorted, "It looks like a martini shaker, hmm?"

Carl nodded, although privately he maintained his own view that it looked like a travel coffee mug. He weighed it with his hand and was surprised at how light it was. It felt as though it contained nothing at all. "What are you going to do with it?"

Mathias's eyes sparkled with mischievous delight. "The billion dollar question," he said, "but, what I think you mean is, to whom do I intend to sell it?"

"The billion dollar question? Most of our customers have only tens of millions to spend, some less."

Mathias nodded. "True."

"Governments would pay billions for sure, even trillions... but could you sell it to them? Even the biggest players have trouble moving that kind of money unseen. Plus it would be dangerous to try. You could start a war instead of merely profiting from one."

"Carl, my dear friend, you're completely correct, of course. It is true that our many clients have, at most, but millions to spend each. But, *together,* well, that's a different story..."

"I don't understand."

That same mischievous smile flickered once more across the German's lips. "This is a once in a lifetime opportunity, Carl, even for me. The value of a weapon such as this is without limit. That said, the finances of our customers, as you point out, sadly, are not. So, I can sell Loose Thread only once, but once is not enough to make it worthwhile. A conundrum, yes?" At this, Mathias reached over and raised the dome from the silver platter, revealing two more identical canisters that winked in the light as the lid was lifted.

"You've made more of them?" said Carl with amazement.

"Not quite. Sadly how Loose Thread works is far beyond me and any scientist I could find. And we could hardly open it up to take a look as we would all be destroyed. We tried x-rays, gamma rays, and every other method of detection imaginable, but simply could not see its contents. I'm told nothing larger than a neutrino can penetrate it, and that hardly helps us. So, as a weapon, it is intrinsically unique."

Carl stared at his friend, baffled. "Then what...?"

Mathias was clearly enjoying himself. "We couldn't duplicate the device. We can, however, duplicate the shell that contains it. These, my friend, are old fashion German Doppelgängers."

"Forgeries?"

"See for yourself," said Mathias, offering him one of the fakes. "They're completely identical to the nearest atom."

Carl placed the original carefully on the desk before accepting its counterfeit twin.

"Same materials, same weight, cast from laser-cut moulds," boasted Mathias, like a proud father. The arms dealer then turned to pour himself a drink at the wet bar behind the desk. "Can I get you anything?"

"No, thank-you, I'm fine," said Carl, clearly struggling with the implications.

"Of course these are only the first two prototypes. There are dozens more on the way."

Carl picked up the second fake to compare it to the first. He found that, as promised, they were absolutely identical. "But people will find out. I mean once they start to issue threats, they'll know they've been duped!"

"Of course," said Mathias. "Cheers."

Carl, still confused, dutifully clinked one of the canisters with Mathias's glass.

Mathias took a measured sip of vintage port. "Each sale comes with a contractual agreement that they will not publicly reveal that they even possess the device, let alone threaten to use it, for at least six months."

"Isn't that suspicious?"

Mathias waved off his friend's concern. "Nothing is suspicious when you've got the world's most awesome weapon in your hands. Power is a blinding light."

Carl wasn't so sure. He put down the first fake, to examine the second more closely. "Regardless," he said, "Sooner or later they'll know they've been duped."

"Indeed. That is why this is my last hurrah. I've spent forty years building an impeccable reputation, and will blow it all up in the greatest confidence job the world has ever seen!" Mathias paused to take in the look of shock on Carl's face. "Oh come now, my friend, our customers are warlords, dictators, and terrorists. Weep not for them!"

"I just... I just can't believe it. Your reputation..."

"You'd have me sell the actual device to one of them? Some of our customers are just crazy enough to actually use it!"

Carl considered this and had to admit it was true. Selling the real device even once was simply too dangerous. Mathias's plan to sell forgeries, even if it cost him his business, was really the only way to go. No one would ever do business with him again, but Mathias wouldn't need them to. "You know," said Carl, "they'll try to hunt you down to kill you."

Mathias shrugged and turned to refill his glass. He was starting to feel a little drunk. "Perhaps, but I think not. They say, in a swindle, a mark will be too embarrassed to admit himself a victim, so will simply let it go. Besides, once they realize I still have it, who would dare come for me? I have the most powerful weapon on Earth, after all."

Carl opened his mouth to express doubt, but found himself staring at the two canisters on the desk before him. One was the original, while the other was the first duplicate he'd put down a moment ago. The problem was, he wasn't sure which was which. Panicked, he looked at the second duplicate in his hand and frantically tried to find a flaw that might help him discern the original from the fake. He glanced up to see that Mathias had turned his back to him. His friend was at the wet bar and was busy fumbling in the ice bucket with a pair of tongs. The slightly inebriated warmonger picked up a chunk of ice, unsteadily. He then squeezed too tight and sent the cube ricocheting across the back of the bar, off the wall, and onto the floor. "Damn it," said Mathias, in German, "who knew ice was so slippery?"

Carl, panicked by the possibility that his friend would turn around and see what a fool he was, snatched up one of the canisters from the desk.

"Absolutely indistinguishable, no?" said Mathias with a crafty smile and a sip of his refreshed drink. For a moment, Carl thought his host had turned around in time to see what he had done but, after studying his friend's face, he knew Mathias had seen nothing.

Carl desperately scanned the two canisters in his hands, once more looking for a clue that might reveal the truth. He'd grabbed the one on the left, which *felt* right, so it must be right, he told himself, before looking at the one that was left.

"Hmm?" said Mathias.

"Yes!" said Carl, "Absolutely indistinguishable. Quite... amazing."

"Don't feel bad, dear friend. If an electron microscope couldn't tell the difference, then how possibly could you?"

Carl nodded and placed the two canisters on the silver platter, and watched as Mathias replaced the lid. They're the fakes, he tried to reassure himself, I'm sure of it.

CHAPTER 11

"Watson, come here I need u, #phone"
– Alexander G. Bell

Somewhere past the depletion region, where the heliosphere meets the edge of deep space, flew the Voyager I spacecraft. Launched on September 5, 1977 and weighing roughly the same as a Renault *Le Car*, the unassuming probe had since roamed far beyond its original mission. Four decades later both it and its twin, Voyager II, continued to function, largely forgotten by the now middle-aged men born at the time of its departure. Of course, its creators did envision the idea that it might someday reach interstellar space, and even be found by alien life forms. To this end, they included in it the Golden Record, so named for being a phonograph record made of gold. It would not have qualified as an official 'Gold Record' in terms of numbers sold. Its sales were non-existent. Only two copies were ever pressed and those were just given away. The metal itself contained images, directions to Earth, and instructions for how to play the record. All of this was in non-lingual form, making it an IKEA instruction manual for aliens. The musical tracks included Mozart's *Magic Flute* and Chuck Berry's *Johnny B. Goode*. Most scientists on Earth declared Voyager I to have officially left the solar system as of August 25, 2012. Some disagreed, preferring to define the solar system as including the outermost comets circling the sun. By that definition, Voyager I would have a mere thirty-thousand more years to go. One is reminded that the universe, in terms of pretty much anything, is really quite large. Voyager I itself held no opinion on this. With its cameras disabled to save energy, it was now blind, unable to see the now distant star that served as Earth's sun. Its other sensors, however, meant that it could still perceive, its high-gain antenna meant that it could still speak, and its three radioisotope thermoelectric generators, powered by plutonium decay, ensured that it would do so for years to come. The sixty-four kilobytes of computing power that served as its brain was less than what could now be found inside a Tickle Me Elmo doll, but had steered it with astounding aptitude from planet to planet. In the time it takes you to read this sentence, Voyager I would have traveled seventeen kilometres. In the vast scale of space, however, it would appear almost frozen in place. If Voyager I could feel, it would also feel frozen. Temperatures here approached minus two-hundred and seventy degrees celsius. Still, the spacecraft, far ahead of its twin, Voyager II, continued its relentless journey into the void, inching towards eternity—ever further, never closer.

CHAPTER 12

"Cloudy with a chance of rain."
– M. Nostradamus

Faith tore the wrapping from the present with sheer joy. She knew what was inside, but was excited in the way that only a six year-old could be. Charlie exchanged a glance with Lisa, basking in the light of their daughter's delight. Faith gasped and squealed as she pulled the box free from its wrapping. Inside, of course, was the artist's set she'd so desperately wanted. Charlie had read the reviews to make sure it wouldn't disappoint. Faith took a moment to examine the colourful box, as if making sure it was real. "Thank-you! Thank-you! Thank-you!"

"It's from Santa," said Lisa, with a wink to Charlie, "Thank him."

"Thank-you, Santa!"

"But we're glad you like it," said Charlie.

Faith opened the lid of the box, spilling the contents at the foot of the Christmas tree. Inside was a folded easel, artist's palette, brushes and a complete set of water colours. It was meant for children "10 and up", but Faith insisted she could handle it. Charlie knew she could.

"I'm going to paint *everything*!" said Faith.

"Except the walls," said her mother.

"Except the walls."

Ping. The 'fasten seatbelts' light came on. The sound of airplane engines intruded into Charlie's consciousness. It was the ever present, underlying white noise of reality. Charlie, forced back to the present, wiped his eyes and drew a deep breath. He knew these daydreams were like a drug, intoxicating in the moment, but so painful to come down from. Like any addict, he didn't want to quit. He wanted instead to escape there forever and never come down again.

The flight from New York to Edinburgh took over eight hours. It did so traveling at fourteen-hundred kilometres per hour, a relatively pokey speed compared to the Voyager I spacecraft. He glanced at the boy asleep in the seat beside him. Alex Graham was years older than Faith would ever be, but still a child. With his eyes closed and his chest rising and falling, he looked more childlike than ever. Charlie forced himself to look down the aisle instead, its long blue carpet illuminated by floor lighting. Someone in the row ahead of him was watching a movie called *Master of Tai-Chi*. It was a low budget comedy consisting mostly of the main character getting beaten up a lot, but being at peace with it. Charlie had read somewhere that Jack Black had turned down the title role.

* * *

Edinburgh International Airport was nothing if not remarkable—and it was *not* remarkable. Despite being Scotland's busiest airport, it was a completely pedestrian terminal. Of course, all airports were pedestrian, in that they required enormous amounts of walking. Like every other major airport, EDI was a vision of ostentatious minimalism consisting of interminable terminal hallways, fitted with moving sidewalks connecting the gates. These were then interspersed with overpriced dining areas to ensure patrons did not actually perish from starvation en route to their flights. The idea was similar to the base camps on Mount Everest, only with more Cinnabon locations. In this sense, Edinburgh was just like every other airport, only more so.

Charlie and Alex navigated the crowded corridors, dragging roller-bags behind them. They were following signs to the car rental locations. As major airports went, Charlie noted, this was a small one with only a single time zone. Deciding they needed food for the road, they paused in the departures area at a sandwich shop called McHegel's Bagels. The two waited in silence while the shop's owner, Hrundi Bakshi, prepared their kosher Scottish smoked lox on rye. Standing still in an airport longer than necessary always had a certain sense of wrongness to Charlie and he remarked on this to Hrundi. Hrundi, who fancied himself an amateur philosopher, said he understood completely. "An airport isn't a destination but a transition," he explained, "so being here is like not being at all. The only way to be in an airport is to be leaving it, to maintain your 'terminal velocity', if you will." Hrundi then asked Charlie if he wanted the complimentary dill pickle. Charlie indicated that they did, as well as some of those tiny packets of salt and pepper. Moments later, they were once more en route, bags of 'nosh' in hand.

"Shouldn't I be in child services or something?"

Charlie looked at Alex in surprise. "You want to be in child services?"

"No."

"Okay then."

"But shouldn't I?"

Charlie shrugged, "Probably. Yes. But you're the only person we have who has actually seen and touched the canister. That's more important."

"More important than my welfare?"

Charlie looked to see whether Alex was joking. He was. After telling the boy of his mother's death, there had been a lot of tears and confusion. The following day, Alex became functional again. Charlie knew from his own experience that this in no way meant Alex was okay, or that he'd already put his mother's death behind him. That would take years. Still, the boy was remarkably resilient. He demonstrated the same sort of dry humour that Charlie enjoyed, and found refuge in. Charlie told himself that it was his own presence that was helping Alex cope. He knew, however, that might simply be what he wanted to believe. He had already pulled up a couch in his mind to ask himself if it was really he who needed the boy, not the other way around. He liked to think the answer was both. "It's the same thing," said Charlie.

"Because if the world ends it doesn't much matter how screwed up I am?"

"Exactly."

They continued their pilgrimage to the car rental desk. En route they passed a contingent of Pō Lights. The relatively new religion had joined the Hare Krishnas in taking up residence in airports around the world. While they also dressed in robes, they were far more reserved. Unlike the joyous Hare Krishnas, Po Lights shunned celebration in deference to their mission. "Are you the chosen ones?" they asked Alex and Charlie as they passed. "No," said Alex. The acolytes nodded graciously and turned to ask an elastic band salesman behind them the same question.

When Charlie and Alex reached the car rental booth, they faced the final task of waiting in the queue. The queue consisted of themselves and the customer currently being served, an American named Donald MacDonald. Don was on vacation to find his family's ancestral roots. Budget Rent-A-Car had lost Don's reservation and was in the process of trying to find it. Alex was of Scottish descent as well, being a member of the Graham clan. He didn't know this, however, as no one had ever told him. Alex assumed all Scottish names either began with "Mac" or ended with "son". In Alex's mind, his family was American and always had been.

"So, why did you tell the customs guy I was your son?"

Charlie hesitated. The CIA had supplied a fake passport for the boy, but it was Charlie's idea to take him and pass him off as his son. "It's easier that way. You're a minor, and the truth is too complicated. The UK doesn't know why we're here. The fewer who do, the better."

"Oh. So, you lied."

"Yup."

"Do you have kids? For real, I mean."

Charlie considered lying again. "Not anymore. I had a daughter, and a wife."

"They died?"

"An accident."

"Car accident?"

Charlie nodded in the same detached way he always did when asked about the crash.

"My dad left us," said Alex bluntly.

"I know." They had tried to locate Alex's father following his mother's death and continued to do so. He had effectively fallen off the grid. Despite people's assumptions about the all-knowing CIA, FBI and NSA, it was still possible to disappear, provided you were prepared to make the sacrifices necessary to do so. Of course, finding the boy's father was not their top priority. To the agency, the boy's role in this whole affair was largely over. Indeed, Charlie's own role had been greatly diminished as diplomatic efforts were underway to locate and apprehend Mathias Boltzmann. Despite his infamous reputation, Interpol had no records of him. Still, the demotion of Charlie and Alex's importance came with a certain degree of freedom. Charlie had been able to convince the necessary people that he should fly to Scotland to locate Project Loose Thread's creator, Dr. Rupert MacGuffin. He had argued that, if he found the scientist, he might tell them how to stop it. Convincing people to let him take Alex along had been a trivial matter. "It was in your file," said Charlie."We did try to find him."

Alex nodded. After a moment he said, "You're lucky."

Charlie stared at him incredulously. Nobody had said that to him since the accident. Even coming from a thirteen-year-old boy, it was offensive. "What?"

"I'm sorry, I don't mean for what happened. That's horrible. What I mean is... you're lucky in that... well, you know they'd be here with you if they could."

The desk clerk had now cleared up the confusion with Donald

McDonald. His reservation, had incorrectly listed him as 'MacDonald'. They were really the same name, she told him, historically speaking. 'Mc' was an abbreviation of 'Mac' for people who found the extra letter simply too much. Donald found it all very interesting and saw it as a part of his quest to learn about who he was. "Next!" said the desk clerk.

CHAPTER 13

"All gay people look alike to me." – V. Putin

Fluß Ruhr Industrial Park, Germany

The black limousine wound its way along the narrow side roads that divided the grey cinder block buildings. It was dawn. The air was clean and crisp. The early morning light had all the nascent promise of a new day. The car's route was intentionally inconspicuous, its destination clandestine. The limousine was escorted by a black BMW X3. The luxury SUV was the perfect vehicle for a family of four, or a contingent of heavily armed henchmen. Inside the back of the limousine, Mathias Boltzmann sat with hands clasped. He was nervous for the first time in over three decades. That was when, at the age of twenty-three, he sold one hundred barrels of cyclosarin gas to a certain Middle East dictator. It had been his first major deal in violation of international chemical weapons laws. It was not his last. He'd sold a lot of sarin, tabun and soman gases over the years and had always done so with a certain degree of patriotic pride. All were invented by the Nazi's in 1938. Originally developed as insecticides, with typical German efficiency, they killed everything else as well. The German word for poison was 'gift'. As Mathias used to tell his customers, Sarin gas was the gift that kept on giving. It wasn't violating the law that had made him nervous that day. Nor was it the large sums of money, or even the possibility that the dictator might use the stuff. What made Mathias nervous was that he'd decided to go on the cheap with the barrels used to contain it. Sitting through a seven-hour flight aboard a transport plane stacked to the ceiling with a compound capable of killing a man in parts-per-million was risky enough. Storing the gas in cheap plastic containers bought in bulk from Real Hypermarket was just plain foolish. From that day forward, Mathias had committed himself to quality full service, including free delivery on all orders over one million euros. Still, when he thought back on those days of shipping nerve agents in an overstuffed cargo hold, he couldn't help but smile. It was a more innocent time. Today was different. Back then, there was only a chance his career might end, albeit with himself flopping on the ground like an asphyxiating fish. This time, he knew it would. With this deal, he was crossing the Rubicon. Once completed, he'd have no other course of action but to continue with the plan. In a matter of months, his reputation would be in tatters. He would have enemies everywhere. These would include the most dangerous men in the world, many of whom he currently counted as friends. He'd also be ludicrously wealthy. Ironically, he mused, his subterfuge could leave some of these organizations so financially depleted, he'd actually be leaving the world a less dangerous place. Of course, his own exit from the stage would help accomplish this as well. Such was the law of unintended consequences. Not that another arms dealer wouldn't soon take his place. No one is irreplaceable, he thought, I'm just a cog in the machine. His grandfather had told him that. His grandfather had been a Swiss banker in World War II. There were an estimated 875 million guns in the world. Mathias had sold maybe ten million over the course of his career. On that scale, Mathias lamented, it was hard to feel as if one were making a difference.

Mathias felt fidgety. Since driving between the buildings, the car radio had dissolved to static. The white noise interrupted his thoughts and added to his sense of unease. He ordered the driver to switch it off. Mathias opened the steel briefcase on the seat beside him and lifted out the osmiridium cast canister inside. He turned it slowly, admiring its flawless surface. It was a thing of minimalist beauty, he decided. Something the Bauhaus might have designed, or Braun appliances. It slices, it dices, it destroys worlds, he chuckled to himself. After a moment, Mathias placed it back in the form-fitted foam interior of the case. He paused to wipe his fingerprints from the metal, then spritzed it with bottled scent. After all, he thought, if you're paying a five billion dollars for something, you expect that new armament smell. The spray dotted the surface, highlighting a hairline fissure in the canister's shell. Mathias blinked. "Stop the car!" he barked.

"I'm sorry sir?" asked the driver.

"Stop the goddamn car!"

The driver halted abruptly, forcing the SUV escort behind to slam on its brakes as well. The henchmen inside, already bruised from a brutal game of punch-buggy after driving the past the Volkswagen plant in Wolfsburg the day before, were flung into windows and seatbacks. They quickly gathered themselves to scan the area for any possible threat. The driver picked up his cellphone to call the car ahead. "Escort 1 to Pandora, what seems to be the problem?"

"Not sure," came the reply. "Wait."

Mathias opened the car door and stormed around to the back of the limousine, clutching the flawed canister in one hand. He snapped his fingers at the driver, who popped the trunk. The guards in the SUV watched in silence. Mathias pulled a second identical steel briefcase from a hidden compartment and, closing the trunk, laid it on top. He entered the combination, 27315, and retrieved the canister's twin.

The air was raw and Mathias could see his own breath as he held both canisters up in the cheerless blue light. He turned the second slowly, looking for the same fatal flaw. He found none. "God damn it!" Slamming the canisters down onto the trunk, he pulled his cell phone from his inside pocket and dialed. "Rufus?" he shouted into the phone.

"Yes, sir?" said Rufus timidly.

"They're not the same!"

Rufus knew immediately what Mathias meant. Rufus was in charge of the canister duplication process. Not because he was an expert, but because Mathias trusted him. "In what way, sir?"

"There's a nick in the side!" There was a long pause at the other end of the phone. "Well?" demanded Mathias.

"Perhaps there's supposed to be?"

"There isn't in the other one, so at least one of them is wrong!"

"You're right. I can be at the lab in an hour and can check the scans then. Or we can check the original when you return."

"It's too late. I have too many deals to do." Mathias paused for a moment to think. Rufus knew his boss well enough to remain silent. "Listen, I don't care what the scans show, people expect this canister to be indestructible and even the slightest scratch says otherwise. Make all of them flawless."

Rufus resisted the urge to argue that even osmiridium wasn't indestructible. "Yes, sir."

Satisfied, Mathias hung up and put his cellphone back in his coat pocket. He carefully laid the unmarked canister back in its case. He then looked around and spotted a nearby dumpster. Lifting the lid he tossed the imperfect canister inside. Mathias then returned to his seat in the limousine. He snapped his fingers impatiently, and the two car caravan rolled on.

* * *

Mathias's limousine and escort pulled into the yard of what had once been an automotive parts manufacturing plant. The sun was out now, brightening the concrete lot and belying the dark purpose of the men gathered there. The terrorist leader, Ali Madda, stood waiting with his entourage before a custom-made stretch Bentley sedan with the license plate "DTH2USA92". He'd wanted the plate to read simply "DTH2USA", but unfortunately there were already ninety-two people ahead of him with the same request. The terrorist leader wore sunglasses on his tanned cherubic face which was framed by a traditional keffiyeh headdress tied with an agal. Ali Madda's wide girth filled out his white Arabic bisht robes like a billowing circus tent that flapped audibly in the early morning breeze. As the arms dealer's limousine rolled to a stop, Ali beamed with beatific delight. His whitened teeth gleamed like polished piano keys. The men behind Ali watched the arriving vehicle with the practiced sullenness of professional minions. They included six armed guards and Ali's seventh son, Ali Junior No. 4. Ali had four sons named Ali. He'd not planned it that way but, caught up in the glorious moment of receiving each child, had decided that this was the special one deserving of his name, only to change his mind again and again. He also had a daughter named Ali, but that was just an honest mistake after too many shots of arak in the maternity ward waiting room. As Ali's grin broadened, his entourage's glowering only intensified. By agreement there would be no arms at the deal, other than those offered up for sale. In reality, no one actually honoured this or expected anyone else to. It simply meant that no weapons would be displayed openly. As a result, Ali's men each wore oversized robes in order to conceal handguns, machine pistols and so on. Mathias's men wore oversized suit jackets. One of Ali's minions, Altair, was attempting to pass off a grenade launcher as an artificial leg. This despite the fact that the exposed muzzle looked nothing like an actual prosthetic.

"Ali, you radical extremist dog you!" shouted Mathias as he stepped from the car.

"Mathias, my infidel swine friend!"

The two men fiercely embraced, slapping each other warmly on the back several times, before stepping back. Each, of course, had been patting the other for a wire.

"Looking good!" said Mathias.

"You mean, looking fat," said Ali with a chuckle.

Mathias waved off the remark. "So you enjoy life."

"Yes, I do, my friend, yes, I do. A little too much, perhaps." Ali turned and gestured to his son, "You know my son Ali?"

"Of course, you brought him last time."

Chaos Theory

"No, no, that was his older brother, Ali, " said Ali. The terrorist then shook his head sadly and added, "Such a disappointment." Ali Junior #3 had 'brought shame' upon the Madda family by announcing that he was a homosexual. Ali Madda maintained that his son was simply "crazy" as everyone knows there are no gay Arabs. Still, when his son Skype video called him from a drag bar in Athens wearing only a pink Hello Kitty burka and eyeliner, it was hard to ignore. Being insane was one thing, but being gay was completely unacceptable. Ali #3 had called to say that, in spite of it all, he loved his father, and to say goodbye. He wouldn't be coming home, he explained, out of fear that his own father would have him shot. "He's being ridiculous," Ali told the boy's mother, "everyone knows the punishment for homosexuality is death by stoning."

"Shall we begin?" asked Mathias.

"Absolutely." Ali Madda snapped his fingers. One of his men lifted a steel briefcase from beneath his robe. Mathias, in turn, lifted his hand, and one of his men stepped forward, holding an identical briefcase. Ali smiled, savouring the moment. "The Loose Thread project, I can't believe it. We'd seen photos, heard rumours, but always assumed it was just a myth. Only you Mathias, could find such a thing. It is truly the Holy Grail of Islamic terrorism, as it were."

Behind him, Ali's men gawked. Ali had told them what they were going to acquire that day. Now, in the presence of such awesome power, they stopped their glowering and simply stared. "Subhan Allah..." gasped Altair.

"I'll show you mine, if you show me yours," said Mathias.

Ali snapped his fingers again, and the henchman opened the briefcase. Inside was, what appeared to be, a pile of mottled translucent

128

glass lumps. The lumps winked in the sunlight as if to say, "I am so much more." Online, Mathias accepted bitcoin, Visa, Mastercard and Diners Club. In person, he preferred the old fashioned feel of uncut diamonds. One of Mathias's men stepped forward, selected a random stone and peered at it with a jeweller's loupe. After verifying the quality of the gem, he replaced it and nodded to his boss. Mathias had known Ali would deliver. He was not only one of Mathias's richest customers, but also one of his oldest and most trusted. They had done more deals than Mathias could count. None, of course, even approached the scale of this one.

Mathias turned to where his own henchman stood holding the briefcase, entered the combination, and lifted the lid. Mathias was nothing if not a showman. He carefully raised the shiny canister from within as if it was indeed the Holy Grail.

"That's it?" exclaimed Ali Junior. "It looks like a tiny trash can!"

Ali struck his son with the back of his hand. "Insolent cur, you have no idea what you're looking at! I should never have named you Ali." Ali Madda turned to Mathias with a penitent smile. "I am sorry my friend. He is a young and foolish boy. He knows not what he says."

Mathias waved off the apology. "Now, you remember our agreement? Keep this under your fez for six months."

"Yes, yes, of course. I don't wear a fez, but you have my word. Before Allah, I swear." This was, of course, the real reason Mathias had selected fundamentalists as his first customers. He could make them swear to their God to keep the device secret. "May I inquire as to why?" Ali asked tentatively.

"Ali, old friend, when you ordered thirty-four toothpaste tubes full of C-4 plastic explosive last July, did I ask what for? No, I did not."

"No, indeed. How do you say it? Discretion is the better part of valour. A thousand apologies, again." Ali was practically salivating at the sight of the canister. "May I?" he asked anxiously. Mathias nodded. Ali raised the device with abject reverence, as if cradling a sacred relic. Mathias said nothing to dissuade this. While the canister was tightly sealed, he'd rather the terrorist leader be overly cautious than needlessly negligent. One of Ali's men stepped forward, offering to authenticate the weapon. The Arab waved him away. "I *know* this." Ali Madda spoke in a hushed voice as if the presence of the Almighty. "I have studied every photograph. I have felt it in my dreams. This...?" Ali clutched the canister fiercely to his bosom and moaned. "This is the key to paradise."

"To each his own," said Mathias, as he watched his men place the diamond filled briefcases into the trunk of his car. Mathias climbed into the limousine and gave a final nod to the enraptured terrorist. Ali Madda failed to notice. The arms dealer signaled to the driver, and he and his entourage drove away.

Ali Madda lingered a moment longer. He was savouring the idea that he was now the single most powerful man on Earth. It was intoxicating. He felt the urge to burst out in maniacal laughter but stopped himself out of a sense of decorum. He then realized that, as the most powerful man on Earth, he could do whatever he wanted. Ali Madda laughed. He then laughed some more. He laughed and laughed until his eyes watered and his belly ached.

"What now?" asked Ali junior skeptically.

"Now? Now, we rule the world!" Ali triumphantly slapped a nearby henchman on the back. Unfortunately, the man whose back he slapped was Altair, who had been gingerly mincing about with the grenade launcher tied to his knee. The henchman stumbled forward and lost his balance. "Whoa whoa!" shouted Altair, as he teetered about on one foot. The others, including Ali, backed warily away. The off-kilter henchman hopped back and fourth in a desperate attempt to regain his balance. Finally, Altair slammed his heavily armed leg down with a *thunk*, which was followed by a *click*. "Uh oh," he said. *BOOM!* The weapon discharged, launching the big man over the fence and into a wall, where he was killed instantly.

There was a moment of stunned silence. Ali Madda then shrugged and got back into the car. Realizing that Altair's coveted front passenger seat was now up for grabs, one of the surviving henchmen yelled "Shotgun!"

CHAPTER 14

"They shoot movies, don't they?" – S. Pollack

The small white ball rolled smoothly across the manicured green and dropped into the hole with a *plop*. "You see, Reverend, another sign!" said the President enthusiastically. No one would normally describe the Commander-in-Chief as a gifted golfer, but this morning he was playing well. He wasn't supposed to be playing at all today. All the forecasters had called for rain. The President, however, had insisted the sun would shine. He'd felt it in his solar plexus.

"Indeed, Mr. President," said Revered Duke Norman, "I should never have blessed your ball."

"True! Very true! Ever since you did, I've been winning."

"It is God's will," the Reverend agreed, nodding sagaciously. The

Reverend then stepped up to his own ball, and began carefully lining up the putt. He lifted the putter to take his shot.

"You know..." began the President.

The Reverend stopped mid swing. He took a calm breath, leaned on his club and looked at the President expectantly. The Commander-in-Chief continued his thought. "First, we have this weapon capable of destroying the world, and now... now we have me sinking this ball. I do believe that someone is telling me something."

"I have no doubt, sir," said the Reverend. The President nodded, seemingly lost in contemplation. The pastor seized the opportunity to focus once again on the ball. He gently lifted the putter to take the shot.

"You know, I think they're trying to tell me my purpose."

Reverend Duke stopped short and lowered the putter to the green. He smiled serenely. "God chose you to be President for a reason," he said.

"I know, but I wasn't sure for what exactly."

"The Lord moves in mysterious ways."

"And as Jim would say, there are no ways more mysterious than the electoral college system of the United States of America."

"Amen, to that." Before the President could interrupt again, the Reverend tapped the ball, sending it on a long unerring arc into the hole where it disappeared with a *ka-lop!*

"Pretty good," said the President, "but you'll have to do better than that to beat me today. Jesus is my caddy."

The Reverend Duke Norman glanced back at Jésus and Fernando, standing at the edge of the green, holding their clubs. "Indeed, sir," he agreed.

The President and the Reverend walked to the next tee. The caddies and Secret Service, as always, kept a discreet distance. The President rarely took the golf cart, preferring the extra time to talk. After all, nobody could rush the President of the United States or ask to play through. This time, however, the two men walked in silence as the President pondered. He thought of his grandfather, whom he'd never met. The President's grandfather had been among ninety-eight Americans held prisoner on Wake Island during World War II. Wake Island was an atoll, a remote speck of land in the middle of the Pacific Ocean. The Japanese had captured the island early and ordered the ninety-eight civilians stationed there into forced labour, until one fateful day in 1943. US Forces bombed the island resulting in heavy casualties for the defenders. In a fit of fury, the Japanese Commander ordered all ninety-eight prisoners machine gunned down in cold blood. It was an act of retribution in direct violation of the Geneva convention. One man somehow escaped. Alone on a tiny atoll less than two miles across, the escapee must have known his freedom to be fleeting. So he did the only thing he could; he left a message, painstakingly carved into a rock next to the mass grave containing the corpses of his comrades. With nowhere to go on that piece of Pacific paradise, the escapee was soon recaptured and decapitated. No one knew who the man was. He did not single himself out in his epitaph. Instead, he wrote simply "98 US PW 5-10-43" or, effectively, *we were here.* The President, however, was convinced that man was his grandfather. He was so convinced, he'd even proclaimed it in speeches during the campaign. It was a claim he couldn't prove, but neither could others refute it. In his heart of hearts, The President simply knew it to be true. That, he believed, was a sign of a great leader; knowing things. The men of his family had always had a purpose. That purpose, he could see, was now culminating in him.

Reverend Duke Norman assessed his next shot carefully. He was actually a superb golfer, having spent his summers as a young man working and playing at the famous Augusta National Course in Georgia. While Augusta wasn't exactly known for welcoming African American members at the time, it did welcome black caddies. As club founder Clifford Roberts said, "As long as I'm alive, all the golfers will be white and all the caddies will be black." The caddies weren't supposed to play, of course, but the young Duke Norman managed to sneak in holes whenever he could. The caddies weren't supposed to sleep with members' wives either, but the young Duke did that too. For the most part, these violations went unnoticed. That was until one day out on the course. That day left a vision forever seared in Duke's consciousness. It was the sight of an angry husband lifting his golf club high into the sky in the midst of an unforecast thunderstorm. The golfer was ready to bash young Duke's bright red brains all over the ninth hole green. The later police report said what happened next was the result of electrical conductivity. Duke knew it was more than that; it was divine intervention. The lightning bolt came from nowhere and struck the golfer's club, killing him instantly. That was the day Duke Norman found God or, as he put it, God found him. The golfer may have been electrocuted, but Duke was electrified. He knew on that day that God had chosen him for a purpose. When he met the President he knew that that purpose involved him. Duke's faith in God and golf skills were the two things he retained from his days at Augusta. As a result, he was a good enough golfer that he could play to the level of whomever he was with. Playing down perfectly was a discipline that came with its own rewards. The Reverend gauged his shot carefully, then swung just a little short. Duke Norman's ball landed in the rough, exactly as intended.

"Oh, what a shame," said the President.

"We all have our crosses..." said the Reverend. He then realized that the Commander-in-Chief was not referring to his deftly foiled shot. Instead, the President was watching a golf cart approaching over the hill. The cart was driven by a secret serviceman. The White House Chief of Staff was riding on the seat beside him.

"I need your support Reverend," said the President. He turned to his evangelist friend with a look of urgency. "There are... doubters."

"I see," said Duke Norman, "you mean..."

They both looked at Jim Hornswell bouncing towards them on the golf cart passenger seat, gripping the sidebar to keep from falling out. The President nodded and said grimly, "I truly believe this is as it was foreseen, Reverend. What does the scripture say? This is the way the world ends, not with a bang, but a whimper."

"I don't think that was the Bible, sir."

"I'm pretty sure it was."

"Yes, Mr. President."

Jim Hornswell pulled to a halt a few feet away. He wore an anxious look on his face. "Mr. President, we need you in The Situation Room right away. Something has happened!"

The President turned to Reverend Norman and said, "I'm thinking of letting my beard grow, what do you think?"

"An excellent idea," agreed the Reverend.

"Mr. President?" said his Chief of Staff anxiously.

"Oh all right, I'm coming," said the President, "but officially I won this game!"

The pastor nodded his acquiescence. "Indubitably, sir."

* * *

The Situation Room was packed. The close quarters mixed with tension and thick suits filled the room with an air of intrigue and body odour. The President, having had no time to change, arrived in plus fours and a golf cap. The tartan on his trousers was that of the MacDonald clan, although he did not know it. He'd picked it out because it looked nice.

Standing at the end of the table, Secretary of State Sarah Maxwell looked grim. On the drive back, Jim had briefed the President, who became fully engaged once he learned it concerned Loose Thread. All other matters were secondary to him now. Who cares about the debt ceiling when the world might end on your watch? Jim looks pale, thought the President, I wonder if he's coming down with something?

"This appeared 30 minutes ago on Al Jazeera and other Arabic television stations," said Sarah. She switched on the wall-mounted TV at the front of the room. On the big screen, appeared the figure of Ali Madda. The rotound Arab stood smiling broadly with his hands clasped across his belly. Beside him, an assistant held a small steel canister. The video was paused, leaving Ali with one eye open and the other half-closed. It was the inebriated look people often had when frozen mid frame. The set looked like some sort of Arabic Home Shopping Network. In this case, the item being presented was the deadliest weapon ever devised.

"For anyone who doesn't recognize him, this is Ali Madda," the Secretary of State explained. "Ali Madda's father, Abd Al Madda, is considered the Godfather of terrorism in Saudi Arabia. We don't believe, however that Ali here is working on his father's behalf. In fact, we believe he is trying to impress his father and more successful siblings. Analysis suggests he wants to ultimately usurp his father."

"An edible complex," said the President knowingly.

"Did you say *edible* complex?" asked Jim.

The President nodded, "As in, to eat one's father. Not literally, of course. It's a metaphor. You know, from that Greek play, *Death of a Salesman.*"

"Don't you mean oedipal complex?"

"Really Jim, now you're just making up words."

His Chief of Staff started to object, but the President waved him to silence. "Please continue, Sarah."

The Secretary of State nodded and pressed play. On screen, Ali Madda's smile grew wider. "You see what I possess? The President of the United States knows what it is. Look closely." Ali waved to the cameraman. The camera zoomed in towards the canister, but went too far. This resulted in the device being half off screen. Ali, who was able to see the live feed on an off-stage monitor, became agitated. "It's out of frame, move left!" Ali shouted in Arabic.

The flustered cameraman and canister holders both moved left, respectively, making matters worse. Now, only the edge of the device remained visible, while the hairy forearm of the assistant filled the display.

"No, not the camera, the device!"

The canister now moved completely out of frame.

"No, no, no, you idiot!" Ali shrieked.

"I knew we shouldn't have done this live," the director muttered off screen.

"Not your left, camera-left, your right!"

The canister moved clear across the screen and off the other side.

"No! No! Stop!" There was a pause then, as the terrorist leader tried to regain his composure. With forced calm, Ali Madda said, "Slowly, slowly, move it back a bit." Slowly the canister inched back into view. "Keep going... keep going... stop!"

The canister was still off center, but fully visible in frame.

"Good enough," said Ali with relief. "Now turn it around to show the markings."

The assistant started to rotate the canister, then dropped it. It clattered to the floor and rolled off stage. Panicked, the assistant leapt across the screen in pursuit.

"Ahhh!" screamed Ali, who began inexplicably slapping a nearby terrorist intern.

The screen blurred into fast-forward mode as the Secretary of State explained, "Sorry, it goes on like this for, um, several minutes." Sarah pressed play once again.

An exasperated Ali Madda, headwear askew, was now holding the canister himself. His assistant was still visible in the background, sitting on a crate, with his head between his knees. He'd suffered a bloody nose and had toilet paper stuffed up his nostrils to stop the bleeding. The intern had run off entirely.

Ali drew a deep breath and continued his rehearsed tirade. "Mr. President, you know what this is because your country made it many years ago. You made it to rule the world, but today? Today, the devil will feel his own tail! This is a weapon far worse than the atomic bomb. You know that, if I open this container, the entire world will be destroyed. There will be no survivors. The infidels will perish and only the holy will go to paradise! And by 'holy', of course, I mean Muslims."

"Pause it," commanded the President. "Is this real?"

The Secretary of State nodded. "We believe so, Mr. President. It makes sense. Mathias Boltzmann has done business with Madda in the past. The canister certainly looks authentic."

"It kind of looks like the coffeemaker they use at the White House dinners," another staffer observed.

"This a disaster the likes of which the world has never seen!" said Jim, aghast.

"I agree..." said the President solemnly. The leader of the free world peered carefully at the frozen image of the Islamic terrorist holding the weapon and nodded, "It *does* look like the coffeemaker they use at the White House dinners."

There were nods of consensus down the table. Jim Hornswell and Sarah Maxwell looked on, dumbstruck.

"Continue" ordered the President. The video began to play once more.

* * *

"We will release Allah's vengeance unless the following demands are met. First, one hundred billion dollars from the United Nations. Second, the release of the following groups of prisoners..." For a moment, Ali Madda feigned peering at a long list. He then looked up with a devilish grin and shouted, "All of them!" The jolly terrorist then burst out into a maniacal laugh, holding his jiggling belly like some sort of diabolical Santa Claus.

Mathias switched off the TV in disgust and threw the remote to the floor.

"We knew this could happen," said Carl.

Mathias glared at him, "No, we did not. Not yet! Now, the

duplicates are worthless!" Mathias swept a dozen counterfeit canisters from his desk. They clattered to the floor and rolled off in different directions. "God damn it! Where has the trust gone? It used to be you could sell contraband munitions on a handshake!"

"We were lying to him too," Carl pointed out meekly.

"That's not the point! The point is..." Mathias paused for a moment, trying to figure out what the point was. "The point is, we had long standing relationship, he and I. I picked him very specifically because I could trust him and he could trust me. The only reason I was prepared to betray that trust was because of the uniqueness of this particular weapon."

"Yes, well... perhaps he felt the same way?"

Mathias stared at his friend for a moment. He wanted to throw a canister at Carl's head. The only canister within reach, however, was the real one and, even with its presumed adamantine shell, winging it across the room still seemed a bit reckless. Mathias picked up the device and, instead of throwing it, paused to study its reflective surface. The curvature of the metal warped his reflection like a funhouse mirror. I could twist off the top and end it all right now, he thought, that would be something.

"Mathias?" asked Carl tentatively.

"Yes? Oh yes. Hmm, well, it's a good thing I didn't give him the real one. He might just be crazy enough to open it!"

Carl blanched noticeably.

"Are you alright, Carl?"

"I'm fine, I, um... you don't think he ever would open it, do you?"

"What's it matter? He doesn't have the real thing."

"No... no, of course not."

Mathias turned and placed the canister in the wall safe where it belonged. He then closed the door, spun the dial, and lowered a painting to conceal it. The painting was an authentic Van Gogh, entitled *The Painter on the Road to Tarascon*. It had been a gift from his grandfather, who had himself "come across it" at the bank one day. The painting, he told Mathias, was a symbol of the common bond they shared.

CHAPTER 15

"My colours, my honour, my colours, my all..."
— Robert the Bruce

"Because it's pointless," Charlie insisted. Lisa rolled her eyes. That's not right, thought Charlie, I'm the one who should be rolling mine. "Look, if you want to go to these classes—"

"Meditation sessions."

"Whatever. If you want to go, then that's fine. I don't."

"You could find yourself there."

"I can find myself here." He patted himself. "See? I already did."

Charlie loved Lisa, but she changed belief systems as often as her outfit. She was on an eternal quest for meaning and had run the gamut from Kabbalah to Faith Crystals. She might have tried Amish but for their "terrible taste in clothes." Lisa's latest fling was with eastern philosophies.

Charlie had inherited his own religious thinking from his father, which is to say, he didn't. "My religion is cattle," his father would scoff, "most religion is sheep." Charlie sighed and said, "Look, I appreciate you wanting to include me, but I don't need it. I'm just an atheist or whatever."

"Buddhism is non theistic."

Charlie sighed. He usually humoured her religion-of-the-week. He considered it a hobby for her. Like most husbands, he was happy to indulge his wife's hobbies. Today, she was into Buddhism, which is what she claimed to have been seeking all along. She explained that she'd read Siddhartha in high-school but had forgotten how awesome it was. A few weeks ago she'd 'Liked' the Dalai Lama Facebook page, and now here she was. The whole reincarnation thing seemed silly to Charlie. Most religions at least made some sense, in that they moved in straight lines. You're born, you live, you die, and then you go to Heaven or Hell. Atheism was the same really, except for the last bit. The idea of going around and around forever seemed idiotic, like circling a metaphysical parking lot for all eternity and never finding a spot. The problem was, this was no longer about Lisa, it was about Faith. Lisa wanted to teach Buddhism to their daughter, and how they raised Faith mattered. From that point, their discussion degenerated into yelling. Lisa accused Charlie of never truly respecting her beliefs. Charlie accused Lisa of being a 'faith tourist', a line he'd thought up while waiting for his coffee at Starbucks the day before. They then began to bicker about whether 'bhavacakra' was the Circle of Life, or some sort of Greek dessert. The fight only ended when Faith came out of her room in tears, begging them to stop. Lisa and Charlie instantly forgot their quarrel and rushed to comfort her. "It's just an argument," Lisa reassured her, "something grownups do."

Charlie agreed. When Faith asked him why, he answered, "Because we're ridiculous."

* * *

"Are those the highlands?" asked Alex.

"I guess so," said Charlie, noticing for the first time the green hills rising before them through the pouring rain. He had the windshield wipers on high, but they could barely keep up with the downpour. Where did this weather come from? he wondered. The forecast had called for clear skies. They'd been driving for over two hours through the Central Lowlands along a blacktop highway, having just passed through another soggy Scottish town whose name he'd already forgotten. Now, they were driving past what looked like a bog. The rain beat across the brackish surface, making the water even wetter than usual. Once he had the hang of driving on the left side of the road, his mind had again started to drift. In an effort to break the habit, he'd started to force himself to think of less ideal moments. He knew his life before hadn't been perfect. He and Lisa had been fighting more and more, while being intimate less and less. He'd found himself noticing women at the agency. He and Lisa had talked about fixing their issues, but never did. Charlie's theory was that, if he dwelt more on the flawed reality than those memories of bliss, he might be able to break this cycle of constantly returning to his life before the accident. So far it hadn't worked. The truth was, even at the lowest points, he was happier then. He knew why. He'd had a purpose, things to strive for. Life was moving forward in a linear fashion, like it was supposed to. Of course, he'd also lived for Faith, so that she could grow up and, someday, have children of her own. That, he realized, was circular. Maybe life is a corkscrew, he thought.

"Hey," said Alex, "did you know I'm Scottish?"

"What?"

Charlie glanced over to where Alex sat in the passenger seat. The boy had his nose buried in a brochure on the clans of Scotland he'd picked up at the car rental booth. "The Grahams were a clan," he said. "I'm Scottish!"

"You're an American, of Scottish descent."

"Still. I think it's neat. I have a crest, a tartan and everything!"

"Well then," said Charlie, "welcome home."

Alex smiled at him. It was the first look of genuine happiness Charlie had seen from the boy. It disarmed him.

* * *

The rain continued unabated as they rolled through the deserted streets of the village of Cockwaddle. "What about there?" asked Alex. He pointed to the warm yellow windows of the Lamb & Lion pub further down the street. Since it was Sunday, the bank next door was closed, so Charlie pulled in there to park. The two then dashed through the downpour to the front door hung with a sign of a lion lying down with a haunch of lamb.

The interior was packed with locals, fellow refuges from the rain. The loud hubbub halted as patrons turned to stare at the new arrivals who stood dripping in the doorway. Charlie and Alex stared back, awkwardly. For a moment, they were the most interesting thing in the room, before being dismissed as misplaced tourists. The room's attention then turned back to the TVs.

"I've never had that happened before," said Alex, "actually silence a room."

"Well, we're off the beaten path here, and we're a couple of strangers."

"Stranger, maybe, but not the strangest," said Alex with a grin.

Charlie smiled back. His smile vanished as he noticed what the locals were watching. The televisions were showing a newscast of what appeared to be massive riots.

"What's going on?" asked Alex.

"Soccer match?" Charlie joked weakly. In truth, the images were much more troubling. One scene was clearly in Tokyo, while another looked like Berlin. Charlie and Alex approached the end of the bar and squeezed in next to the brass service rails, the only place they could find an opening. After several minutes of waiting, it became clear no one was coming to help them. "Hello?" said Charlie to the barman, "Hello?"

The barman sighed, put down the pint glass he'd been wiping and trudged over, "Ay?"

"I'll have a pint of bitter please."

"Which one?"

"Whatever you recommend. Oh, and an iced tea for the boy.

"I don't drink iced tea," said Alex.

"Good," said the barman, "cuz we 'an't got noon. We got coke, we got water, an' we got beer."

"Do you have diet coke?"

"Pansy Coke? No, we dunna got pansy Coke."

"Okay, Coke, please."

"Pepsi a'right?"

"Um, sure."

The barman proceeded to pull Charlie's draught and Alex's Pepsi.

"Wet out," said Charlie, hoping to draw out a conversation.

"Is it?"

Charlie hesitated, unsure if the man were joking. His expression betrayed nothing.

"Very. Do you know if it'll clear up?"

"Fellow on telly said sun tomorrow."

"Oh, Good."

"Ay, but it's a cheap telly, so tha n'er knows." The proprietor finished filling their drinks and placed them on the bar. He didn't let go of the glasses, however. Instead, he held them firmly along with Charlie and Alex's attention. "Drink up, eat if you moost, then you and yur lad best be goin'. Folks may be less than friendly wit' what all's goin' on."

"What's goin'—going on?" asked Charlie.

The barman's watery blue eyes told Charlie he'd have to find his answers elsewhere. Charlie nodded to indicate that he accepted the barkeep's terms. "Okay. Maybe some fish'n chips to go?" asked Charlie.

"Fine."

"How much do I owe you?"

"It's on the house."

"I'm happy to pay."

"It's on the house."

Charlie nodded again, and the barman walked away. Charlie sipped his pint of bitter and peered about the bar. It was warm and cozy, and likely two hundred years old at least. The flat-screen TVs and Super-Nudge slot-machines had presumably been added more recently. The televisions, he noticed, were all tuned to either the BBC or CNN International. The riots onscreen were clearly global. Wolf Blitzer spoke before an image of a burning car in Boston, while Anderson Cooper looked down upon a wall of riot police in New York. The closest screen, however, was out of earshot. Charlie looked to see whether he and Alex could move closer. All the tables were full, and it was hard to even stand near a set without blocking someone's view. The last thing Charlie wanted to do was give cause for a local to be annoyed.

"Tha's all yur fault, tha' knows?"

"I'm sorry?" said Alex.

Charlie turned to see an old man in a wool cap waggling his finger at them from a nearby barstool.

"Tha riots! All yur fault," he said with a Scotch braw so thick it could be mixed with oatmeal and used to stuff a sheep's stomach.

"I don't understand," said Charlie. "Our fault?"

"Och aye. Is lak tha poet says, the best laid schemes o' mice 'n men..."

"I'm sorry," said Charlie. "I really don't know what you're talking about."

"Either does he," muttered Alex with a smirk. "Crazy old coot."

At that moment the image on screen switched to the video of Ali Madda threatening to destroy the Earth. CNN had been playing it repeatedly since it first aired. Initially, they had no information on it and had spent the entire time speculating. The assumption was that it was all some sort of hoax. Despite this, the Cable News Network had cleared the deck of all other news stories and begun round-the-clock coverage. CNN brought out their best pundits and began describing how, in theory, the world might end were the device actually real which, they occasionally reminded viewers, it almost certainly was not. The Republican spokepeople blamed the

Democrats, the Democratic pundits blamed the Republicans. No one knew what was happening, but were quite confident whose fault it was. It soon degenerated into an argument as to whether the 2nd amendment included doomsday devices. The result was a fear feeding frenzy. That was when the riots began and, suddenly, there was a lot more news to cover.

"Tha'! Tha' fella on telly!" yelled the old Scott. He'd now taken to his feet and was spitting on them as he shouted. "Sayin' he's goin' ta blow up world with what weapon yoo Yanks made fifty-years ago. Now thar's riots and sooch all o'r world. I's absoloot chaos!"

"Calm down Tinker!" ordered the barman. He pointed to Tinker's barstool to indicate that calming down also meant sitting down.

"Why should I, A.D.? They dunna leave alone, now doo they? They think they know't all and they dinna ken nuthin! Nuthin! They just... bah!" Tinker shot the pub-owner a defiant glance but did as he was told. He sat on his barstool and scowled at them like an ornery old hound.

Charlie glanced about to see that they had, once more, become the most interesting thing in the room. Dozens of faces eyed them from every nook and corner of the public house. The barman received a pair of newspaper wrapped bundles from a barmaid and tossed them on the counter. "Here's yur fish'n chips. Yu'd better go, lads, a'fore there's trooble."

"Thank-you, " said Charlie. He gingerly picked up the hot bundles, now translucent with oil. "What we actually need is directions. We're looking for a Lucy MacGuffin, Dr. Rupert MacGuffin's widow?"

The barman looked surprised, then amused. "Lucy MacGuffin?"

Charlie nodded.

"Well, if it's MacGuffin farm you want, keep going, up road ten miles. You canna miss it."

"How will I know it?"

Now, the barman chuckled outright. "Oh, I think you'll know't. It's a very... distinctive stroocture." The others at the bar within earshot laughed at this, with the exception of Tinker, who continued to eye them suspiciously. "Guid luck!" the barman said with an amused smile.

"Thank-you," said Charlie, wishing he knew what was so funny.

*　*　*

Charlie drove the rented Volkswagen along the gravel road that wound its way between the high hills that gave the land its name. The rain had lifted and left a low hanging mist in its place. The result was an air of damp Scottish romance, like a copy of *The Bride of Lammermoor* dropped in a puddle. Even Alex, who had always protested when his mother told him to stop playing with his iPod long enough to look out the car window, could not help but wonder at the soaring landscape around them.

Only BBC Radio 1 served to remind them of whatever it was that was passing for reality these days. "... while UN and United States officials are down-playing the threat. The President of the United States has yet to explicitly refute the existence of such a weapon. Many experts suggest that this is purely a hoax concocted by Ali Madda precisely for creating the type of terror seen in streets around the world today. If so, then—"

Charlie switched off the car radio. His brain was unable to process it anyway. Instead, it was overwhelmed by the massive grey edifice that loomed out of the mist before them. At six hundred and forty feet tall, the structure stood shoulder to shoulder with the highest of the surrounding hilltops. Despite its details being lost in its own shadow, there was no mistaking the concave contours of a nuclear cooling tower. Both Charlie and

Alex struggled with the incongruity of it all.

"Do you think that's what he meant by distinctive?" asked Alex.

* * *

As they drove closer to the tower, they could see that it was badly weathered and in need of repair. Cracks were visible across the surface. In places, the outer layer of cement had actually sloughed off, revealing the steel rebar skeleton beneath. The ominous shadow of the man-made mountain draped the entire valley in permanent dusk, resulting in grey grass and brown briar at its base. There were none of the other buildings one would expect with an operating nuclear facility. Instead, at the foot of the tower was a quaint little croft cottage, surrounded by a dry stone dyke wall. Alex, who had needed to go to the toilet for the past twenty-minutes, noticed an outhouse visible to the side. He hoped it was an unused relic, but decided he would make do if need be. Smoke dribbled from the chimney and meandered off into the sky. *Someone* was home. Charlie pulled in to park next to the rusting remains of a ramshackle 1957 Morris Minor.

"I still don't get why we're here," said Alex. "I mean, isn't the mad professor dead?"

"Missing. Presumed dead."

"But you think he's alive?"

"No, we're here to see his widow." With that, Charlie lifted the iron ring door knocker and let it fall with a surprisingly loud *ka-lock!*

"Dead or not, that'll wake him," said Alex with a grin. He then leaned over to peer through an adjacent pebbled glass window, only to be yanked back by Charlie.

"Don't be rude!" said Charlie.

Alex looked peeved. "You can't see anything anyway."

"Uh huh."

The door was opened by an elderly, but robust woman in her eighties. She looked them up and down with keen blue eyes, then nodded. "From the goov'ment are ye? Right then, ya better coom in."

Several minutes later, Charlie and Alex found themselves in the sitting room of the cottage. Alex had been relieved to learn that the home did indeed include indoor plumbing. Inside, the dwelling was every bit as cozy and charming as one could imagine. The only oddness was the perpetual sense of dusk created by the cooling tower's shadow. This sense of anomaly was further heightened by the sight of sunlight on nearby hills, clearly visible through the windows. The low ceilings had forced Charlie to stoop when entering, but he now sat comfortably ensconced on a sofa. Charlie glanced about the living room. It was crammed full of antiques. Just like their owner, he mused. Alex sat on the other end of the sofa, staring at a pewter statuette on the mantle above the fire. It was of the American mythical figure, Rip Van Winkle, aroused from decades of slumber to find his beard grown long. Their host, satisfied they were comfortable, was visible through the kitchen doorway, preparing tea. She was a handsome woman, Charlie decided, and must have quite attractive in her youth, although unusually tall for a woman. The dress she wore, patterned with intertwining thistles, looked to be an antique as well. Still, it suited her, he thought.

"You sure I can't help you with that?" Charlie called out.

"No, I'm fine. Thank-ye mooch."

Her accent, Charlie noted, was not strictly Scottish, but a mix. He recognized Yorkshire and even some American. The result of living in many places from a young age, he mulled.

Mrs. MacGuffin stepped from the kitchen carrying the tea tray, then stopped. Her hands began to shake. The teacups began to tremble. Charlie leapt from his seat to help. "Is a might heavier w' so mooch water," she said, "I'm not used havin' coompany." Together, they placed the tray down on the coffee table. Mrs. MacGuffin sank down into her seat with a sigh. "Right then, we'll just let that infuse a bit."

"Mrs. MacGuffin... may I call you Lucy?"

"No."

"Um, okay. Mrs. MacGuffin, we are here because we need to ask you a few questions about Dr. Rupert MacGuffin."

Mrs. MacGuffin nodded, "Well, I didna suppose you came to ask me about ma-self." She then glanced at her watch. "Right then," she said, "I think that's time." She began arranging the teacups on their saucers.

Charlie stared at the watch on her wrist. That looks like an antique too, he thought. He was right. The watch was one of the original Santos men's watches designed by Louis Cartier in 1904. "Lovely watch," he said.

"A memento," Mrs. MacGuffin explained. "Before he departed I never wore a watch. Time was always Rupert's concern. When he went, I simply put it on. I dunna ken why, exactly."

"When he went... you mean when Dr. MacGuffin died?" asked Charlie.

"I meant what I said, and I said what I meant." She responded. "You may call him 'departed' and he is most surely 'late', but he is not, to my knowledge, dead. Milk?"

Charlie decided it would be improper to press the matter. She's clearly in denial, he thought. "Yes, please. No sugar."

Mrs. MacGuffin poured the milk, which Charlie noted, was yellow with cream.

"And you, young man?" she said addressing Alex. "How do you take your tea?"

"I don't," said Alex with surprise. "My mother says—said, I 'm too young for caffeine."

"Nonsense, it's good for a growing lad," she said. "Tea'n Gin'll keep ye thin. Tha's what me moother taught me."

"Listen lady, I said I don't want—" Charlie kicked Alex under the table. Alex started to protest, "I don't have to..." Charlie sternly stared him to silence. Alex scowled and sank into the sofa in a sulk.

Mrs. MacGuffin proceeded to fill a cup two-thirds with milk and added just a splash of tea. "There you go, young man" she said with a warm smile. "Tea for beginners."

Surprised by the warmth of her smile, Alex begrundingly accepted the cup. They then waited while Mrs. MacGuffin poured for herself. Alex tried a tentative sip, decided it was harmless, and relaxed.

"Do you know about something called Project Loose Thread?" asked Charlie.

"Of course, dear, there's ne'er day goes by I dinnae think about it."

"Then you know that it's resurfaced?"

"Oh, aye. I've been expectin' it."

"You have?"

"Well, it was always just a matter of time, weren't it? I mean, it couldn'a be destroyed."

"Oh right, I see," said Charlie. Charlie considered this for a moment and decided that, despite her doddering appearance, Mrs. MacGuffin knew and understood a great deal. "Of course, I've read the documents," he said. "But the science is far beyond me. Can you explain how it works exactly?"

"Nay. The science is beyond me too, and everyone else for that matter. All you really need t'ken is t'open the cask would be very, very bad."

"They say it could destroy the world. Of course, I've always assumed that wasn't exactly, well... accurate."

"Well, no, I suppose that's not strictly accurate," said Mrs. MacGuffin reflectively. "Saying it would destroy the world would be lak saying the black death made a few people feel poorly. More accurate would be to say it would destroy the entire universe."

Alex choked on his tea. Charlie simply let his mouth hang open.

"Don't catch flies, dear," said Mrs. MacGuffin. She reached across and gently lifted Charlie's jaw shut. "Now then, where are my manners?" She then offered up a plate of cookies. "Biscuit?"

"No, thank-you. Mrs. MacGuffin, can you be a little more specific as to how it could destroy the entire universe?" asked Charlie.

"Well, I suppose I could explain it to you the same way Rupert used to explain it to other layfolk."

"Please. That would be very helpful."

"Right. Well, the first thing you need to do is to stop taking existence so literally. That was always a stumbling block right there for his colleagues. The Nobel Laureates, ach, they were the worst. Right boonch of empiricists, they were. Always waving their medals around and going on and on about how clever they all were—"

"Got it."

"Right. Next forget everything you know about quantum mechanics."

"Done," said Charlie. Since neither he nor Alex knew anything about quantum mechanics, this was really quite easy.

"And math."

"I failed math last year," said Alex helpfully.

"Good for you, dear," said Mrs. MacGuffin. "Well then, let's get started..."

CHAPTER 16

"Finally, a practical use for physics."
– Harry S. Truman

The Pentagon, Virginia. Tuesday, September 5, 1956.

The meeting room was a cumulonimbus cloud of cigar and pipe smoke hovering about the heads of the twelve men gathered there. Most of the men were soldiers. They were among the highest ranking officers from all four of the US armed service branches, Army, Navy, Marines and Air Force. Each wore a phalanx of medals on his chest. The room itself was located on the fourth floor of the Pentagon's A-ring, with a large picture window overlooking the facility's five-sided courtyard. This was the semiannual meeting of the Joint Chief's Weapons Advisory Board. Membership on the JCWAB (pronounced "Jcwab") was largely offered as consolation prize for not being appointed directly to the Joint Chiefs of Staff (pronounced "Joint Chiefs of Staff"). The group's unofficial motto was "no hard feelings." Still, they had what most considered a fun job, providing recommendations to the Joint Chiefs on which weapons research projects to fund. In other words, they got to unwrap all the new toys before Christmas. Their attention was focused on an overhead projector slide showing the predicament they faced. The Soviets had, again, conducted an underground test of a bomb that appeared to be bigger than any in the current US arsenal.

Doug Nolan, DOD AWD Director, having finished the core of his presentation, now took his seat. Doug was one of only two civilians in the room. He carefully placed the experimental 'laser pointer' back into his briefcase. Still needs work, he thought. At two feet long, it wasn't much shorter than a conventional pointing stick anyway, and the laser itself definitely needed calibration. In the ten minutes Doug had been talking, the pointer had burned a hole in the projection screen, set fire to the drapes and sliced Colonel Clarkson's tie in half. Colonel Clarkson, fortunately, had laughed off the incident.

"So, we just build an even bigger bomb," said General McKoy, brushing aside the concern. General James L. McKoy was the board's chairman. "Hell, we already have two in development."

"Come on J.L., you know the problem," responded Nolan, pausing to take a sip of ice water. "The atomic bomb, the hydrogen bomb, the neutron bomb—every time we up the ante, the Russians meet us and raise."

The General puffed his pipe for a moment, then nodded. "You're right. Costs us a Goddamn fortune too. Those penny pinchers in Washington are beginnin' to ask questions." The General broke in a mock whine, "What about education? What about healthcare?" He stopped to snort phlegm from one side of his nose, then continued, "Goddamn bunch o' whiners if you ask me. They don't understand that none of that matters if the Ruskies turn their precious hospitals and schools into smoking craters and we have a bunch of radioactive mutant babies on our hands. Still, if I go to Admiral Radford sayin' we just need bigger bombs, he'll wonder what the Hell we're doin' all day." The others nodded their agreement. The ever escalating cost of the arms race was a growing concern. Mutually assured destruction, it seemed, had a downside. "What I don't understand is, how a bunch of commies can keep up with us? We're America fur Christ's sake!"

"Slave labour," muttered General Dimmler knowingly.

"We had slave labour once," said Colonel Clarkson.

"I suggested that," said General McKoy. "The President said 'no'. The losses in the North would outweigh the gains in the South. But by Jesus's jockstrap, we gotta do something!"

Once more there were nods of consensus around the table. Everyone, of course, hated the communists, but no one more so than General J.L. McKoy. His son, a former marine, was one of the few direct casualties of the Cold War. Private 1st Class Billy McKoy had been accidentally squashed flat by a runaway ICBM that had rolled free of its mooring. Since then, no idea was 'off the table'. The General had once held a meeting to discuss the possibility of turning the pentagon itself into a giant pentagram. The theory was that a large 'military grade demonic symbol' might be used to summon the devil himself with whom some sort of deal could be struck to destroy the Soviets. The plan was scrapped only after the President himself got wind of it and pointed out that some might consider a pact with Satan 'unAmerican'. That decision simply confirmed General McKoy's opinion about 'mealy mouthed' politicians. General McKoy eyed the AWD Director suspiciously. "So, what exactly are you proposin', Doug?"

Doug smiled and leaned forward, eyes bright. This was the moment he had been waiting for. "A new kind of bomb. A bomb so big that no one, not the Russians, not the Chinese, *no one*, can build one bigger."

There was a moment of silence before General McKoy broke it with a resounding raspberry. "Impossible! No matter how big the bomb, someone can build a bigger one! It's a simple law of physics. I shouldn't have to tell you eggheads that!"

The other officers nodded in agreement and exchanged smirks and chuckles.

"Actually they can'na," said a new voice. It was the soft-spoken Scottish lilt of Dr. Rupert MacGuffin. The physicist had, until that moment, been sitting silently. Despite his tall, lanky physique, he tended to fade into the background when not actually talking. "Because there's no such thing as something bigger. And, to be honest, because it's not really a 'bigger bomb' anyway. First of all, it's not an explosive and, second of all, it's actually quite tiny. Only its effect is big."

"Allow me to introduce Dr. Rupert MacGuffin," said Doug, "our most brilliant physicist and the genius behind this particular project." There was a moment of surprise as the large military men around the table stopped to stare at the scientist. Until that moment, they'd assumed Rupert was simply Doug Nolan's assistant or perhaps his live-in male companion, like General Dimmler's 'personal private' Andrew who sat knitting quietly in the corner. Rupert, slight, pale, redheaded and dressed in tweed looked more like a university student than destroyer of worlds.

"It's not a bomb?" asked Admiral Hawkley skeptically.

"Not technically, no."

"Well, what the hell good is that?" demanded General McKoy, slamming his fist on the table. "The only thing the Reds understand are bombs. Bombs are the God damn international language! You know what 'Ka-boom!' is in Russian? Ka-boom!"

The other officers around the table began making explosion noises to show their support, and because it was fun.

"This is much, much worse," said Rupert quietly.

"I mean if it doesn't blow up, then the Ruskies just don't..." General McKoy trailed off mid-tirade. "I'm sorry... did you say worse?"

"Or better, depending on how you look at it."

There was a moment of stunned silence before General Paulson asked skeptically, "Worse than the bomb dropped on Hiroshima?"

"Oh aye."

"Worse than the H-Bomb?"

"Aye."

"Worse than the neutron bomb?" asked an incredulous General Kray.

"Moost assuredly," said the scientist.

"Ooo..." said Admiral Hawkins, clapping his hands excitedly.

General McKoy wasn't convinced. Still, the eggheads had always delivered in the past. "I'm listening..."

Rupert looked at Doug. His boss nodded for him to proceed. The reedy scientist stood up and walked to the large picture window. In the polygonal courtyard below, the DOD Glee Club could be seen performing a round version of Jolsen's *Mammy* for the benefit of Pentagon staff on their lunch break. They did so in full costume, complete with black face. This in spite of the fact that three of the members were, in fact, black. They were a talented group thanks to their leader, Captain Seymour Higgs, and the pride of the DOD. There was concern at the department that Higgs was unstable and, if he left, the entire Glee Club could fall apart. Rupert, of course, didn't know or care about any of this. Instead, he looked to the sky. After a moment he pointed and said, "Do you see that cloud?"

"The one with the bite taken out of it?" asked Admiral Hawkins.

"No, next to it."

"The one that looks like a bunny?" asked General Kray.

"Exactly," said Rupert, "the one that *looks* like a rabbit. It's really just a mass of water vapour, of course, but it happens to look like something."

"Say, is this some sort of weather control device?" asked Colonel Clarkson. Nolan noted the Colonel's tie was still smouldering slightly from the unfortunate laser pointer incident.

"No."

"Because a weather control device could be really useful."

"Especially for golf," said General Paulson.

A chorus of agreement ran down the table.

"It's not a weather control device!" snapped the flustered physicist.

"Then what the hell are we talking about clouds for?" demanded General McKoy.

Rupert hesitated. He then took a deep breath, found his inner calm and explained, "Because, the clouds are just a metaphor."

General Paulson snorted. "Well, Hell's bells, if I knew I was going be in English class I woulda brought my textbooks!" There was a series of guffaws about the room. Rupert stood with his eyes closed, waiting for the moment to pass. General McKoy looked at the scientist sternly and said,

"Get to the point, man. Is this really about anything?"

"Yes!" said Rupert excitedly, "It's about *everything*." The officers looked baffled by this, so Rupert decided to take advantage of their confused silence and plow on. "Listen, you know how Einstein said that all matter was made up of atoms and that these could be split to create your precious atomic bomb?"

"Yes," said General McKoy, still dubious but encouraged that they seemed to be moving the right direction.

"So I've gone deeper. Past atoms, past neutrons and electrons, and past quarks. I've walked 'the planck', as it were, and I've discovered the truth about the universe. It's all *chaos*."

"It's all what?"

"It's all chaos. Chaos that isn't matter or energy or something or nothing. It neither is nor isn't. There are no laws of physics or rules of any kind. It's all just chaos that, right now, happens to look like stuff."

"Well, that clears things up," said Colonel Clarkson with a snort.

The room burst into laughter. Even Andrew in the corner put down his half-knitted baby booties to titter derisively.

General McKoy wasn't laughing. He leaned forward, tapped out his pipe in the ashtray and said grimly, "Get to the part that goes *bang*."

"All right. So the point is, everything and I mean everything from this table to you and me, to your precious atomic bomb, are just illusions."

"Maybe you should ask the folks in Hiroshima if that felt like an illusion we dropped on 'em," sneered Admiral Hawkins.

"Okay," conceded Rupert, "maybe not an illusion per se, but, suffice it to say, everything's really just chaos that happens to have momentarily formed to look like something—like that cloud right now looks like a rabbit."

"Everything?"

"The universe, plus any extra dimensional planes that may, or may not, exist."

"Temporarily?"

"For a few trillion years."

"A trillion years? But we want to destroy it now!" whined General Kray.

"Give or take a trillion. Of course, it could have all coalesced five minutes ago, there's no way to know. Still, probability suggests it formed in a much simpler initial state, before the Big Bang, but who knows? The point is, you, me, the sun, the stars, are all just cloud bunnies on a cosmic scale." Dr. MacGuffin paused a moment to let this sink in. After a moment he realized he was only allowing the confusion to permeate. "The point is, I can create a device that can create a tiny bit of chaos when detonated."

There was a murmur of excitement at the word 'detonated'. General McKoy paused from re-lighting his pipe and said, "And what exactly does that mean, son?"

"Well, if you imagine the universe is a giant sweater..."

"Oh! Oh! Another metaphor!" shouted Colonel Clarkson, who then settled back into his chair, feeling rather pleased with himself.

"Once I create a peace of chaos it becomes like a loose thread that keeps getting pulled. Slowly at first, existence itself starts to unravel."

"Like a sweater!" exclaimed General Meer who had only just now started to pay attention.

"Well, yes, that's what I just said."

"Wait..." said Admiral Hawkins, light dawning in his eyes. "Without sweaters, the Russians will get cold and it's very cold in Russia. This could work..."

"Indeed."

"Yes, very cold."

Rupert held up his hands. "Remember, gentlemen, the sweater is just a metaphor. Anyway, once it starts it can't be stopped. Like that bunny rabbit cloud dissipating in a strong wind."

"Now you're mixing metaphors," said General Paulson.

"Forget the damn metaphors!" shouted Rupert, exasperated.

General McKoy put down his pipe and leaned forward. There was a look of real excitement in his eyes. "So, you're saying, you could build us a weapon capable of destroying the entire universe?"

"Yes!" shouted Rupert with relief. "Theoretically, yes. I haven't done it yet. It needs more work and funding, of course, but... yes, that's exactly right. We could destroy the entire universe."

The room watched as General McKoy pondered this possibility while scraping out the bowl of his pipe. After a moment, he looked up with a broad grin and said, "Well then, what the blazes are we waitin' for?"

CHAPTER 17

"I think, therefore it is." – Brandon Carter

Charlie and Alex hurried to keep up with Mrs. MacGuffin, who moved at a surprisingly brisk pace for a woman of her age. After she'd finished explaining what Loose Thread was, Alex asked what had happened to Professor MacGuffin. Mrs. MacGuffin expressed surprise. "Daen' ya ken? A'knoo those goov'ment agents dinna believe me, but I'da thought they'd at least put it in their reports. Aye, they moost really o' thought me a right nutter. Ah, well, I suppose I'd better show you." With that, she'd stood up and walked out the front door of the cottage, leaving Charlie and Alex scrambling to catch up.

"Where are we going?" Alex called after her.

"Did ya nae notice the rather large thing in me backyard, dear? Well,

I dunna live next to it for the view." With that Mrs. MacGuffin disappeared around the corner of the cottage. Charlie and Alex followed and found themselves facing the concrete base of the cooling tower. Both stopped to gaze up at the massive grey structure. They craned their necks to see how it soared—its curvature only visible when viewed in its entirety. The enormity of it all left both man and boy feeling inconsequential by comparison. Mrs. MacGuffin unlatched a small gate, on which hung a sign that said simply 'Keep Out'. Mrs. MacGuffin, who had been living with the tower for years, thought of it as a nuisance when she thought about it at all. It was only when she turned to hold the gate open that she noticed her two visitors staring up in stunned silence. "Aye," she said, "it's very, very, big. It's also dirty and dark and a downright pain in the neck if you moost ken. Now then, you've had a good gawk, so coom on in." Charlie and Alex shook off their trance and followed her through the gate. At the foot of the tower, a set of metal steps led up to a long landing, followed by a second set of stairs leading to a small, unremarkable steel door. As they followed Mrs. MacGuffin up the steps, the entire staircase shook. "Dunna worry," she assured them, "it's quite safe."

Mrs. MacGuffin reached the door where she lifted a small panel, revealing a security keypad. She entered a code, and the internal mechanism unlocked with a *ka-lunk!* She then swung open the rusted steel door, its hinges keening loudly for oil, and disappeared inside.

Charlie and Alex followed warily into the dim interior. "Hello?" shouted Alex. The interior echoed a polite response, "...lo...lo...lo". For the second time they were struck by the size of the tower, this time by its enormous interior. The soaring walls left most of the space lost in shadow while, far above, the top was roofless. The opening formed a giant circular portal to a world of azure sky and soft white clouds that seemed at once both immediate and unattainable. The effect was between some sort of holy site, an ancient observatory and an enormous camera obscura set to capture the heavens. If the outside had made them feel insignificant, the inside made them feel like they were the focal point of the universe. Charlie's neck began to hurt from looking up too long. "Holy crap," said Alex, "it's one big room!"

Charlie nodded. He knew nothing about what a nuclear cooling tower should contain, but he was pretty sure it should contain something. The room wasn't entirely empty. The concrete base was cluttered with piles of fallen debris and random refuse. Here and there small green shoots and tufts of grass sprouted through cracks in the concrete. Above their heads, massive steel support beams bridged the interior in various places, silhouetted starkly against the cameo of sky. Here and there were, what looked to be, recent renovations, presumably to keep the decaying superstructure from collapse. There were also numerous catwalks traversing the space, as well as safety-ring ladders and stairs along the walls. These all ultimately led to a bizarre apparatus that was clearly the focal point of the facility. Over two hundred feet above their heads a giant steel ring hung parallel to the ground. When Charlie squinted, he could see that the ring, a dozen yards across at least, was suspended from the walls by a series of steel cables pulled taut. Against the interior tower gloom, the cables were almost invisible, making the shiny ring appear to float in midair, as if by magic.

"Shit!" yelped Alex, as he sidestepped a splatter of white from above.

"Oh aye—swallow shite, to be precise," said Mrs. MacGuffin. "Sorry about that, lad, I shoulda warned ya. I use to try to keep them out, but eventually gave up." As Charlie's eyes adjusted to the murkiness he could just make out the dim shapes of birds perched on the tops of girders and mud wattle nests clustered along the undersides. "Bahn swallows, see?" she explained, "I tried to tell them this were no bahn, but they would'na listen."

With that, the old woman walked to a rickety ladder and began to climb. The ladder led to a catwalk above, then more steps, which in turn led to another ladder, catwalk and so on, circumnavigating the vast interior. "Wait, we're climbing that?" asked Alex. He eyed the corroded metal suspiciously.

"I do it all the time, dear. It's perfectly safe."

Alex wasn't so sure. Charlie tried to gauge his own weight against that of the old woman, as well as the strength of the clearly rusted supports, fasteners, and bolts that held the ladder to the wall. "I'll go first," he said, "if it can carry my weight, it can carry yours." Alex sucked in his courage and nodded. Charlie began after Mrs. MacGuffin, who was already working her way up the subsequent set of stairs. He carefully wiped off any cobwebs as he went, concerned they might alarm Alex. The boy followed, telling himself it was like a video game on PlayStation. A classic platformer, he thought, like *Donkey Kong* or *Super Mario Brothers*. All I have to do is scale the ladders from tier to tier to complete the level and win. He then imagined Mrs. MacGuffin as the digital gorilla, rolling barrels down upon them. He chuckled to himself.

Several minutes later, both Charlie and Alex were out of breath as they began the ascent of yet another set of steps. Mrs. MacGuffin continued ahead with unflagging resolve. "Do we really have to do this?" asked Alex.

"Aye, if you want to know the truth," said Mrs. MacGuffin. "You wouldn'a believe me if I just tell ye."

"Try me," muttered Alex.

Charlie leaned over the guardrail to look at the floor below. They were already over a hundred feet above the guano splattered concrete base. He noted an overturned forklift, previously hidden behind a heap of rubbish. Completely crusted in droppings and dust, it had clearly been there for years. "How high are we going?"

Mrs. MacGuffin simply pointed, past the giant suspended ring-thing, to a large steel platform another hundred feet up. While mostly square in shape, there was a long single panel that extended out into the center of the chamber. To Charlie, it looked disturbingly like a diving board. Alex noticed it as well, although in his mind it conjured images of sailors being forced to 'walk the plank'. It was impossible to see what was on the platform from where they stood. Charlie opened his mouth to protest, but Mrs. MacGuffin had already resumed her steady ascent.

As he climbed, Alex thought about his mom. Her face filled his vision, drawing him in. Ever since she'd died, he felt as if he'd been plunged into a dream world. He felt as though he'd fallen down a hole into a land where nothing made sense. No matter how stressed or confused his mother was, she always took control. She always took care of him. Here, grown-ups didn't have all the answers and ran around like confused children. It was a world without common sense, or any sense at all, for that matter. Here, the threat of Armageddon loomed like a monster, with eyes of flame, so real he could feel it whiffling closer. It was the scariest thing imaginable. No, thought Alex, scarier is the sense that no one's in charge. That was a hard thing to accept. With that, his thoughts went to the coziness of his house in Michigan, with its teak furniture, familiar smells and TV sounds. He remembered the warmth of his mother giving him a hug on the school steps the day before she died, even as he pushed her away for fear of being seen by his friends. Alex bit his lip and forced back tears. He focused instead on Charlie, trudging ahead, glancing at his watch. Charlie, at times, seemed as confused and lost as anyone, but he also seemed to care and he kept moving forward. He was someone to follow. Alex needed someone to follow. He needed someone to be in charge. He wasn't ready to give that up yet. It felt like a dream, but it wasn't. I'm not asleep, thought Alex, I can't wake up and I can't go home.

Alex suddenly realized they'd reached the platform. The air was cooler here and, despite their altitude, the damp concrete walls smelled obversely like a dank cellar. Charlie stood waiting for Alex, smiling. Alex smiled back. It was good to finally stop climbing.

"Aven't been oop 'ere in moonths," Mrs. MacGuffin explained, brushing the dust from some sort of control console. The instruments looked like something from the set of a 1950s science fiction film. Instead of touch-screens and sensors, the galvanized steel panel consisted of switches, dials and cathode ray tubes. An actual ignition switch sat next to a keyboard that looked like it had been lifted from an old Smith Corona typewriter. The console took up one entire side of the platform. In front of it sat an upholstered red bar stool for its operator. Finally, atop the console was an array of clocks, one for each timezone around the world, New York, Tokyo, Greenwich, and so on. Charlie and Alex tentatively stepped to the platform's edge. A guard rail was the only thing that stood between them and the long lethal plunge to the concrete floor below. A latched gate led to the narrow extension they'd observed from below. Now, even more so than before, it reminded Charlie of a diving board. The giant steel ring suspended beneath formed an imaginary swimming pool. Diving off, of course, would soon dispel any such illusion, as one passed clear through the ring en route to an abrupt end on the concrete floor below. "Dr. MacGuffin, he built all of this?"

"No, no. The goov'ment built the tower years before, but the project ran out of mooney. It were a bit'o scandal at the time. When we arrived, Rupert's reputation was sooch that he were able to convince them to let him have the use of it indefinitely, as well as some funding for his little research project. It let the politicians off the hook, you see?"

"Oh I see," said Charlie. It made sense. Building such a tower would have been an enormous endeavour, costing millions of dollars. Once built, however, tearing it down would cost millions more. Turning it over to the famous physicist was undoubtedly a way of saving face. Charlie also knew that the professor had no shortage of personal funds to finance his experiments. Besides his pioneering work in physics, Rupert MacGuffin had tangentially developed a new theory of economics he called 'Quantum Accounting'. This was the idea that, electronically, money might both exist and not exist at the same time. While laughed at by economists, he used these ideas to build himself a personal fortune on the NYSE. These same 'crazy' ideas would later go on to become the foundation of modern accounting practices on Wall Street. As with subatomic particles, he argued, at the digital level, money can exist in more than one place at once, provided that it remains unobserved. Unfortunately, also like quantum particles, it was possible to transition to a lower state. Knowing this, Rupert MacGuffin had pulled all of his money out before this actually occurred.

Having cleaned the console, Mrs. MacGuffin pulled a key from her apron pocket and said, "Ya dunna wanna git up here and forget the key, I tell ye. Very tiresome!" She inserted the key into the ignition switch and turned. Numerous indicator lights blinked on and off and a large digital clock on the console began flashing '12:00'. At the same time, the entire platform, started to vibrate and hum like a giant leather massage chair. Charlie suspected that contributing to the din were thousands of loose screws and corroded components. He wondered once more about the soundness of the entire enterprise.

"Look at that!" said Alex with excitement. He was pointing to the giant steel ring. The inner band of the circle had begun to glow blue like an enormous neon halo. As they watched, the glow intensified. Unlike the rest of the antique technology around them, the luminescence was utterly intangible. It was at once both entrancing and unearthly. It didn't just glow, Charlie observed, but appeared to jump and jitter in an uncanny way. He tried to put his finger on it. The best he could manage was that it was like watching a movie where the film reel had come loose, causing the image on screen to flicker in and out of sync with the world around it. The effect continued to expand, threatening to leap from the movie screen and into the audience. Suddenly something snapped into focus. The white-blue energy continued to crackle and hum, but now seemed safely contained within the hoop. The air inside the ring's confines shimmered sporadically as passing through some sort of charged field. Charlie became alarmed at the prospect of what this all meant. The absentee professor had a history of playing with fire. "What is this for?" he asked warily, "More chaos stuff?"

"Oh, no dear," said the old woman, as if the answer were perfectly obvious. "It's for time travel. This is a time machine."

Charlie and Alex stared at her blankly. In any other circumstance, such a claim would have been preposterous. "Of course it is," said Charlie.

CHAPTER 18

"I can't say, I told you so." – R. Dawkins

Donna Craig, the White House Press Secretary, stood in her customary spot behind the podium, trying to tame the middle-aged lions that were the White House press corp. She looked around the room of half-raised hands and pointed to NBC News correspondent, Chuck Todd. "Yes, Chuck?"

"Same question as yesterday, does the President have any plans to bring in the National Guard to help quell these riots?"

Donna put on her patient face. "Not at this time. The riots, as we all know, have been decreasing. The violence has reduced. Local police might have been initially caught off guard, but have been doing a first rate job in restoring order across the country. The President thanks them, and all first-responders, for their service."

"What about Cleveland?" someone shouted.

"The standoff in Cleveland is regrettable. The President is following it, and all events, very closely. Introducing the army at this point however, would not help alleviate the situation. In fact, he believes it could escalate it further." Donna looked about the room for another of her favourite reporters. This was the time-tested protocol of the press corp—you can ask pointed questions but, if you want to get called on again, make sure they're not barbed. She spotted Julie Conner from Fox News and gave her the nod, "Julie?"

"Is the White House still denying the existence, or at least authenticity of Weapon X?"

This was another question Donna had already answered many times before. She sometimes wondered if reporters learned their craft from her ten-year-old son, asking for something again and again in the hope of wearing her down. 'Weapon X' was the name the media had given to the alleged weapon held aloft by the terrorist Ali Madda. No one could accuse the media of originality. CNN's Wolfe Blitzer had been running 3D holograms of the device, opening it to show it containing glowing green isotopes which would then explode. CNN would then cut to a graphic of desolated cities. They even ran estimates, based on 'expert analysis assumptions', also known as 'complete fabrications', about the number of survivors. They advised their viewers to "go to their basements" and "duck and cover" in the event of detonation. Donna now assumed her motherly calm look, it was the same face she used when comforting her young son. "One of the reasons that the riots have been controlled is that the initial fear has subsided. People have realized how silly it is to panic the moment some terrorist claims to have a mythical 'doomsday device'. Remember, chaos is what the terrorists want. People who spread fear are helping the terrorists win." This was the tactic that had been decided on prior to the press conference. First, dismiss the danger. Next, make it clear that only fools and conspiracy theory nuts could take the existence of such a weapon seriously. The Vice-President himself had been on ABC News the night before joking about how the same people who believed the 1969 moon landing was a hoax, now believed we'd built a weapon capable of destroying the Earth years prior. "We can't do that now, let alone in 1957! And making it the size and shape of a 7-11 Big Gulp Slurpee? Impossible!" Even the subject matter experts on CNN agreed with that, and began showing a 3D graphic of how many Cherry Slurpees it would take to fill a single 1950s era nuclear warhead. The real discussion, however, centered on the fact that the Vice-President seemed to think that Big Gulps and Slurpees were the same thing. His critics said this showed that he was out of touch and merely trying to pander to the electorate. Even PBS's *Washington Week* panel agreed, saying that the gaff "fit the narrative for the Vice President" and "could spell trouble for him on the campaign trail."

* * *

Ali Madda pried his fingernails carefully into the seam and pulled. After a moment, the shell popped open. He popped the pistachio into his mouth and reached for another. All the while he watched the White House Press Conference on Al Jazeera with barely suppressed glee. It felt good to be talked about, and ever since issuing his threat, all the world did was talk about him. He spent almost every waking hour glued to his TV or iPad. They were obsessed with him, and so was he. I feel important, he mused, like how a 'Real Housewife' of Orange County must feel.

"Susan?" asked the infidel White House Press Secretary in her blasphemous pantsuit.

"Can you confirm reports that the President has been spending a lot of time with members of the Holy Church of Preordination, specifically leader Reverend Duke Norman?" asked the burkaless blonde reporter.

Karim switched off the TV. He was seething. "You see? You see? They do not believe us! If they do not believe we have the weapon, then we might as well not have it at all!" He gesticulated wildly as he said this, pointing at the small metal canister sitting on the nightstand. "We must make them believe us!"

Ali Madda, who had raised his hand to cover his face, scowled at his fanatical friend. "Stop spitting, Karim! You alway spit when you talk." They were sitting in the master bedroom of his luxury estate. The estate was on the man-made island of 'New Brunswick' in the archipelago known as 'The World'. The World was a collection of three-hundred artificial islands in Dubai designed to be sold off as lots to the uber wealthy. Handcrafted by indentured servants out of sand and hubris, the archipelago had one fatal flaw. Every one of the artisanal islands was now slowly sinking back into the sea and threatening to take their opulent dwellings with them. Some islands were sinking faster than others. For now, New Brunswick remained solid enough to serve as a home base for Ali Madda and his entourage. Ali Madda had never been to the real New Brunswick in Canada, but he imagined it to be an exotic and magical place.

"I'm sorry, Ali," said Karim, wiping his chin, "but we must prove to them our might! We must show the infidels. Allah gave us the weapon that we might use it!"

Ali who was now struggling with a particularly stubborn pistachio, shook his head. "Your father used to spit on me too. It used to hurt him in the organization. People don't want to listen to people who spit."

Karim threw up his hands in frustration. He stomped angrily over to the wall of windows that formed a panoramic view of the rest of The World. From there they could see England, Norway and Jamaica. They shouldn't be able to see Jamaica, of course, but that particular island had begun to drift a month prior and was now sliding into Europe, leading to an unexpected border dispute between Jamaica and Ireland. "Ali, please. You don't understand, if they don't fear us, then..." Karim trailed off as he saw his friend's face flush red with fury. He had overstepped his bounds.

"You, Karim, do not tell me what I do and do not understand," Ali snarled. He paused to pick up the canister, then waggled it at Karim as he spoke. "The people who matter believe us. The President of the United States knows we are telling the truth. His allies in Europe suspect it. If we heard the rumours of this device then so did they. Whatever people say in public, make no mistake—they are terrified." Ali spoke these last words with deliberation, as if daring Karim to contradict him.

"I'm sorry! I am so, so sorry!" said Karim, bowing obsequiously. "I intended no disrespect."

"Apology accepted," said Ali with satisfaction. He resisted the urge to pat his friend on the head. Instead, the terrorist leader lifted the canister high into the air, then brought it down like a hammer. The blow split the pistachio shell where it lay on the table. It also had the unfortunate effect of demolishing the nut inside. "Damn it," Ali grumbled, "I really need to be more careful."

* * *

"Well, it's obvious we're never going to understand the math," said Charlie.

Alex gazed at the diaphanous fabric of space-time suspended matter-of-factly in the ring below. It reminded him of the Native American dreamcatchers he'd made in elementary school, but without all the feathers and stuff.

Mrs. MacGuffin hemmed for a moment, then nodded. "So, with time travel, it's lak space and time is a giant ca'pet and we're all boomps in't."

"A giant carpet?"

"Aye. You push down a boomp and it just poops up in another spot."

Alex snickered at the old woman's pronunciation of the word 'pop'. Charlie threw him an admonishing glance. Alex pointed at a silver module covered with dials. "What's that do?"

"Tha'? Oh, tha's just the geolocation compensator."

"The geo-what?"

Mrs. MacGuffin sighed. "So, if you watch your science fiction films, you 'd think you can just go back in tam and poop up in the same place. People forget that the Earth rotates at aboot a thousand miles per hour. So if you go back in tam just one hour you'd end up—"

"In Russia?" asked Charlie.

"Other way actually, a better guess would be somewhere in th' Atlantic Ocean. But tha's wrong too. Donna feel bad. It's the same mistake Rupert made when he first tested it and sent poor Doris back in tam. He never forgave himself for tha'. Poor Doris. You see, not only is the Earth spinning, but it's also orbiting the soon. On top of tha' the universe itself is expandin'. So the GC figures that all out and accounts for it. Tam travel, it turns out, is actually quite complicated."

"Imagine that."

"Anyhoo, if you want to end up in the same place, your tam machine really also has to be a teleporter as well—a space-time machine if you will."

"Um... what happened to Doris?" asked Alex.

"Who knows? She went somewhere, I s'pose. Moost unfortunate." For a moment she stared sadly into space then added, "Did I mention Doris was a hamster?" Alex and Charlie shook their heads 'no'. "Look, all ya really need ta ken is that it wurks. You go through that hole and you coom out somewhere and somewhen else."

"Okay," said Charlie. He understood that, but still struggled to believe her. The idea that time travel could actually work seemed preposterous.

Mrs. MacGuffin read his expression and sighed. "Fine, dear, I'll show ya. Give me yur shoe, if ya please." Charlie looked at her skeptically. "Just let me 'ave it a sec, you'll get it back soon enoof." Charlie untied his left sneaker and handed it to her.

"Thank-ye," said Mrs. MacGuffin. She spun a dial on the console, then turned and strode out onto the diving board platform. She held out his shoe by the laces and, before Charlie could object, unceremoniously let go. His footwear fell one hundred feet to the giant temporal hoop below and was gone. Charlie and Alex both blinked. The shoe had simply vanished. There was no effect; no flames nor bolts of lightning, nor was there any sound of it hitting the ground below. Instead, it had simply ceased to be. If this was time travel, thought Alex, it was rather anticlimatic. "Um... where's my shoe?" asked Charlie, who was, at that point, teetering on one foot like an oversized uncoordinated flamingo. Time travel, he thought, looked suspiciously like being vaporized. It also seemed to have a rather distinct odour, he noted, the smell of burnt toast.

"Not where, when," said Mrs. MacGuffin. She put on her reading glasses to view the dials. "1926. Same date'n time as now since tha's the default and I only changed the year."

Charlie stared at her. His flamingo impersonation was becoming more and more desperate. "So... how do you bring it back?"

"Bring it back? Oh no, we canna do that. I mean, things come through the other way sometimes, but tha's mostly luck. Tha's where the swallows came froom—1702, South of France, a farm outside of Toulon. Aye, after that we kept it closed unless we were usin' it. As Rupert used to say, today it's sparrows, tomorrow it could be Richard III. Who knows? Anyhoo, the gate is unpredictable on the other side, so it's really a one way trip."

"But you did say I could have my shoe back, didn't you?" asked Charlie, suddenly concerned about the prospect of hopping down all those stairs and ladders.

"Oh aye, dear me," said Mrs. MacGuffin. She then stooped beneath the console to unlatch a compartment. The inside was cluttered with equipment parts, ragged manuals, a one armed Boris Yeltsin action figure and other various nicknacks. The old woman rummaged about for a moment before extracting a small brown box from which she blew several decades worth of dust. She then opened the box and extracted a single blue running shoe. The fabric was noticeably aged, but it was clearly Charlie's missing sneaker, long lost only moments ago.

"Wow," said Alex.

Charlie accepted the shoe dumbly. Both he and Alex looked at the old woman with new found astonishment. The recovered shoe felt like a parlour trick, but one he could not explain away.

"Rupert found it in a field round back about twenty-years ago. He suspected it might be from the future. As soon as I saw your shoes, I knew what I had to do."

"But then... we could go back in time and fix everything!" Alex exclaimed. "We could save my mother!"

We could save my family as well, thought Charlie. He became aware of his emotions rushing like water under dangerously thin ice.

"Oh no, " said Mrs. MacGuffin. "Most certainly not."

Both stared at her. Charlie felt a flash of anger. How could this woman so easily dismiss the possibility of saving his daughter's life?

"You canna go back an' change time. It's simply impossible."

"What? Why?" asked Charlie.

Alex had seen enough time travel movies to draw his own conclusion. "Because of the paradox. If we go back in time to change something, then we change the future—including the fact that we went back in time. If my mother didn't die, I wouldn't be here right now."

"Well, yes and no," said Mrs. MacGuffin. "There's no paradox because it canna happen. If you go back in time to change something then you will fail. Because it *did* happen, your mother did die, so you moost have failed to stop it. There's no other explanation. It was, because it was, as they say. Unless of course, you buy into the alternate reality stoof, but Rupert always felt that was nonsense."

"So wait, I go back in time to save my mom, and..."

"And get hit by a boos."

"Hit by a boos? Oh, a bus."

"Or summat else. It dunna matter, either way you'll fail. You canna stop it happening because we know it happened. Paradoxes are just misunderstood cognitive dissonance. There are no true paradoxes, otherwise, they would'na be paradoxes. Which sounds somewhat paradoxical, but isn't."

Charlie wasn't convinced. His whole being shouted at the prospect of going back in time to save Lisa and Faith and wouldn't be silenced. It deafened him.

"Anyway," said Mrs. MacGuffin, "It would'na work at all right now. It's on the fritz."

"It's broken?" said Charlie. "But you just send my shoe back to 1926!"

"Yes, but living things aren't survivin' the trip. Rupert's supposed to be here to fix it, but he has na coom back. Tha's why he's late. So I've been trying to fix it m'self. I think I've almost got it, but not quite. Come back next week. Or year, y'know, depending."

"So if we went through today?"

"You'd arrive, but all jumbled up. Y'know, lak an anagram, but mooch messier."

"Oh..." Charlie's heart sank. He wasn't at all sure the old woman would ever be able to fix it herself. Neither was he confident that anyone else could. He knew, from the dossier, that Rupert MacGuffin had tried to explain his ideas, only to be mocked or dismissed as a once brilliant mind gone to jelly. He'd told his fellow physicists they were all hobbled by their assumptions and thought only in terms of the universe, when they needed to "think bigger." He wrote in an open letter, "You all still believe physics and metaphysics are separate things. Al told you space is curved. I tell you space is *imaginary*, having imagined itself to exist." Charlie's cell phone rang. He glanced at the display. It read, 'CIA Director Morely'. "I have to take this," he said as he stepped away.

Alex tried to fathom everything they'd seen and been told. Mrs. MacGuffin switched off the machine. Inside the steel ring, the suspended field of unreality collapsed to a pin prick, then vanished like the final dot of light on a black and white TV. "So that's where your husband went?" asked Alex. "Back in time?"

"Yes and no," said Mrs. MacGuffin in what seemed to be her stock contradictory reply. "He did go back in time, tha's true, but Rupert MacGuffin's not ma husband."

"He's not?"

"No, his waf, Lucille, died a year a'fore he went. Dr. Rupert MacGuffin is ma father. But I understand your confusion. I never called him Dad, just Rupert. He was never one for titles an' sooch."

Alex tried to figure this out. "Wait, he was your father in the present, or in the past? And you said it was a one way trip, how will he—?"

"Alex," said Charlie. "We have to go."

"What? Why?"

"They've located Ali Madda and the canister—and they need our help."

CHAPTER 19

"Ceci n'est pas une citation." – R. Magritte

The President stood in the Oval Office looking scruffy. Jim had been trying to persuade him to shave for days, but the President would have none of it. In the end, the Chief of Staff had decided to spin it. "The President is losing sleep and won't even stop to shave until this crisis is resolved." In truth, the President was distracted, irritable, and had taken to making strange pronouncements he expected to be written down for, what he called, his *Gospel*. Jim told the staff members that the President was simply working on his memoir. He glanced down nervously at the memo he'd intercepted just that morning before it was released. It was a short verse

God is a man, not a woman as some say

which isn't to say a man, like Adam, of clay
But that he's a he, and not a she nor an it
He's the Holy Father, as in The Book is writ

It didn't even sound like the President, at least not the President that Jim knew. Lately, however, the Commander-in-Chief had been more lyrical. At yesterday's finance meeting he'd begun speaking in rhyming couplets, such as 'budget' and 'fudge it', or 'veto' and 'neat-o'. He'd also asked the Secretary of Defence, Frank Holbert, if the United States had iambic pentameter capability. Frank immediately reassured the President that they had "the best damn iambic pentameter capability in the world." Jim decided that the Secretary of Defence didn't have the slightest idea what they were talking about. Beside the oddness of The President writing poetry at all, Jim didn't need a focus group to tell him that the theme of this particular verse might not go down well with women voters. He also didn't need anyone to tell him that Duke Norman's almost constant presence wasn't helping the POTUS either. The problem was, the Reverend had completely usurped Jim as the President's confidant. Jim feared that challenging the preacher, at this point, would only cost him his own job. He dared not make the President unhappy and, right now, the President was frowning. "But this is good news, Mr. President," said Jim. "Very good news!"

The President gave a "harrumph" and turned to gaze out at the Rose Garden.

"I understand you're concerned, sir. We all are. After all, it's still a very tenuous situation and something could still go wrong."

The President brightened somewhat. "Yes, I suppose that's true isn't it? Something could go wrong..." Jim was puzzled by the President's reaction, but nodded. The Commander-in-Chief was under a lot of stress, more than any President since the Cuban Missile Crisis. "So what's the plan then?" asked the President, tugging pensively at his growing whiskers.

"Robert will brief you properly but, basically, the RCOA is a stealth operation. We go in, get it and get out."

"RCOA?"

"Recommended Course of Action."

"I see. And what are the chances for something going wrong?"

"Well, RA says any number of things, but that the risk of inaction is greater. Each day—"

"RA?"

"Research analysis, sir. So, as I was saying, each day these nut jobs have the WMD is a day one of them could decide to open it. The biggest threat to the MO, besides the obvious risks of detection, is that we get the wrong TO. We don't want to get it back here only to discover they nabbed a propane tank or water filter or such. So, just like we did DNA analysis on OBL, we'll have AG on hand to ID LT on site."

"What the heck are you saying?" said the President, "What does any of that mean?"

"What does what mean?"

"All those acronyms!"

"I didn't use any acronyms."

"Sure you did... OBL?"

"Those are initials. Osama Bin Laden."

"Okay, *those* are initials, but what about MO?"

"Modus Operendi. Also just initials. To be an acronym initials need to be pronounced as a word, such as RADAR, LASER, POTUS..."

"Those are words."

"Yes and no. Technically they're—"

The President raised his hand to stop him. "This is why I hate you, Jim."

"You hate me? I... I'm sorry, sir, I only use initials to save time. I'll send you a complete list of the initials used, immediately following this conversation."

"Great, then I'll know what the heck we talked about. For now tell me who or what is AG. Is he or it an acronym?"

"No, sir. He's Alex Graham, the boy who first found LT, I mean, Loose Thread. He's the only person we have who's actually seen and held it."

The President shut his eyes, then nodded and said, "Ah, yes, the *innocent child.*"

"I'm sorry, sir?" Jim noted with alarm that the President had gone to his 'distant place'. It was a place he seemed to be spending more and more time in lately, as opposed to the real world or, for that matter, the White House.

"Nothing. Proceed."

"You don't want to first see IMPACs from the CIA, DOD, JCOS, or..."

"I've heard enough. Proceed."

"When?"

"Immediately."

"Meaning..."

"ASAP."

"Yes, Mr. President."

Chaos Theory

∗   ∗   ∗

The stealth helicopter swept over the Persian Gulf like an Egyptian osprey. Charcoal clouds blanketed the sky, blocking out the moon and stars and turning ocean waves to ink. The forty-billion dollar flying machine itself was black, rendering it as imperceptible as five tonnes of flying steel had any right to be.

In the cockpit sat the pilot and mission coordinator. In the cabin behind, huddled three men and a teenage boy. The interior was illuminated only by scattered LED equipment lights and the iPad screen on which Alex Graham was busy playing *Emoji Inquisition*, the current hottest game for download. There wasn't supposed to be any civilian equipment on board for a mission where every ounce had been weighed to ensure fuel capacity. Charlie, however, had argued it a necessity to keep his young ward from "totally freaking out". Now, he found himself watching the game over Alex's shoulder in an effort to do the same. While inspired by the Spanish Inquisition, the game's cartoon victims made it hard to take their suffering seriously. Charlie resisted the urge to tell the boy when to 'rack' and when to 'flay' to turn the smiley faces :-) into sad faces :-(and, hopefully, elicit a full confession :-O. Alex chose instead 'toca', the sixteenth century version of water boarding. He was rewarded with a full conversion +:-o, along with twenty bonus points.

"Seven minutes," said the pilot over the intercom.

With the exception of Charlie and Alex, all of the men in the cabin were Navy SEALs. They were not, as Charlie had expected, the famed SEAL Team 6, aka the best of the best. Instead, they were from an even more elite subgroup of that unit, formed after the operation that killed Osama Bin Laden. These were members of SEAL Team 6², composed of the best of the best of the best. For the most part, the SEALs had remained in total silence during the flight. They had all been thoroughly briefed and the mission had been planned as best as possible given the available recon. Ali Madda's compound had been easy enough to spy on from the outside. The interior required more guesswork. They had, however, acquired word-of-mouth descriptions primarily from a source known only as 'Wetmop'. Wetmop's identity was unknown, but was widely suspected to be Ali Madda's former cleaning lady. She had provided detailed descriptions of all the rooms, but most especially the bathroom and kitchen areas. She had also provided a complete inventory of the contents of his sock drawer, which turned out to be socks of various styles and colours, including a disturbing predilection for toe socks. The place was palatial, including its own bowling alley, Bikram yoga room, and Dancersize studio. It was not, however, impregnable. They would enter with just two soldiers. The fear was that a large squad would be detected more easily and might lead to the device's detonation. The SEALs in question had been hand picked as the best of the best of the best of the best, aka SEAL Team 6³. Charlie and Alex did not know the two men's real names, only their code names. Everyone on the mission had code names. The mission itself had a code name which reflected its intent to infiltrate and infect the terrorists. That name was 'Operation Infectious Disease'. The mission theme was then used by a Pentagon computer to generate theme related identifiers for all of the individuals involved. This meant that, for the purpose of the mission, Charlie was known as 'Gall Stone', while Alex's alias was 'Whooping Cough'. Clearly the automated software had some drawbacks. Neither, however, was complaining. They knew it could be worse, as the two Navy SEALs seated next to them, Chicken Pox and Pink Eye, could attest to. Chicken Pox sat next to Charlie, eyes closed as if sleeping. Pink Eye sat hunched across from him, dressed entirely in charcoal grey fatigues, with his night-vision goggles pulled up over this head. He was singing softly under his breath. So softly that Charlie couldn't make out the tune, although there was something oddly familiar to it.

"You ready?" Charlie asked.

Pink Eye nodded. Pink Eye kept nodding. Charlie noticed the familiar white iPod earphones dangling from under the soldier's helmet. Pink Eye was nodding to the music in his head. Charlie tapped the SEAL's knee. Pink Eye pulled the earbuds from his ears, allowing the tinny sound of Rogers and Hammerstein's *The Surrey with the Fringe on Top* to escape into the cabin. "Yo, 'sup?"

"Let me give you Herpes," said Charlie, using the assigned codename for the item in question.

"Sure."

Charlie reached into his bag and retrieved a shiny steel container. It was a perfect replica of the Loose Thread device. Perfect, save for being made out of stainless steel instead of osmiridium. That was simply too tall an order on such short notice. Still, provided no chemical tests were conducted it would fool Professor MacGuffin himself. Alex agreed, he could see no differences between it and the original. Charlie handed it to Pink Eye, who slid it safely into a satchel at his side. "Remember, making a swap is secondary. All that really matters is that you and Chicken Pox get Restless Leg Syndrome. If you can give Ali Madda Herpes, well, that's just icing on the cake."

Pink Eye stared at Charlie with a sort of withering look that said, I'm the best of the best of the best of the best, do you really think you need to remind me of our mission objectives? Charlie stopped talking. He heard someone snicker and glanced to see Chicken Pox smirking at him.

"I still don't get why we're doing a swap," said Alex.

Charlie shrugged and said, "Orders from on high. I'm not sure myself. Ours is not to wonder why..." Charlie stopped himself. He realized Alex didn't know the rest of the line and decided it was better that way. What they were doing was incredibly dangerous. It wasn't his decision to bring the boy, but he suddenly felt sick at the thought of it. He thought of Faith. He'd never have let her be put in such a dangerous position. Yet somehow he'd failed to protect her too. Of course, if they didn't retrieve the device, the whole world would be in danger. I'm out on a ledge here, he thought, I guess we all are. Alex had told him where he'd found it. The canister had been wedged under a rock in a river for more than half a century. I guess we've all been on this ledge the whole time, thought Charlie, we just didn't know it.

* * *

The stealth helicopter descended over the roof of Ali Madda's estate on the island of New Brunswick in The World, Dubhai. The artificial landmass had little in common with its namesake province. For example, while the island featured an abundance of palm trees and Islamic terrorists, the province had considerably more potatoes and Canadians per capita. Commonalities included: being land, being land near water, and a relative scarcity of Albanians. The helicopter halted thirty feet above the roof and began to hover. The muffled craft wasn't entirely silent, but the waves, wind and sound of a Yusuf Islam dance remix thumping from the windows below provided sufficient cover. Ropes dropped to the rooftop and almost instantly two dark figures rappelled down. The house was oddly Spanish in style, chosen on a whim after Ali Madda spent a drunken weekend in Tijuana during his pre-terrorist youth. Despite the fragile clay shingles, the two Navy SEALs landed silently, and immediately surveyed their surroundings. Everything was exactly as expected. There were no guards on the roof, nor any cameras. As far as the interlopers were concerned, Ali Madda might as well have left the key in the front door.

"Pink Eye, Chicken Pox, get yur fingers outta yur noses and get yur butts in gear!" growled a voice in their helmets. "Now, move to the access vent to your left" The voice belonged to 'Irritable Bowel Syndrome', the acting mission coordinator. Sitting upfront alongside the pilot in the helicopter, Irritable Bowel Syndrome was their eyes and ears. He also came with an attitude that embodied his codename. Still, there was nobody better, so the two SEALs were glad to have Irritable Bowel Syndrome for the duration. Chicken Pox spotted the rooftop air vents and pointed.

"Got it, IBS," said Chicken Pox. The two men moved to the vent and began immediately, in tandem, unscrewing the corner bolts. A sudden gust of wind buffeted them, nearly knocking Chicken Pox over. Both men glanced up and noticed, for the first time, the black storm clouds above their heads.

They're pregnant with rain, thought Pink Eye, and it looks as if their water's about to burst. Pink Eye thought this, but decided not to say it. "Nobody talks that way," his wife told him when he said things like that. Pink Eye loved metaphors. He loved mixing them like drinks and serving them like jury duty. Pink Eye wanted to be a writer. I just want to do something important, he thought. Instead, here I am stuck unscrewing bolts on some terrorist's rooftop in Dubai. "Looks like rain," he said.

"In Dubai?" said Chicken Pox.

"Forecast's all clear. Weather will *not* be a factor," said Irritable Bowel Syndrome irritably.

"Um, okay," said Pink Eye. He wanted to point out that the storm clouds might have different ideas. Instead, he let it go. Concentrate on the mission, he thought, focus like a Buddhist monk, focus like a camera. With the last bolt extracted, the vent was easily pried free.

"We're in," said Chicken Pox.

The second floor of the Ali Madda estate was decorated in the sort of Versailles grandeur beloved by tinpot tyrants from Moammar Gadhafi to Donald Trump. Gold leaf lay over every piece of furniture and moulding. Original artworks covered every inch of every wall. These too were covered with gold leaf, rendering them, ironically, less valuable. A friend of Ali Madda had once observed that these were hardly the trappings of a humble warrior or devout Muslim. Madda disagreed, saying that, "if we're all going to paradise, what was wrong with bringing a piece of paradise here? A 'paradise preview', as it were, to help inspire us to greatness." Ali Madda championed the view that the warriors of Jihad, and generals such as himself, should not suffer the same restrictions as the average Muslim. "If Allah intended us to be equal," Ali argued, "he would not have given so much money to some and so little to others." Ironically, he first conceived this philosophy while accidentally watching Christian minister Joel Osteen preaching the 'Prosperity Gospel' on television. At the time, Ali Madda was in his suite at the Waldorf Astoria in New York, eating nachos in his underwear and was too busy picking hot melted cheese out of his chest hair to change the channel. He later said that the searing pain of liquid Velveeta helped inspire him. Specifically, it inspired him to personally avoid pain. Ali Madda was glad to be a Sunni Muslim if only to avoid 'Tatbir', the Shia

Muslim practice of hitting oneself on the head with a sword.

A lone guard, armed with an AK-47, paced the long, red carpeted hallway. Silently behind him, a grill dropped from the ceiling but did not hit the floor. Instead it stopped short, suspended by a pair of cable clamps, which then retracted. The grill disappeared back up into the ceiling vent. A moment later Pink Eye and Chicken Pox descended quietly to the floor below. Pink Eye immediately trained his silencer on the sentry. The guard, unaware of the laser dot dancing like a nervous gnat on the back of his cranium, continued his patrol.

Chicken Pox counted doorways to find the one they wanted. "Found it. IBS, I need the door code."

"571."

"All caps?"

"Lower case 7."

Pink Eye remained focused on the guard. Should the guard turn unexpectedly, his finger would simply squeeze the hair trigger.

"Damn it!" Chicken Pox swore under his breath. His gloved fingers had forced him to mash a typo on the numeric keypad lock.

The guard reached the end of the corridor and stopped. Pink Eye's finger tightened on the trigger. The red laser gnat on the back of the guard's skull grew still. The guard paused to light a cigarette. Pink Eye imagined the bullet shattering the sentry's skull like a honeydew melon dropped down a mine shaft on a Tuesday. Or maybe a cantaloupe, he thought, yes, maybe a cantaloupe. The only other melon he could think of was a watermelon, and while the colour was right, the shape was totally wrong. That and the fact that watermelons were largely just empty calories. Whatever the melon, Pink Eye knew, if the guard moved, that's when the fireworks would happen.

"Got it!" whispered Chicken Pox.

The two Navy SEALs disappeared through the doorway, which they shut silently behind them.

The guard turned and began to trudge back down the hall.

Inside was darkness. Both men pulled their night vision goggles down over their eyes. And now, thought Pink Eye, the unseen becomes seen, the invisible becomes visible, and the obscure becomes scure. He made a mental note to check later to see if 'scure' was really a word. It must be, otherwise obscure made no sense and Pink Eye would have to question the underlying logic of the entire English language. The 'scured' room was clearly Ali Madda's office, just as Wetmop had promised. The details were exactly as she described, down to the discarded socks on the sofa. "Why he can't just keep them in his shoes I don't know," said the informer, "I mean, if you don't like socks, why put them on in the first place?" The sofa was part of a complete living room set. It looked expensive even in the monochromatic green of the goggles. Opposite, was a massive executive desk that looked as if it had been cobbled together from several smaller desks and a side table or two. They looked past all of this, however, to their objective. "We're in Urinary Tract Infection and have spotted Stendhal Syndrome." Urinary Tract Infection was, of course, the office itself, while Stendhal Syndrome was the safe on the wall behind the desk.

"Good job," said Irritable Bowel Syndrome. "Be careful."

"Roger that."

The stealth helicopter still sat surreptitiously suspended in the air above the roof. The muffled beat of its propeller panted 'wuh wuh wuh' like an asthmatic bloodhound. Syphilis, the pilot, sat at the controls, ready to move at a moment's notice. Irritable Bowel Syndrome watched a row of small monitors that provided everything from satellite views, to recon data, to a live camera feed from each of the SEALs' helmets. Charlie and Alex both leaned over the seat backs to get a glimpse of what Irritable Bowel Syndrome was seeing. "Is everything going to be okay?" asked Alex anxiously.

"Sure," said Charlie. At that moment lightning flashed, flooding the helicopter in white light. Thunder boomed and a coarse rain began pelting the windshield and hull. "Or not."

In the second floor hallway, the guard continued his monotonous routine. To pass the time he'd begun humming the cha-cha in his head and sashaying his way along the carpet. To his right were doors leading to various bedrooms, the master's office and study. To his left was the bannister and a twenty-foot drop to the marble floor of the front hall. He could hear the muffled rhythm of *Ah be Kardsim* from the party room below. It seemed like a new version, he thought, with some sort of offbeat going on that didn't quite fit. One of those new Arab ska dubs that were so hot in the Riyadh speakeasies right now, he figured. The rain whipped against the glass front of the house. The entire foyer of the Spanish / Bauhaus-revival fusion structure was two-story glass, offering a panoramic view of the wind whipped palm trees and storm churned gulf waters beyond. The occasional lightning strike brought this all into stark relief, making briefly visible the neighbouring islands of England and Belgium. An unexpected storm to be sure, but a nice break from the mind numbing monotony of guard duty. He hadn't signed up for this. When he'd joined the Jihad he hadn't envisioned spending it patrolling the halls of a rich man's house, even one as important as Ali Madda. He'd wanted to be on the front lines, fighting the good fight, blowing up schools or setting fire to heretics. In other words, making a difference. The sentry brushed cold rainwater from his hair and continued several feet before stopping. Rainwater? The guard walked slowly backwards while looking up, until the wide open ceiling vent came into view. "Intruders!" he yelled, "Help! Intruders!" He then slapped the remote in his pocket, causing alarms to blare and strobe lights to flash.

"Keep going," urged Pink Eye. He didn't look at his partner as he spoke. Instead, he kept his focus on the office entrance, pistol aimed, ready to shoot.

Downstairs dozens of guards ran for their guns. Blinded by flashing lights and dry ice from the dance floor, several crashed into each other. Others then tripped over those who had already fallen. Someone shouted that whoever had thought strobe lights in the event of an emergency was a good idea was a "complete idiot." The fact that several of the guards had been drinking didn't help either. None of the complaints, nor attempts to organize for that matter, could be heard regardless. This as a result of the incessant alarms and the fact that no one had thought to turn the music off.

"Got two out of three cherries," said Chicken Pox. He was waiting for the electronic safecracker to complete its work. The digital device was using magnetic pulses to hack the computerized locking mechanism. This was only possible because of the intel received that had told them exactly what model of safe Ali Madda had purchased from Amazon.com. Whatever people might say, the NSA had its uses. "Bingo." Without hesitation, Chicken Pox yanked open the thick steel door. "We got Restless Leg Syndrome." He reached in to grab the shiny canister, while simultaneously pulling the counterfeit from his bag. "Making the switch..."

At that moment the door to the office flew open, instantly flooding the room with light. To the two men in night-vision goggles, it was as if someone had set off a flash bulb in their eyes. The goggles automatically re calibrated, but the SEAL's eyes could not. Pink Eye fired blindly into the light. The terrorist guard fired back. As his eyes adjusted Pink Eye was able to see the silhouette of the sentry and unloaded the rest of his clip. The guard staggered backwards until his hips met the bannister, and he toppled over. He was dead before his body hit the marble floor below.

"Chicken Pox, we gotta—" Pink Eye stopped as he saw his fellow soldier slumped behind the desk, head lolled. A Pollock of blood splattered the wall behind him. Chicken Pox had pulled the night vision goggles from his face and his eyes now stared with the look of someone surprised to find himself the guest of honour at a funeral. In each hand Chicken Pox clutched an identical silver canister. As Pink Eye stared in shock, Chicken Pox convulsed in a death rattle, relaxed his grip, and let go. The two canisters clattered and rolled. Pink Eye instinctively stopped one with the toe of his boot. The other came to a rest just out of reach beneath the massive desk.

"Upstairs!" someone shouted in Arabic.

Pink Eye deliberated, distressed by what to do about Chicken Pox. Never leave a man behind, he thought. This time, however, the stakes were simply too high. He picked up the canister at his foot. As he did he noticed the blood running down his own boot. For the first time, he realized that he too had been shot. A quick look at the wound showed it to be soft tissue only. Did he have the real device? Pink Eye's mind raced. He must have, he decided, there was no time for the alternative. Pink Eye shoved the canister into the satchel and ran for the office door.

A contingent of over a dozen guards cautiously climbed the stairs to the second floor. Some were in various states of dress, having been either roused from bed or the party below. All were armed with AK-47's. When it came to weapons, Ali Madda was a traditionalist. He loved the reliability of the AK-47, calling it the "Toyota Corolla of guns." The guards proceeded cautiously down the hallway towards the open office door. They had all stepped or stumbled over the corpse of their fallen friend in the hall below and none had any desire to join him. Feeling a draft, one of the guards glanced up to find himself staring into the open air vent in the ceiling. He could see there the bottom of the wounded Navy SEAL's boots as he struggled to ascend the shaft.

"Up here!" he yelled and raised his gun to shoot. As luck would have it, a drop of blood fell from Pink Eye's boot and landed squarely in the guard's eye. The terrorist fired blindly, spraying the surrounding ceiling with bullets and forcing the other guards to drop to the floor. Pink Eye pulled himself up and rolled onto the roof, safely out of sight from the floor below.

For a moment, Pink Eye simply lay there on the rain soaked roof, heart pounding, staring at the helicopter hovering overhead, unable to move. I'm like a beached whale, he thought, and if I don't move soon, my goose will be cooked. The Navy SEAL forced himself up, stood swaying for a moment, then staggered forward, waving for help. Despite the danger of striking a nearby satellite dish and signal tower, the pilot lowered the helicopter to within a foot of the rooftop. Charlie crouched at the side door, then jumped down. "Quickly!" he shouted as he ran foreword. He grabbed the wounded SEAL's arm to help him navigate the wet piping and cables that snaked the roof top. The stairwell door swung open, and a contingent of terrorist guards who had been frantically trying to pull on the push door, spilled out onto the roof.

"Take it, leave me," Pink Eye gasped, offering up the satchel.

"No."

Amid confused shouts, the terrorists began shooting erratically at the two men, the helicopter and various rain drops. Several shots struck Pink Eye's body armour, causing him to stagger. A single shot found a gap and drove deep into his torso. Another bullet hit Charlie in the shoulder. He registered this only as an abstract burning sensation. The endorphins flooding his brain softly reassured him "don't worry, it's only a flesh wound." Charlie helped Pink Eye to the helicopter door, then, with adrenaline fuelled strength, heaved him inside. As he followed, several more bullets struck Charlie's own kevlar vest, throwing him face first onto the steel floor. Both men were then pinned by the sudden acceleration of the helicopter as it hurtled high into the sky. Alex stared at them, in shock, trying to process everything that had just happened. Numbly, Alex accepted the satchel offered by the outstretched arm of the Navy SEAL. Charlie lifted his head in time to see Pink Eye spit blood and mumbled broken words "You need... know... made... switch..."

"You made the switch?"

The Navy SEAL opened his mouth to speak, but began to cough uncontrollably. Charlie held his hand, turned to Alex and shouted, "Is that it?"

Alex opened the satchel. In the dim green cabin light, he could just make out the sheen of the canister it contained. Outside, a smattering of bullets continued to clatter against the steel helicopter hull.

"Well?"

"Um, I think so?"

"Do you *know* so?"

Alex wanted to say he couldn't tell for certain. How could he? He stared at Pink Eye, now dead at his feet, yet somehow still staring back at him expectantly. Alex looked into Charlie's anxious eyes. "I know so."

Acting on impulse, Charlie reached up, grabbed the boy and hugged him fiercely. It was the first time he'd hugged a human being since before the funeral. The pitch and yaw of the helicopter made him feel as if he were teetering on the brink of everything and nothing. The ocean filled the open door on one side of the chopper, while dissipating clouds filled the other. He felt like a snowflake in a storm that had somehow found a twin despite the soul crushing improbability of it all. At that moment one last bullet ricocheted off the roof of the cabin and drove neatly into Charlie's back. He collapsed into Alex's arms.

"Charlie? Charlie?" shrieked Alex.

Back on the roof, two-dozen terrorist guards stared forlornly into the night. The helicopter had vanished from sight several seconds earlier. The ruin had finally broken and exposed the moon, an iridescent crescent in ascent.

One of the guards threw his gun down in frustration. "Twenty of us shooting and still they escape? Did any of you attend the training camps? Hmm? I always said the webinars wouldn't work! Virtual monkey bars are not the same as real monkey bars!"

"You were shooting too, Mousa."

"I had infidel blood in my eye," he shouted. "Do you know how hard that is to get out? It's not like the blood of martyrs you know. It clots."

"Oh, yes?" chimed in another of the men. "Because you're such a marksman with both eyes? I've seen you at the range. Every time, the poor Jihadist is full of bullet holes. Meanwhile, the woman and child? Not a scratch!"

"Take that back," demanded Mousa. "Take that back!"

"Oh, I'm so afraid! What are you going to do, shoot me?"

The others broke out into snickers and snorts. Mousa seethed and clenched his fists angrily.

"Enough."

The men turned to see Ali Madda standing at the rooftop exit. For a moment he glowered at them sternly, like a disappointed father. Then, slowly, a sly smile traced his lips. Lifting his ample thawb robe, he unveiled the shiny metal canister within. He began to chuckle, then laugh maniacally. His henchmen cheered. Ali Madda lifted the device high above his head in and shouted "Allah!" The men gave another cheer, followed by shouts about God's all around greatness and tossed their guns into the air in celebration. They were then forced to cover their heads and run out of the way as the weapons fell back to Earth once more.

CHAPTER 20

"Tea with sugar's often the answer, but always a solution."
– M. Hatter

The President had once more written a poem, and his Chief of Staff had once more intercepted it. There was now an understanding with trusted staffers to redirect all of the President's so-called 'memos' to Jim's desk. It made perfect sense and followed protocol, but was clearly not what the President intended. Still, he seemed to be forgetting these things as quickly as he wrote them down. There were no questions, no follow-up, no wondering what the public's reaction had been to his mad musings. Instead, he simply spent the day fingering his growing whiskers, and walking barefoot through the Rose Garden, sometimes with Reverend Norman, sometimes alone. It wasn't just that the poems were inappropriate or bad, they were outright inane.

Chaos Theory

> **2nd Amen-dment**
>
> *The flag is made with stars of light*
> *Like a tyger burning bright*
> *What immortal hand or eye,*
> *Could shoot that tyger?*
> *Die! Die! Die!*

Jim crumpled it up and tossed it into the fire. After watching it burn a moment, he raked the coals to ensure no evidence remained. While some might argue that it was harmless, or even charming that the President had taken to writing nonsense poems, Jim saw it as potential political dynamite. Poetry was the province of artists and elite ivy league academics, not 'real Americans'. Worse, this poetry wasn't charming or folksy, it smacked of intellectualism. Of course, the President had gone to Princeton. That had all come up during the primaries but, as the then-candidate explained, he was young and foolish at the time. During the debates he'd joked that, "while I experimented with academics, I didn't inhale." Jim smiled. He'd written that line himself. There were scurrilous rumours that the President had once been a closet intellectual. The claim was that, realizing how damaging this could be to his political ambitions, he had undergone hypnotherapy to suppress these tendencies and replace them with dogmatic beliefs. Being an intellectual, after all, was a choice. All of this had supposedly happened years ago, before he and Jim had met. The campaign denied it all as malicious lies spread by political opponents, and staunchly maintained that the President was "no smarter in the past than he was today." Still, Jim had to admit, the President did have a way of occasionally slipping up in ways so ironic, they seemed almost unconsciously intentional. Such as the time he'd referred to Wall Street investors as "job cremators" during an interview on CNN. Almost, but not quite as bad as being accused of being an intellectual, was the notion that the President might be clinically insane. Privately, Jim had concluded that the Commander-in-Chief was now as nutty as a fruitcake. Still, he was the President of the United States and one had to respect the office. Regardless, Jim had taken an oath to serve him to the best of his ability and that was exactly what he was going to do.

* * *

The President wandered in the desert, sipping on an iced tea. Reverend Duke Norman walked beside him. The Reverend was wearing a suit and was sweating profusely, dabbing his forehead with a silk handkerchief. He'd assumed they'd stay inside the President's air conditioned house the whole time, not take a constitutional around the grounds in the sweltering one hundred and seventeen degree heat. After all, he thought, who goes for a stroll in Palm Springs in the summer? One of the secret servicemen had already collapsed from heatstroke and been carried away. The Reverend guzzled his own tea and began crunching the crushed ice between his teeth. They were in Rancho Divertido, the President's private retreat, just a few miles from the Rancho Mirage home that had once belonged to President Gerald Ford. The scorching sun, however, wasn't the only thing burning. The decision by the POTUS to take a few days vacation amid the current crisis had sparked a political firestorm in Washington. The President, despite this, seemed blissfully unconcerned. He strolled over the baking sands, wearing just a loin cloth and belly length beard, as if he hadn't a care in the world. He even seemed untroubled by the rapidly reddening skin on his shoulders. Officially, the Reverend was here for a prayer meeting in the tradition of Billy Graham. In reality, he was here to help the President reach his 'true potential'. For years, the Reverend and his fellow faithful had only dreamt of having a 'true believer' in the highest office. Again and again, even the most faithful Presidents had disappointed them, picking politics over God every time. Separation of church and state, Duke Norman believed, was the greatest mistake the founding fathers had ever made. It made sense to separate the bad religions like Islam, of course, but not Christianity. He called it "the madness of Madison" in his sermons. "America is the chosen land," he preached, "and yet, again and again, it fails to choose itself." Finally, it seemed, they had a President who realized this and had the guts to do something about it, whatever the cost. If it took the end of the world to save America, then so be it.

On the surface, Duke's chief adversary was Jim Hornswell. He knew Hornswell didn't trust him and felt that he was a political liability for the President. Hornswell might even believe that the pastor was responsible for the President's current 'leap of faith'. The Reverend, however, saw himself as merely a humble, spiritual guide, facilitating the President's ordained fate. Jim Hornswell believed in nothing except politics. Nevertheless, to Reverend Duke Norman, the Chief of Staff still served one critical purpose —to help keep the President in power long enough to achieve salvation. The problem was that the President's childlike enthusiasm could, at times, be prematurely self-destructive. Rumour had it that, just two days earlier, Hornswell had barely kept the President from being both politically and literally exposed. It seemed that the POTUS had dashed from his shower to greet a White House tour group without stopping to put on pants. He'd wanted to welcome them personally and explain his idea to finally bring peace to the Middle East. The plan, apparently, involved a lot of hugging and the Commander-in-Chief thought he could demonstrate how exactly that might all work. "To get the ball rolling," he told the bewildered and somewhat traumatized tourists. After ushering the President out, Hornswell assured the visitors that this was not the President of the United States, despite the striking similarity. He told them it was a body double performing a security exercise. "You can tell it's not the President," he said, "because the President wears clothes." Hornswell then told unsettled staff members that the President was somehow asleep and therefore didn't think he needed to put on trousers. He reassured them that the President was "solidly pro-pants" having worn them on many occasions. It was an argument few could dispute. The incident had been a close call, averted by the Chief of Staff's quick thinking. A deposed President was no good to anyone, on that Duke Norman and Jim Hornswell could agree. So for now, they were unwilling allies.

"I am somewhat concerned, Mr. President" said the Reverend.

"So am I," said the President.

"What are you concerned about, sir?"

"Judas."

"Judas?"

"Judas Hornswell. He might have to go."

"I see," said the Reverend. This was exactly what he had feared, that the President might wish to prematurely fire his Chief of Staff. A few days earlier, the Reverend had found what he suspected was the President's list of possible successors to Hornswell scrawled on a napkin. Several of the candidates were fictional characters, and two of them were deceased. Even if he could persuade the President to choose a more qualified replacement, whom could they trust? Jim Hornswell may be a secularist damned to Hell, but at least he was the devil they knew. This was a situation that even the Reverend had to deal with carefully, lest he too be seen as suspect. Managing the Commander-in-Chief was a constant game of chess, except that the President wasn't playing chess. He was playing Yahtzee and could, at any moment, roll his dice across the board and declare "war." In other words, the President's rules were constantly changing. You had to be careful lest he take your king, demand a triple letter score or decide to pass go and collect two hundred dollars. This wasn't entirely a metaphor, the President really did confuse which rules applied to which game, making poker night at the White House an often bewildering affair. Still, he was the most powerful man in the world and that made the game, whichever it was, worth playing. "Why does he concern you, Mr. President?"

"I believe he will betray me."

"I wouldn't worry about him, sir."

"No?" The President turned to face the Reverend, studying him carefully. As he did so, he inserted his index finger into his nose and extracted a bead of mucus. He then carefully placed this into a No. 10 envelope. The envelope contained that morning's collection of nose-pickings which, the President was convinced, contained traces of brain-matter. It wasn't that he wanted to keep the snot for himself, so much as he wanted to prevent it from "falling into the wrong hands". Later the envelope, along with others, would be mailed to an underground bunker in New Mexico. It was the same undisclosed location where Dick Cheney had spent much of the Bush presidency. The interior was still decorated as the former Vice-President's 'man-cave'.

"Sir, I think Jim Hornswell is simply concerned with keeping you in office. His motives may be... impure, and he may not appreciate the, um... magnitude of your destiny, but his interests are unwittingly aligned with ours. That is why you're so clever to keep him around."

"Hmm, yes, I am clever. Keep your friends close and your enemies closer," said the President, nodding his head thoughtfully. "Jesus said that, didn't he?"

"Well, someone certainly did, but yes, exactly, Mr. President. Brilliant." The President, happy with this, nodded enthusiastically. Duke Norman saw an opportunity to both change the subject and address his own, growing concern. "If I may, sir... you are attracting a good deal of attention. Some are suggesting your recent behaviour is... eccentric."

The President looked surprised, "Eccentric? How?" As he said this, he carefully folded the snot-filled envelope and tucked it into the crotch of his loincloth.

"Well..." began the Reverend. He paused for a moment, unsure whether to remove his hand from his knight and make his move final. With the President, every turn involved a certain amount of guesswork. It was possible that, just when Duke Norman thought he was going to declare 'Checkmate', he'd be told to 'Go Fish'. "You know Washington; it could be any little thing."

"Hmm," said the President, accepting this. "You give good council, dear friend. It won't matter, when the time comes. Unless, that is, one of these doubters ruins it all by saving the day. Judas insists we must make every effort to stop it. That failing to do so might cost us votes. He said if the world ends we'll be crucified in the election."

"Indeed, sir. It would be a tough thing to spin."

The two men walked on in silence for several moments. The pastor noticed that the President's skin was actually starting to sizzle. Right now, however, he had more pressing concerns. While the potential end of the world was on everyone's mind, there were other issues he needed to discuss with the President, specifically, the explosive growth of the Pō Lights. The cult's rapid expansion was culling members from every religious flock, including his own. Having some upstart religion led by a bunch of rabble rousers babbling on about a 'messiah' was an anathema to what Christianity was all about. Having the group's tax exempt status revoked might do much to stem their growth. Once again, however, the President needed to be played like Parcheesi, not pushed. "Have you considered my request, sir, regarding the pagan Pō Lights?"

"What? Oh right, the tax exempt thing. Yes, yes, we'll make that happen. You're sure you don't want them simply thrown to the lions?"

The Reverend stared a moment before he saw the trace of a smile on the President's lips. "Oh, right, you're joking, sir. Very good. Ha-ha!"

The President chuckled. "Of course I am. PETA wouldn't allow it; one of the lions might get sick. They'll get their own, along with the rest of the heretics, when the time comes. I'm not crazy, you know?"

"No, no, of course not, sir."

Even after all these years, the President could still surprise Duke. The Reverend had first met the POTUS at his inauguration. The President had been a long time fan of Duke Norman's *Pray to Power* television program and podcast. He asked Duke to lead a national prayer breakfast event. At the breakfast, Duke was offered the role of White House Spiritual Advisor. Duke Norman's appointment was not without controversy. The doubting-Thomas news media questioned the goings on of his televised church and his great personal fortune. He responded to these critics by scolding them for being obsessed with such matters. Duke Norman explained that, like Jesus, he was unconcerned by wealth. The fact that he had so much of it was "neither here nor there." When they pointed out that he'd been paid over nine million dollars by his church in the previous year alone, he responded that his salary worked out to only pennies per parishioner. Surely, he admonished them, they would not begrudge a few cents to save a soul. As with all teapot tempests, it soon fell from the front-pages, aided by a salacious scandal involving a Senator and his pet poodle named 'Noodles'. Duke Reverend Norman had since grown to know the President as a man of passionate faith. The President, in turn, increasingly looked to Duke for guidance. "Sometimes, Mr. President, life will hand you a square peg that doesn't fit into the round hole of your faith. Do not be deterred. Hammer that peg until it fits, or toss it away. Never question what you believe. It is the peg that is wrong." They were words the President took to heart. Critics decried the Commander-in-Chief taking guidance from an unelected clergyman over matters of state. Duke argued that he was hardly the first such confident to offer advice to a sitting President. Appearing on *Charlie Rose*, he reflected on Joan Quigley, the Reagans' astrologer. At the time, alarmists questioned the President of the United States running the country by horoscope. None, however, could doubt the political efficacy of his presidency. Would Ronald Reagan have been as good a leader were he a Capricorn or Pisces? Only the stars could say.

As he followed the POTUS through the desert landscape, Duke cringed uncomfortably at the sight of white blisters now bursting fourth on the Commander-in-Chief's shoulders. "If I may, Mr President, perhaps it is best to... play along. After all, whether or not the world ends is ultimately in God's hands, not yours or mine."

The President stopped, considering this for a moment. He looked down at his own hands, opening and closing them like an infant wondering what they might be capable of. "What, exactly, do you mean by 'playing along'?"

"Well, to start, perhaps by wearing pants. You know, to assuage people. People expect the President to wear pants. It's just one of those things."

The President nodded, accepting this. "Fine. I will wear your pants, if that's what it takes, although it sounds like the kind of political pandering Judas Hornswell might suggest."

"Heaven forbid."

"On a more important note," said the President, "I think it's time we start planning the 'Going Away' party."

"Indeed, sir?"

"Invite all the participants. The witness, the innocent child... oh, and that fellow from the CIA."

"That fellow from... Draper? I believe he's unconscious."

"So? He can be unconscious anywhere."

"A very good point sir. Why not? The time foretold is approaching."

The President nodded with satisfaction. He then sniffed. "Reverend, may I ask you something?"

"Of course, Mr. President, anything."

"Do you smell barbecue?"

CHAPTER 21

"Never go to bed angry." – Clytemnestra

"I told you about this a week ago," said Lisa impatiently.

"No, I don't think you did," said Charlie, as he loaded the dishwasher with dishes he'd already washed in the sink. This was the eco-efficient model that featured a water-saving mode only. It meant that the dishwasher conserved water, but required dishes to be washed first. "Clean dishes in, clean dishes out," the salesman had promised with a smile that Charlie had insisted was more of a smirk.

"Yes, I did," Lisa insisted. "In fact, you were doing exactly what you're doing right now. I'm doing yoga on Tuesday, I said, so you'll be looking after Faith."

"I..." Charlie hesitated. He couldn't prove that she hadn't told him this and, since it was his job to load the dishwasher each night, her description was plausible. "Well, regardless, my thing is a work thing."

"So?"

"So, I think my job is slightly more important than your burkha shake-weight class."

"It's *Bikram* Shake Weight," said Lisa, rolling her eyes. She closed her bag and fastened her yellow yoga matt with a Velcro strap. Bikram-Shake Weight was Lisa's current passion. This involved engaging in high temperature yoga, while using the as-seen-on-TV spring-loaded barbells known as 'Shake Weights'. She loved the combination of the physical and the spiritual or what Andrew, her instructor, called the 'chakra shakera'. It was all part of the new mind-spirit-body fusion workout trend. Fusion-fitness was the new big thing from California. The first fusion-fitness viral fad had merged Kangaroo Shoes with Shake Weights. That particular variation had been banned after an epidemic of injuries and the hospitalization of a celebrity. The problem was that the combined kinetic energy of the oscillating shake-weights and equally spring-loaded kangaroo shoes had proven overly volatile. This culminated in Gwyneth Paltrow being launched out of a second story studio in Venice Beach, ricocheting off a car roof on Abbott-Kinney Boulevard and hurtling through a furniture art store window on the far side of the street. Despite this disaster, the combination trend continued unabated with Swing-Stick Spinning, Aqua-Zumba Tai Chi and Bikram Shake Weight Yoga. "See, this is your problem," said Lisa. "You think work is more important than life. Work to live, Charlie, don't live to work."

"You just read that on Facebook."

"And I *liked* it. So what? It's true."

"The point is, we need my job to pay for stuff like our mortgage, food, and bikram yoga-whatever classes! Oh, and, as we agreed, so that you could stay home to look after Faith."

"During the day, not twenty-four-seven. Not so you could go to meetings at eight o'clock at night."

"The CIA isn't a nine-to-five job."

"Neither is being a parent."

"Exactly!"

Lisa's eyes narrowed. Both glanced towards the living room where Faith was watching television. They couldn't see her from where they stood, but the noise and image of *Yo Gabba Gabba* reflected in the window was enough.

"Look," Charlie pleaded, "my boss is expecting me. Go to class tomorrow night."

"There are no good teachers tomorrow night. Besides, Andrew is expecting me."

"Your yoga teacher? So what? There are other students."

"Andrew's very... he promised to give me... one-on-one instruction tonight. He's going to help me find my chi." They stared at one another for a long moment. Charlie resisted the urge to say he didn't know she had a 'chi', let alone that she'd lost it. Inane TV noises from the other room filled the void. "Fine," said Lisa. "I won't go. I've only been waiting weeks for solo time with him, but whatever."

Charlie realized he was now in the classic no-win scenario. He'd try to escape, although he knew from experience, escape was impossible. If he went to his meeting now, he'd pay for it for weeks. "No, look, I can tell Bryan that I'm not feeling well, or that Faith's not feeling well. We can reschedule."

"Don't be silly, your job's more important, right? Like you said, it pays the bills." She put the words 'pays the bills' in air quotes.

"It's not that it's more important, it's just that..."

"It's just that what? It's fine, Charlie, you made it quite clear what you think."

Charlie felt like a gazelle that had stumbled and now finds itself in the lion's maw. There's no escape, he thought. Simply relax, fighting only makes it worse.

"Lisa, please go to your yoga class. I *want* you to go."

"No, you don't."

"Yes, I do. Please. Look, I should be spending more time with Faith anyway. I've been so busy, even when I am home I barely acknowledge her. If not for me, for her sake, go."

Lisa hung her head. In Charlie's mind the lion was pondering whether to play with the gazelle some more, or mercifully snap its neck. "Fine," she said, "because you're right, you don't spend enough time with her, but this better not come back to bite me."

"No, of course not. As I said, I want you to go."

Snap! The truth of it was, he had no moral high ground. Charlie was lying. He didn't have a work function. Once in a while he simply felt the need to escape. He'd blame work events or other excuses. He would then walk around the city, visit a museum, or have a few drinks in a bar. He didn't get drunk or look at other women; he just needed to get away. He fantasized about not going back, but he loved his family too much for that. The fact that he even thought this way sickened him. That was what his father had done. After years of preaching responsibility and telling Charlie to 'be a man', his father had simply gone out one night and never returned. Charlie despised him for it and, when he felt like doing the same the same thing, he despised himself too. Hate father, hate son, he thought.

* * *

"Who lives in a pineapple under the sea?"

"Spongebob Squarepants!"

Alex stared at the cartoon rerun impassively. He'd seen it before and, even if he hadn't, he wasn't exactly in the mood. As a kid he'd loved the show. It and The Simpsons were his go-to TV shows for a sense of normality. Spongebob was trying to explain something to his friend Patrick. Patrick was a talking starfish. The joke was that Patrick was too stupid to understand, but it should be noted that, in terms of real echinoderms, Patrick was nothing short of a genius. Of course, as a plastic sponge, Spongebob's intellect was even more impressive. Spongebob Squarepants, however, was rarely watched for its zoological accuracy, in spite of being created by a marine biologist. Spongebob and Patrick were now joined by Squidward, the show's token cephalopod.

"My kids love that show."

Alex turned to see that the nurse had reappeared. Her name, according to her tag, was Ronnette. Ronnette, or Ronnie to her friends, was a large black woman, with a generous smile. Alex liked her much better than the bitter blonde on duty earlier. "Me too," he said.

Ronnie flashed that warm smile and proceeded to check on Charlie. His catheter bag was only half-full and his IV was getting low, but not empty. She adjusted his pillow and gently rolled him on his side to prevent bed sores. "You don't need to stay here, sweetie. You know we'll call you when he wakes up."

"That's okay."

"It's a beautiful day outside."

"Is it?"

Alex picked up the remote and changed the channel to CNN. Scenes of violent riots on the streets of Chicago filled the screen. A gang of marauding investment bankers were intent on overturning a purple Prius in what could only be described as an impromptu act of mob performance art. Wolf Blitzer narrated "... overwhelmed police in every major city across the globe. The unprecedented rioting was clearly set off by leaks from the White House that the threats by Ali Madda are, in fact, real." The crowds, in a paroxysm of nihilistic angst, were intent on destroying everything they could. They had gazed long into the abyss, and the abyss had gazed back. Finding one another attractive, the mob and the abyss had decided to hold hands and 'go steady'. CNN cut to an "on the street" interview with a rioter. The rioter had taken a break from beating a mailbox with a wooden baseball bat to speak to the reporter. The mailbox, being made out of steel, remained undented, while the rioter remained undaunted. The ruffian was panting and mopping his forehead from the effort of his, as yet ineffective, attempt at wonton destruction. "Yeah we're angry," he snarled, "angry because the governments let this happen. We're all going to die, so what's it matter? Do what you want is what I say! Do whatever the hell you want and damn the consequences!" To illustrate his point he took a dramatic swing at the mailbox. The bat rebounded off of the steel frame, clocked him in the forehead and knocked him out instantly.

"Now you turn that off," said Ronnie.

Alex started to argue, but decided there was no need. The news was all the same anyway. He switched off the TV.

"I was watching that," Charlie protested weakly.

Both Alex and Ronnie turned to stare. Charlie managed a weary smile. Alex flung himself on Charlie and hugged him. Charlie, despite his overwhelming fatigue, weakly hugged him back. For a moment, both felt whole.

CHAPTER 22

"...and, nose for a nose and the world goes anosmic."
– M. Gandhi

The Azylum Mahall, with its soaring sand-white walls and sparkling azure domes, shone like an opal above the beaches of the Persian Gulf coast. The palace was the envy of even the most eminent of emirs and had been in the possession of the Madda family since the days of the Ottoman Empire. The only exception had been a brief period in the sixteenth century when Muyassar Madda had lost it in a game of cards to famed British industrialist Sir Archibald Pennyworth. The palace was soon returned to the Madda family, however, after the Englishman accidentally chopped off his own head with a scimitar. Ali Madda, stout and cherubic even as a child, was the youngest of fifteen sons. As such, he suffered from all of the usual concerns of being the youngest. Even Akbar, brother number fourteen, referred to Ali as 'the baby'. This meant, his opinions were rarely heard and readily dismissed. Ali was seen as the dreamer and irresponsible one, best left to console himself with his hobbies; his car, plane and Beanie Baby collections. Ali Madda had no interest in being so easily ignored. As the de facto black sheep of the family, he became more and more involved in the activities of his former classmate and bocce ball teammate, Osama. Osama introduced Ali to the underground radical Islamic scene and encouraged his discontented friend to "just try Jihad". With youthful fervour, Ali threw himself into his new found faith and came to see Jihad as necessary to defend the tenets of Islam. "The fact that blowing up people is fun," he said, "is simply a nice perk."

The Diwan Room occupied much of the second floor of the palace. With its decorated stone columns and elaborate arabesque floor, it served as the palace's party room. Today the party was in full swing. Famous terrorists and their entourages chatted, laughed, and exchanged suspicious sideways glances at one another. These included such notables as Akbad the Bad, Omar the Dentist of Qatar and Boom-Boom Bahir, who, having recently lost both hands, now built bombs using only his teeth. They mingled with wealthy donors dressed in thawbs and business suits. Most of the donors were Middle Eastern, but many were from elsewhere, including Europe, China, and even the USA. "You can't blow up buildings without bombs, and bombs need backers," Ali explained, "so, we mix business with pleasure." Notably absent where any members of ISIS or the Taliban. Ali scoffed at these groups. "ISIS is too uptight and little bit crazy, you know? And the Taliban are just plain backwards. The problem with most extremists is that they're extremely dull. Terrorism today needs to live in the 21st Century AD, not the 1st Century AH!" On one wall, big screen HD TVs obscured ancient

Persian frescos. Each was tuned to a different news channel, from Al Jazeera, to the BBC, to CNN. All showed riots and chaos from around the world. The feeling inside the room was festive, as attendees sipped multi-coloured arak cocktails or plucked tasty canapés from passing plates. The idea of alcohol at such at gathering might seem hypocritical, heretical, and, incidentally, illegal. Ali Madda, argued that such rules were really for those less worthy than they. He'd learned to love liquor during his two years as a dissolute at Oxford, from cream sherry to Pimms on ice. He'd spent his time there pretending to write a dissertation on the history of pocket lint. This complete waste of time was made possible by his family's donation of twenty-million pounds. "Osama has his porn, I have my booze," he used to say, "all's fair in love and Jihad." The only things absent from the party were women. That, of course, would have been wrong.

"You see? Everywhere, it is the same. Anarchy! Truly a triumph of terror," said a gangly terrorist. As he spoke, he waggled the glowing blue tip of his e-cigarette at the televised mayhem as if assessing an artwork.

"The infidels go mad when faced with their own oblivion," nodded another, stroking his salt and pepper beard and sipping a glass of sidique. A servant approached with a tray piled high with duck liver paté on gluten-free crackers. The elder terrorist waved him away while patting his stomach. "No, no, please don't tempt me. I'm on a low carb diet."

"Really?" asked the first terrorist. "How's that working for you?"

"I'm down to a size-7 thawb," said the other, pirouetting slowly to show that this was true.

At that moment, the great doors of the diwan swung open revealing Ali Madda himself, flanked by members of his entourage. Among them was Karim looking conspicuously less jubilant than the rest. The room fell silent, then erupted into applause. Their rotund host grinned broadly, basking in the adulation of his peers. He was a rockstar among terrorists now. And not just any rockstar, Ali thought, I'm Kanye West, Justin Beiber, and Beyonce Knowles rolled into one. He lifted his hands to silence them. "Gentlemen, please, you're too kind. Welcome, and thank-you all for coming!"

"We love you Ali!" someone shouted.

Ali laughed. He then lifted his hand as if grasping an invisible vessel and said, "First of all, I would like to propose a toast." A cowering servant scuttled forward to insert a flute of champagne between the terrorist leader's outstretched fingers. "A true reign of terror does not happen without help. Oh sure, everyone knows the famous ones by name; the suicide bombers, the mass-murdering gunmen, the beheaders... But, we can't all be lucky enough to be martyrs partying in paradise with seventy-two virgins—am I right?" The audience broke into laughter and nods. "Let us not forget, that behind every successful strike are the planners, the explosives makers, the arms dealers, the recruiters, the imams, the moms, and, of course, the sponsors of terrorism both state and private. You, each of you, are truly the unsung heroes of Jihad. And so, I raise my glass to you... To you all!" With that, Ali drained his glass with a single loud slurp.

"And to Allah!" added Karim anxiously from the side.

"Yes, yes, yes, and to Allah too," said Ali with a listless wave of his empty glass.

Karim scowled.

For a moment, the crowd broke into excited babble until Ali loudly clapped his hands. A large projection screen descended from the ceiling. On it, the nations of the UN Security Council, represented as sad stick figures, bowed before a happy Arab stick figure. "You see, even as we speak, the western and eastern nations tremble at our feet! I did try to get a tremble animation going on here, but it turns out it's quite tricky to do in PowerPoint."

"But do we truly triumph?" someone shouted. The room turned to see who had dared doubt Ali. The question came from a disaffected Libyan named Daib. The veteran Jihadist had fought in five wars and lost a limb in each. As a result, he sat propped up inside a wicker basket with only his eyes visible above the rim. Daib, whose name meant 'happy fellow', sneered contemptuously at the crowd. "Well, do we?"

"We were guaranteed a return on our investment by now, mate," said an Australian banker named Bob. Bob managed a private hedge fund that had heavily invested in Ali Madda's terrorist enterprise. As he'd explained in the prospectus, "Nobody likes the idea of global extortion, but the expected returns are excellent and we have a responsibility to our shareholders."

"Despite this supposed leak, the Americans still officially deny your canister is what you say it is," shouted a Syrian.

Ali raised his palms and smiled beatifically. He had anticipated doubters and was ready for them. "Oh, it is the real thing, my friends. Publicly the Americans deny it, but the other countries of the world know that they are lying. You see, America's poker-face has a 'tell'. When America mobilizes all three branches of her military, you know that she is bluffing. As of this morning I have received word from leaders around the world that they are more than willing to talk."

Another backer, an oil executive from Kuwait, was emboldened enough to ask. "But how? Europe, Asia and the Americans all swear they will never negotiate with terrorists."

"Ha! A purely public stance," Ali assured them. "No one believes in paying ransoms until they themselves become the hostage. The game is young, and yet we have already raised an obscene amount of money."

"Really?" asked Bob. "How obscene?"

Ali's chubby cheeks spread into a broad grin as he clicked to the next slide. "Seven-hundred-billion dollars." On the screen, the number in question swooped in for a landing while animated dollar signs jumped up and down enthusiastically.

A collective gasp drained the oxygen from the room. The only sound was that of the TV news commentators covering the riots. The exception was Fox News, which had taken a break from the mass burnings in Belgrade to run a commercial for Goldline. Gold had exploded in value since the crisis began. Buyers saw it as the only investment that might hold its value in a post planet Earth world. As Fox's Jim Cramer said on his show Mad Money, "Gold is the silver lining of the dark cloud that is Armageddon. Be prepared to make some serious moolah."

A wealthy Texan, known only as Tex, tentatively broke the silence. "Can we... have some?"

Ali laughed and patted his belly like a halal Santa Claus. "You can cash out anytime, my friend, if that's what you really want. Just download and print off the forms from our website. Meanwhile, eat, drink, enjoy!"

"Allah-u-Akbar!" shouted Karim. "Allah-u-Akbar! Allah-u-Akbar!" he continued in a vain attempt to rouse the crowd to chant. Instead, the attendees buzzed with delight at the thought of so much money. Nobody wanted to cash out. Ali listened for a moment to the excited rhubarb, then smiled with satisfaction. Deflated, Karim sank down in a sulk, brows knitted in a wool muff of frustration.

Minutes later, Ali mingled with a contingent of Russian billionaires who were admiring his 16K Subatomic Resolution HDTVs. "Prototypes," he explained, "able to show parts of the colour spectrum visible only to insects and certain types of birds. Simply marvellous! I can't even look at a 4K TV now. Samsung doesn't ship these until February, but I can get you one next week, if you like. We had them hung there so we can watch TV and face Mecca at the same time." The Russians walked over to examine the displays. Seeing his opportunity, Karim grabbed Ali's arm with alarm. "What about the hostages?" he demanded.

"What about them?" said Ali, instinctively raising his hand to shield himself from Karim's spitting.

"Did you negotiate for their release?"

"Of course, I... I mean, maybe... I mean... You know, Karim, I can't be expected to remember everything I did or did not negotiate. It's all being handled by Goldman Sachs anyway." Ali approached a table piled high with hamburgers. Karim followed so closely Ali cringed at the fanatic's smell. Saliva, b.o. and cumin breath, he rued, a perfect storm. "You should try these, Karim. We have them for the backers, but they're really very good and not at all Ḥarām."

"What about the pullout of foreign troops? The lowering of sanctions?"

"Karim, relax, and please go away. You're spitting on my food."

Karim opened his mouth to object, but Ali began loudly squirting catsup on his burger. Livid, Karim turned and, shoving aside a drunk Afghan warlord doing the Penguin Dance, he stormed from the room.

CHAPTER 23

"Nuclear weapons don't kill people, people kill people."
— K. Jong-un

Charlie sat uncomfortably in the wheelchair trying not to wince from the pain in his side. The White House staffer had taken them into the President's Personal Secretary's office to wait. Alex could barely contain himself. "This is awesome!" he said for the fourth time. He then pointed at the door to the Oval Office. "So the President of the United States is right through there?"

Judy, the President's Personal Secretary, nodded with a smile. Anywhere else in the country she would be given the title 'Administrative Assistant' for job such as this, but the White House was not given to change. Besides, it wasn't as if there was any lack of prestige in the position. Yes, she did have to bring her boss coffee, but her boss was the self-described 'leader of the free world'. Primarily, her job was to shield him from the constant barrage of requests for appointments and personal favours. Lately, that had extended to protecting the President from himself. It was Judy who, at the Chief of Staff's request, had been intercepting her boss's increasingly odd orders and proclamations. This was arguably illegal, but Hornswell had assured her that he would take responsibility if it ever came to light. The President had been inexplicably morose since the success of the mission in Dubai. His poems, for the most part, had ceased. This morning's missive, written on a sticky note, was largely stolen from Jim Morrison.

> *This is the end,*
> *My only friend, the end.*
> *I call him Phil.*

"This is so freakin' awesome!" said Alex.

"It is exciting to meet the President," Charlie agreed. It was exciting for him as well, but he found himself taking more pleasure from Alex's anticipation than his own. He knew the feeling. It was the same feeling he'd felt watching Faith jump up and down while waiting to see Santa Claus. He knew he had no right to see Alex as his son, but it seemed that the feeling was somewhat mutual. Alex would never replace his daughter, nor would he replace Alex's mum but, still, they both needed family. So what was the harm?

"I'm sorry, but the President needs a few more minutes," said Judy.

"No problem," said Charlie.

Alex, unable to remain seated, went over to admire the painting of the Statue of Liberty that hung beside Judy's desk.

"It was a gift from France," said Charlie.

"The painting?"

"The statue."

"Some guy on TV said we saved their asses in World War II."

"They saved us in the American Revolution."

"Oh."

"That's history for you. What comes around, goes around."

* * *

The President was not in the Oval Office—that had been a lie. Lying was part of the President's Personal Secretary's job. Most of these were white lies, but many came in varying shades of grey. The President was on the ground floor in the Situation Room once again, literally biting his nails. Intelligence had unearthed the possibility that Mathias Boltzmann might still be in possession of the original Loose Thread canister. The lead came from an informant attending a lavish party at the arms dealer's mansion outside of Munich. He had reported that a close confidant of Boltzmann, an American citizen named Carl Weiss, had blabbered while in a drunken stupor. Weiss had insisted that Boltzmann had secretly made several copies of the device, intending to sell the fakes and keep the original for himself. Weiss, confessed, amid snivelling sobs, that he himself had "mixed them up" and that Ali Madda might actually have the real one. "Stupid! Stupid! Stupid!" he'd sobbed, while banging his head on a dresser. He then went on at length about how he had "failed his friend", was "pathetic" and "a poor excuse for an Aryan." Bizarrely, he then agreed to lead the informant and several other curious guests, down to Boltzmann's private office to which he knew the key code. There, they found a half-a-dozen identical canisters in a row on a shelf. Intoxicated as he was, Weiss then announced that he wanted to open up all of the canisters to "see if they were real." At that point the informant and the other partygoers were forced to restrain Weiss as he began furiously unscrewing lids. This, apparently, tripped a silent alarm and Boltzmann's guards arrived to escort them all out. Boltzmann himself appeared at that point and explained that the canisters were not weapons at all, but rather humanitarian awards he'd received for several years running. Any resemblance to Ali Madda's device, he said, was "purely coincidental." He dismissed Carl Weiss's claims as the "ridiculous ramblings of a drunk." The informant, however, insisted that the canisters were identical in every detail to Loose Thread. Even if there was only the slightest chance that the real thing was in Boltzmann's possession, there was no option but to go in and get it.

So now, here they were; The President of the United States; Jim Hornswell, his Chief of Staff; Sarah Maxwell, the Secretary of State; Joint Chiefs Commander, General Troy, and CIA Director, Robert Morely. All were huddled closely in the projection room staring at a live satellite view of Germany. The President, having missed lunch, had ordered bags of popcorn brought up from the White House kitchen. Morely, who was attempting to quit chewing tobacco, impulsively shoved fistfuls into his mouth.

"Excellent," said Sarah into her cellphone. She paused to listen, then replied, "Well, as we agreed, the allies need only understand that the weapon is real but that, thankfully, we have the means to stop Ali Madda from using it... Okay... Yes.... That's easy, just tell the ambassador that we would like to protect them, but we're just not sure we can protect everyone... Correct, that's when you mention the changes we want in the trade agreement... It's not a threat. It's a realistic analysis of a critical situation over which we don't have complete control and must exercise our natural inclination to offer protection first to those with mutually beneficial economic interests. He'll understand... Perfect... No need, I'll brief the President myself... Yes, briefly." With that Sarah hung up the phone and smiled, not at the President, who was lost in his own world, but at Jim. The Secretary of State and Chief of Staff had always had a rocky, competitive relationship. Somehow, however, since the crisis had begun, that relationship had pivoted. In an after-hours meeting in the Roosevelt Room, in the midst of an argument over the relative merits of chemical weapons research, their eyes had met and they truly saw each other for the first time. In that magical moment, they'd realized that they shared a special connection. Since the impending Armageddon, they had moved to consummate that connection several times in the West Wing, including once in the Oval Office, on the President's desk. It was hardly the first time that someone had sex on that particular piece of furniture, but that was usually a privilege reserved for the President himself. This President, however, for all of his flaws, was faithful and quite possibly sexless. The First Lady was not, having found comfort in the arms of her Secret Service detail. Sordid rumours aside, Sarah and Jim had found what they believed was true love—love of politics, love of power, and, quite possibly, love of one another.

Jim smiled back. He then turned to Morely and said, "So, Bob, are we good to go?"

The CIA Director, who had just crammed another handful of popcorn into his mouth, began to choke. Desperate, he grabbed a bottled water and gulped it back, The others waited. Finally able to talk, Morely spat soggy kernels as he spoke. "We're good to go. US Intelligence units are positioned around Mathias Boltzmann's estate along with the German police.

Seeing as he is an arms dealer, we're ready for anything. By which I mean, guns."

"Alrighty then."

General Troy turned to wave at the AV operator, "Zoom in!"

On screen, the satellite image flew past clouds to offer a direct overhead view of Mathias Boltzmann's estate. Mathias owned a multitude of luxury properties around the globe. These included a Scottish castle, a private island in the Caribbean, an estate in Africa and a three bedroom apartment in New York City. His home in Munich, however, was his original home. As such, it was simply a large, well appointed mansion in an upscale neighbourhood. It was not without amenities, however, including a swimming pool, tennis courts and a private helipad. All of these were now in plain view on the Situation Room projection screen. Also in plain view were three figures sitting on deck chairs on the backyard patio. A fourth man, presumably a guard, stood against the wall of the house.

Morely explained, "Our on-the-ground recon tells us that Boltzmann is in the deck-chair on the left while his primary financial partner—"

"What the Hell is going on next door?" asked Jim.

"Language!" objected the President, demonstrating for the first time in several minutes that he was awake.

They all peered at the screen to better see what was happening on the other side of the wall separating Boltzman's yard from his neighbour's. The overhead perspective and distance made the details blurry, but there was no mistaking the bountiful flesh romping gleefully about the neighbour's garden.

"Are they naked?" asked General Troy incredulously.

Morely explained, "Intelligence indicates that Boltzmann's

neighbours like to engage in, uh... free spirit social gatherings.'"

"There must be fifteen people there!" said the Secretary of State.

"Yes, well, it is Germany."

For a moment they all stared at the screen, briefly forgetting why they were there.

"It looks like they're f-f-f..." Sarah caught the President's disapproving glare, "frolicking?"

"They're fornicating," snapped the President with disgust, "Truly these are the days of Saddam and Gomorrah!"

"I believe it's Sodom, not..." Jim also caught the Commander-in-Chief's withering gaze and fell silent. Sarah had been teaching him to know better when to shut-up.

"They have been particularly, um, frisky, since the whole end-of-the-world thing started, " Morely added. "Day and night really."

"Okay then," said Jim snapping back into focus, "we're about to give them a cold shower like no other. Right, Mr. President?"

The President nodded and gave the codeword as he remembered it. "Go Hotdog!"

Sarah relayed the order into her phone, "Commence Operation Frankfurt."

Instantly, an army of police appeared on screen. They leaped from cars, parked vans, and nearby houses. An army of officers scaled walls into the neighbour's yard en route to the primary target. Chaos erupted in the garden of earthly delights, as naked people ran shrieking in panic amid a militarized force that was, in fact, just passing through.

* * *

Chaos Theory

Mathias Boltzmann, Carl Weiss and Philippe Vandross sipped mojitos on the back patio. They squinted in the afternoon sun and savoured the sweetness of the icy cold drinks. Carl still squirmed inside when he thought of the events at the party three days prior. He had apologized profusely to his friend for his bizarre behaviour. Fortunately, Mathias had not heard everything. He'd missed the part where Carl had confessed to mixing up the canisters. If Mathias learned that, Carl knew, he'd never be welcome here again. He didn't put it beyond the realm of possibility that Mathias might even have him killed. He felt sick at the thought of it all. On the other side of Mathias, Philippe slurped loudly on his straw. He then accidentally inhaled a clump of muddled mint, and began to cough. Philippe was an effete aristocrat from Amsterdam with white-blond hair and translucent skin. He'd inherited "more money than God" and liked to dabble in the arms trade as "something to do". He didn't actually like to get his hands dirty, so he invested only indirectly in Boltzmann's string of shadow companies. Carl couldn't stand Philippe, but was hardly in a position to complain given his own recent behaviour. Still, he smirked at the thought that, even if Philippe did get his hands dirty, he could simply send them out to be cleaned. Both of the dutchman's hands were flesh-coloured plastic prosthetics. Philippe, a man of many affectations, was an 'uber foodie'. This meant he was no longer content with merely exotic or strange cuisine, but lived in the world of 'culinary relativism'. As such, he belonged to a unique group of fellow enthusiasts called the Ouroboros Club. Members of the elite and secretive club embraced the notion that eating human flesh was the ultimate taboo to be broken. Cannibalism, after all, had been widely accepted in many cultures and who were we to judge? Some argued that it should be counted as part of the 'paleo diet'. Ouroboros Club members carried this idea one step further, to eating *themselves*. Of course, even this wasn't entirely new. After all, placentophagy had been embraced by the celebrity set in Hollywood for years. This meant the group, in pursuit of true sophistication, had to go one step further and engage in the long term goal of eating themselves in their own entirety. Such self-indulgence presented a variety of challenges, however, even for the absurdly affluent. These culminated with the problem of literally dying of consumption. Club Members, therefore, strove for the next best thing—they would all eat each other. The idea was that, if you are what you eat, then you could blur the notion of yourself and others through 'mutually assured digestion'. Since its inception, over a half-dozen members had been served. Others were in process, having lost their soles to soul food, their scalps to scaloppine or, as in Philippe's case, his fingers to finger food. It was only when an outbreak of spongiform encephalopathy struck several members that the diners' club was forcibly dissolved. Collective cannibalism may be avant-garde, but mad cow disease was not. As a result, Philippe had retreated to a more pedestrian diet of near extinct animals. It wasn't as exciting as eating oneself, but somewhat more sustainable.

"Do you hear thumsing?" said Philippe.

"No," said Carl.

"Hmm..." said Philippe, as he did when he felt he knew better. He then lifted his glass to drink, only to have it flip and spill in his lap. His cutting edge prosthetic hands had cost upwards of a million dollars. They were agile enough to play piano and could transmit synthesized tactile senses to his brain. Despite this, a design flaw in the wrist pins caused the hands to spin freely at the most inconvenient moments. "Oh dwat!" shouted Philippe, brushing crushed ice and mint leaves from his pants. "Dwat! Dwat!

Dwat!"

"Philippe is right," said Mathias, "I hear something too..."

"It's just the neighbours," chuckled Carl. "They've been at it all morning!"

"No," said Mathias with a look of genuine alarm, "it's not."

Shouts and screams sounded from behind the neighbour's hedge. All at once, police officers and german shepherd dogs were clambering over the garden walls. A black police helicopter loomed overhead, creating a maelstrom of leaves, cocktail napkins, and detritus. Instantly, dozens of red laser-sight dots danced on the chests of the three men. The guard standing against the wall behind them, in an admirable act of fealty coupled with a woeful lack of risk assessment, drew his weapon. He was shot fifteen times before hitting the ground.

Philippe leapt from his seat in panic. "Oh! Oh! Oh!" he yelled. At that moment, the pin in his other plastic wrist gave out and both of his hands began to spin in the turbulence of the hovering helicopter like twin propellers on a plane.

"This is the police!" shouted a voice in German over a megaphone. "Get down on your knees with your hands behind your heads!"

In his eagerness to comply, Philippe threw his hands up into the air. Unfortunately, this turned out literally to be the case, as one of his hands flew off, then fell back down and punched him in the head. He collapsed unconscious to the ground. The sight was so startling, so unexpected that, for a moment, nobody did anything at all.

"This is the police!" the megaphone repeated, "Get down on your knees with your hands behind your heads!"

"I'm an American!" shouted Carl.

For several seconds, the helicopter simply hovered. The only sound was the *whup! whup! whup!* of the propeller blades. Finally, a voice came over the megaphone once more, this time in English. "This is the police. Get down on your knees with your hands behind your heads!"

Carl, realizing it was time to bring in the lawyers, knelt on the ground.

Mathias abruptly turned and ran into the house. In that moment, in the whirling chaos, he'd surmised that the police would have orders not to kill him. He was right.

Mathias stormed into the main hallway of the house to find Colonel Rynard Gruber rallying his men. The large house contained a garrison of a dozen mercenaries as well as the Colonel, who alone counted as a dozen more. Gruber buttoned his kevlar vest and shouted at his men, "They are the weak—the puppets of the state! We kill them or die trying!" With several spare belts of ammunition slung over his muscular shoulders, the mercenary heaved up an enormous Dillon M134 Gatling gun. Colonel Rynard Gruber then paused to light a cigarillo with a skull head lighter, licked his lips and whispered "Endlich." He did so with a smile, as if he'd been waiting for this moment his whole life—which, in fact, he had.

CHAPTER 24

"Nacht, nacht. Who's there?" – S. Freud

Sankt Herman Catholic School, East Berlin, Germany, 1977

"Sit up straight!" the nun snapped, cracking a metre stick across Rynard Gruber's fingers as they lay upon his school desk. The edge of the ruler split the skin across his knuckles. His instinct was to put them to his mouth, but he would not give Sister Ophelia the satisfaction. It was not the first time the twelve year-old boy had had his knuckles rapped, nor would it be the last. The nun glared at him with rapier eyes, expecting him to cry. Rynard stared blankly ahead. He could feel her eyes burning into his skull. He would not goad her, but he would not grovel either. After a long moment of silence, Sister Ophelia moved on. The other boys in the classroom smirked and snickered, but Rynard would not acknowledge them either.

They called him 'freak', but for the most part they left him alone. If the latter required the former, than Rynard was fine with it.

"Fractions and percentiles," said the nun as she approached the front of the class. "If seventy-five percent of the people in this class are dummkopfs, then how many dummkopfs are there in this class?" She spun about and glared at the room, as if daring someone to answer. There were no volunteers. "Perhaps Herr Gruber would like to redeem himself in the eyes of The Lord?"

Rynard considered this coldly. He knew there was no redemption. He wasn't even sure if answering correctly was better or worse than getting it wrong. "That depends..." he said.

"On what exactly?"

"On whether or not 'this class' includes you, Sister."

* * *

Rynard walked home along The Wall, still smarting from the belt marks on his back. He smiled. This sort of pain pleased him. Not in a strange, creepy way like his Uncle Rudolph, but in the sense of satisfaction that it gave him. He hated the nuns at his school, and he revelled in every small frustration they felt, even when it cost him in terms of bruises or blood. The school was allowed to function only by the grace of STASI officials who were, themselves, closet Catholics. As he walked, Rynard gazed up at the soldiers patrolling the crumbling barrier that divided east from west. Graffiti covered almost every inch except where the surface concrete had fallen away. The wall would stand forever, they said, but it was hard to believe the structure could last another ten years. Rynard's eyes were for the soldiers themselves atop the grey barricade. He had to squint to see them silhouetted against the setting sun. To him, their uniforms and glinting weapons represented the infinite army. "There will always be war," his father had told him, "and therefore there will always be soldiers, no matter what the side, no matter what the country. Hitler, Stalin, Brezhnev? Leaders come and go, and causes are just fictions they create to get their men marching in the same direction." The boys in school had cast doubt on whether Herr Gruber was Rynard's real father. The boy was already tall and ruggedly handsome, while his father had been described as "nasty, brutish and short." They began a rumour that Rynard's mother had slept with Satan and that Rynard was the devil's bastard. Before Rynard could ask him about this, Herr Gruber was squashed flat by a reversing tank during manoeuvres along the river Elbe. His last words were, "What are those idiots shouting and waving their arms for?" As per his instructions, his ashes were flushed down the toilet.

Young Rynard arrived home and ran inside. He ignored his mother's shouts from the kitchen and headed straight upstairs. Ostensibly the family subsisted off his father's military pension and his mother's job as a music teacher. His mother, however, had found a magical way to earn extra income and address her chronic nymphomania at the same time. It consisted of bringing strange men back to the house each night and waking up the next day a hundred marks richer. Rynard found it disconcerting that so many of her clients were soldiers like his father. When he complained about her nightly activities, or "Eine kleine Nachtmusik" as she liked to call it, she told him "don't believe the communists, darling, even in East Berlin, money makes the world go 'round." She insisted that her moonlighting paid for his education and put extra food on the table. Rynard loathed her all the more for this pretence of virtue. In his eyes, she was a whore who deserved to burn in Hell, assuming Hell was real and somehow worse than East Berlin.

Upstairs, by contrast, was Heaven. Rynard's older sister, Anna, was an angel. She was deeply pious, yet abhorrent to judge others. In this way, she seemed the direct opposite of the nuns at his school. In his eyes, it made her beautiful both inside and out. She refused even to judge their mother, which Rynard struggled to understand. Anna sat on her bed, her long blond hair in meticulous braids. She sat, as she always did, cross-legged to conceal the club foot she'd been born with. "Did you have a good day at school, Bärli?" she asked him. Bärli was Anna's nickname for Rynard since, when was very young, he used to growl like a 'little bear'.

"What do you think?" he said, sitting cross legged on the oval rug at the foot of her bed. He fought the urge to light up a cigarette knowing Anna didn't like it. "Children shouldn't smoke," she'd say.

Anna looked up from her needlepoint and embraced him with that bathwater warm smile she had. "You know they just want to teach you."

"They just want to beat me, you mean," he said, "and they do." With that he lifted his shirt enough for her to see the purple welts across his ribs.

Anna winced. "Did you do something to make them mad?"

"Sure, I refused to crawl in the dirt and kiss their feet."

"I don't imagine that's exactly what they asked you to do, Bärli."

Rynard shrugged and helped himself to the remains of schnecken left on a plate on her dresser. The nuns had withheld his lunch, so the cinnamon roll tasted delicious despite being slightly stale.

"You know, life could be a little easier for you if you didn't insist on fighting everyone."

"I don't care," he mumbled with his mouth full, "I really don't. There are only two things I've ever cared about in this world. One of those things was Papa. The other is you. The rest of the world can go to Hell."

"Rynard, please!"

Rynard flushed, "I'm sorry, Anna. I get... frustrated."

"Well, that's no reason to use that word. And as for what you were saying, you simply need to find things to care about. The world is full of beauty."

"We live in East Berlin."

"Nevertheless." Anna reached down and stroked his cheek. The startling warmth of her touch defrosted his disposition. "Don't let your heart turn to stone, Bärli."

Rynard rolled his eyes and tossed back the final bite of pastry.

"Promise me," she said sternly.

Rynard saw then how serious his sister was and swallowed. He looked into her eyes, nodded earnestly, and gave his word.

* * *

The following day, Rynard's unwilling penance continued. All of the nuns chided him and pushed him to break. Throughout it, he held his tongue, determined not to give them an excuse to punish him further. They didn't need one. He was kept after school without explanation, and forced to work with Father Klauss, proofing pages for his new Papal Dictionary. Klauss, a former Vatican scholar, had amassed copies of every document ever written by Popes that contained a misspelled word or typo. The priest's assertion was that, since the Pope was infallible, ipso facto, these could not be errors. They must, therefore, be documented as legitimate new spellings of these words ordained by God himself. Most of these typos, of course, were in Italian and Latin, as put fourth in Klauss's initial thesis *Eradoom X-libris*

Addendumb. Since, however, the Popes were often required to speak in unfamiliar tongues, this meant the Holy Fathers often transubstantiated words in those languages as well. This resulted in a series of articles published in the theological journal *Cummunio*, including *Holy Rightings: Papal Spelinks of Englich Frases and Wrods*. The priest saw his work as a sacred labour. Rynard Gruber did not. He resented his detention as well as Father Klauss himself. The obese clergyman smelled of tea tree oil and sacramental wine and had no hesitation in putting the school children to work on his new *Vadigan Too Digshunary*. Still, Rynard thought, at least, unlike Futher Braun, he keeps his hands to himself.

Father Klauss was particularly inspired that evening, having recently discovered that, by implied Papal decree, the English words *there, their* and *they're,* were, in fact, interchangeable. He was devoting an entire chapter to the subject and required Rynard to search out as many supporting instances as possible. By the time the boy was permitted to leave, it was growing dark. Before Rynard reached home, night had fallen. He entered by the backdoor and headed upstairs to see his sister. "She's not home!" his mother yelled from the kitchen.

"Where is she?" he asked.

"Church."

Rynard's heart sank. He felt that it was his job to escort Anna to evening mass. This was not only for safety's sake, but also because he enjoyed it. Missing this, he decided, was his real punishment. Still, he thought, at least I can walk her home. Without a word, he ran out into the night.

Rynard jogged along the main road which was now lit by regularly spaced street lights. He soon reached St. Eunich's Cathedral. All three sets of doors were flung wide with the end of the evening service, casting a trinity of light beams onto the cobblestone street. Most of the worshippers had already left, although a few still mingled. There was no sign of Anna. Rynard recognized a teenage girl named Elsi, who knew Anna, and approached her. As he did so, he assumed the pretence of shy insecurity he used to make adults feel more at ease. "Fraulein Elsi?" he asked.

"Why hello Herr Gruber," she said with a laugh.

"Have you see my sister?"

"She left a long time ago," said Elsi. "She never stays to chat. You should tell your sister to be more sociable."

Rynard nodded. He knew this. Anna regarded mass as a time for spiritual kinship with God, not gossip.

"You're getting to be quite big, Rynard," said Elsi. "Soon you'll be a man."

Rynard ignored her, turned and headed for home. Since he hadn't seen Anna on the way there, she must have taken the north road. From what Elsi had said, Anna had a good start, but her crippled foot meant she moved more slowly. Rynard was certain he could catch her.

The north road was a longer, darker route. Despite her difficulties walking, Rynard knew why Anna chose to take it sometimes. She enjoyed the bit along the river where the moon made the water sparkle. She thought it was beautiful. Anna could always find beauty in even the darkest path. As he walked briskly along the winding streets, snow began to fall for the first time that December. Rynard barely noticed. River or no, he couldn't imagine what would possess his sister to go that way, alone at night. He was wondering that still, when he passed the alleyway and heard a girl's whimper. He listened for a moment as the blood froze in his veins. Filled with ice, he plunged into the black abyss between the buildings. For a moment he could see nothing then, with heart-stopping horror, he spotted his sister's unmistakable foot.

The man had offered to walk Anna home. It was not the first time. He'd escorted her safely the night before, although she'd told no one. He'd expressed the desire to come in. She said 'no', that she was not that kind of girl. He asked her whether he could walk her home the following night as well, and she'd replied, "Yes". Despite his impropriety, she couldn't help herself. He was so handsome and charming and he didn't seem to care about her unfortunate foot. That night, as they passed the pitch black alleyway, he shoved her inside. In the dark his five friends were waiting. He had his way with her, followed by each of the other men. When they left her, they left her for dead, crumpled on the cobbles, strangled with her own rosary.

At the hospital Rynard sat beside his sister's bed, along with his mother, in numb, naked silence. For all their brutality the men had somehow fallen short of murder, at least in the legal sense. His sister was, for now, alive. She was, however, hemorrhaging internally and would die soon enough without expert intervention. Fortunately, the doctors told them, there was such an expert. Dr. Zufällig was on his way from Potsdam and would most certainly be able to help when he arrived in the morning. "Thank God," said Rynard's mother, crossing herself for the first time Rynard could remember.

They waited all through the night. Outside, the first flurries of winter gathered strength and began to blanket the earth, Rynard held his sister's hand, noticing how cold it felt and how, by morning, it had begun to quake gently. In the morning light he could see the deep drifts of snow that had formed in the dark. When he saw the look in the doctor's face, he knew what the physician was going to say. "I'm afraid the blizzard has made the roads impassable. Dr. Zufällig's unable to get through. I'm sorry, there's nothing we can do. It is an act of God."

Later that morning, Anna quietly slipped away. She never said anything, or even woke up. He so desperately wanted her to open her eyes and call him "Bärli" one last time. Instead, just once, she squeezed her brother's hand, held it tightly for a moment, then released it forever. The boy knew it was more likely a death spasm than any last conscious act. Rynard stood up with calm deliberation. He bent over and lovingly tucked in Anna's blankets, as if she were simply sleeping. He then kissed her gently on the forehead and said, "I'm sorry, Anna, I cannot keep my promise."

The twelve-year-old boy then turned and, without acknowledging his sobbing mother, headed out into the frozen world, never to return home again.

CHAPTER 25

"You make me want to be a better person."
 — A. Hitler (to E. Braun)

Mathias Boltzmann's Estate, Munich, Germany, Today.

Rynard Gruber's grey crewcut was spiked with sweat into a buzz-saw blade as he unleashed round after round at the rear doors of the house. Finally, he released the trigger and let the rotating gun barrel spin itself out. The back wall of the hall was nearly disintegrated with bullet holes. The doors themselves were shredded to sawdust and every pane of glass was reduced to powder. The air was thick with gun smoke and the pungent reek of gore. Just inside the doors, were the crumpled corpses of a half-dozen German police officers. They lay in a swelling pond of blood that flooded the floor and ran in rivulets between the tiles. In his enthusiasm, Rynard had reduced several of the invaders to pulp. He panted, wiped the perspiration from his brow, and calmly awaited the next wave. It was work, but it was good work. Beside him, two of his men simply gawked at the Colonel as if in the presence of some primordial god. To them, Rynard had become death, destroyer of worlds, and they loved him for it.

* * *

In the White House Situation Room, the atmosphere was tense. Every eye was fixed on the projection screen where police, paramedics and naked people ran amok on a well-tended lawn half a world away. While they couldn't see inside the structure, clearly resistance was fierce with reports of several officers down. Still, General Troy insisted, it was just a matter of time. His was an 'old school' strategy, employed by army ants and perfected by the generals of World War I. The idea was to simply throw wave after wave of bodies on the pile and, eventually, the side with the most to lose wins. To that end, a small army of German Landespolizei were on hand. There was also a busload of US operatives, as backup. The Americans weren't supposed to be needed. Now, however, reports were suggesting that while the strategy of shock and awe was working, it was working in the wrong direction.

"Gummy bear?" asked General Troy, offering bag full of bright coloured candies to the Secretary of State.

Jim moved to take one, then hesitated. "Where are all the red ones?"

General Troy looked somewhat embarrassed. "I ate them," he said. "They're my favourite."

"Never mind then," said Jim, waving the bag away.

"The black ones are good."

"I hate them. I hate liquorice."

"Oh. Orange?"

"We're done here."

General Troy hung his head in defeat.

"The President likes liquorice," Bob suggested, his teeth full of popcorn.

"Ah..." said Sarah, glancing about, "where *is* the President?"

The men looked around the room. Jim went so far as to steal a glance under the table. The President, unnoticed by anyone, had simply slipped away. His Secret Service detail, who had also been enthralled by the on-screen action, whispered hurriedly into their lapel mics. "The President is back in the Oval Office, sir," one of the agents reported, hoping to make it sound as if he'd known this all along.

"Then why aren't you?" asked Jim pointedly.

"Um..."

"Never mind, we'll all go up together." Jim turned to Robert Morely and asked, "Do we know how this ends?"

"We always do, Jim."

"Good."

The Secretary of State stormed from the room flanked by the two somewhat sheepish Secret Service agents. His fear was that the President had actually nodded off and wandered away. The President had been prescribed Ambian, months before, to help him sleep. Jim's theory was that the drug explained much of the Commander-in-Chief's peculiar behaviour since then. He first considered this when noticing that the President's poetry and other missives always seemed to be left on his secretary's desk between three and four in the morning. Clearly the President was sleep walking, sleep writing and even making sleep phone calls, including one to the President of

Georgia, asking him to change the country's name to something "less confusing". It certainly explained the poems that read as if written by someone else. Jim himself had been in several meetings with the President, only to suspect twenty minutes in that his boss was actually asleep. The fact that his eyes were open and he was capable of carrying on a conversation made it difficult to be sure. The President seemed confused by it as well, and Jim had noticed him pinching himself at times as if checking. The Chief of Staff had tried to get the President to stop taking the drug, warning him that he might be a "somnambulist". The President told Jim to stop talking gibberish, declaring, "I don't know the meaning of the word!" Jim had little doubt that this was true.

As they marched down the hall, The Chief of Staff received an encrypted text message on his phone. American Carl Weiss had been arrested at the scene. Damn it, thought Jim. Weiss was a major campaign contributor. They had been hoping that the businessman would simply be shot. It would be so much cleaner, he thought, now there will be questions to answer. Weiss was too prominent to just disappear into a black site in Bucharest. Jim's phone chirped again. A prominent Dutch businessman had apparently been shot dead after grabbing the ankle of one of the arresting officers, this despite being several feet away at the time. Jim frowned at the confusing account, but decided to ignore it. He had more important things to worry about.

* * *

The party was over at the Azylum Mahall. Most of the guests had departed by limousine, helicopter, or private jet, while others had taken advantage of Ali Madda's offer to 'crash'. "Friends don't let friends drink and jihad," he said, imploring them to stay in one of the palace's seventy-two bedrooms. The palace was so large, it might be days before some of them would be seen again.

As the sunrise seeped over the horizon, Ali Madda, three fellow terrorists, and three foreign backers were the only ones left in the party room. Technically there was one more, a Syrian passed out under a sofa whom no one seemed to know and no one wanted to touch as he'd vomited down his front. The seven stragglers sat in a lounge area in front of one of the big screen TVs, sipping beverages and snacking on pita chips. Ali himself was sucking on a Cuban cigar with one hand, while cradling a glass of warmed cognac in the other. He was wearing a Texas Rangers baseball cap that belonged to Dallas oilman Howard Crawford. Howard was slumped in a nearby armchair, in a state of alcohol induced slumber. He was wearing Madda's keffiyeh backwards on his head, so that the cloth covered his face and fluttered each time the fat man snored. The Texas tycoon suffered from sleep apnea and would occasionally stop breathing for seconds at a time before resuming with a loud snort. Howard had initially joined Ali Madda's cause for his own ideological purposes. He believed that America needed an existential threat to remain strong and ready. Since joining, however, he and Ali had found they shared much in common and had become fast friends. He'd even promised to introduce Ali to the Koch brothers, believing they'd also "hit it off like gangbusters." For now, Ali and the others bathed in a warm tidal pool of self-satisfaction. "I think..." Ali announced, "I think I will buy England."

A grey haired Russian snorted derisively. "I'd rather own Yugoslavia," he said, "or whatever the stupid Yugos are calling it now-a-days." As he spoke, he sloshed a glass of vodka about, spilling it down his sleeve.

"England? Why England?" asked an Iraqi warlord. "The reason the English built the empire was to get the hell out of England. It rains there all the time! Trust me, I grew up in London."

"He has a point," the Russian nodded, "Why else would someone want to conquer Iraq?"

Madda shrugged and tasted the cognac with his tongue. "I miss England. I suppose you could call it nostalgia for my college years, sipping bitter in the local pub, chanting death to America over a basket of fish & chips... It was a good time, a time of dreams, foolish, ideal dreams."

"My head is really starting to hurt," moaned Ali #2, one of Ali Madda's many sons. "You really shouldn't mix arak and wine... especially in the same glass."

"Well, I'm from England," argued a British backer from Bristol whose name Ali had forgotten. "And I wouldn't live there. If it's an island you want, I recommend Tahiti. Lovely girls there, beaches... It's bloody brilliant."

"If it's girls you want... " began the Russian. He then trailed off. He'd been trying to pat down his vodka soaked arm, whilst holding a cigarette between his fingers. Consequently, he'd managed to set fire to his sleeve. In a panic for something to extinguish the flames, he'd reached for a nearby bottle of Stolichnaya vodka. One of the other terrorists grabbed his arm before he could self-immolate, suggesting he use a seltzer bottle instead. "Thank-you!" said the Russian, shaking his head with amusement, "I would have been pretty red-faced, had I—"

"What the Hell?" shouted Ali, sitting up in his chair and pointing anxiously at one of the ultra HD TVs. On screen was Karim flanked by masked jihadists. They were holding what appeared to be a press conference. Karim was speaking, but the television was on mute. Ali rifled through a coffee table drawer filled with remotes. "DVD player... VHS... lights... ah ha!" He clicked a button. Outside the lawn sprinklers started up. "God Damn it!"

"Is that it, old fellow?" asked the Englishman, pointing under Ali's chair.

The terrorist leader snarled, retrieved the remote and tapped the volume button.

"... our great leader, Ali Madda, has lost his way," said Karim, shaking his head sadly. "This is the problem of western evil. It corrupts all who touch it. In the end, evil cannot be redeemed, it must be destroyed. Fortunately, Allah has blessed us with the means to do so." With that Karim reached beneath his robes and withdrew a shiny steel canister. "Allahu Akbar!" he said.

Ali stared in shock. "Is that...?" He reached for another remote and entered his secret code, "1 2 3 4". This caused a hidden panel in the wall to rise up, revealing an empty velvet pedestal in the alcove within. "God damn It!" he swore, flinging the remote against the wall and inadvertently changing the channel to *The Real Housewives of Bucharest*. "That... lunatic!"

"He couldn't... well, I mean, he wouldn't really... would he?" asked the Englishman.

"You don't know Karim," moaned Ali, putting his face into his hands.

"Can we watch something else?" whined the Russian. "I've seen this one already."

Chaos Theory

* * *

Charlie and Alex sat silently in the President's Personal Secretary's office. It had been a half-hour, and the initial excitement had since faded. Now both began to wonder what the holdup was. Still, it didn't seem right to complain when the President of the United States keeps you waiting, so they continued to sit. Charlie was now on page thirty-two of a New Yorker article on the history of melba toast. The article was so engrossing that he failed to notice when Judy stepped out and Alex snuck a memo from the stack of papers on her desk. The letterhead indicated that it had come from the desk of the President himself. The content of the letter, however, made that hard to believe. It was a poem, and the margin was full of bad ballpoint pen drawings of tanks being bombed by airplanes.

The Worm
by the President of the United States

The Gecko walked along the road,
And complained of great regret.
His companion, the ancient Tortoise,
Recalled how he could n'er forget,
And so they wandered in the darkness
Long after the sun had set.

The Gecko told a wistful tale
Of the many tails he'd lost.
The Tortoise babbled on forever,

For, to him, time bore no cost.
"The further we go, the further we are
From the many men we've crossed."

They chanced upon an old Potato,
Just sitting in the road,
Its eyes were blind as blind could be,
And it spoke an odious ode.
"I am a spud of science" it said,
"And I've solved the secret code."

"I've run a small experiment
Of seeing what I can see
And through the power of observation,
Deduced you two simply cannot be.
Now I know that may be hard to hear
But it's advice I give for free"

I exist," cried the Tortoise,
"Always have and always will.
You see I am immortal,
In a thousand years I'll be here still!"
"I done the math," sneered the root insipidly.
"The odds of that (rounded up) are nil"

"I exist even more," declared the Gecko,
For he truly felt that this was true.

Chaos Theory

"Chop me up in tiny pieces,
And make me into stew
I'll simple grow myself back,
All without a drop of glue."

"We hate you, oh Potato,
For what you've said of us is lies."
They decided then to eat him,
Whipped, mashed or chopped as fries,
But first they chortled with delight
And plucked out all his eyes.

The Potato then cried out for real,
About this dreadful dream.
In the end they chose to bake him,
Served with a side of sour cream
"You did this to yourself," they said,
As he began to scream.

The two friends then tucked in their bibs
And carved up the little bloke
The Tortoise took an enormous bite
But then he began to choke.
The Gecko found he was allergic,
And proceeded there to croak.

The Gecko breathed his final breath

Then fell upon the ground
The Tortoise sank into his shell,
Never more to make a sound
So none could greet the Worm that came
To feed on what he'd found.

What a stupid poem, thought Alex. He decided it must have been written by a small child, perhaps a nephew or niece of the President. Alex knew the President, himself, was childless. It had been an issue in the campaign.

He was still wondering when a commotion sounded in the hallway. All at once, Judy, along with a television news crew, crushed through the doorway into the small office. Alex realized he'd stepped too far from the desk and was forced to stuff the poem into his pocket. Charlie and Alex both stared with surprise. "Is that...?" Alex asked. Charlie nodded. They'd both instantly recognized Chuck Todd, Chief White House Correspondent for NBC News. Chuck looked at them as well, trying to decide if they were involved in or incidental to the reason he was here. Since Chuck hadn't actually been told why he was here, he realized he'd have to figure this out later. The news crew consisted of a cameraman and his assistant. Both were currently testing their signal for what was going to be a live broadcast. "Test... test... test," the assistant said into a microphone.

"Peter picked a peck of pickled peppers," said Chuck, trying to wake up his tongue.

"Test... test... test."

"Sally sells seashells by the seashore."

"Test... test... test."

"Eustence euthanizes eunuchs by the eucalyptus tree."

The cameraman gave a thumbs up.

Judy picked up her desk phone. "Chuck Todd from NBC News is here, Mr. President... Yes, sir, and Charles Draper and Alex Graham... Yes, sir." Judy hung up the phone and walked between them to open the door to the Oval Office. "You can go in now."

"All of us?" asked Charlie.

"Yes," said Judy.

"Who are they?" asked Chuck. Before anyone could answer, they were all in the Oval Office, live on national television. The question, for now, was forgotten.

The President was sitting behind his desk looking like a bewildered hermit. His beard was down to his belt now, its end tied with a baby blue bow. He was wearing what appeared to be some sort of Hebraic robe. In all of his years reporting on Washington, Chuck Todd had met several Presidents and seen his share of scandals. Nothing, however, could prepare him for this. For a moment, any questions or even intelligible words were simply obliterated from his brain. NBC News Anchor Lester Holt's questions in his earpiece failed to register. "Um, uh...Chuck Todd... reporting from the Oval Office?" It shouldn't have been a question, but somehow it was. "Mr. President?" Again, a question.

"Is that the Duke Norman guy?" the assistant asked. Chuck's assistant wasn't supposed to speak on air.

"It is indeed," proclaimed the President. Despite his bizarre appearance, he still possessed the deep, commanding voice that had served him so well on the campaign trail.

Reverend Duke Norman, with his signature tinted glasses and

whitened teeth, stood beside Commander-in-Chief like a sort of spiritual bodyguard. Behind them both stood two burly men, one black, one white, also in suits and sunglasses. Officially, they were acolytes of Duke Norman, but the word 'henchmen' seemed more descriptive. Why they were here in the Oval Office instead of the Secret Service was a mystery. "Welcome, gentlemen," said Reverend Duke Norman with a beneficent smile.

The President turned his attention to Charlie and Alex. Both were dumbfounded. Charlie felt as if everything he'd believed in was on fire, while Alex felt as if the world were suddenly made of smoke. Charlie put his arm around Alex's shoulder in an attempt to say, okay, we're lost, but let's not get separated. "CIA Agent Charles Draper! And you... you must be young Alice."

"Alex. I'm a boy."

"Don't correct the President!" snapped Duke.

The President waved him off. "No, no, it's fine. He can be Alex if he likes. Welcome! I wanted you two here as the chosen ones who helped bring about this great moment. To bring it full circle, as it were." The President turned to the camera to explain, "Alex first found the holy vessel known as Loose Thread, and delivered It unto the world. Mr. Draper here, was his appointed shepherd—his guardian angel, as it were."

Back at the NBC anchor desk in New York, Lester Holt, who had been trying to fill dead air, now checked back with Chuck asking, "Chuck? Are you there, Chuck?" Chuck Todd opened his mouth to speak, but at that moment the Chief of Staff, Jim Hornswell, entered the Oval Office via his own office. He wore of look of grave concern. "Mr. President, I don't understand..."

"Yes, Lester, uh, Chuck Todd for NBC News, in the Oval Office in an unexpected, unprecedented, apparently unplanned, and completely bizarre event. When I say, unplanned, I mean by anyone other than the President himself. You can see his Chief of Staff, Jim Hornswell, appears to be completely surprised."

Jim shot the correspondent and news camera an aghast look and groped for an explanation. "The President is unwell."

"What exactly is he sick with?"

Jim was unsure what illness could explain these symptoms. He knew a cold or flu wouldn't do it. Still, he needed something not so serious as to depose the President. "Dutch Elm Disease."

"Really?"

"Well, I'm not a doctor. The point is, the President doesn't know what he's doing."

"Mr. Hornswell, are you saying the President is mentally incompetent?"

"I'm saying... I'm saying... " Jim didn't know what he was saying.

"I'm saying," said President, taking up the slack, "Welcome. Welcome young innocent Alex, welcome Charles, welcome Jim, welcome Chuck, and welcome my fellow Americans to this... this, is Judgement Day!" As he made this declaration, the President of the United States lifted his hands into the air and stood like a holy figure framed by the window behind.

"I'm not sure we got that," said the cameraman. "The feed may have cut out."

"I'm sorry, Mr. President," said Chuck, "Could you say that again? You know, the bit about it being Judgement Day?"

* * *

In the upstairs master bedroom, Mathias Boltzmann was busy. Outside came the irregular percussion of gunfire in rapid bursts and single shots. Occasional explosions thudded below, shaking the marble floor and sending a snowfall of plaster dust from the ceiling above, while making the chandelier swing. Mathias ignored it all and heaved another pile of papers into the fireplace, where a blaze now roared. He grabbed his laptop from the bed. A deletion routine was already zeroing out the data on the drive and launching viral eradication scripts to obfuscate and erase any information from remote accounts. The progress bar showed minutes more to complete. Mathias tossed the computer onto the pyre, where the plastic quickly melted and sparks flew. This event was unexpected but not unplanned for. In the illegal arms business if you don't prepare for the possibility of a sting, you're living in a fool's paradise. There were secret accounts behind anonymous accounts, refuge properties in countries without extradition, and lawyers, so many platoons of lawyers. It was hardly ideal, but everything would be fine. If all else failed, left on the bed was a single shiny steel canister. It was the ultimate bargaining chip.

The double doors of the bedroom flew open under the impact of a single, powerful kick. Colonel Rynard Gruber materialized through a noxious cloud of smoke and tear gas that filled the threshold. His shirt was torn from one shoulder, and several pieces of shrapnel had minced the meat of his exposed pectoral. He wiped his benzyl bromide reddened eyes and surveyed the room. Despite the unsurmountable odds he now faced, the unforgettable soldier appeared to be calm, even enjoying himself. Having exhausted the ammunition from his original minigun, Rynard now carried a double-barrelled shotgun in one hand and his trusty Mauser pistol in the other. Between his teeth he still chewed a cigarillo, despite the fact that its tip had been shot off and was now dangling by a paper thread. At the sight of Mathias he grinned and grunted, "Grüß Gott." Rynard then turned, shouldered his shotgun, and swung closed the double doors. With the lock shattered, the Colonel dragged a loaded dresser one-handed to act as barricade. Mathias knew it was in part adrenaline, but still couldn't help but marvel at the soldier-for-hire's seeming superhuman strength. Outside, a police attack helicopter descended level with the windows, summoning a hurricane that flung wide the curtains and flurried papers about the room. Mathias gripped a bedpost and tried to think above the din. They know we're in here, is what he thought. He knew the weaponry that such a helicopter possessed. It could level the room in seconds.

Rynard Gruber strode nonchalantly to the bedroom wall where a rare platinum-plated AK-47 signed by Kalashnikov himself was mounted. He tore the weapon from its braces and tossed it to Mathias, who instinctively caught it. "We are going to die now," said Rynard, matter-of-factly, "So you might as well die on your feet."

Mathias threw the weapon to the floor as if it were burning hot. "We're not going to die," he said. By 'we', he meant himself, of course. There was probably little he could do to protect Gruber given the sheer number of polizei the mercenary had killed that morning alone. "Unless I'm holding a gun, in which case they may well shoot me."

Rynard frowned, assessing his employer. "Perhaps, I shoot you myself."

"Are you insane?" shouted Mathias. "There's a clause in your contract that specifically forbids that!"

Rynard laughed so hard his eyes watered. Mathias tried to join in as if they were simply old friends enjoying a joke. "Look, Colonel, this is what lawyers are for. Put down your gun and we'll be out of jail by this afternoon. Tomorrow at the latest."

Rynard stopped laughing. He wiped away the tears and pointed at the canister half-buried in the king-sized comforter. "Give me that," he ordered.

"What... are you insane?" asked Mathias.

Rynard lifted the shotgun to within an inch of Mathias's face. The metal barrel hole hovered between the businessman's eyes. Mathias could smell the acrid stench of hot steel, gun oil, and smoke. Puppeted by fear, he fumbled blindly behind himself, felt the canister and numbly handed it over. "You'll kill us all," he said.

Rynard Gruber held up the device, somewhat surprised by its lightness. He'd been expecting something with at least the heft of a munitions shell. "When I die, the world dies with me," he said with a shrug, as if this explained everything. He then squeezed the trigger. Mathias Boltzmann's head exploded like a pomegranate in a pressure cooker.

* * *

Reverend Duke Norman was in heaven. In all of his years of preaching on television, never once had he spoken to a global audience. In the Oval Office itself, there were less than a dozen people present, even including the Secret Service and Duke's own minions. Duke knew, however, that they were now being carried live on every TV news channel in the country and likely the world as well. "And so the Lord has chosen this time and this great man..." As he spoke, he nodded towards the President of the United States. The camera followed. The Commander-in-Chief, unfortunately, had chosen that moment to pick his nose again and was too engrossed in the excavation to notice. The Pastor persevered, "...and myself, to expunge the evil from the world and save the souls that dwell within it."

"Wake up, Mr. President!" shouted Jim from the side, hoping that his boss was asleep. "Wake up!"

Chuck Todd added his own observations, commenting in a hushed voice into the microphone. "I think it's safe to say that this is the greatest political scandal since or even including Watergate. The President's mental state appears to be in doubt. His Chief of Staff, Jim Hornswell, seems convinced that the President is in some sort of... trance, perhaps? It's hard to say."

Duke Norman continued, "For as each day passes, the moral cancer that has rotted the souls of Americans and the world for the last half-century continues to spread. Each day delayed towards salvation, another thousand souls are lost to the sex, violence, and impropriety that permeates our airwaves, our streets, and our schools under the guise of liberalism, love and tolerance. We thank the Lord for giving us the key to the gates of heaven and placing it in the hands of one strong enough to turn it." He nodded once more to the President, who, thankfully, was now paying attention. "...and wise enough to ask me for guidance. Amen."

"Amen" said the President.

"Amen," Duke Norman's acolytes said together like a Greek chorus.

"Amazing," said Chuck, "we've actually just heard TV evangelist Duke Norman give a full on sermon right here in the Oval Office. So much for the separation of church and state."

The Reverend, overhearing this, interjected, "A separation is not a divorce, Mr. Todd. Today is a day of reconciliation!"

The President then pointed at the NBC White House Correspondent and decreed, "Your job, man with two first names, is to act as scribe. That is why you have been summoned here. Judge not, lest ye be judged. Just as the books of Bible recorded all great acts before, so it is your job to record this moment for posterity. You may call your scripture *The Book of Chuck* or *The Book of Todd.* Both are equally terrible."

Charlie, who until this moment had been too stunned to speak, said, "Wait... you're recording the end of the world for 'posterity'?" For a moment, the entire room turned to look at him. "I mean, it's madness. Right?"

On TV screens around the world, billions of people were now following the live broadcast, from living rooms in Omaha, to the sidewalks of Times Square, to the bordellos of Bangkok, to a satellite TV in a one room schoolhouse in the Solomon Islands. They were scared, confused, and perplexed. They were also angry. They were angry that an American President was apparently announcing the end of the world. In Milan they were more angry that the President had preempted a football match with Barcelona but, still, they were angry.

The President of the United States turned and gazed directly into the camera. He then spoke with unwavering calm. This was the same voice he'd used to reassure the country during the nationwide yellow die no. 5 shortage two years prior, when Americans were shocked to discover that dill pickles were actually green inside and not, in fact, the colour of processed uranium. "My fellow Americans, citizens of the world," he began. On CNN, which had picked up the broadcast, Wolf Blitzer interjected to explain to viewers that the President of the United States had just addressed the American people and the citizens of the world. The President continued, "For today is a day I address *all* of humanity." Wolf Blitzer explained that the President appeared to be addressing all of humanity which, he added, presumably included all humans, but not animals. CNN pundits then began a fierce debate about whether this did include household pets which "often think they're people" in so many adorable ways. This then served as a segue to the top kitten videos currently trending on social media. "Today is a day that will live in infamy and, indeed, outfamy. As your President, I have seen the destiny that awaits all true believers and I know my duty. As Jesus once said, with great power comes great responsibility. I own up to that responsibility this very day." With that the Commander-in-Chief lifted his robe to reveal the shiny canister concealed within. This had the unintended consequence of revealing more than just the device. The result was that the weapon itself went momentarily ignored as audiences gasped, and journalists tried to explain the significance of the President of the United States exposing himself to the world. Oblivious, the President held the shiny canister aloft and proclaimed, "For today is the day foretold of by John the Apostle and foreseen by Jack Van Impe many, many, so very many times. Today is the day of Revelations!" This proclamation had the effect of returning global attention to the shiny container. The only exceptions were Fox News viewers who were now treated to a panel discussing the President's genitalia at length under the banner 'Flashpoint!'. All subsequent proceedings in the Oval Office were relegated to a ticker along the bottom of the screen.

"Is that what it appears to be?" gasped Chuck Todd.

"I hold in my hands," said the President, "the key to Heaven itself."

"You hold in your hands the key to the Apocalypse!" shouted Charlie. As he said this, he struggled to lift himself from his wheelchair. His hands shook with the effort, and stabbing pain paralyzed him. As he reached for the device, one of Reverend Duke Norman's acolytes stepped forward to block him. The second acolyte drew a pistol from his jacket and aimed it directly at Charlie. Charlie collapsed back into his chair, caught by Alex.

"You can't have guns in the Oval Office!" shouted Jim Hornswell indignantly. He then added, weakly, "...or doomsday devices, for that matter."

The President shook his head sadly. "You never really did believe in the second amendment, did you, Jim?"

The Secret Service drew their own weapons. For a moment they were confused as to whom to point them at, and consequently waved their guns about in a noncommittal manner. It was Charlie, after all, who had threatened to attack the President, but it was the acolytes who had drawn weapons. On the other hand, the President seemed to be threatening everyone in the world, including himself. Still, shooting him just *felt* wrong.

"Put down your weapons and get out!" ordered the President. The Secret Service codename for the President was 'Bubble Wrap', and the agents knew that obeying a direct order from Bubble Wrap was rule number one. Reluctantly, they re-holstered their firearms and backed slowly from the room, eyeing everyone with equal suspicion.

"Upside... there must be an upside to this..." muttered Jim in a panic nearing mania. This will actually help us with the doomsday prepper vote, he thought, and with any religious nuts excited about the Rapture. In other words, anyone actually looking forward to Armageddon as a day to gloat. Still, he decided, that can't be anywhere near a majority, except possibly in Texas. Even without poll results he felt fairly confident that most people of either party didn't want the world to end or, at least, not their half of it. At that moment, the Chief of Staff's phone buzzed.

"My fellow Children of God," the President continued, cradling the steel canister like a holy relic, "We are all God's children. As Jesus said on the sermon of the mount, I love you, you love me, we're a happy–"

"Mr. President," Jim blurted, "I think you'll want to see this."

The President looked peeved. He jabbed his thumb towards the cameras and muttered under his breath, "Not now Jim. I'm speaking to the world!"

"I realize that, sir, but something is happening right now that has a direct impact on what you're doing." With that, Jim pressed a button on a small remote control. Hidden panels slid up in the bookshelf opposite the President's desk, revealing the three television screens behind. Jim pressed a second button, and the first TV turned on. "Who lives in a pineapple under the sea?" Jim changed the channel to Al Jazeera showing a live broadcast from a television studio in the Arab Emirates. On screen was a terrorist, looking unsettlingly similar to the President with his long beard and flowing robes, standing behind a podium. Karim glanced down at his notes and continued, "... and to Abbas, and Abdel, who never stopped believing in me and the cause. We did it fellas!" At this Karim gave a heartfelt thumbs-up to his offscreen co-conspirators.

"What the hell is this?" shouted the President.

"In yet another twist in this growing scandal we're now calling *Heavensgate*," Chuck Todd explained, "Jim Hornswell has turned on what appears to be some sort of... terrorist awards ceremony, perhaps?"

"Thank-you," said Karim, choked with emotion. "Thank-you all. For without your support we could never have reached this day, this wonderful day, this day of absolute triumph!" With that Karim thrust his own metal canister high above his head. Camera flashes strobed the moment. Tears of joy ran down Karim's cheeks.

"I don't understand," said the President of the United States, staring back and fourth between the canister in his hands and the identical one on TV. "Loose Thread is a People's Choice Award? What does that even mean?"

"It means, it's a trick," asserted Duke Norman. He glared at Jim accusingly.

Jim didn't notice. His phone was once more playing *Lollipop*, the ringtone he'd assigned to high priority Defence Department alerts. "Yes?" he answered. "What?" Jim's incredulous expression silenced the room. "No, put it through to the Oval Office on line one." Jim hung up and stared back. He opened his mouth to say something then, finding no words, simply lifted the remote again and turned on television number two. The screen filled with what was a live feed from a drone helicopter hovering outside Mathias Boltzmann's estate in Munich. The bird's-eye-view showed Colonel Rynard Gruber on the outside terrace, surrounded by a ring of German police. Rynard was shirtless; his body battered from numerous shrapnel fragments and gunshots. His muscular physique glistened with sweat and blood. For all his many wounds, he appeared unaffected. Instead, he moved with the tenacity of a cornered cat, his head darting back and fourth constantly. While a dozen men in blue flak jackets surrounded him, it was clear he would not be blindsided. Despite the untenable odds, it was Rynard who was in control of the situation. In his hands, he clutched a shiny steel canister.

"Who the hell is that?" screeched the Commander-in-Chief.

"That is Colonel Rynard Gruber. A mercenary in the employ of Mathias Boltzmann, the arms dealer who originally obtained the canister. So the reports were true. Like us, Boltzmann thought to make copies."

"We made copies?"

"Just one, Mr. President. You ordered it."

"I did?"

"You may have been asleep at the time."

"Oh," said the President, nodding. "I do move in mysterious ways..."

"It was a clever idea."

"Hmm, that does *sound* like me."

"Then that must be the real thing!" Alex exclaimed.

"Alex's right," said Charlie. "Boltzmann must have sold a replica to Ali Madda and kept the real thing for himself."

"Not if Carl Weiss mixed them up as also reported, but possibly. If so we switched a fake for a fake," agreed Jim.

"No! No!" protested the President. "I refuse to accept this. I'm the President of United States! If anyone's going to destroy the universe it should be us! We made it!"

"The universe?" asked Alex.

"No, the bomb!"

"Technically it's not a bomb..." said Jim.

"Ahhh!" The President almost threw the canister at him. He stopped himself and lobbed a commemorative pen instead. His Chief of Staff ducked.

"Don't be fooled, sir," shouted Duke Norman. "*Everyone* in this room is lying to you!"

"*You're* in this room," said Jim.

"Well, yes, but—"

"He's opening it!" shouted Alex, pointing at the TV. On screen Karim was trying, unsuccessfully, to unscrew the lid of the device.

"That heathen, he can't get to open it!" screamed the President. "Well, not if I open mine first!" With that the President also began frantically tugging at the canister lid. Charlie, unwilling to risk that the President might have the real thing, tried once more to lunge forward. Again, an acolyte intervened, this time slugging Charlie in the belly. Charlie doubled over in agony.

"Stop!" Alex screamed as he threw himself at the burly henchman, only to be tossed easily to the floor. Alex attempted to jump up. Charlie, despite nearly blinding pain, grabbed Alex's arm to hold him back.

On TV, Karim was now alternating between trying to twist off the top, and banging it on the floor to loosen it.

"Mr. President, let me try," offered Duke.

"I've got it!" insisted the Commander-in-Chief. The President then sat in his chair, placed the canister firmly between his legs, and began pulling with all of his might. His face grew first red, then purple from the effort. The President then began to make squeaking noises like air escaping a balloon. He paused to rest a moment, panting, "God damn it!"

"Mr. President," chided the Reverend.

"I mean, gosh darn it."

"We may have welded it shut," Jim pondered. "I honestly don't remember."

"He's going to open it!" exclaimed Alex.

"He's going to try," said Charlie.

"No, on TV, the German guy!"

All eyes turned to the first television where Rynard Gruber was now holding the canister high above his head like a trophy. One hand gripped the bottom, while the other gripped the top. The Colonel threw his head back, looked directly at them and laughed.

"Shoot him! Shoot him now!" Jim shouted into his phone. "No, no, not the hellfire missile, just bullets, lots and lots of bullets!" The order should have come from the President, or at least the Secretary of State, but the men on the other end of line weren't arguing.

The German Landespolizei opened fire. They were joined by several unseen German snipers, US operatives, and the drone itself. The blistering barrage of bullets boiled the skin on Rynard Gruber's body. All the while Gruber's maniacal grin never wavered, even as he was tossed about like a human lawn sprinkler, flooding the green grass with bright red blood. The force of the gunfire was so fierce it actually sawed his torso in half. The shooting stopped. Amazingly, the shredded mercinazi still stood for several seconds more. Then, like a felled ironwood, the top half of Rynard Grubber crashed to the concrete floor of the terrace. In his hands he still clutched the two ends of the canister. For a moment his lower half continued to stand before, slowly, its knees buckled and the half man sank to a kneeling position. There it remained, still overflowing with blood, flooding the terrace like a gruesome zen fountain.

"Ech," said Jim.

The President gaped.

Duke Norman gagged, covering his mouth with a silk handkerchief so as not to vomit on his suit.

Charlie clutched Alex's head to his chest, shielding his eyes. The boy was in shock. He'd seen worse in movies, but somehow knowing it was real was different.

"That was close," said Charlie.

One of the German police officers stepped forward to reach for the device. He tried to tug it from Rynard's grip but found that he could not. Stymied by what he assumed to be rigor mortis, the officer let go to gain a better grip. Rynard blinked. The officer stared in shock as a final grin traced itself across Rynard's lips. Rynard's hands then spasmed violently and yanked the two halves of the canister apart.

There was a collective gasp from around the Oval Office.

Nothing happened.

The devil light in Rynard's eyes guttered and dimmed to the defeated, distant gaze of the dead.

The German policeman kicked the bisected corpse to make sure it was finally, truly deceased. He then bent down and picked up the silver container and its lid. Even from the drone camera they could see that it was empty, save for the small note Mathias Boltzmann had inserted in all of the fakes that read simply, "Bang!"

"Ha! Stupid kraut!" shouted the President of the United States at the television. He then turned and shook his finger at the assembled guests. "I knew it; I've got the real one. Hee! Hee! And you all thought I was crazy!"

On the other television, Karim and his entourage had their canister on the floor and were busy shooting at it. One of his men nursed an arm maimed by a ricocheted bullet.

Seeing this, the President turned and started whacking his own canister upside down on the Resolute Desk. "This normally does it with pickle jars!" The Acolytes closed ranks to warn off Charlie or anyone else who might attempt to stop him.

"The Arab guy has his off too!" shouted Alex, pointing at the screen.

The gunfire had dislodged the lid and Karim was now holding the open canister and peering inside, puzzled. His men began shouting excited and confused suggestions in Arabic. Seeing nothing, Karim turned the container upside down and whacked the bottom several times with the butt of his pistol. When nothing continued to happen, he threw the canister to the ground and he and his men resumed shooting at it.

With everyone in the Oval Office transfixed by the TV, Charlie saw his chance. He reached out and karate-chopped the gun from the nearest acolyte's hand. Before the man could react, Charlie then launched himself from his wheelchair, straight at the President of the United States. Too weak to fight, he allowed his momentum to carry him, landing a head-butt directly into the Commander-in-Chief's gut. The President flew backwards into his chair, tossing the canister high into the air. For a moment everyone froze and simply watched as the device seemed to spin in slow motion up to the ceiling. There, it dislodged a chunk of plaster from the Presidential Seal, before falling back to Earth. Duke Norman tried to catch it but tripped over Charlie, who was now on his hands and knees, contorted in agony. The other acolyte reached for it as well, but fumbled the catch with one hand and butter-fingered it with the other. This did, however, redirect the device under the desk. There, Alex dove and caught it by the top, inches from the floor. For several seconds the room held its collective breath. Alex nodded and said, "Got it." The room exhaled. At that moment, the bottom detached from its lid and landed on the floor below with a *clunk!*

"I loosened it," said the President.

Everyone in the Oval Office stared in silent alarm. The NBC cameraman zoomed in. The cameraman knew that, if he caught the end of the world on close up, he was a shoo-in for an Emmy. The world watched and held its breath as the canister bottom rolled in decreasing concentric circles, until it came to a stop. Once more, an astonishing amount of *nothing* happened.

"Well, I'll be," said the Commander-in-Chief.

"Ahhhh!" screamed Jim. The White House Chief of Staff pounced on the President of the United States, throwing him to the ground and began pummelling him. The two men rolled about in a heap, like schoolchildren in suits. The President pulled off Jim's glasses, while the Chief of Staff had his boss firmly by the beard.

"Yeeee!" screeched the President, who then began vigorously slapping the Chief of Staff's bald head.

The Secret Service, hearing their master's voice, burst into the room. Assessing the bewildering scene, they holstered their weapons and began trying to separate the two men. By this point, the Chief of Staff had the President of the United States's hand in his mouth and was biting it hard. "Yow!" shouted the President. Reverend Duke Norman began looking for an exit, but found himself blocked by Chuck Todd and his crew. "I have a few questions I'd like to ask you," said the reporter.

Alex helped Charlie slowly to his feet and back into his wheelchair. Once successfully seated, Charlie closed his eyes to cope with the pain. He clutched Alex's hand. His grip was too tight, but Alex didn't care. Alex was still trying to make sense of it all. "So if it wasn't Boltzmann, or Ali Madda, or The President, who has the real thing then?"

"It must have been a hoax," gasped Charlie between breaths. "Maybe it stopped working. Maybe it never worked in the first place."

"But why?" asked Alex. "Why make up such a fraud?"

The Secret Service by this point had pulled the two men apart. Jim's shirt was open and missing three buttons, and his tie was pulled loose. His glasses, while recovered, were bent cockeyed on his face. The President of the United States was worse off, having lost a tooth and a good chunk of his facial hair.

"Well," said Charlie, "it was the Cold War. Bluffing was the name of the game. It was a weapon they could never use anyway, so as long as the Soviet's thought we had it, then that was probably enough. Then again, maybe Dr. MacGuffin just had a great sense of humour and it was all a big joke." At that moment, Charlie realized he was on camera. He waved the news crew away.

"And there you have it," said Chuck Todd. "Was it all just a giant joke? The theatre of the absurd at play on the world stage? Who's afraid of Virginia Woolf? Perhaps we all are. One thing we can say for sure, things are not looking good for this President going into the midterm elections." Behind Chuck, the President now sat defeated on the corner of his desk. He was hopelessly trying to reattach a dislodged tooth the Secret Service had found on the floor. This was an effort made all the more futile by the fact that the tooth they'd found wasn't his, but rather belonged to Gerald Ford. "Back to you, Lester," said Chuck Todd, "back to you."

* * *

The old woman wandered along the narrow alleyways of the Fluß Ruhr Industrial Park in Germany. She was dressed in layers of sweaters, despite the warmth of the summer night. She pushed the requisite shopping cart issued to homeless persons the world over. A miniature schnauzer trotted faithfully at her heels, pausing to sniff the occasional scent, before hurrying to catch up again. Regularly spaced floodlights created bright pools of light, holding off the weighted darkness from above and joining the places between with shades of grey. The bleak factory-filled suburb of Frankfurt was originally built as part of the rubber boom in the early twentieth century. The park had been a critical component of the Nazi war effort, cranking out tires for cars, trucks, and anything else with wheels. Consequently, it had been blasted to rubble by Britain's 'Bomber' Harris. The park had then been replaced with poured concrete, uncomplicated by any of the character the original factories might have possessed. It would be easy to get lost amid the moulded grey blocks if not for the large numbered identifiers painted on every street and building. Fluß Ruhr Industrial Park was not so much a place, as a system of organizing space.

The old woman's name was Eva Braun. She owed her notorious name to the fact that she was born Eva Klauss and had the misfortune to fall in love with a man whose last name was Braun. Consequently, Eva had spent much of her adult life answering the question, "Not *the* Eva Braun?", to which she would patiently reply that this was highly unlikely as *the* Eva Braun had met her end, along with her maniac husband, in a Berlin bunker in 1945. In the past ten years, Eva had clearly fallen on harder times. She had lost her husband, her sanity, and her home, although not necessarily in that order. All she had left were the possessions she'd piled into the shopping cart and her dog, Atom. Atom was so-named for his tiny size as a puppy. Even for a miniature schnauzer, he was small. He had been the runt of his litter.

One of Eva's remaining possessions was a white transistor radio she'd duct-taped to the handle of her cart. She had been listening to a radio report about a massive police raid in Munich. According to the report, a small army of Landespolizei and helicopters had descended upon the mansion of a wealthy drug lord. The coverage included exciting sound bites of intense gunfire interspersed with questions of "How could this happen in such a respectable neighbourhood?", "Who exactly was this Mathias Boltzmann?" and "Is it true he's really Swiss?" As she walked between two tall buildings labeled 'Gebäude 16' and 'Gebäude 17', the radio descended into static. The old woman shrugged. It's becoming like the United States here, she thought. Thanks to Hollywood and American rap music, Germany was now a place where bad things could happen. She switched the stereo from radio to CD. Nina Hagen belted out a cover from her new collection of public domain classics, entitled *Öffentliches Gut*. The song she sang was *The Daring Young Man on the Flying Trapeze*. She sang it in English but with a thick German accent and, as always, the voice of an asthmatic chain-smoking angel.

He'd smile from the bar on the people below
And one night he smiled on my love.
She wink'd back at him and she shouted "Bravo,"
As he hung by his nose up above.

The old woman drew alongside her current objective, a green dumpster on the back of Gebäude 16. The industrial park was a void of human activity at night. In the city proper there was the Landespolizei who would ask questions and possibly take her downtown. Worse, there were the roaming gangs of Burgessün, young thugs dressed in long johns and lederhosen, who would beat her half-to-death for fun and the other half out of a sense of German work ethic. Here the streets were empty, the dumpsters largely unplundered. It was a concrete garden, unspoilt by the presence of humanity. Eva climbed on top her shopping cart, in order to make herself tall enough, and peered inside.

The interior was swallowed by darkness. Eva was forced to switch on the LED keychain flashlight she kept for such purposes. This served only to illuminate the largely disappointing contents. Inside were boxes of discarded sponges, an old office chair and tubs of liquid latex that had been thrown out for being the wrong colour. Atom sniffed about beneath the dumpster, then began scratching furiously.

"What is that you've got there, Atty?" asked Eva. She climbed off of her perch and joined her dog on the cold ground. Aiming her flashlight into the shadow, she saw the object of Atom's interest. It was a discarded sandwich bag from Die Kaiser Kaiser. She pulled it out and opened it up. Inside were the remains of an apple strudel. She took a bite, then dumped the contents onto the pavement. Atom began to eat. She then noticed something else. The bright light of her keychain caught the glint of metal, shiny and flawless.

Eva peered at the inscription on the side of the canister that read 'Property of the United States Government. Top Secret'. How peculiar, she thought. Its size and excellent condition ruled out the possibility of it being an unexploded bomb. Those were still popping up from time to time in farmers' fields, but were usually the size of a bathtub and rusting to bits. Eva considered the possibility that it had come from a US Army base. The nearest, however, was miles away, in Wiesbaden. Eva suffered from undiagnosed schizophrenia, but she was far from stupid. Eva knew it was possibly a very bad idea to open the canister. She considered that it might be dangerous and that if she opened it, she might even be killed. Inside her head, however, a voice told her that she would not die. It told her that she would know 'the truth', whatever that was. Even before her life had disintegrated, Eva had always believed that everything happened for a reason. Since then, she told herself that her current bleak existence was simply a purgatory meant to prepare her for something better. She also believed that a super-intelligent hedgehog, named Hermann H, was sending her coded messages through discarded newspaper clippings. Eva gave the lid a twist. For a moment it refused to budge. Then, suddenly, it began to turn quite easily and came off in her hand.

There was a faint *pop!* like the sound one's ears make when changing altitude in an airplane. Eva peered inside and was surprised to see what appeared to be a splotch of floating television static. 'Snow', her father used to call it. She lowered the canister to get a better look and found that the static remained where it was, hanging in the air like a scratch in reality. It confounded her eyes. Its surface was simply black and white noise. Walking around it, Eva could see that it clearly occupied three-dimensional space, yet seemed to have no surface and appeared flat from every angle. Despite looking like static, it made no such sound. It wasn't silent, but the sound it did make was a B-flat too low for the human ear. It was the same exact tone that a black hole makes, were anyone there to hear it. Atom began to bark at the static, just as he did the vacuum cleaner.

Eva was both alarmed and intrigued. Here was something she simply could not explain. Once more, her curiosity got the better of her. The voice spoke with slurred S's. "Sssstick it," the voice said, "sssstick it!" At the very least she should have known to use an actual stick or some other object to prod it. Instead, she reached out and touched it with her finger. "Yessss..." said the voice.

The tip of her finger instantly turned to static. Eva didn't feel any pain, thanks to the wonder of endorphins. Instead, she simply stared in shock and tried to withdraw her finger. She found that she could not. She found that her finger was stuck, as if in a Chinese finger trap. What's more, the static appeared to be creeping slowly up over her knuckle. She watched in horror as it reached her hand. In a panic, she leaned backwards with all of her weight, but could no more break free than tear off her own arm. Atom, in an effort to protect his mistress, leapt up and bit the static. His head instantly vanished, and the dog was left dangling dead in midair. Eva screamed.

Eva continued screaming, unheard, for the next twenty-five minutes, as the static slowly spread up her arm until she passed out from blood loss. Without clotting to protect her, her circulatory system ensured that all of the blood in her body was soon pumped into the static. By this time, Atom was completely consumed while Eva, now dead, hung there for over an hour, until her corpse too collapsed into chaos.

CHAPTER 26

"Numbers are meaningless, but they're better than nothing."
– Ed Platzberg

Firstring, Virginia, Winter, six months prior.

The world had already ended when Charlie awoke that morning, he just didn't know it. Lisa's side of the bed was empty, but there was nothing odd about that. She was always an early riser. He got up, showered, shaved, and headed downstairs.

Downstairs there was no sign of either Lisa or Faith. He tried to remember if there was something 'on' that morning. He didn't think so, but, truth be told, he frequently didn't listen when Lisa was talking. It's not that I don't care, he told himself. Still, he couldn't explain it otherwise. Why don't I listen? Maybe I don't care, he thought. He then immediately banished the idea. It's probably something to do with Brownies, he decided. The Girl Guides were always doing some sort of fundraiser or event. He was somewhat sad to not see Faith but, truth be told, it was nice to have the house to himself.

He dropped some bread into the toaster and filled a glass with orange juice. He then stood at the counter, reading the New York Times on his iPad, waiting for his toast. The timer on the appliance was broken, so if he didn't watch it constantly the bread would burn. It was also a relief *not* to see Lisa because of the night before. It had been one of their loudest fights ever. The yelling had ended only when Lisa had flung a crystal fruit bowl at the kitchen floor. Charlie instinctively glanced down to make sure there were no more shards of glass. The bowl had been a wedding gift from his uncle who thought that people still cared about crystal. As usual, the fight was over something stupid. Charlie commented that Lisa was spending so much time at her Yoga classes that it was amazing Faith even knew who she was. It was a cheap shot and didn't even make sense. Charlie spent far more time in his office at Langely, and bringing their daughter into it was just wrong. He would apologize eventually, but he hadn't last night. He didn't even know why he was so mad. They'd been drifting apart for a long while, but it was hard to say who was the boat and who was the shore. Perhaps they were both boats. Charlie smelled burnt toast. "Damn it!"

He flicked the switch and up popped two smouldering briquets of bread. "Damn! Damn! Damn!" he muttered as he plucked them out quickly but carefully, to avoid burning his fingers. He then spent several seconds scraping off the top layer before concealing the damage under a smear of marmalade. "Damn."

Charlie sat at the table with his iPad, juice and burnt offerings that would have to serve as breakfast. In another life he might have eaten at the kitchen counter, but years of domesticity had taught him to sit at the table 'like a civilized person' to avoid spilling crumbs on the floor. For some reason, he appeased Lisa best when she wasn't around. He bit into his toast and perused an article about a man in Yonkers who'd murdered his newlywed wife. The man had disposed of the body over the course of several days by feeding her in bite-size pieces to the pigeons of Central Park. He'd have gotten away with it too, had one of the birds not choked to death on her wedding ring. Upon being arrested, he'd confessed to his crimes. He stated that at least he had proven once and for all that the pigeons of New York would eat anything, even "bride crumbs." Charlie moved onto the sports section to see how the Washington Capitals were doing. It was only then that he noticed the envelope in the middle of the breakfast table. On it was his name, in Lisa's handwriting. Putting down his toast, he reached for the envelope and tore it open. As he unfolded the handwritten note inside, the doorbell rang.

Charlie put down the letter, brushed the crumbs from his palms and headed for the door. He decided it was Jehovah's Witnesses. He imagined them mistaking the smell of burnt toast for Brimstone and fleeing in a panic. The thought made him smirk. Through the glass, he saw a police officer waiting. The officer was fidgeting, looking oddly nervous. It was then that Charlie felt the first pang of alarm. What happened next was a contradiction; stark reality with every detail ingrained into Charlie's brain and, at the same time, a kind of dream. The young man, no more than twenty-five, explained that there had been an automobile accident, involving Charlie's car, wife, and daughter. The officer then explained that his wife had been taken to a hospital where she had died almost immediately. His daughter was dead at the scene. The car was in surprisingly good shape.

On the drive down to the morgue, he convinced himself that there was some sort of mistake. They can't be dead, he thought, it's not possible. He continued this line of denial while sitting the waiting room, waiting. He told himself this right up to the point where they lifted the sheet from his daughter's face. She looked as small and fragile as a china doll. The only external sign of injury was a purple bruise on the side of her temple. He reached out to touch her cheek. Instead of being warm and soft, it felt tensile and refrigerator cold. For Charlie, it was at that moment the world ended.

CHAPTER 27

"You complete me." – A. Turing

The sky above the Highlands was suitably stormy. Still, no actual rain fell. Instead, torrid clouds hung over the darkened landscape like a mantle of black wool. Occasional flashes of veiled lightning infused the gloom with light, turning the clouds diaphanous, followed by the distant rumble of thunder. The air crackled. The normally green grass of the Scottish hills appeared cerulean and undulated with an unnatural wind. It appeared to presage the end of the world, and that's because it did.

Charlie and Alex drove once more over the rolling, once idyllic, landscape. The atmosphere was wholly different now and everything felt wrong both inside and out. It had been two weeks since a woman in Germany had somehow obtained and opened the Loose Thread device. With it's cosmic cord yanked, the fabric of space time itself was beginning to unravel and there was no stopping it. No one really cared what Charlie and Alex, or anyone else, did now. Of course, for many, life continued as it was. Most people on Earth still went to work and carried on as if nothing had changed. Some of these people lived in denial, while others lived in hope that somehow it would all be fixed. Most simply didn't know what else to do. In some parts of the world, people didn't know anything had happened at all. In North Korea, it was business-as-usual; the trains ran on time and executions continued to be executed. Charlie and Alex were still able to board a flight to Scotland. At the start of the flight they were told to fasten their seat belts, and what to do in the event of a sudden loss of cabin pressure. They landed safely and were able to rent a car. The rental was even discounted, owing to the impending global economic collapse. It was a good time for bargain hunters.

Not that this meant life was anywhere near normal. The news continued to be filled with horror stories of murder and mayhem as those who had simply been waiting for an opportunity to destroy without fear of reprisal got to work. Mostly, however, people appeared to be lost. Mount Everest was said to be littered with bucket loads of bodies from people rushing to complete their 'bucket lists'. As Charlie and Alex passed through the quiet town of Cockwaddle, they could see graffiti on the walls that read, "The End is Nigh". The town's long abandoned, dark satanic mills, appeared as quaint relics of a simpler time. Every church they passed was packed. The faithful and the lapsed now prayed to be saved either before the world's end or shortly thereafter.

Charlie had the radio tuned to BBC1 where an announcer had pledged to report right up until the end. "... Missiles, lasers and all sorts of other armaments have been fired into the cloud to no effect. The cloud, which now measures 1.2 miles in diameter, simply absorbs everything that is thrown at it and continues to spread." Journalists had taken to referring to the chaos as a 'cloud', even though this was scientifically ridiculous. It wasn't a cloud, it just happened to look like one. "We have with us here, Dr. Malcolm McBreigh, physicist with the University of Edinburgh. Dr. McBreigh, welcome."

"Thank-you fur havin' me," said the professor, "and please, call me Malcolm."

As Charlie and Alex exited the town, they drove past a fallow field. A dozen locals ran naked through the clover, clutching bottles of wine, and laughing. They were clearly drunk and appeared to be happy. At least the towns and villages are less scary than the cities, thought Alex. "So then, Malcolm," the interviewer continued, "we have now learned that NATO intends to drop a nuclear bomb on the cloud. What effect you expect this to have?"

"None."

"None? A nuclear bomb will have no effect at all?"

"Nay. It's the nature of chaos, tha knows. Everything you throw at it, whether it be matter or energy, wull simply become part of it. It'll take awhile, but eventually this cloud will consume the earth, the soon, the galaxy, black holes, stars, light, heat and even dork matter."

"I'm sorry, did you say *dork* matter?"

"Yes, exactly, dork matter and dork energy. Proportionally speaking, you know, the universe is mostly dork."

"I see."

"Anyhoo, as I was saying, simply put, this chaos will consume all of existence. So, when you consider what's on its menu, a nuclear weapon's naught more than what a French scientist would call an 'amuse bouche'."

They passed a farmer, on the road, dressed in drag. He was leading a cart horse. The horse was wearing a man's necktie.

"Of course, we'll all be dead long before that," the professor added. "In the next few weeks, the cloud, as you call it, will burn a hole right through the earth's crust. That's when things'll get a right bit nasty."

They rounded a hilltop and a lone tree came into view. Four bodies dangled in nooses from a single, large outstretched branch. "Don't look," said Charlie, although he knew it was far too late for that.

"Is there nothing we can do?" asked the announcer.

There was a long pause. The professor then said in a near whisper, "Go home. Go home to your wife, your kids, your parents... whomever. Go home and tell 'em that you love 'em. In the end, it's the best any of us can do."

*   *   *

Mrs. MacGuffin had sent a message that read simply, "I've fixed it" and invited them to come. The plan was to step through the portal and go back to a previous time. Charlie had called to confirm. "Oh aye," she said, "Yur more than welcome. I've invited all manner o' kith'n kin to do the same, so there'll be others as well."

They saw the line even before they saw the tower. It wound along the side of the road, down the gully, across a small bridge, and up the next hill towards the valley where Mrs. MacGuffin's cottage lay. The narrow road itself was now clogged with discarded cars, trucks, and even a few bicycles. The people in the line were almost entirely local, but from every walk of life. They included farmers, policemen, firemen, road workers, doctors, nurses and more. There were individuals and whole families. Station and class clearly played no role; you simply took your place at the end of the queue. Seeing no other option, Charlie pulled the rental car to the side of the road, next to an abandoned glazier's truck, its racks still full of plate glass. "What do we do now?" asked Alex.

"I guess we get in line," said Charlie.

Alex nodded and the two walked to the end of the queue. They were surprised to find themselves directly behind Tinker, the cantankerous pub patron from Cockwaddle. He eyed them suspiciously. "You all ag'in?"

"We're friends of Mrs. MacGuffin," said Charlie

"Oh, aye, aren't we all? Place'll be overrun if word gets out."

"What's it matter to you as long as you get through?" asked Alex.

"Don't need a boonch o' filthy foreigners ruinin' the past as well as present is all. The good ol' days is where I'm goin'. When laf was fine an' noble."

"Where, I mean, when is that?"

"Middle Ages. Time o' glory and chivalry 'n sooch. When men were men and you could marry yur first cousin w'out so mooch as a blink of an eye. An' don't you even think of followin' me." As he said this waggled his finger at them in a threatening manner.

"We won't," promised Charlie.

After that they stood in silence. Just ahead of them in line was a group that loudly identified themselves as the local branch of the Clan Donnachaidh Society. They wore kilts and hoisted bottles of Scotch, having thought to bring an entire case to celebrate their relative good fortune. They were drunk and happy until, in the midst of singing Auld Lang Syne, one by one they burst into tears of remorse for friends and family not present.

"Is that Mrs. MacGuffin?" asked Alex incredulously. He was pointing to a motorcycle with a sidecar weaving its way between abandoned vehicles on the road towards them. Its driver was wearing goggles and a pink scarf but there was no mistaking their octogenarian hostess. She reached the end of the line and smiled and waved at those waiting there. Mrs. MacGuffin jumped off the bike with the same spryness that had surprised them before. She then pulled a sign from the otherwise empty sidecar seat and began pounding it into the dirt with a rubber mallet. The sign read, "No queue jumping. No place holding. Be polite. Wait your turn."

"Mrs. MacGuffin!" shouted Alex.

Mrs. MacGuffin turned around in surprise and spotted them with a smile. They were no longer at the end of the line. A busload of Mrs. MacGuffin's distant cousins from Skye had arrived, as well as a dentist from Dublin. The line had also moved, and they'd almost reached a small shrub Charlie had marked in his mind as a milestone.

"So glad to see you made it!" she said with genuine delight. "I was'na sure if there were flights still froom America!" She gave them both hugs and paused to beam at Alex. "Especially you, yoong lad, you've got a full laf to live." After giving the signpost a final whack, she straddled her motorcycle, revved the engine once, and patted the empty sidecar. "Well, come on then, the both of ya."

"But what about..." Charlie nodded to the sign, then to the somewhat disgruntled faces of those in line ahead of them.

"I have front-of-the-line passes," she said, then shouted to the others, "Don't you all fuss, you'll get through." Mrs. MacGuffin then turned back to Charlie and Alex. "Right then, you, young fella, in the side. Mr.

Draper can ride on the seat wi' me."

A moment later they were racing past the relentlessly long line of temporal refugees. Charlie guessed there to be five thousand or more people waiting. He wondered how many had gone through and how many more would make it. "I'm amazed you aren't even more inundated," Charlie shouted, hoping to be heard above the din of the engine.

"Well, it's not like it's widely known," she shouted back over her shoulder. "And even of those that have heard, few believe it to be true. Based on the time it takes for people to go through, everyone here in line will make it. But, there'll come a time when there's those that won't. I daresay, if word got out far o'field, some that came might not be so civil as to wait their turn."

Several times before they reached the rise, Mrs. MacGuffin slowed or stopped to greet friends in the queue. Some petitioned her to jump ahead. She simply assured them they were safe and told them to wait their turn. Charlie wanted to ask how she decided whom to invite, but he suspected he knew the answer. There was no way to pick who would survive and who would not. Whoever showed up could get in line and as many as made it through before the end would survive. It was as fair as system as any. "So your father, he knew this would happen?"

"Oh aye," she said. "He was ne'r good at knowin' difference 'twixt *could* and *should* in science. Only after he'd built the device, did he realize its use was inevitable. It couldn'a be destroyed. As sure as Pandora's box, some way, someday it would be opened. He felt a might bit foolish then."

They breached the crest of the hill and saw again the massive nuclear cooling tower standing incongruously in the midst of the Highland dale. Now, with the fantastical storm clouds surging above and the weaving procession of people leading to its base, it seemed strangely to make sense. As visible threads of lightning danced across its top from the boiling sky, the tower appeared to Alex like an enormous peg, pinning down the circus tent universe that was threatening to blow away.

"So he built the time gate, as a means to escape?"

"Aye. Once you ken the true nature o' the cosmos, time travel is'nay hard." She then added with a wink, "At least if yur name's Rupert MacGuffin."

"And we really can't go back in time to stop this all from happening?" asked Alex. "I mean, I could go stop myself from listing it on eBay."

"Nae," she said firmly. "As I told ya afore, you can visit the past, even live yur laf there, but you canna change things you know to be true. Try and you will fail. You might even die."

As they drew close and entered the veil of its shadow, the awesome structure filled their sight. Mrs. MacGuffin parked the motorcycle at the bottom of the steps and dismounted. Charlie helped Alex out of the sidecar. The people in line stepped aside to let them pass. No one wished to risk offending the timegate's keeper, however amiable she might appear.

Entering the cavernous shell of the tower, they found the queue continued. Folks wound about the interior as if waiting for a ride at Disneyland. The inside was loud with the echoing voices of nervous pilgrims. Above all, was the persistent hum of the timegate ring suspended far above. The blue white halo filled the hollow structure with near daylight and the odor of time travel. Once again Charlie was struck by the smell of burnt toast, only now it hung thick in the air like ozone. The line continued up the interior steps and along the circling catwalks. Charlie felt a pang of fear that the aging structure might suddenly give way and send dozens of people plummeting to their deaths. At the very top, the line continued right out onto the platform. "Look!" said Alex, pointing eagerly. A family of three was ready to go. The father punched in a date at the control panel, then joined his family at the edge of the temporal diving board. Their daughter, who looked about twelve, was clearly terrified. Her father put his arm around her shoulders and all three covered their eyes. Someone shouted "Go already!" and they did. All three stepped from the platform and plunged through the ring below. They entered on one side and simply failed to exist on the other. Despite knowing what would happen, Alex blinked. Charlie glanced down at his sneakers, one nearly new, the other cracked with age.

"So that's it? We just a pick a date? Any date?"

"Well, the future would be a bit pointless tha knows. And if you dunna go far enoof into the past there's a chance you'll just have to go through again. There's soom here through a second time. I see you Robert!" Mrs. MacGuffin waggled her finger playfully at an elderly man who looked back sheepishly.

"Have you seen my younger self?" Robert asked hopefully.

"Already gone through," she said. "Make sure you go far enooff back yurself this tam."

"Tha's not so far now, m'lady" he said with a sad smile.

With Mrs. MacGuffin leading the way, they made their way up the long creaking superstructure. At one point they were forced to squeeze past actual circus clowns, in full greasepaint. Charlie couldn't imagine why they would be in costume, but there was no time to ask. Alex almost tripped over an enormous clown shoe and was forced to catch himself on the precarious railing. Charlie felt self-conscious at jumping the line, but he saw little or no resentment on the faces they passed. Instead, there seemed mostly to be a palpable sense of relief. After all, he realized, what did they have to be resentful for? These people had won the fate lottery. Of all living humanity, billions around the world, they would make it. They alone had been chosen to be saved, even if they had no clue as to why.

They reached the platform and felt, for the first time, the waft of warm air emanating from the iridescent ring below. Evidently, the longer the machine was on, the more heat it generated. As before, the air occasionally crackled and Charlie noted a faint metallic taste on his tongue. He also heard a sound like distant wind chimes and felt the hair on his arms and neck stand up. None of these things made sense but that, he decided, made sense.

Mrs. MacGuffin held them back a moment as an older gentleman and his dog prepared to make the leap. The Labrador retriever had lain down and was refusing to move.

"So we can go *whenever* we want? We could go to Ancient Greece? Or to watch knights fight in Medieval England?"

"Technically, yes," said Mrs. MacGuffin. "Now, a lot of people get romantic notions like that, but I advise you to think about it very carefully. Wherever you go, you'll be spending the rest of your life there and the past is a lot less romantic when you have to live in it."

Finally, the man resorted to scooping the dog up in his arms and stepping off the edge. The dog panicked and struggled for a moment, then both were gone. A woman stepped forward to take her turn.

"Sarah, do you mind?" asked Mrs. MacGuffin. "I wanted my friends to go next."

Sarah, already nostalgic for the future present, was happy to spend a few more minutes there. She nodded and stepped out of the way.

At that moment Mrs. MacGuffin's cell phone rang. She answered it and said, "What? Oh dear. Well, then I suppose I'd better coom down." She then hung up her phone and said, "I'm sorry, but I've got to go. Good luck. Have a loovely tam, whichever one it is." With that she vigorously shook Charlie's hand, then leaned over and gave Alex a kiss on the cheek. The next moment she was gone, stomping her way down the steel steps to the tower exit below.

Suddenly abandoned, Charlie and Alex both became conscious of time. Those next in line watched them expectantly, as did dozens more from the stairs and catwalks. It was a momentous moment that would decide the rest of their lives, and yet it was a decision that needed to be made swiftly. "Where, er, when are we going to go?" asked Alex. He looked to Charlie anxiously, clearly wanting him to make the adult decision.

Charlie knew what he wanted to do. "I need to go back ten years."

"What? Ten years? That's not enough time."

Charlie had somehow managed to avoid thinking this through. Of course it wasn't, well, not for Alex anyway. "I need to go back to when my daughter was born."

Alex stared at Charlie in shock. "Are you..." he then stopped and considered his words carefully. "We'll just end up back here again!"

"I know," said Charlie, flustered. From the moment he'd learned about the timegate, he'd thought endlessly about going back to see his family again. He'd obsessed about it. Despite this, he'd never once thought how that would impact Alex. "Several times. Again and again. I don't expect you to understand, Alex. You don't know what it's like to have a daughter and to lose her."

"I know what it's like to lose a mother."

"And you could see her again too!"

Alex stared at Charlie. "How? From outside the window? Creeping about? You heard Mrs. MacGuffin, *we can't change anything.* We can't interact with people we knew. We'd just be hanging around, watching them, like ghosts."

Charlie reached out for him, but Alex flinched and drew back. "Alex..." Charlie said.

"Keep moovin'!" someone shouted.

"Every minute wasted, means people who dunna make it throo!" yelled a woman.

Charlie looked at Alex pleadingly. He didn't want to hurt him, but he couldn't just let go of his wife and daughter. He felt as if he'd been holding on to them for a year, dangling over a cliff, his arm aching in agony, only now able to pull them up. "I have a chance to see them live again."

Alex shook his head firmly and said, "That's not living."

With that he turned and ran towards the platform edge.

"Alex!" Charlie shouted and ran after him.

Alex never looked back. He simply reached the end of the diving board and leapt off into empty space. He then plummeted through the halo and was gone. Charlie halted himself at the edge of the precipice, flailing his arms to avoid carrying over the edge. Part of him wanted to follow, but part of him could not. "Where did he go?" he asked frantically of Sarah who, of course, had no idea. The others waiting, stared blankly at him as well. Charlie ran to the console and looked at the dials. He found the display vacant. There were no numbers, no dates selected. The system had reset. "What does that mean?" Charlie staggered back from the console and stared at the emptiness inside the glowing ring.

"Can I go?" asked Sarah tentatively.

Charlie, unable to answer, simply, walked past her. Those next in line stepped aside to let him pass. In a confused daze Charlie descended the rattling steps. For the second time in his life, every thought in his head, every inkling of who he was, had been vaporized.

On the platform far above, Sarah entered the date 'June 28, 1914', and stepped off into space.

CHAPTER 28

"I'll just take one last look..."   Mrs. Lot

They were buried side-by-side. Everyone told Charlie that the service was lovely, but he could see nothing lovely about it. It was a closed casket service and he knew why. Lisa's beautiful, soft face had passed through the hard windshield. The other driver had been killed as well. That was good, Charlie thought. The other driver was drunk. He could go to Hell.

After the service, friends and family had gathered at the house. Not his friends and family. They all belonged to Lisa and Faith. He had none of his own. A few colleagues from the agency showed up, the people who felt they should. There were no children. The parents of Faith's friends didn't want to shock them, to expose them to the 'idea' of death. Charlie couldn't blame them, he'd have done the same.

Someone had arranged for the catering and the flowers. Bill, the neighbour, tried to warn him about being "taken to the cleaners" by the funeral home. "They prey on grief" he explained. "They know you're in a weak place, and they overcharge for everything. They tried that with me when mom died. I mean, who needs a mahogany coffin for Christ's sake? You're just going to stick it in a hole to rot." Charlie punched him in the mouth. Bill got a bloody lip and lost a tooth. Charlie hurt his hand. It was good to feel pain. That was when everyone left. Charlie later settled with Bill for twenty-five thousand dollars, or rather his lawyer did. He knew he'd been 'taken to the cleaners', but he didn't care. Punching that idiot was worth it at the time, just to drive everyone away. After they'd left, Charlie sat alone on the ottoman in the living room, massaging his hand and trying to cry. It didn't happen. All he felt were sore knuckles.

A week later he did cry. It was when he let himself finally enter Faith's bedroom. He sat on her tiny pink bed, held her tiny pink socks, and broke into uncontrollable sobbing. After that, he couldn't leave the house or talk to anyone for days.

Everything Lisa or Faith had touched became a holy relic. He kept every drawing his daughter had done, every toy she'd played with. Most of all, he stared at the photographs. To Charlie, they were magical imprints of light that had once bounced off of their perfect faces. They were frozen fragments of time. He sat and stared at a picture of Lisa holding Faith at age two. Faith was wearing a yellow shirt with the words 'Mommy's Monkey' on it. He tried to imagine himself there, taking the picture, telling Faith to look up, and reminding Lisa to smile.

It was fully a month before he realized something was missing. Lisa's sister, Karen, asked about the letter Lisa had left. It had been there after the funeral, when the guests had arrived. For some reason Charlie hadn't read it. He hadn't even touched it. He wasn't sure why. It was an obvious thing to do. Karen had asked him about it at the time, and he'd told her he'd look at it later. Later, it was gone. He hadn't even noticed. "It must be somewhere," Karen insisted. Charlie couldn't argue with her logic. Still, it wasn't on the table, where he'd left it. Nor was it on the floor. There'd been a lot of people in the house after the funeral, but it seemed like a strange, heartless thing to steal. Nevertheless, it never turned up again. "That's crazy," Karen insisted. She was upset that her sister's last words might be lost, but even more upset at Charlie's apparent ambivalence. "Don't you want to know what she wrote?"

"Of course," he said. "but it's gone, and it's not like I can go back in time to get it."

CHAPTER 29

"I think we're going in circles..." – S. Guatama

The line to the tower was growing now at twice the speed it was consumed. There was a nervous energy of those joining it. Would they get through in time? For now, the consensus seemed to be 'yes'. It felt, however, as if some sort of tipping point was approaching. The tipping point between hope and fear, order and chaos.

When Charlie exited the tower, Mrs. MacGuffin was nowhere to be seen. He jogged down the length of the line which, at its current stretch of three miles, took some time. When he reached the end of the line, he did not find her either. Instead, he found her motorcycle, its sidecar empty, abandoned in a ditch. On questioning those waiting nearby, he learned that some men had arrived in a black helicopter. They had accosted Mrs.

MacGuffin and demanded that she go with them. She did so, peacefully. No one knew where. Someone said the men spoke strangely, but coming from the local Scots that had the effect of ruling out only other local Scots. Charlie turned and watched erratic lightning streak across the sky. It seemed the end of days was determined to look like the end of days. He'd only once felt this alone, this lost. He considered walking back to the front of the line. People might let him through, having seen him earlier with Mrs. MacGuffin, but they also might not. Besides, he decided, he needed time to think. So he joined the end of the line.

Hours passed, and Charlie had almost reached a large rock. This was his current milestone. His next was an ornery looking thistle and beyond that a hillock. The line was moving with the slow, inexorable progress of a bank line that stretched for miles. It continued as well, to lengthen, this in spite of it now being nine o'clock at night. The rural road had no lights, and the intermittent flashes of lightning provided only moments of high contrast and stark relief. The moon was utterly obscured by the cloud cover, cloaking the land in featureless black. The only other lights on the road were a few kerosene lanterns and the dancing rectangles of cellphone screens. There was no service here. The woman in front of Charlie was playing Scrabble on her iPhone. The woman was stumped. She failed to notice that, with six of her letters, she could complete the word 'teleology' and earn a triple word score to boot.

Charlie noticed none of this. He was immersed past his eyes and ears in a pool of his own misery. He was anxious to make a decision, yet unable to decide what it was he wanted to do. Consequently, he jumped when someone tapped his shoulder.

"I'm sorry," said the man in an unplaceable accent, "I didn't mean to startle you."

"It's fine," said Charlie. He was as surprised by the man's appearance as his presence. He instantly recognized the robes, shaved head and question mark tattoos of a Pō Light.

"May I have your name?" asked the Pō Light.

"Um... why?"

"For the record. I assure you, it won't be used for marketing purposes."

"Oh, okay. It's Charlie, Charles Draper."

"American?"

"Yes."

The acolyte carefully wrote this down on a pad of paper. Peering over the top, Charlie could see that it was indeed, a long list of names and other information. "Religion?"

"Presbyterian, I guess. Not now, but that's what I was raised."

"What are you now?"

"Not sure, really. Does it matter?"

"It could be the most important thing in the universe, but probably not."

"Can I ask what this is for?"

"It's a census."

"For Mrs. MacGuffin?"

"No, but she said we could do it. May I ask when and where you're going?"

"I don't know that either."

"Undecided, again. Right then." The Pō Light turned to the next person in line.

"Listen, why are you doing this? It's the end of the world. Surely compiling some big list of who's here and where we're going doesn't matter."

The acolyte stopped and stared at him as if Charlie had just started meowing like a cat. For the first time, Charlie had a good look at the man. The Pō Light had a baby face and wide eyes that made his age ambiguous. Charlie suddenly felt very stupid, and to make matters worse, he didn't know why. Of course, at the heart of it, Charlie didn't really care. What this man said and thought was of no consequence given the monumental decisions Charlie was trying to make. His thought process there, however, was at an impasse. Charlie simply didn't know what to do about Alex versus Lisa and Faith. It was pathetic. Finally, he had been given a choice about his life and he couldn't make it. So he continued numbly on with the conversation, exactly as he had with the people at the funeral. "So why does it matter?"

"Do you know what the tenets of my faith are?"

Charlie had absolutely zero interest in Pō Light doctrine. It was considered, even by religious standards, an extremely silly faith. Not as silly as Scientology, perhaps, but still, quite silly. It was said that there are three types of people you never invite into your house, Jehovah's Witnesses, vampires, and Pō Lights—in that order. The first will try to save you, the second will try to kill you and the last will bore you. "Don't know, don't care," said Charlie emphatically.

"Our great prophet, Ed Platzberg of Winnipeg, Manitoba, had an epiphany we refer to as *The Deselection.*" Charlie turned away. He had neither the inclination nor emotional state of mind to listen to some cult member's sanctimonious blather. The Pō Light, however, was used to indifference and continued undeterred. "Ed's great revelation was to realize that among all the many religions and peoples of the world, Christians, Jews,

Muslims, Mormons, Scientologists, Snake Handlers, Hindus, Americans, Russians, the Swiss, Wall Street Investment Bankers, Vegans, Cross Trainers, Baby Boomers and so on, was one common universal belief. This was the belief that, in all the cosmos, there was one special group, a *chosen people.*"

"Yeah, themselves," a voice said unto them. The voice spoke in a thick Cockney accent. It belonged to Sam, the next person in line. Sam was a scrap dealer from London who had been listening in. "What an amazing co-incidence!" said Sam with an exaggerated eye roll. Sam had been hauling scrap along the road to Cockwaddle when he'd spotted the long queue. Once he'd heard what it was for, he'd joined in, right behind Charlie. Up until then he'd been joking that it must be the line for the new iPhone.

"That's true," agreed the acolyte. "Still, this idea that there are a 'chosen people' who will be saved is, in itself, universal."

"If you say so," said Sam. Charlie was trying not to listen. He thought of Alex possibly lost and alone in some unknown time and space, or worse. He felt as if he'd wandered onto the stage of a play by Sartre and now couldn't find the exit.

"What is not universal, as you point out, sir," said the Pō Light, "is the idea of who the chosen people are. There's basically no agreement on that point whatsoever."

"Now that is true."

"Which means every religion, group, nation, *but one,* is wrong."

"You're right!" said Sam, eyes wide.

"*Ed* was right," said the Pō Light, with humility. "Ed saw no reason to think that he was a chosen person. He soon found others who felt the same; people who realized that they too were utterly unremarkable or, as Ed put it, *extraordinarily ordinary."*

"That's a paradox."

"And yet it is not."

"I see," said Sam though, in truth, he didn't see at all.

"Anyway, that was the foundation of our religion. He gathered together those who shared his belief in their own insignificance and gave us a quest. That quest was to discover the true 'chosen people' and their messiah."

"Really?"

"Well, the messiah bit is optional. In the meantime, since we don't know who the real chosen people are, we go around being as civil as possible to everyone. We start on the assumption that everyone we meet is better than us, rather than the other way around, as most people do."

"That's nice."

"And, once we find the true chosen ones, we will recognize and serve them."

"Oh."

"We also plan to ingratiate ourselves in the hope that we too might be saved. Ed called that 'collateral salvation'."

"Ah, well that makes more sense." Sam thought about this for a moment, then said, "Sort of like hedging your bets, in a way?"

"In a way."

Charlie thought about Lisa and Faith. He thought about seeing them again. He thought about reliving those lost moments, albeit from afar. He imagined the photographs come to life, Lisa holding Faith, while he took the picture. He even fantasized about ignoring Mrs. MacGuffin's warning and trying to speak with them. He imagined hanging outside Faith's school and watching her in the playground. He'd have to be careful not to be spotted by them or anyone else. If someone saw him watching, they might report him to the police. "So," said Sam, trying to appear disinterested "the 'chosen people', any luck with, you know... finding them?"

"Why yes," said the Pō Light with surprise.

"Oh! Oh, well, um, out of curiosity, who might they be?" As he said this, Sam leaned in while casting about furtive glances in case 'they' might be somewhere nearby.

"They're *you.*"

"Me?"

"Yes, and everyone else here in line. At least those who make it through in time."

"Me? I'm a chosen people?"

"Chosen person, and yes. Of all the billions of people on Earth, you and those around you, are the only ones who will be saved. Unless, of course, there's another time portal we're not aware of." Now it was the Pō Light's turn to glance about on the off chance that there was another time portal nearby and he'd simply failed to notice it.

Charlie, unable to think with the inane conversation taking place beside him, turned with a burst of real anger. "Can you shut the Hell up and take your ridiculous religion elsewhere? The people in line here aren't 'chosen', they're just here by random chance. They're people who live in the area, are related to Mrs. MacGuffin, or just happened to pass by. It's not because of their religion, race, nationality or their local God damn sports team. There's nothing special about you, me, or anyone else here in line!"

"Mmm, yes," said the Pō Light, glancing down at his list, "that does seem to be the case."

"And we're not in line to be 'saved'. We're in line to go back in time to take one last ride on the merry-go-round. None of it matters because the world's going to end and everyone's going to die, sooner or later."

"Ah, well, that's where you're wrong."

"Really? You're telling me the world's not going to end?"

"Oh, no. No, no, no, goodness no, which is to say, yes, of course it is. I meant about it not mattering. You see, that was the second epiphany of our prophet."

"Ed Platzberg," Sam interjected, to show that he'd been paying attention.

"Yes," said the Pō Light. "You see, Ed's daughter contracted a brain tumour." Charlie, who had been opening his mouth to yell some more, closed it. Suddenly the zealot's dissonant rambling had struck a chord. "At first he was lost... wandering in the desert, "the Pō Light continued. "Outside of Albuquerque, I believe. They have a cancer treatment centre there. Anyway, the prognosis was grim. They realized they couldn't help her and that she was going to die. Of course, Ed couldn't rail against God, as a chosen person might. After all, who was he? A nobody. Likewise, he'd raised his daughter a Pō Light, so she was a nobody too. They were both nobodies. Well, to God, anyway."

Charlie was speechless. He turned away to hide his face. He felt as though the life marrow had been sucked from his bones. "So what did he do?" asked Charlie, feeling unsteady on his feet.

"He had that epiphany, I mentioned. He asked himself if his daughter had an immortal soul. Chosen people believe they do. They think that's what really counts. Ed, however, realized something very important. He realized that it didn't matter."

"It didn't matter?" asked Charlie incredulously. He'd often found himself wondering if Faith was somehow still there. Sometimes he felt her. Other times he felt he was fooling himself. He'd reach down to touch her shoulder, only to touch air.

"Ed asked himself then, what is the difference between immortal existence and mortal existence?"

Charlie began to feel annoyed again. He wasn't interested in some sophomoric theological debate. "And?"

"And what?"

"And what is the difference between immortal and mortal existence?"

"Oh right. Um, length."

"What?"

"Or 'duration' if you prefer. Basically, one is around forever and the other for, well, less."

"That's it?" It was, Charlie decided, the stupidest thing the Pō Light had said so far.

"Yes. That's it. He then realized that length doesn't matter."

"Well, sometimes it does," Sam snickered.

"I mean, er, Ed meant, length doesn't define value."

"What does then?" asked Sam.

"We do. Even if we aren't 'chosen'. People over complicate things, by which I mean existence."

Charlie stared at him, trying to decide if this was all nonsense. "What about going back in time?" he asked.

"The merry-go-round? What's it matter *when* you live? The past will become your present. Just because the world will end someday, doesn't make it pointless. Pō Lights believe in living. We love life. 'Live for as long as you can, because existence is the best thing there is!' Ed said that. He also said, 'we are all imperfect clones of our former selves', but people think he may have been drunk at the time."

Charlie nodded, trying to absorb the thoughts swirling in his head. The Pō Light turned to leave. "Wait," said Charlie anxiously, "what happened to Ed's daughter?"

"In conventional terms? She died." said the Pō Light. "Of course, Ed would never say it that way when people asked him that."

"How did he say it?"

"He'd say, *she lived.*"

CHAPTER 30

"I believe in moral relativism" – Cain

Charlie watched Faith work. The seven-year-old diligently scooped wet sand into the bucket with the yellow plastic shovel, patted in down, and levelled it off, just as he had taught her. His daughter then lugged the now-heavy container to a corner of the castle and flipped it over. She gave the bottom of the bucket exactly two whacks and pulled it away, leaving a squat sand tower in its place. Finally, she poked narrow windows in the side with a stick. Arrow slits, he'd told her. She sat back to admire her work. She then turned and smiled at her father, squinting in the morning sun.

"Is it finished?" Charlie asked.

Faith nodded and looked once more at the sprawling palace she'd created. Five walls, five towers, and a keep in the center, with a twig for a citadel. "Can you help me make the moat?" she asked.

"Of course." Charlie put down his book and crawled over to her side. "You dig over there and we'll meet up by the water."

Faith nodded and scrambled to the far side. With that same diligence, she began to scoop out a six-inch-wide trench. Charlie did the same. He felt the sand beneath his nails. He breathed in the ocean breeze. The air smelled of salt and sun dried sea weed, but still tasted like the cleanest air on Earth. Further down the beach a man was yelling at his dog to come back in from the water. Soaking wet, frisbee in mouth, the dog would come when it felt like it. The dog wasn't being difficult, it was simply too happy to hear him. Charlie wondered for a moment where Lisa was. They'd come to the beach together, but Lisa had wandered off looking for something. She's probably collecting pebbles, he decided. Lisa often did this at the beach. She'd collect shiny stones, only to be disappointed when, later, they dried off dull.

A few minutes later, Charlie and Faith's trenches met as planned. "It needs to go all the way 'round, Daddy," said Faith, brushing the hair from her eyes.

"You're right." Charlie crawled back to quickly connect the top part of the ring, completing the moat. "Good?"

Faith nodded. "Can we do the peace resistance now?"

"Of course," said Charlie with a smile. She was asking for a trick he called the "pièce de résistance". It involved digging a connecting canal to the ocean, so that sea water would fill the moat. It completed the castle. Charlie and Faith together dug the tiny trench, making sure it and the moat were all lower than sea level. They carefully left a final dyke intact.

"Is it ready, Daddy?" she asked. Charlie marvelled, as he often did, at her perfect small face and bright green eyes. She was so small, in her little red bathing suit.

"Yup."

Faith broke into a grin and proceeded to smash the tiny dyke with her shovel. A gentle wave lapped over the sand and instantly flooded the moat with briny sea water. Charlie spotted a point where the water failed to fill. He leaned over and dug out some more sand. The water rushed in. The circle was complete.

He turned to look at Faith, who was admiring the castle they had built. She then turned to him and smiled. She nodded her approval. "It's perfect," she said.

At that moment a rogue wave rolled in. It rushed past their ankles and swamped the sandy structure. As the water rapidly receded it melted the castle turrets and walls, reclaiming the sand for the sea. Charlie looked at Faith with sympathy. He was surprised to see that his daughter seemed unconcerned. "You're not upset?" he asked.

Faith shrugged and smiled. "I had fun building it," she said.

Charlie nodded. "So did I."

CHAPTER 31

"I paint what I see" – H. Bosch

Once more, Charlie ran the length of the line, this time back towards the nuclear cooling tower. In the night, it appeared as a black silhouette against the eigengrau sky. The clouds had parted, revealing a patch of stars. In the heavy dark of the Highlands, the stars appeared as pin pricks of light so brilliant that it astonished Charlie even as he ran. He was used to the ambient light of cities obscuring or hiding the universe altogether. You forget it's even there, thought Charlie.

As he ran past, the people in line regarded Charlie with looks of surprise, curiosity, and, occasionally, indignation. He wasn't the first to try to jump the queue, and they assumed he'd be sent back like the others. Charlie desperately needed to find Mrs. MacGuffin. He'd heard a rumour that she'd been spotted near the front of the line. Of course, since information was being passed along the queue in a massive game of 'broken telephone', there was no telling how accurate or recent it was. Still, he knew now what he had to do. Charlie had never expected the words of the crazy cultist to help him. He had little time for dime store philosophy. He'd heard enough of it at the funeral. Telling someone that 'everything happens for a reason' is about the worst thing you can say to someone who has just lost his family. He'd rather believe the universe was a cold empty place without purpose, than something that had caused *that* to happen. Even so, the Pō Light's words were cold comfort at the thought of what he was going to do or, more precisely, what he would give up in doing it.

The rumour was true. Charlie found Mrs. MacGuffin at the front of the line and waved to her. She look slightly disheveled and was clearly surprised to see him. Despite this, she smiled curiously and waved back. He vaguely noticed a black helicopter abandoned in a nearby field. Charlie was relieved to find her, but now felt fear at what she might tell him.

"Hello Mr. Draper!"

"Are you all right?"

"Oh aye. I've had quite the adventure!" she explained. She was clearly exhilarated by the experience and delighted to have someone to tell it to. "There was a disturbance at the end of the queue. Some Roosian billionaire and his entourage had flown in. A boonch a Cossack thugs if you ask me. Anyhoo, they were demanding that I take them to the front of the queue."

"I see," said Charlie. "Listen I need to ask—"

"They had goons," she said, too excited to notice Charlie's desperate state.

"Goons, Cossack goons, yes, but—"

"Machine-goons."

"Oh, guns, right."

"And a helicopter, and gold bullion, and diamonds. And they insisted I coom with them. They said if I didn'a coom, they'd kill me, and if I did, they'd give me a million euros. As if money's wurth anything now!"

"Mrs. MacGuffin..." Charlie wasn't the least bit interested in her adventure, however exciting. He needed to know what had happened to Alex. Mrs. MacGuffin, however, was inebriated with adrenaline and misinterpreted Charlie's anxiety as interest. Charlie realized he'd have to let her speak.

"He said his name was Sergey and that he was going to go back to New York, 1930, right after the market collapse. He would take his gold with him and use it to buy up all the blue chip company stock he knew would survive the depression. He wanted to go live his laf even richer than he was now. So I did as he demanded, I took him to the front of the line. He then held a goon to me head and made me enter the date while he watched. He told me he would shoot me dead if I didn'a do it. What a most unpleasant gentleman!"

"But he's gone now?"

"Oh aye, he is. Just lak he said, gone back to New York, 1930..." Mrs. MacGuffin then smiled mischievously and added, *"B.C."* Mrs. MacGuffin began to chuckle. "My only regret is not getting to see the look on his face when he got there! Oh dear, he's long dead 'n' dust now, I s'pose. God rest his soul."

"Mrs. MacGuffin!" Charlie pleaded.

Mrs. MacGuffin saw, for the first time, the pained look on Charlie's face. "What is it dear? Why aren't you and yur lad safely in the past?"

Charlie explained what had happened.

"Oh dear," said Mrs. MacGuffin. She then smiled and began to chuckle once more.

"I don't see what's remotely funny about—"

She touched his hand sympathetically. "I'm sorry dear, I don't mean to laugh but, well, you said he jumped through the gate without entering any date or location?"

"Yes, exactly. The display was blank."

"Well, that's because it resets after each joomp. Rupert made it that way for safety's sake."

"Resets? To when... and where?"

"Well, to here... and now, of course."

"You mean Alex is here?" cried Charlie.

"And now," Mrs. MacGuffin assured him.

*   *   *

It took about twenty minutes for them to find Alex. Here, it turned out, meant a farmer's field about a kilometre away. The latitudinal and longitudinal settings of the gate were only precise to within a few thousand meters. Alex had walked back to the gate where he'd learned that Charlie had not gone through at all. He had been searching for Charlie ever since. People in line had tried to be helpful, but had instead sent him on various wild goose chases. When Charlie finally found Alex, the boy was cold, exhausted and his boots were caked in sheep manure. Otherwise, he was fine. The man and boy fell into each other, both in tears. Charlie hugged Alex desperately, saying again and again how sorry he was. Alex apologized for being stupid and insensitive to Charlie's loss.

"There will be plenty of time fur words later," Mrs. MacGuffin pointed out. "It's all in the past now." She enjoyed the puns that time travel allowed for speech. She liked to refer to them as a 'tense situation'. Charlie and Alex nodded.

Mrs. MacGuffin led them once more into the tower. There was mounting anxiety for those in line and word of numerous scuffles and confrontations further back in the queue. It would be a good while before the world actually ended, but already the fighting had begun. "I still don't get why you don't go through" said Alex.

"Things are going to get ugly here," Charlie agreed.

Mrs. MacGuffin nodded. "Aye," she said. "It won't be all the band playin' while the ship goes down, I ken tha'. Still, I figure, while I'm here I can at least help to keep folk in line. They ken I can shoot it all down. It'll still get nasty towards end, but 'til then... I guess it's all I can do to make up for what Rupert did. It's all his fault tha' knows. You canna give a bomb to a baby and blame the child for what happens next."

Moments later they stood at the platform. A convent of nuns from nearby Neighbrook stepped aside to let them through. The nuns were in a state of religious confusion and were happy to let them pass while they continued to debate whether entering the gate was a form of blasphemy. "What would Jesus do?" asked one sister. Another nun suggested they go back to 0 A.D. and find out.

Mrs. MacGuffin entered the time of their choosing, Jan 1, 1920. The idea was to benefit from the relative comfort of the twentieth century, while giving Alex time to live. They would use their knowledge of the future to avoid the pitfalls of the Great Depression, but not try to change anything that might lead to problems. As it turned out, their plan would work out well. Under an assumed identity, Charlie would eventually find work with US Government intelligence. He would excel there with his 'forward thinking' and go on to become a founding member of the OSS during World War II. His career would later culminate with him as a director with the newly formed Central Intelligence Agency in 1947. He would legally adopt Alex as his son. Alex would grow up and become a successful science fiction writer. He would write stories of a far off future he knew would never be. Alex would later marry and have two children. It would be a family secret that would be passed down, that each successive generation must make its way to Scotland, should it live to a certain date. Eventually, one winter day, both Alex and Charlie would trudge through deep snow and biting Michigan cold to watch a small convoy of military vehicles drive by. They were unable to intervene, but both wanted to bear witness. Charlie would be in his seventies then, and Alex would have to help him through the deep drifts. But before and after all of that, both of them held hands and stood on the precipice. Charlie steeled himself. He knew what he was doing. He knew where Lisa was going when she drove off that morning with their daughter. Most of all, he knew that Alex was right. He had to let go of Faith, except as the memory she was. There was no going back, even with a time machine. That, he decided, was the real paradox, accepting something he knew to be true on faith. He gripped the boy's hand and nodded. The two then stepped from the steel platform, fell through the glowing ring and were gone, forever and never.

* * *

Two years later, the Earth was gone. The Sun was also gone, as were all of the planets. In its place was *chaos*. The chaos was of varying diameter. On average, it was over six billion kilometres across now. It could also be described as forty 'astronomical units' but, given that *au* was defined as the mean distance from the center of the Earth to the center of the Sun, that could only be seen as anachronistic now. Because of the exponential growth of the chaos, it had swallowed the rest of the solar system in about the same time in took to swallow the Earth and moon alone. Of course, owing to the enormity of the ever expanding cosmos, it would still be a very long time before *everything* was gone. In distant galaxies, civilizations would rise and fall, oblivious of the dissolving doom. Voyager II was gone. That left Voyager I as the lone relic of humanity, dutifully beaming back reports to a planet that was no longer there. In and of itself, this was not a great tragedy as, ever since leaving the solar system, these reports had effectively read "more of the same..."

In mere minutes, the chaos would expand enough to absorb Voyager I as well and, thereby, erase the last vestige of mankind from existence. Seconds before that happened, however, an event occurred of mind boggling improbability. It was something so astronomically unlikely that it could only have happened for a reason. This apparent portent, however, was then confounded by its own complete and utter irrelevance. After four decades drifting through space, Voyager I was struck by a piece of space debris. This was not a stray meteor nor part of a comet. The debris was a deceased hamster named Doris. Doris, now frozen solid at 4° Kelvin, exploded into ice crystals upon impact. This random event destroyed Voyager I's central processor and effectively killed the tiny probe. A moment later, the inexorable chaos spread and both the Voyager I spacecraft and the pulverized hamster were gone.

Chaos Theory

Fin.

APPENDIX A: THE 5.5 EPIPHANIES

Ed Platzberg created the Pō Light religion, more or less by accident. This wasn't the first time a religion was created inadvertently. Jesus had no intention of creating Christianity and that worked out fairly well. Or rather it did, until St. Paul ruined it all by intentionally creating the Church. Intentionally created religions include Scientology and Apostolic Socialism. The former was created by science fiction author L. Ron Hubbard in what, one can only assume, was one of the greatest practical jokes of all time. So great, in fact, that it is still going on today. The latter was created by Jim Jones, who showed us that, when life brings you lemons, make Kool-Aid. So, all in all, accidental religions would seem to be the way to go. If the road to Hell is paved with good intentions and, presumably, bad intentions aren't exactly the asphalt of salvation, that leaves unintended consequences as the only building material left.

Chaos Theory

Ed Edward Platzberg was named for his father, Ed, and his grandfather, Edward. His family, however, called him 'Ted' in reference to a beloved great aunt of the same name. To everyone else, he was simply 'Ed' or, sometimes, 'Eep!'. Ed was a moderately successful tie salesman living in Winnipeg, Manitoba, Canada. He had worked for the Breakneck Tie Co., based in Cincinnati, Ohio, for over twelve years, selling ties of every stripe, colour and occasional polka dot. Ed was proud of his job. "Pants separate people from the animals," he used to say, "but ties separate people from people who aren't wearing ties."

One day, while sitting in a sales and marketing meeting, Ed learned an interesting fact. He learned that his home town of Winnipeg was the most important test market in North America. It owed this distinction to the fact of its being completely *average*. To a marketer, this meant that if a product made it in Winnipeg the odds were pretty good that it would make it in other cities as well. This was the reason Winnipeg got Chicken McNuggets, Cherry Pepsi and adult onset diabetes before they became popular elsewhere. Of course, plenty of people know this, but Ed learned something else that day, something very specific to himself. He learned that he too was completely average, even by Winnipeg standards. He was average looking, he was of average height and weight, he was the average age and wore average clothes and read average books. His income was average and he had average kids. His wife was also average and they lived in the single most average part of the city, in an average house. Whatever it was, Ed was the average of it. Mathematically this could also be described as the 'mean', but he didn't like to think of himself as a mean person. Ed realized then, with his average intelligence, that he was conceptually the center of the universe, provided the center was defined as the average. An idea then occurred to him. This idea was that he was 'extraordinarily ordinary'. Something else then occurred to him, that all of this inherent mediocrity was *okay*. Ed decided to share his idea online. Ed had two-hundred and eight Twitter followers, the average number for a Twitter user at the time. When he began to post his ideas he never expected them to resonate so much with the average Twitter follower, but they did. He certainly never expected those followers to then retweet his thoughts to an average of two-hundred and eight more followers each, but they did that as well. Suddenly, there were tens of thousands of average people who had finally found what they were looking for, someone to acknowledge that they weren't special or chosen, but that this was okay. To his followers, not having to live up to the notion that they were somehow preordained for something wasn't depressing, it was liberating. They then turned to Ed and asked him to be their leader. Ed told them "no", that he wasn't special enough to lead them but, if they liked, they could go in the same direction he was going, provided they didn't talk too much or ask a lot of questions. So they did, and that was when something *extraordinary* happened — a new religion was born.

The name of the religion, it is worth noting, was also an accident. One morning, Ed was posting a comment on Facebook about his breakfast cereal. His iPhone, however, auto-corrected the word "frosted mini wheats" as "Pō Light". No one knows why. Some say it was fate, while others say it was a bug in the text interpretation algorithm. Almost certainly it was one or other. Whatever the reason, the post went viral and, by the time Ed realized his mistake, the name had stuck. Several of his more enthusiastic followers had already tattooed it on various parts of their bodies.

Before compiling *The Blog*, the collection of internet postings that comprise the central tenets of the Pō Light faith, Ed wrote *The 5.5*

Epiphanies. The former is too long to be included here. The latter is not. *The 5.5 Epiphanies* were the foundation of the faith and have been compared to the Ten Commandments. This is a poor comparison. For one thing, there are only five and a half of them. Secondly, they're not commandments. They are more like vague suggestions of things you might like to do or think about, provided you're not too busy. Lastly, they weren't handed down from God, a burning bush or even an overheated houseplant. Ed freely admitted to having simply "made them up"—some, quite possibly, while drunk. Cynics have argued that this simply makes the Pō Light religion typical, rather than atypical. Calling a Pō Light typical, of course, is like calling a Lutheran dull. What follows here are those epiphanies, in their original text. Since their first posting, they have been copy-pasted by candlelight by monks in monasteries around the world. They have been shared, re-tweeted, liked and turned into animated gifs. They have also been machine translated, and retranslated into hundreds of different languages and, in some instances, into entirely new religions.

The 5.5 Epiphanies

1

*We are not the chosen people. While there may be people chosen by God(s)
who are better than the rest and postmarked for salvation, it's almost
certainly not us. We have no reason to believe we're special, but that's okay.
We were created this way. Recognizing this frees us up to look past ourselves
to find the true religion and the true chosen people. If you don't see them
nearby, try elsewhere, in the next room perhaps. In the meantime, be nice to
people. There's a fifty-fifty chance they're better than you, and even if they're*

not, it's nice to be nice anyway.

2

We are all (increasingly) imperfect clones of our former selves.

3

There is at least one other force in the world besides Good and Evil, and that force is 'Jerry'. Jerry is my neighbour and he is this thing, so I've named it after him. Jerry, is not good or evil or even neutral. He's just, well, Jerry. Jerry is the umami of being. You can't quite put your finger on it, but you know what it's not. If evil is black, and good is white, then Jerry is chartreuse. When you meet someone like Jerry, you'll know what it is. Until then, it's like trying to explain what B-flat tastes like to a mollusk. It's quite possible that Good and Evil don't really exist, that they are constructs of the human mind. Jerry, on the other hand, is real. I've met him. He still has my weed whacker.

4

Numbers are meaningless, but they're better than nothing. Nothing, on the other hand, is better than anything. If we can't understand the meaning of words, how can we possibly understand the meaning of life? Once you know this, you'll really be onto something.

5

The only truly honest experiment is a triple-blind study. This is similar to a double-blind study in that both the subject and those conducting the experiment don't know what is going on. The difference is that, in a triple-blind study, no one looks at the results either. If you think this doesn't apply to you because you not a scientist, think again.

5.5

There is a truth in the world that can lead to real, lasting happiness and that is *

---

*It is said that Ed was writing this down on a cocktail napkin when his pen ran out of ink. By the time he had the waitress's attention and she gave him another pen, which also didn't work, and she had to go find another waitress and borrow her pen, Ed had forgotten what it was. Nevertheless, he kept it here in the hope that, someday, it will come back to him. Somedays he thinks really hard about it but, so far, no dice.

APPENDIX B

This appendix was inflammatory and has been removed.

APPENDIX C: THE PRESIDENT'S POETRY

The book includes three examples of poetry written by the President of the United States. The Commander-in-Chief, however, was quite prolific, writing verse both short and long. The longest was his attempt to rewrite *The Divine Comedy*. He believed that Dante got it all wrong, at least in terms of who was in Hell and who was in Paradise. Hoping to appeal to a broader audience, he called his version *The Divine Situation Comedy*. Most critics agree that, on analysis, the President likely never read the original. He appeared to have based his interpretation on a video game, a dream sequence from an episode of *Happy Days* and his own assumptions. While that particular work is too long to be included here, a few shorter examples are not.

My Brother's Keeper

On the day, before tomorrow,
I met a man filled with sorrow
He said he'd lost his brother's twin,
I told him, he should look within.
He waved his arms and began to shout,
"I dare not let that person out!"

Time Peace

A man gave me a thing precise
A magical mechanical device
It was a golden watch and fob
To keep it going was my job
But then I found this thing he gave
Became my master, I, its slave
Though t'was my fingers task to wind
In its cold, metallic hands I'd find
My railing, desire to break and bend
And make that infernal ticking—

Jabberwocky 2

T'was frollick in the tulgy wood
With hurbled brandies indagrabe,
W'ilt pseudosinkers fullen stood
Elst bethot mimsy in the wabe.

The Jaberwock raised its head
Despite a wounding most severe

Chaos Theory

Turns out t'was not truly dead
With head in hand, as t'was severe'd.

Resuscitated by grave plot device,
Some staples and a glob of glue,
Some therapeutic massage and ice
A tenacious beast, that much is true.

"Come fight again, oh beamish boy
You think that you're so tough?
I was just warming up, oh joy
I'll tell you when I've had enough!"

Again th'lad turned to face the foe
His vorpal sword snicker-snack'd aloft
It's brainbox balanced on its neck just so
A simple tap sent it tumbling off.

"Oh dang!" the creature turned to pursue,
Seeking to retrieve its rolling head.
The beamish boy stabbed until he slew,
Which is to say, the Jabberwock, dead.

Oh wondrous day, this is sublime
You've done it twice, you've done it well
(Something, something else to rhyme)
Post to Facebook, LOL!

Chaos Theory

T'was frollick in the tulgy wood
With burbled brandies indagrabe,
W'ilt pseudosinkers fullen stood
Elst bethot mimsy in the wabe.

APPENDIX D: THE MACGUFFIN EQUATION

It is, of course, impossible to include Dr. Rupert MacGuffin's many papers here or even offer any sort of meaningful explanation of his work. His theories were broad, controversial, and brilliant beyond comprehension. At least that was the assumption, given that *ipso facto*, the people saying this didn't know what they were talking about. It has even been suggested that some of his theories were so brilliant, that he himself did not understand them. Sometimes, however, his theories were surprisingly simple. One example was his view of multiple universes. Some physicists argue that the Big Bang may be cyclical, having occurred an infinite number of times in the past and set to occur an infinite number of times in the future. Others have argued for fancy pants multidimensional models, with different universes existing concurrently in different planes of reality. Rupert believed that, if there were other universes, they were probably just adjacent to our own or, as he put it, "a little to the left." He figured that at some point, when we were able to view our universe externally in some totally inconceivable manner, there'd be an 'ah-ha' moment, when someone would notice another universe next to it. "Oh that universe" they'd say, nonchalantly, trying act is if they'd known it was there all along, "Well, yes, I suppose there is always *that* universe." Of course, Rupert MacGuffin wasn't the only physicist to conceive of infinite universes beyond the 'cosmological horizon', but he was the first to coin a term for the idea of multiple Big Bangs. He called them 'Splats'. He dubbed our own universe *Splat No. 37.* When asked why 37, he responded, "Well, we're not the first and we're not the last, so 37 seems as good a guess as any. Why? Have you got a better number?" This term was largely ignored by the scientific community and remains in disuse to this day.

Of course, he threw away all of this thinking as merely transitory when he developed his *Theory of Complete and Utter Chaos.* This should not be confused with the similarly named *Chaos Theory* of mathematics, after which this book was unscrupulously misnomered in the hope of selling more copies to people who don't read blurbs. As the nature of the theory is explained elsewhere in this book, there is no need to do so here as well. What is not included elsewhere, however, is the professor's famous *Complete Chaos Formula.*

$$42\Lambda \ V([purple] + 2)$$

Here 42 = the number 42; Λ = the Cosmological Constant; V = the Cosmological Variable; [purple] represents the colour purple; and 2 represents the number 7. When asked about the use of a colour in his equation, Rupert explained that purple is the only hue that doesn't appear in the light spectrum* as it is, in fact, a mixture of violet and red, which are at opposite sides of the rainbow band. When further asked if he was then referring to its wave length values, he replied, with annoyance, "If it could be represented by a simple number, I would have done that. This is why we use Greek symbols in math, people, because otherwise things get lost in translation. *Purple* means purple. Once you understand that, the rest of the equation pretty much explains itself. ὅπερ ἔδει δεῖξαι"

---

* This is not to say that it doesn't appear in nature, but simply not in the actual divided spectrum of white light. Obviously it does, unless you're colour blind, in which case it does not.

APPENDIX E: ALTERNATE ENDING

"But wait, what if he didn't die?" – St. Paul

Note: If you have a pair of scissors handy and some glue, feel free to cut the following paragraph out and stick it before the words "The End" in the last chapter, should you prefer it. If you're reading this on an e-reader, you'll need something stronger than scissors.

Sadly, the obliteration of all existence included not simply the present, but the past as well. This meant that none of this actually happened. The nature of Chaos, after all, is, was, and will be to transcend not simply space, but time itself. An egregious error meant that this fact remained unforeseen even by Dr. Rupert MacGuffin himself. That oversight and everything that happened subsequently was the result of his failure to carry the '3'. Not that any of this mattered, of course, as it wouldn't have happened anyway.

      The author decided to omit this as simply too depressing. More importantly, it would have the effect of rendering the book you hold in your hands a mere work of fiction.

THE END

"We read to know we are not alone."
C.S. Lewis

About the Author

Colin Robertson was born in Toronto, Canada in 1969. Determined not to be ruined by success, he decided to become an indie author in 2012 with the publication of his debut novel, *The Siege of Walter Parks*. He is the author of several short stories and optioned screenplays and currently lives with his wife, son, daughter and very loud wheaten terrier in Culver City, California.

Also by Colin Robertson

The
Siege of
Walter Parks

a novel
by Colin Robertson

GIN&TONICPRESS

For cool free stuff, like books, short fiction and book extras visit:

GinTonicPress.com
with links to buy at amazon.com
itunes.apple.com/iBooks
www.barnesandnoble.com

and sign up for Colin Robertson's newsletter to get news on future books, the
occasional amusing email and more...

Made in the USA
Middletown, DE
29 December 2015